CLEMENTINE FOX

AND THE GREAT ISLAND ADVENTURE

LEIGH LUNA

graphix

An Imprint of
SCHOLASTIC

All rights reserved. Published by Graphix, an imprint of Scholastic Inc., *Publishers since 1920.* SCHOLASTIC, GRAPHIX, and associated logos are trademarks and/or registered trademarks of Scholastic Inc.

The publisher does not have any control over and does not assume any responsibility for author or third-party websites or their content.

Library of Congress Control Number: 2022939581

ISBN 978-1-338-35625-0 (hardcover)
ISBN 978-1-338-35624-3 (paperback)

10 9 8 7 6 5 4 3 2   23 24 25 26 27

Printed in China 62
First edition, May 2023

Color flatting by Andrea Bell and Tyler Johnson

Edited by Cassandra Pelham Fulton
Book design by Steve Ponzo
Creative Director: Phil Falco
Publisher: David Saylor

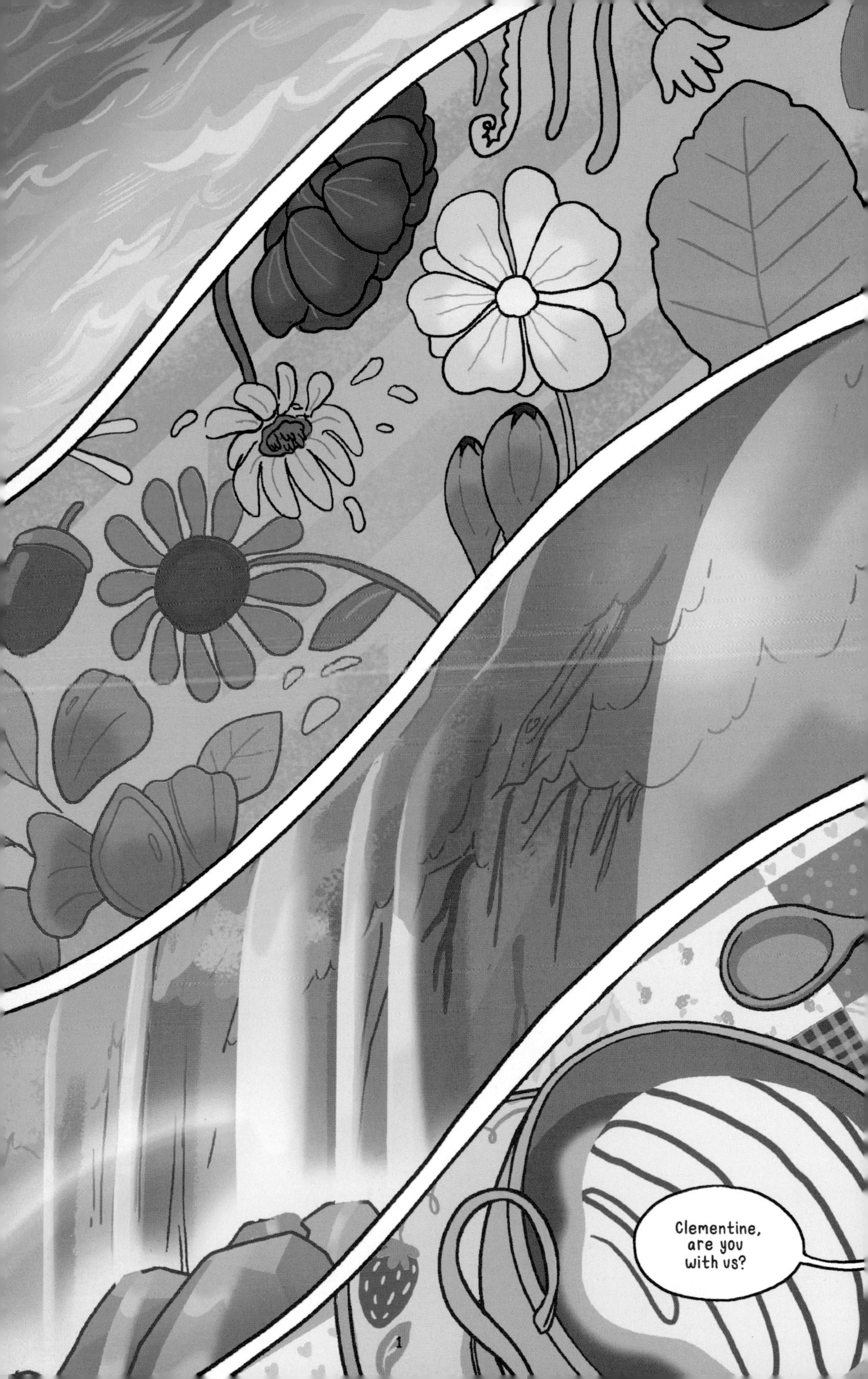
Clementine, are you with us?

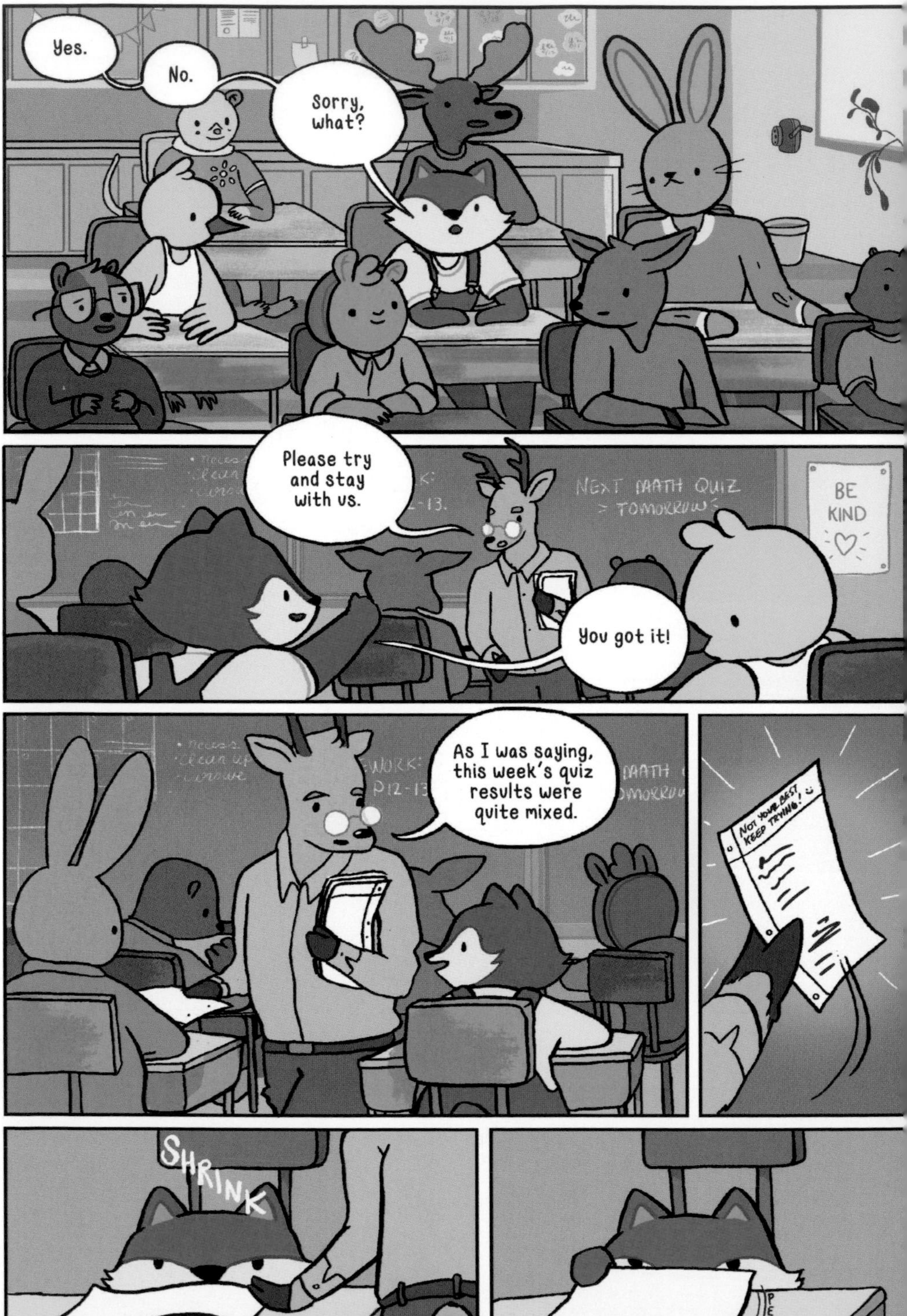
Yes.
No.
Sorry, what?
Please try and stay with us.
NEXT MATH QUIZ
TOMORROW
BE KIND
You got it!
As I was saying, this week's quiz results were quite mixed.
NOT YOUR BEST. KEEP TRYING!
SHRINK
PEEK

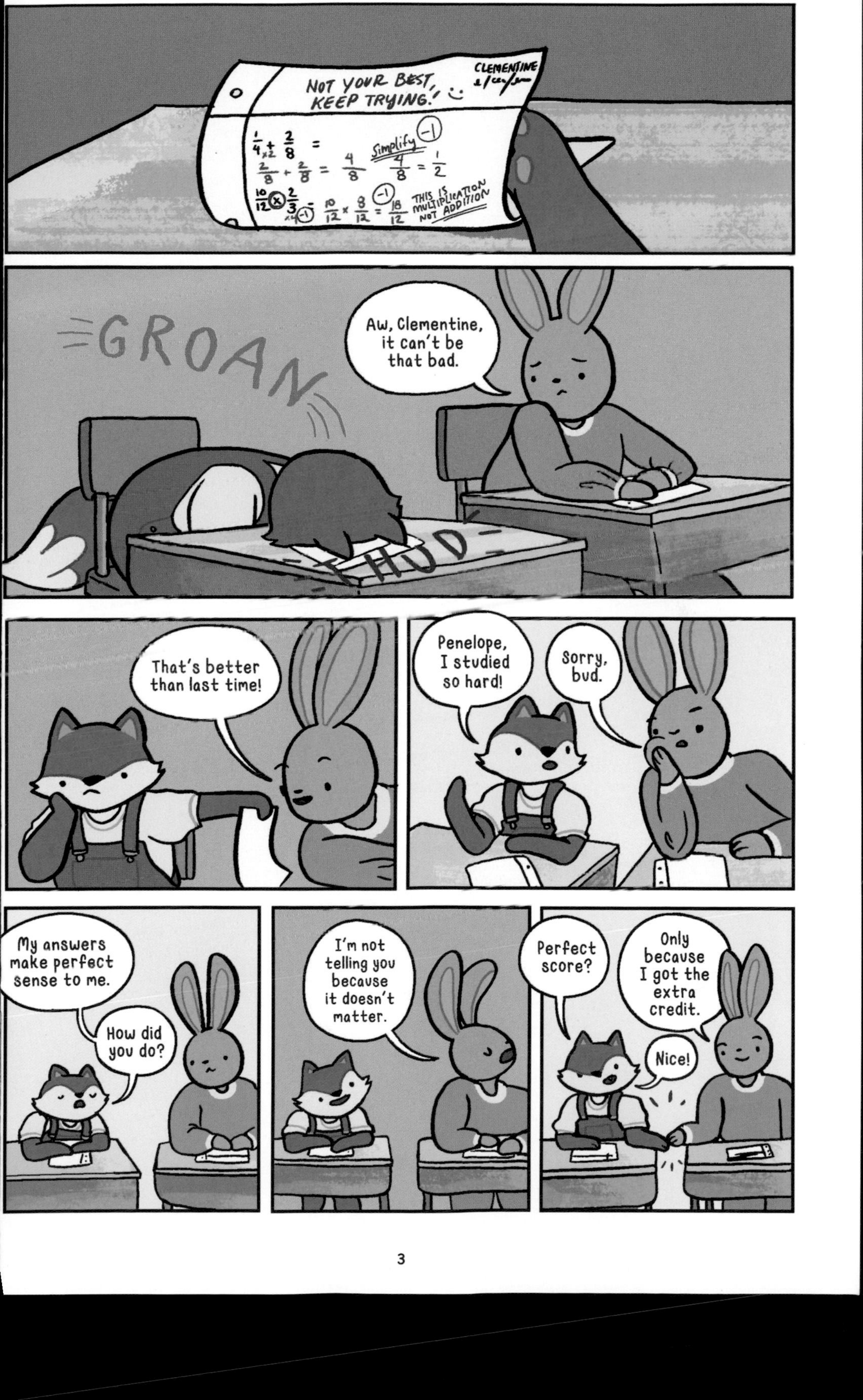
CLEMENTINE
NOT YOUR BEST, KEEP TRYING! :)
Simplify
THIS IS MULTIPLICATION NOT ADDITION
GROAN
Aw, Clementine, it can't be that bad.
THUD
That's better than last time!
Penelope, I studied so hard!
Sorry, bud.
My answers make perfect sense to me.
How did you do?
I'm not telling you because it doesn't matter.
Perfect score?
Only because I got the extra credit.
Nice!

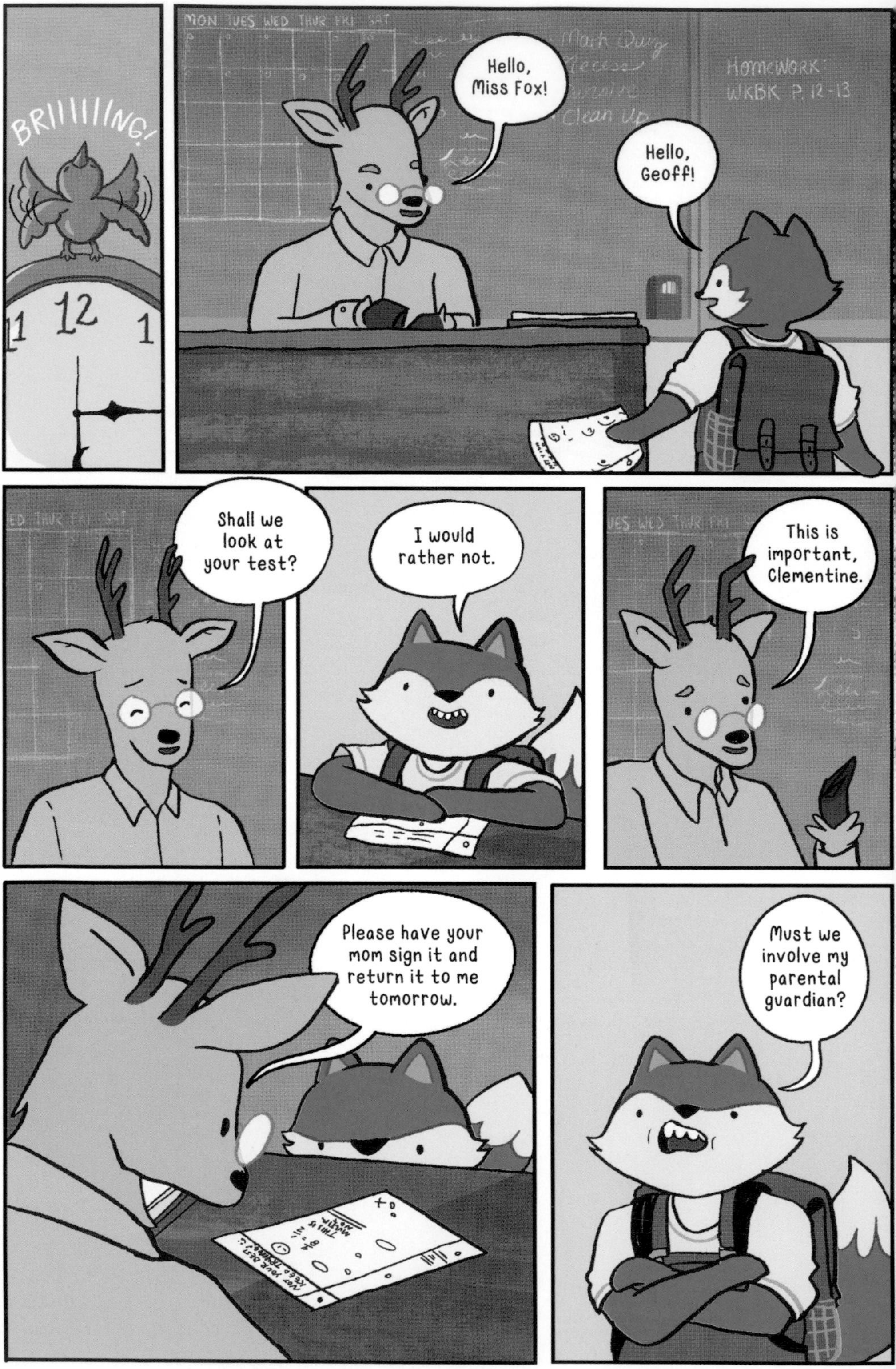
BRIIIIIING!
MON TUES WED THUR FRI SAT
Math Quiz
Recess
Clean Up
HOMEWORK: WKBK P. 12-13
Hello, Miss Fox!
Hello, Geoff!
Shall we look at your test?
I would rather not.
This is important, Clementine.
Please have your mom sign it and return it to me tomorrow.
Must we involve my parental guardian?

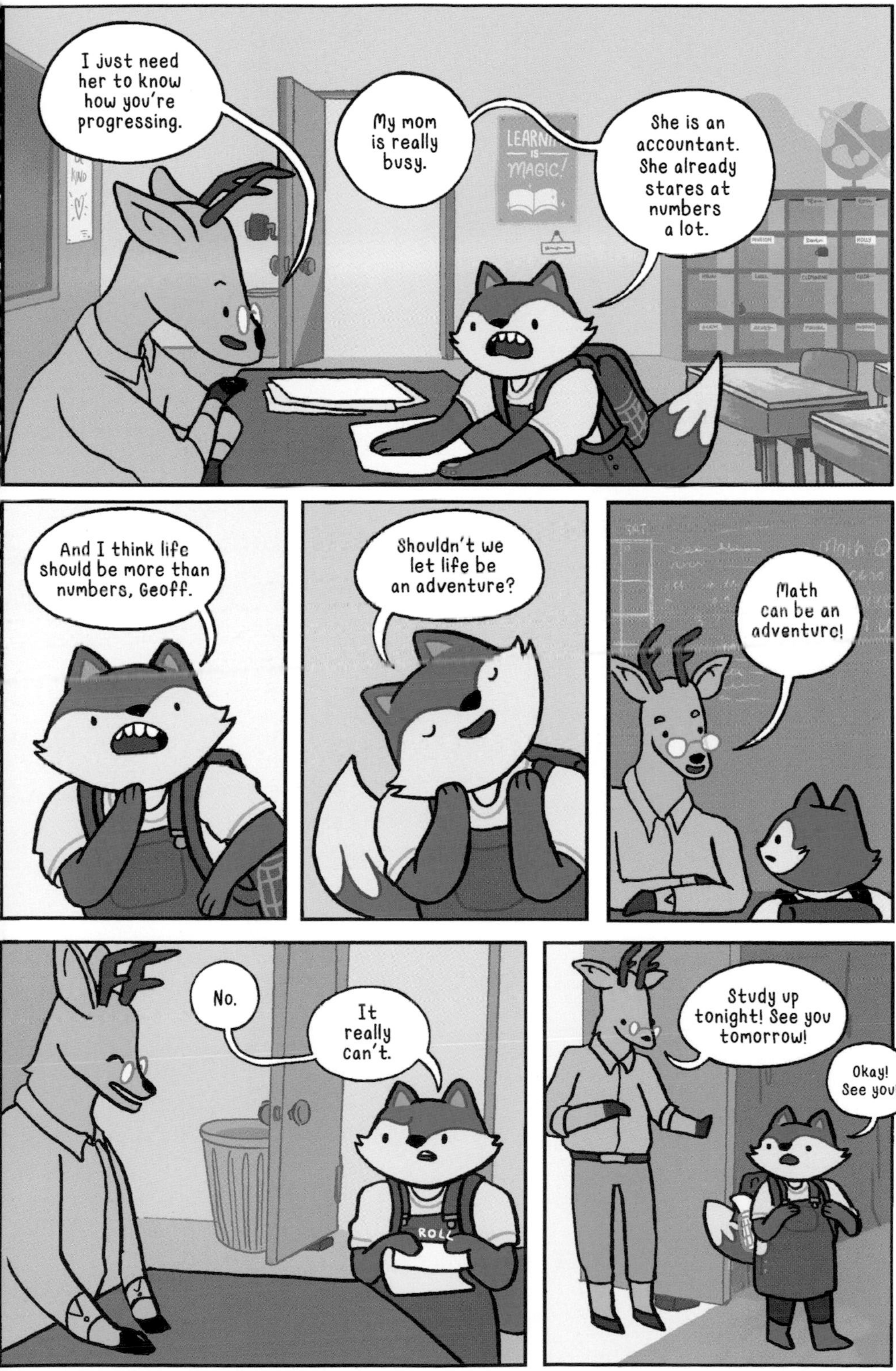
I just need her to know how you're progressing.
My mom is really busy.
She is an accountant. She already stares at numbers a lot.
LEARNING IS MAGIC!
And I think life should be more than numbers, Geoff.
Shouldn't we let life be an adventure?
Math can be an adventure!
No.
It really can't.
ROLL
Study up tonight! See you tomorrow!
Okay! See you!

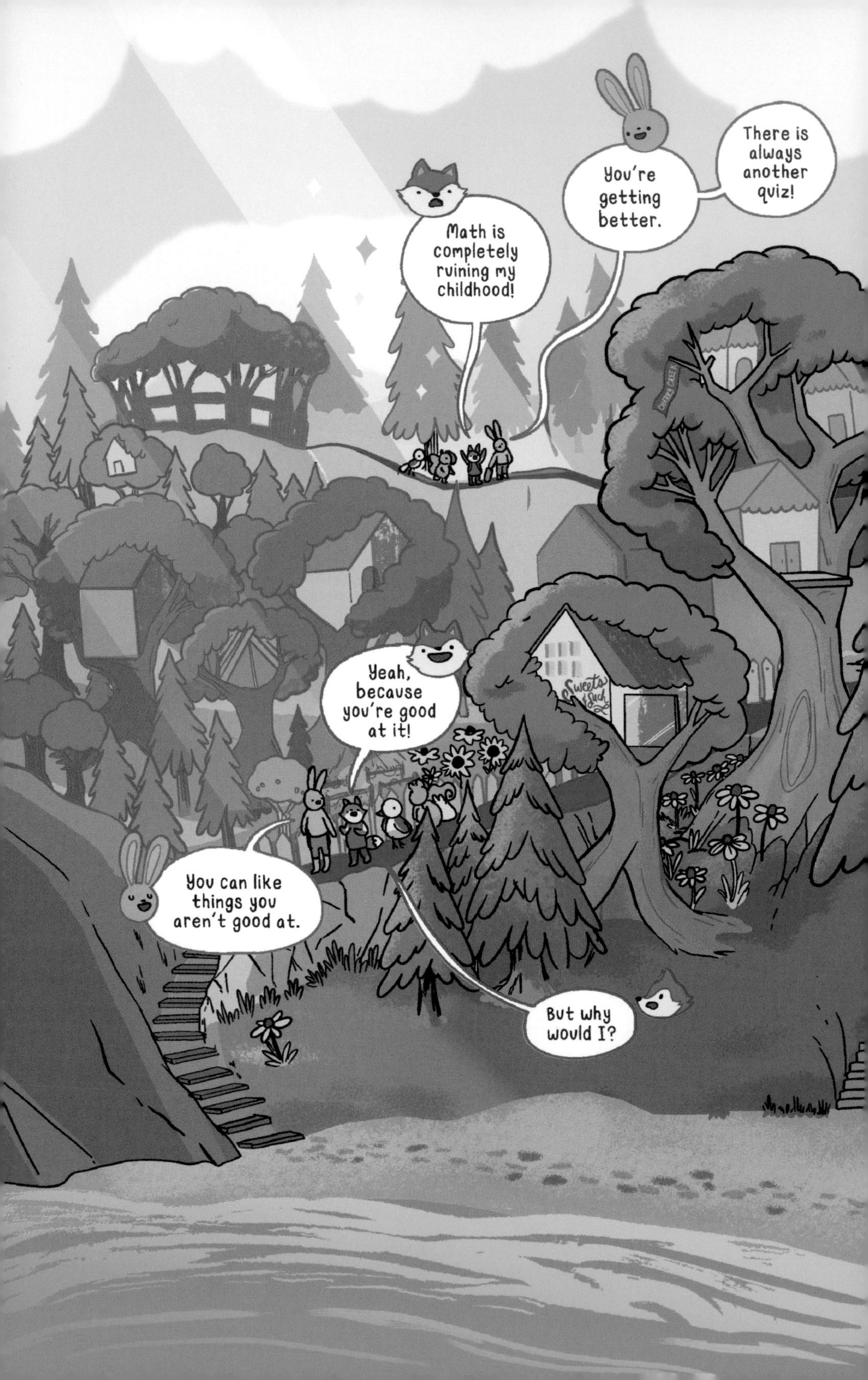

Math is completely ruining my childhood!
You're getting better.
There is always another quiz!
CHERRY CREEK
Yeah, because you're good at it!
You can like things you aren't good at.
But why would I?

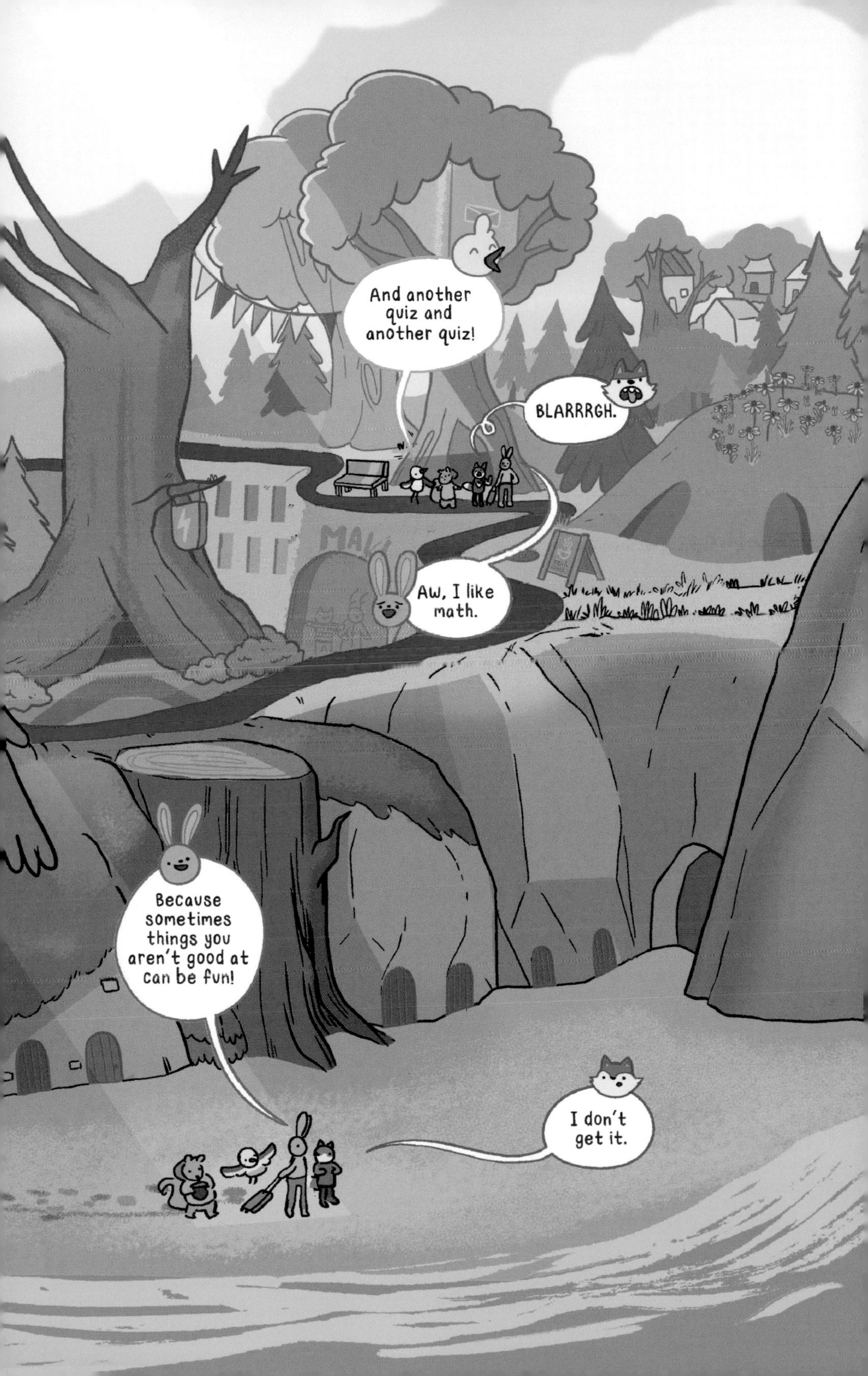
And another quiz and another quiz!
BLARRRGH.
Aw, I like math.
Because sometimes things you aren't good at can be fun!
I don't get it.

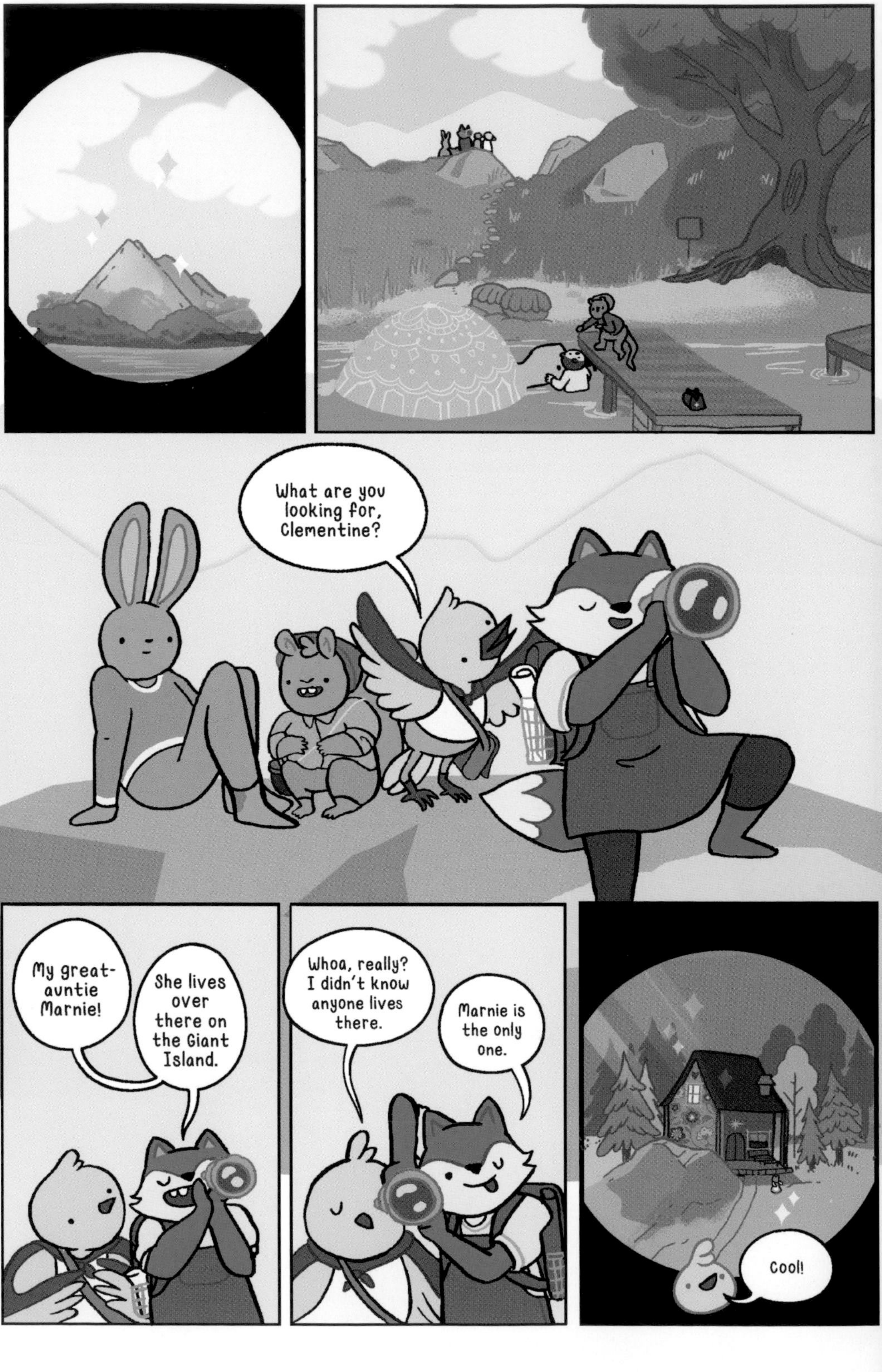
What are you looking for, Clementine?
My great-auntie Marnie!
She lives over there on the Giant Island.
Whoa, really? I didn't know anyone lives there.
Marnie is the only one.
Cool!

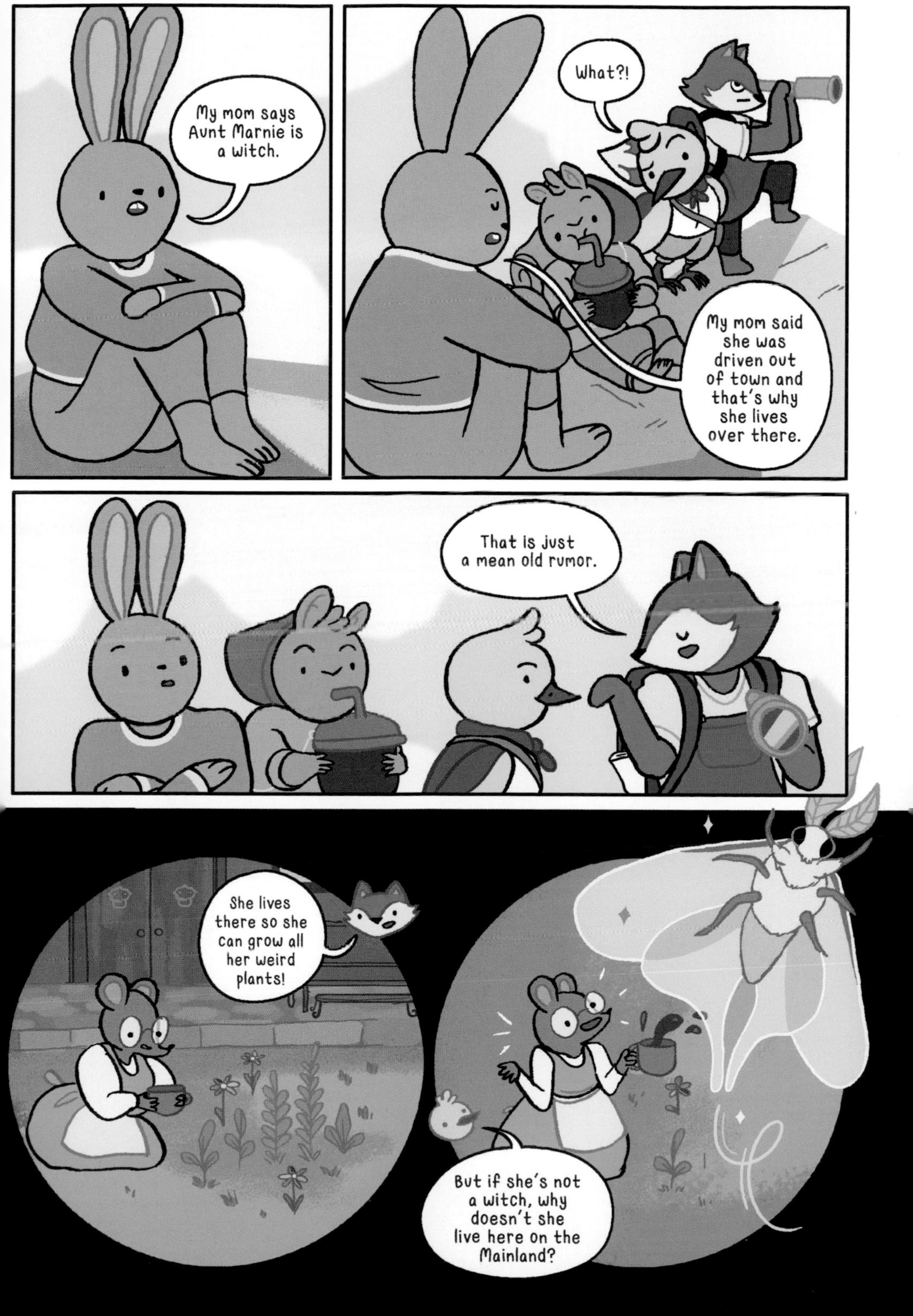
My mom says Aunt Marnie is a witch.
What?!
My mom said she was driven out of town and that's why she lives over there.
That is just a mean old rumor.
She lives there so she can grow all her weird plants!
But if she's not a witch, why doesn't she live here on the Mainland?

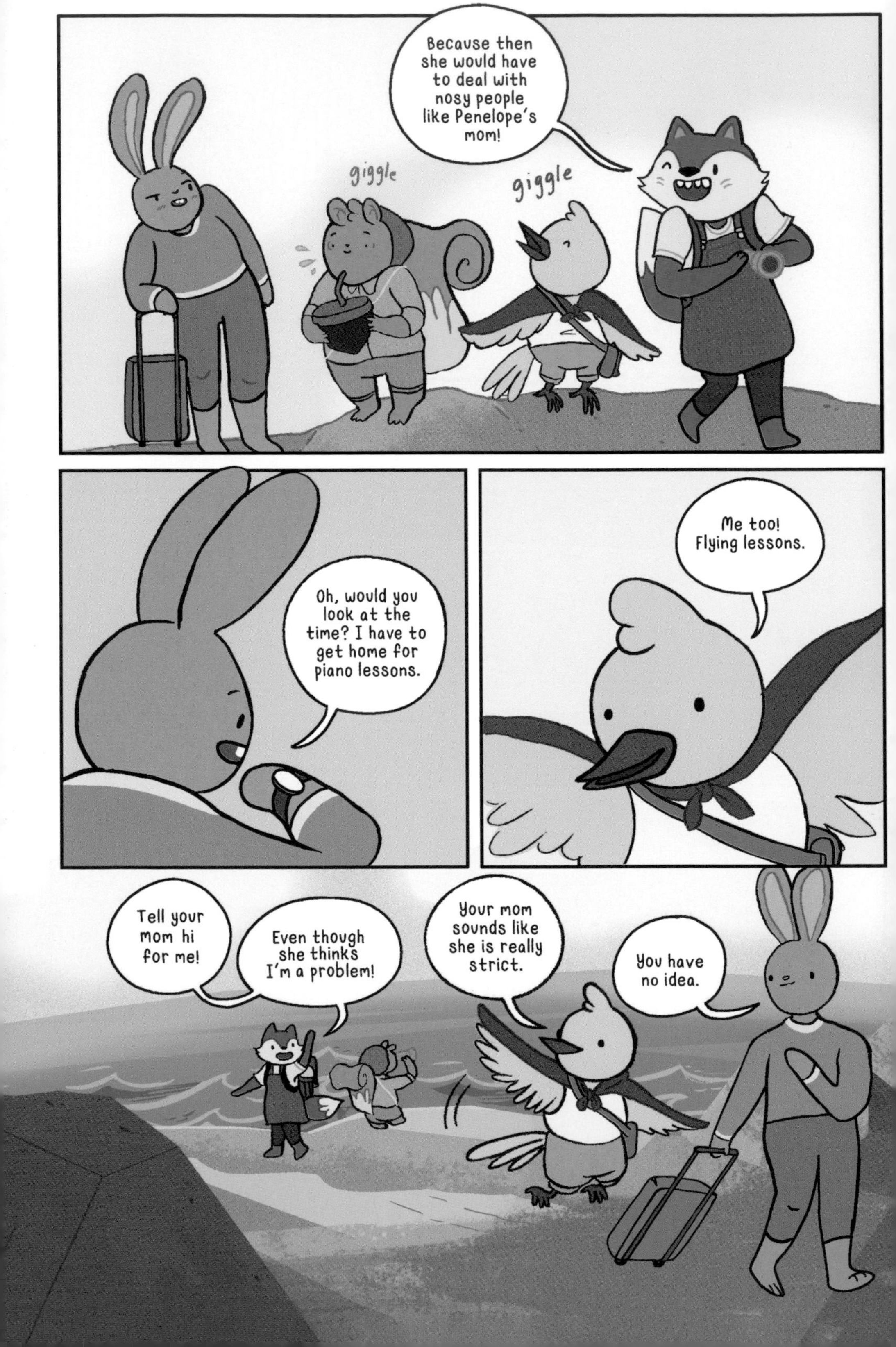

Because then she would have to deal with nosy people like Penelope's mom!
giggle
giggle
Oh, would you look at the time? I have to get home for piano lessons.
Me too! Flying lessons.
Tell your mom hi for me!
Even though she thinks I'm a problem!
Your mom sounds like she is really strict.
You have no idea.

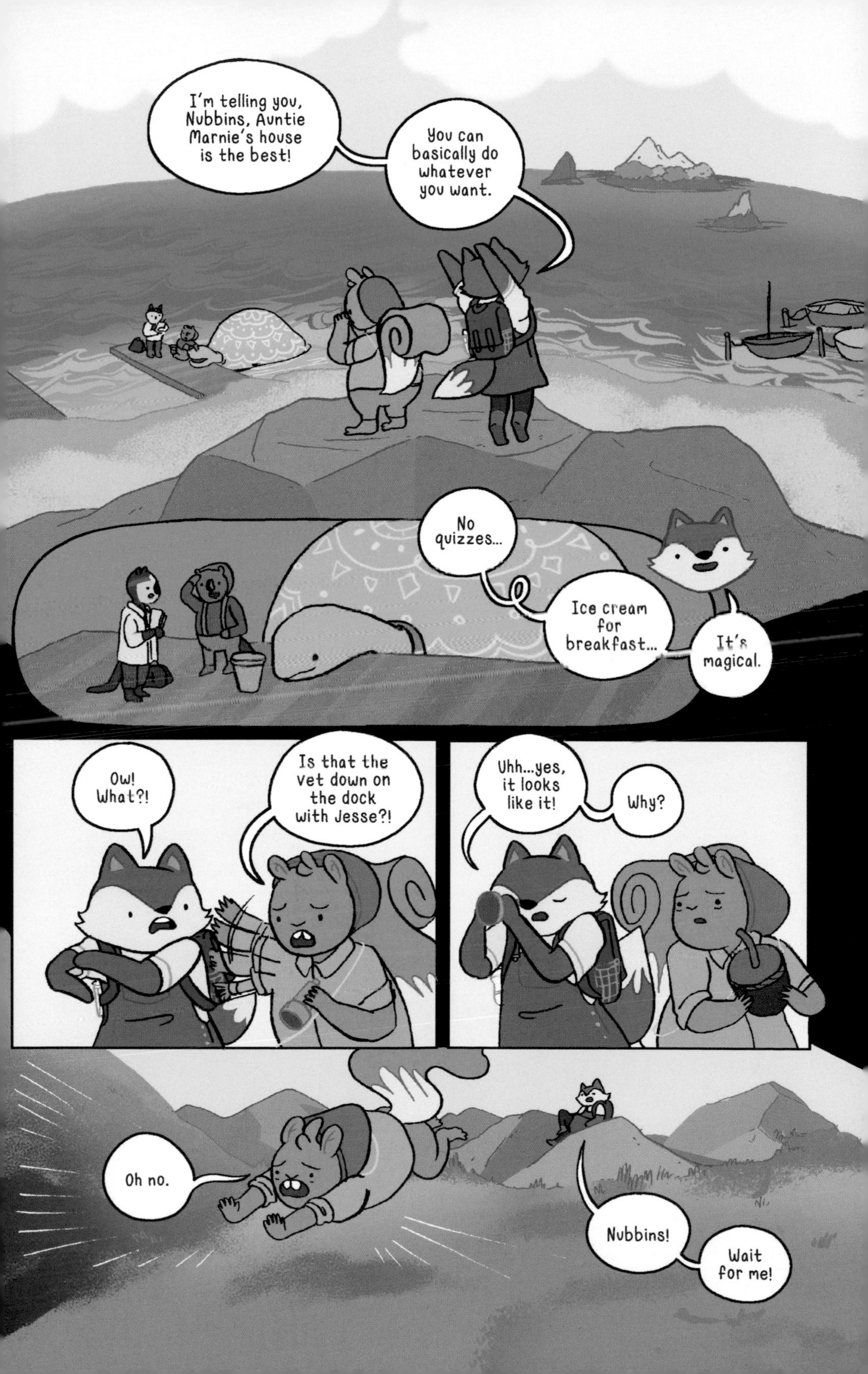
I'm telling you, Nubbins, Auntie Marnie's house is the best!
You can basically do whatever you want.
No quizzes...
Ice cream for breakfast...
It's magical.
Ow! What?!
Is that the vet down on the dock with Jesse?!
Uhh...yes, it looks like it!
Why?
Oh no.
Nubbins!
Wait for me!

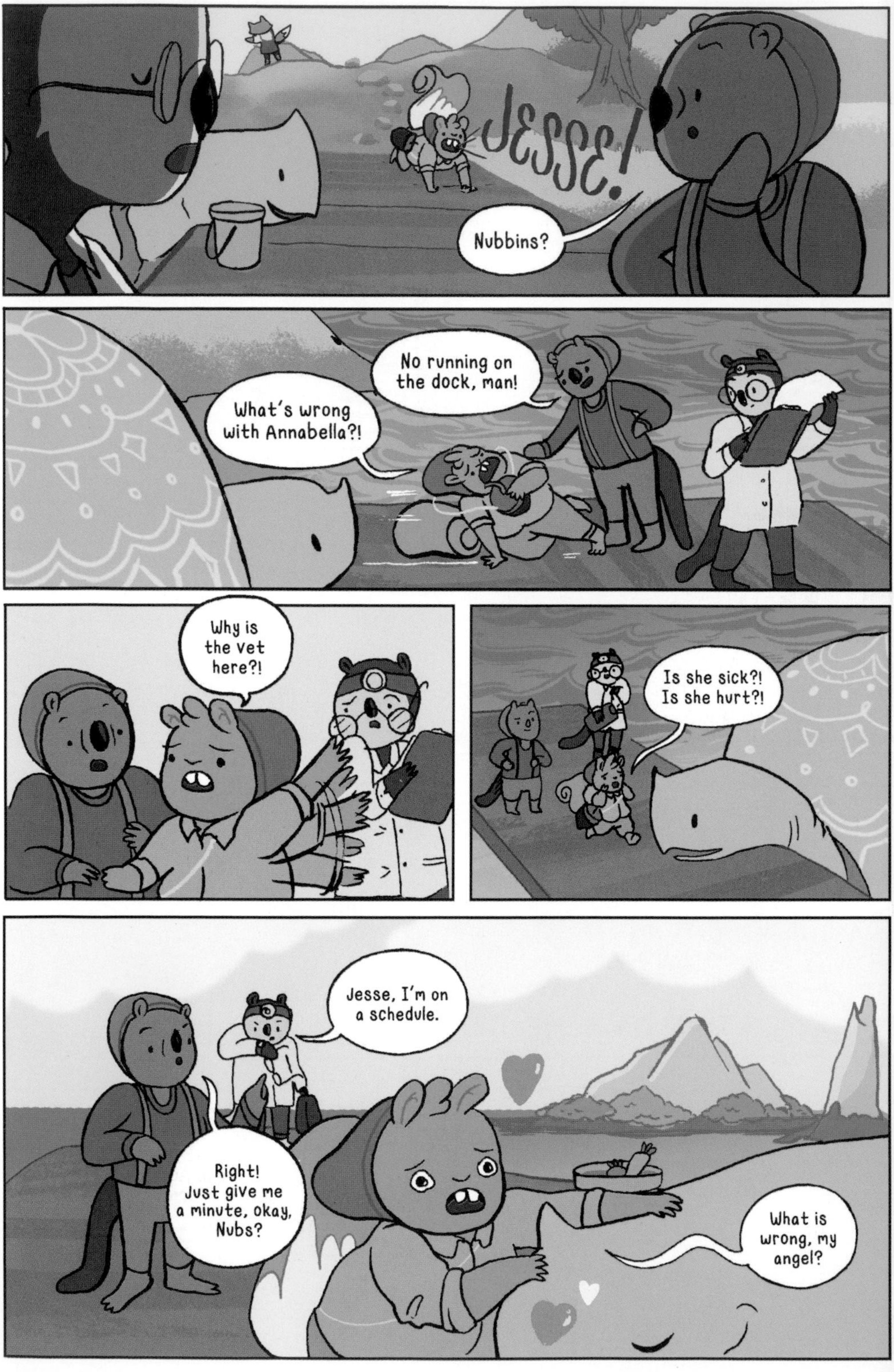
JESSE!
Nubbins?
What's wrong with Annabella?!
No running on the dock, man!
Why is the vet here?!
Is she sick?! Is she hurt?!
Jesse, I'm on a schedule.
Right! Just give me a minute, okay, Nubs?
What is wrong, my angel?

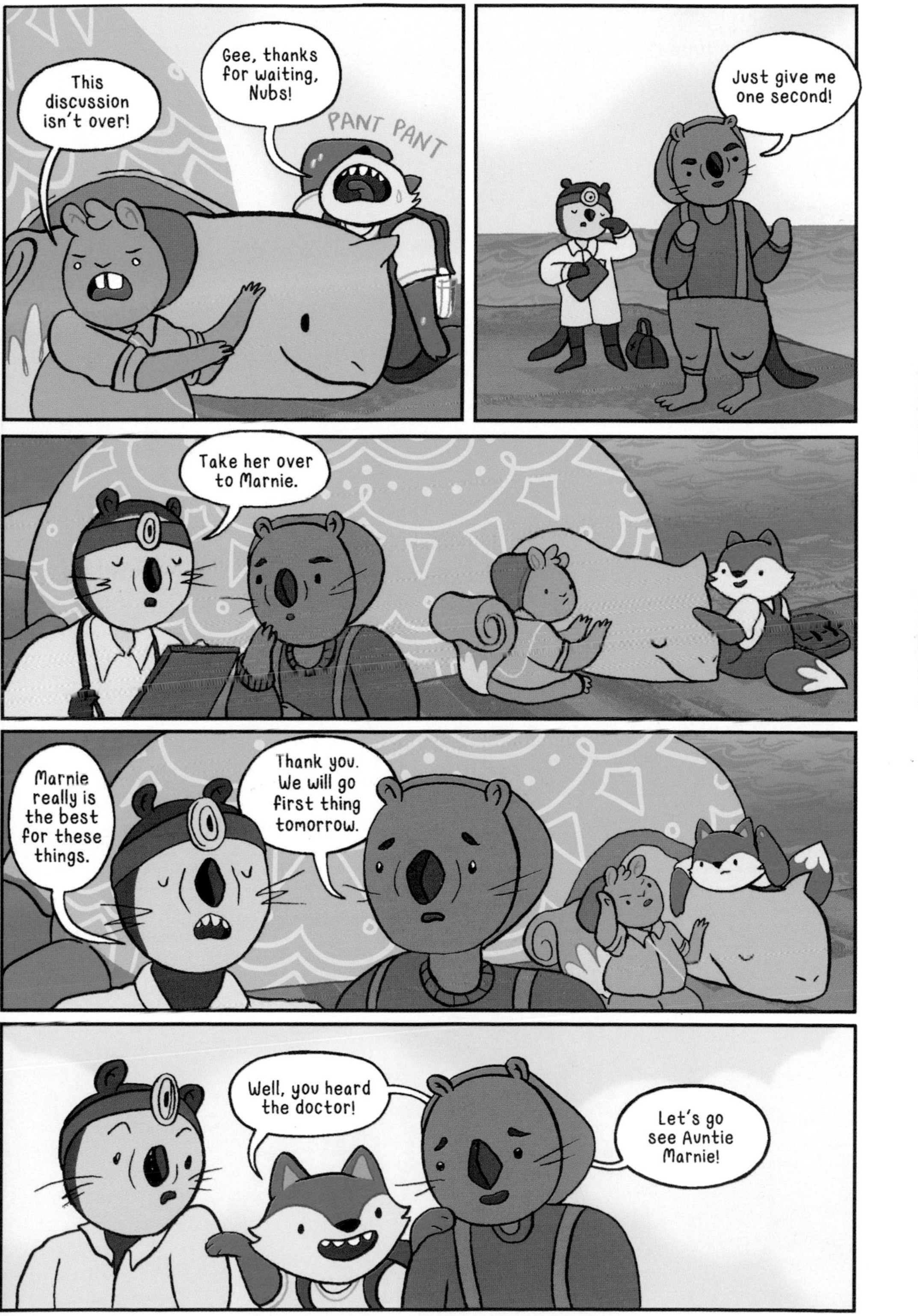
This discussion isn't over!
Gee, thanks for waiting, Nubs!
PANT PANT
Just give me one second!
Take her over to Marnie.
Marnie really is the best for these things.
Thank you. We will go first thing tomorrow.
Well, you heard the doctor!
Let's go see Auntie Marnie!

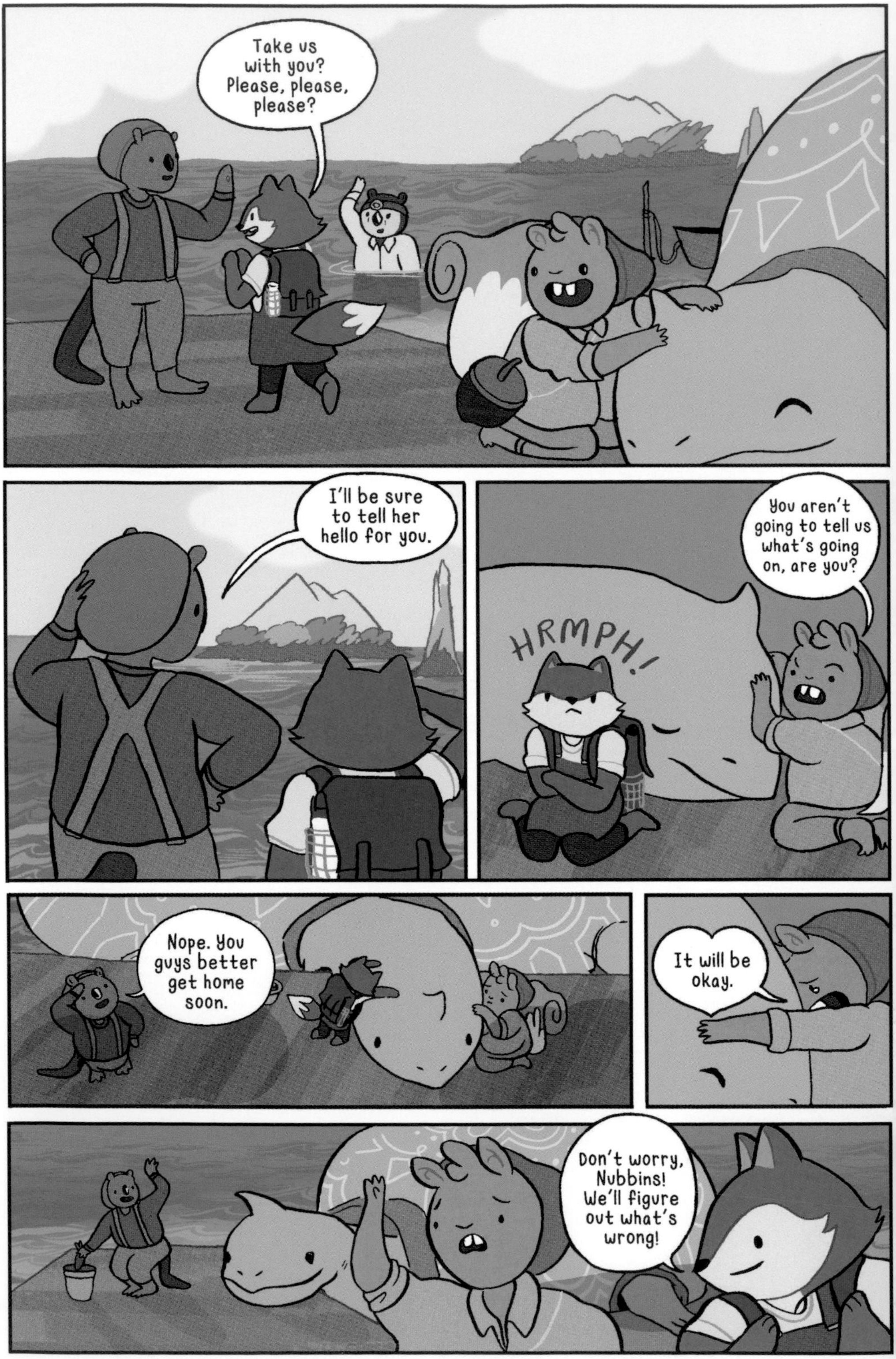
Take us with you? Please, please, please?
I'll be sure to tell her hello for you.
HRMPH!
You aren't going to tell us what's going on, are you?
Nope. You guys better get home soon.
It will be okay.
Don't worry, Nubbins! We'll figure out what's wrong!

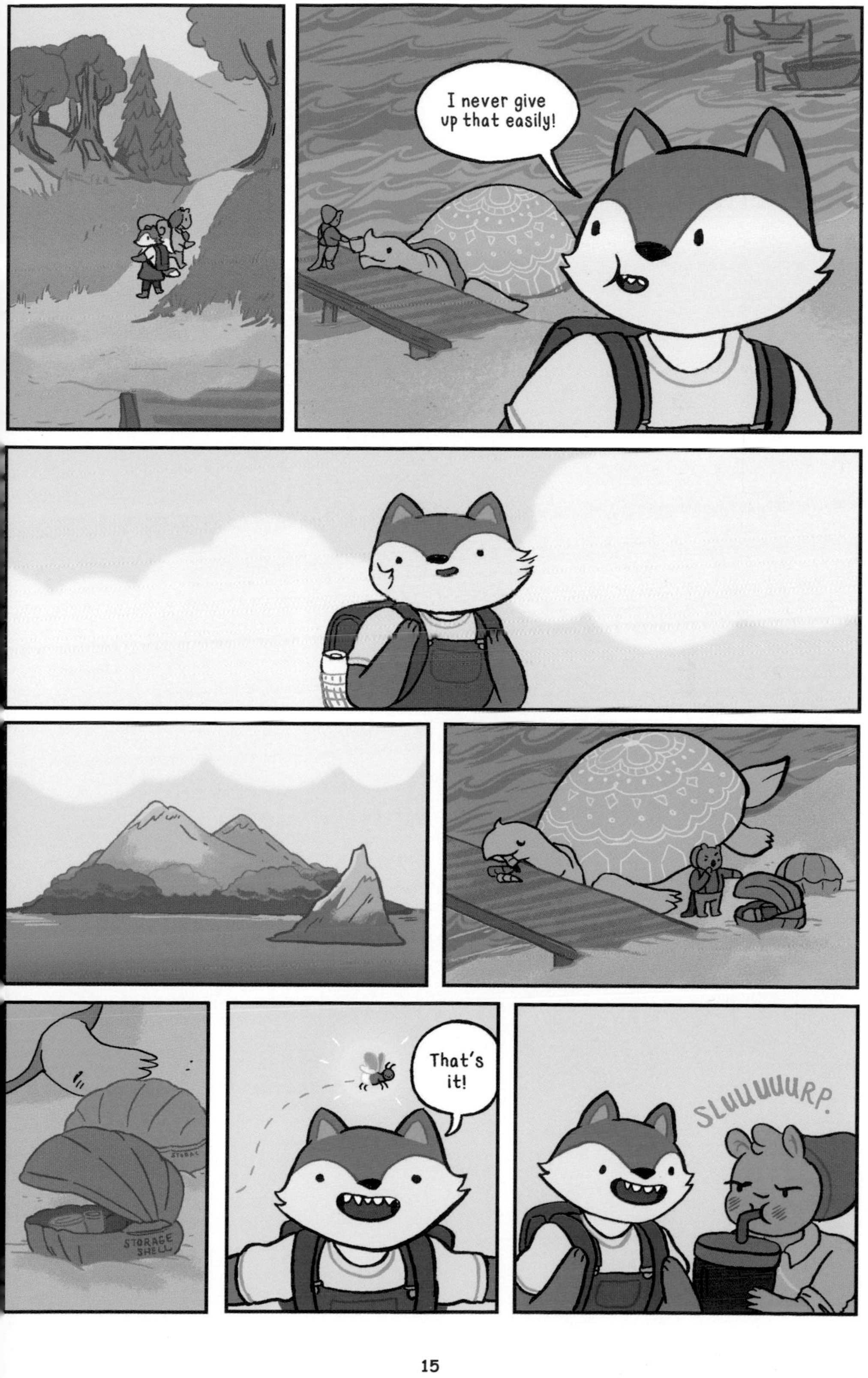
I never give up that easily!
STORAGE SHELL
That's it!
SLUUUUURP.

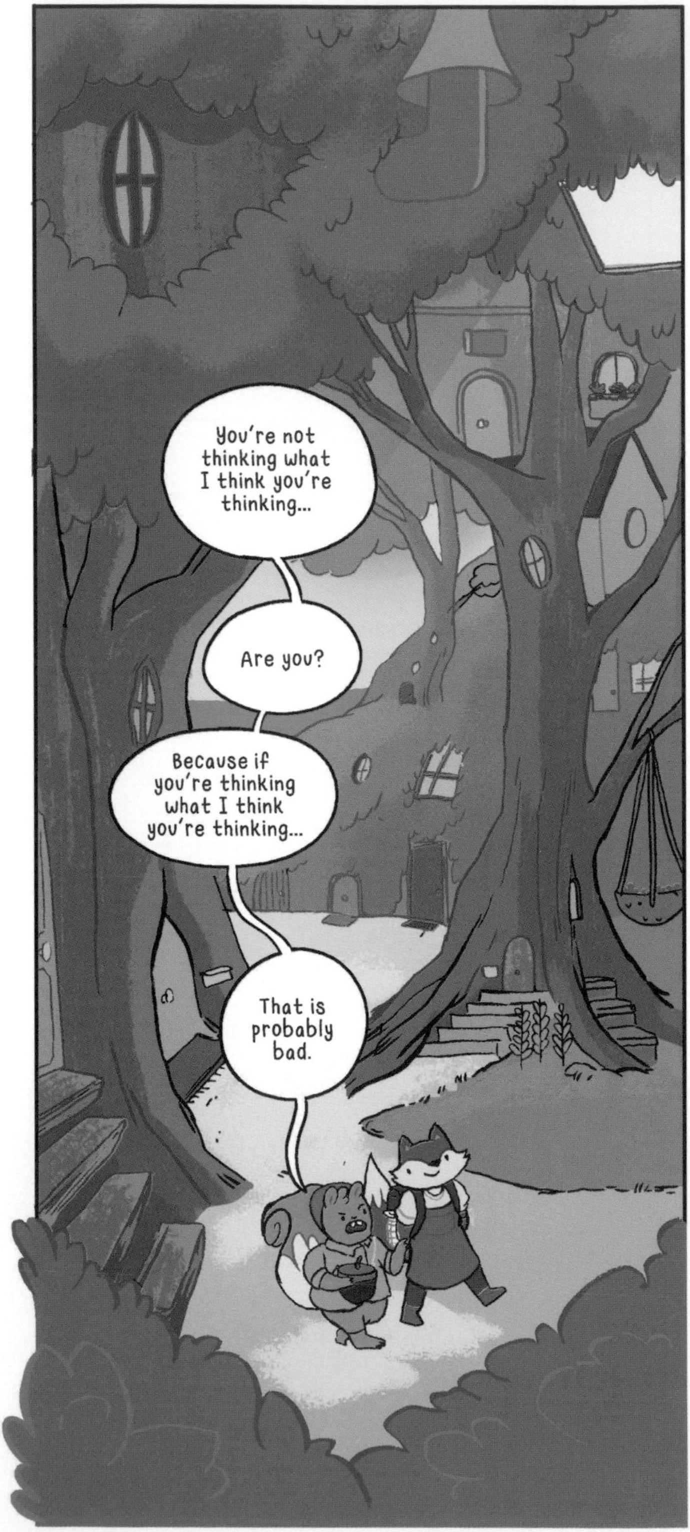
You're not thinking what I think you're thinking...
Are you?
Because if you're thinking what I think you're thinking...
That is probably bad.

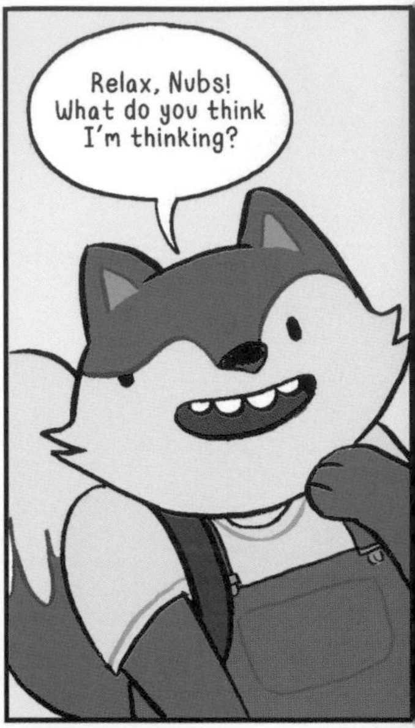
Relax, Nubs! What do you think I'm thinking?

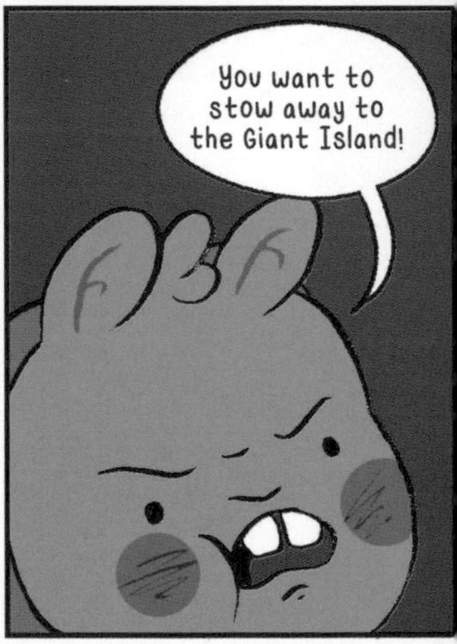
You want to stow away to the Giant Island!

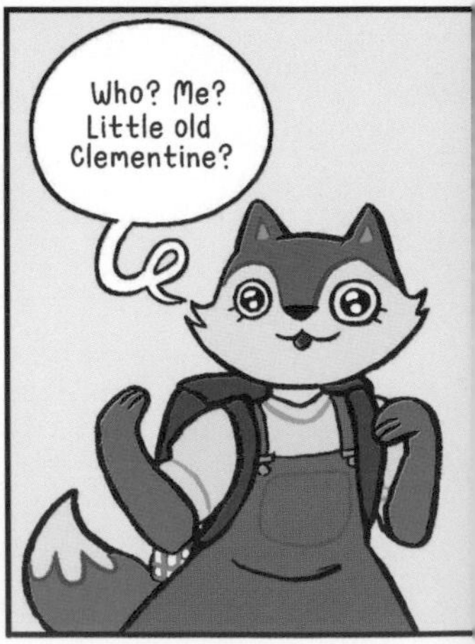
Who? Me? Little old Clementine?

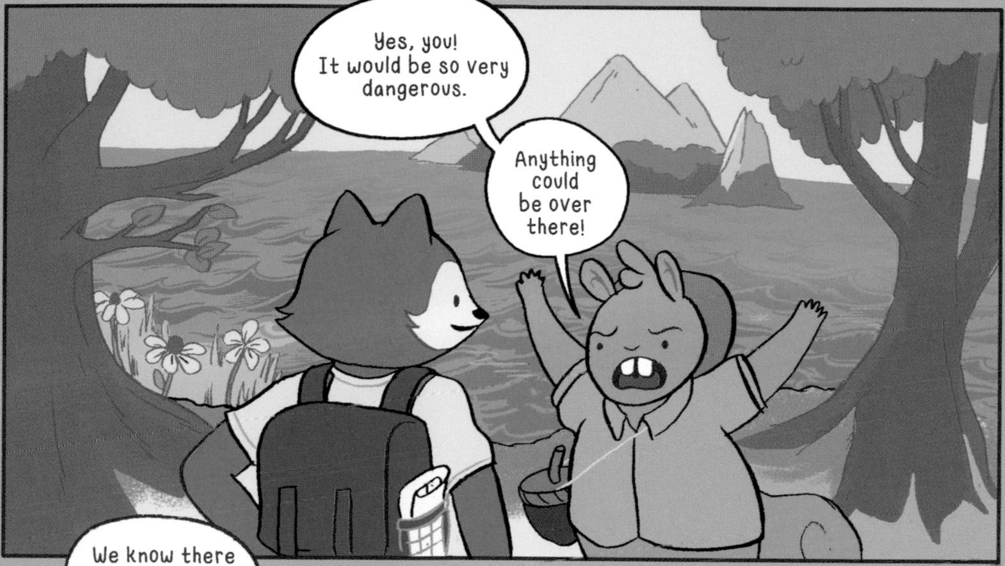
Yes, you! It would be so very dangerous.
Anything could be over there!

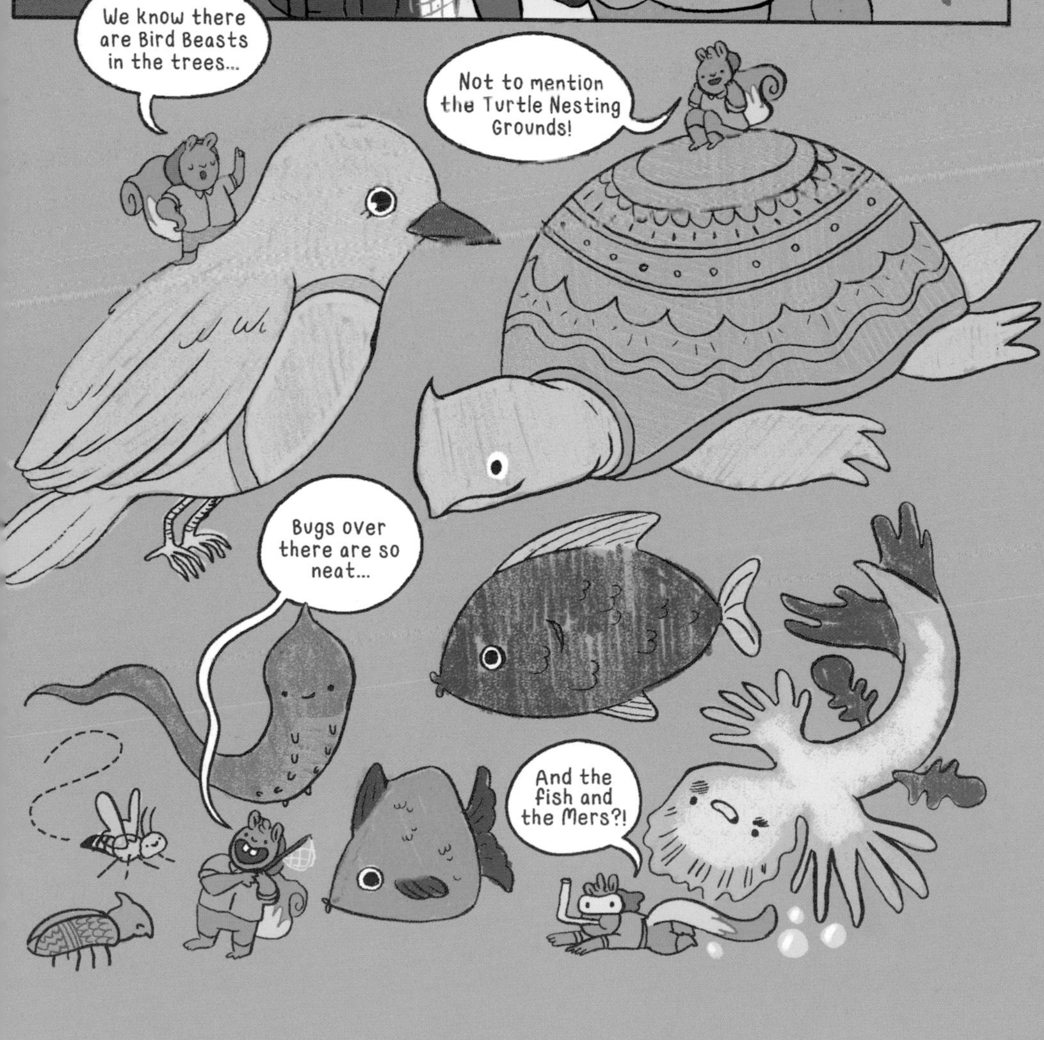
We know there are Bird Beasts in the trees...
Not to mention the Turtle Nesting Grounds!
Bugs over there are so neat...
And the fish and the Mers?!

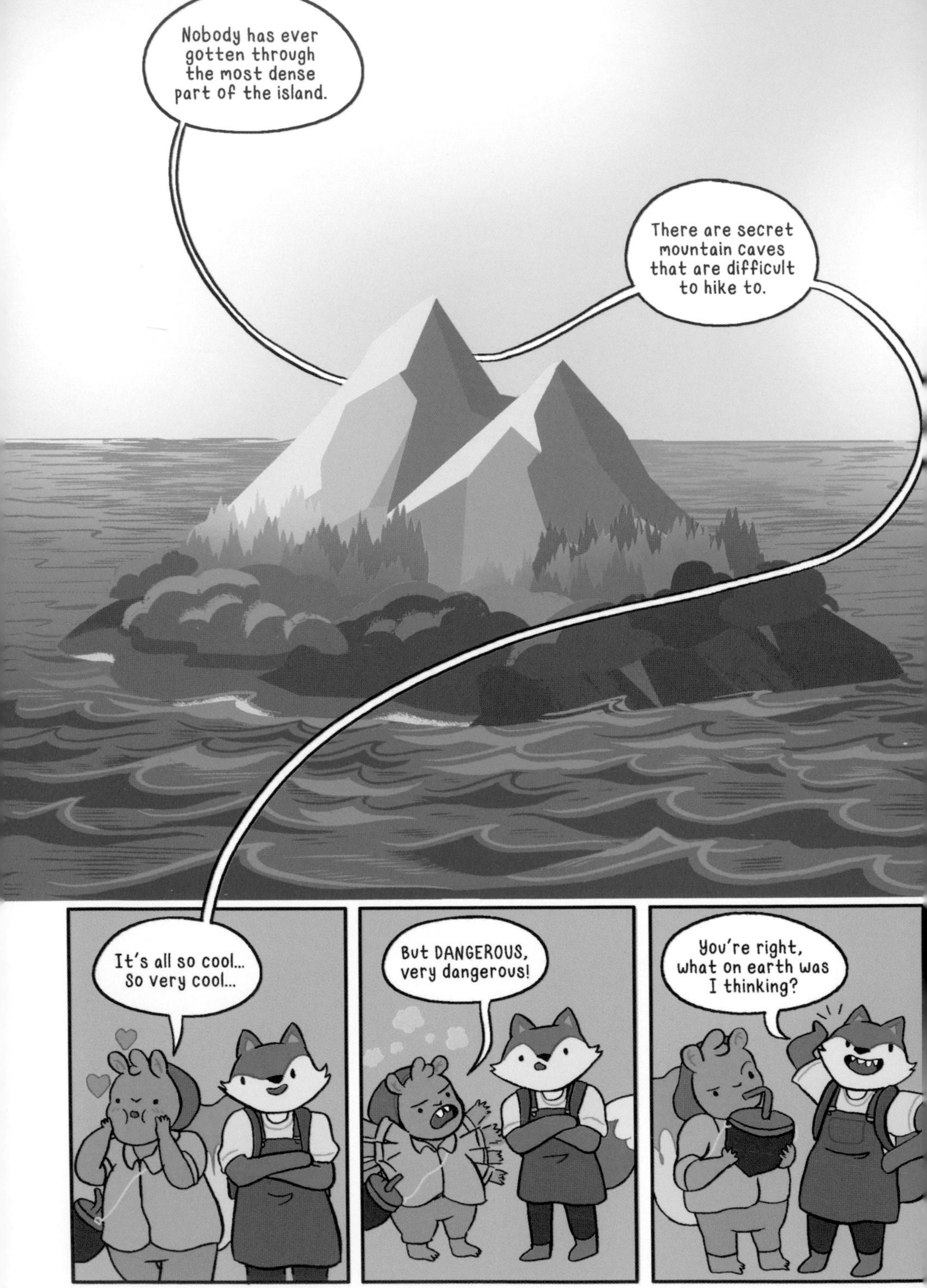
Nobody has ever gotten through the most dense part of the island.
There are secret mountain caves that are difficult to hike to.
It's all so cool... So very cool...
But DANGEROUS, very dangerous!
You're right, what on earth was I thinking?

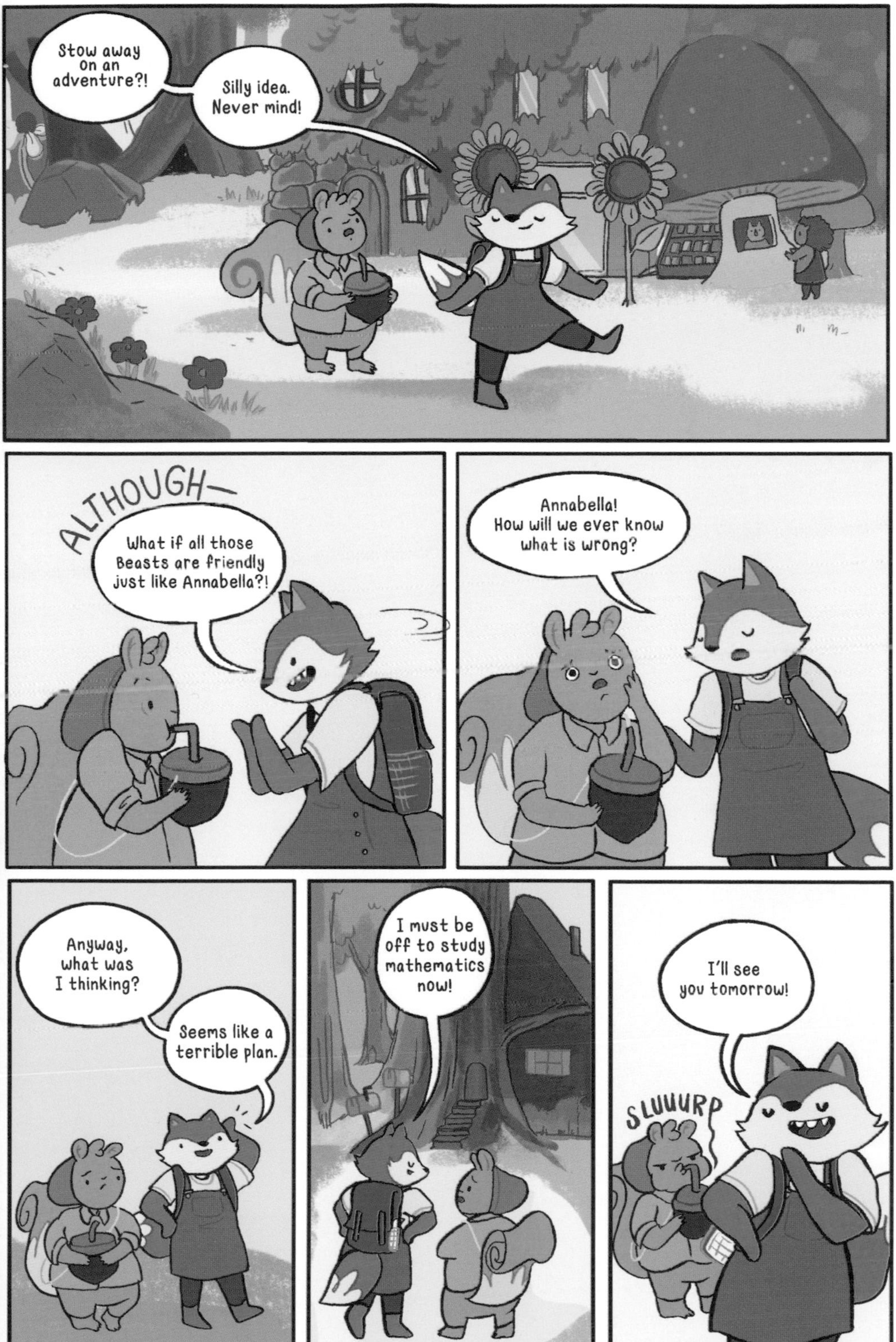

Stow away on an adventure?!
Silly idea. Never mind!
ALTHOUGH—
What if all those Beasts are friendly just like Annabella?!
Annabella! How will we ever know what is wrong?
Anyway, what was I thinking?
Seems like a terrible plan.
I must be off to study mathematics now!
I'll see you tomorrow!
SLUUURP

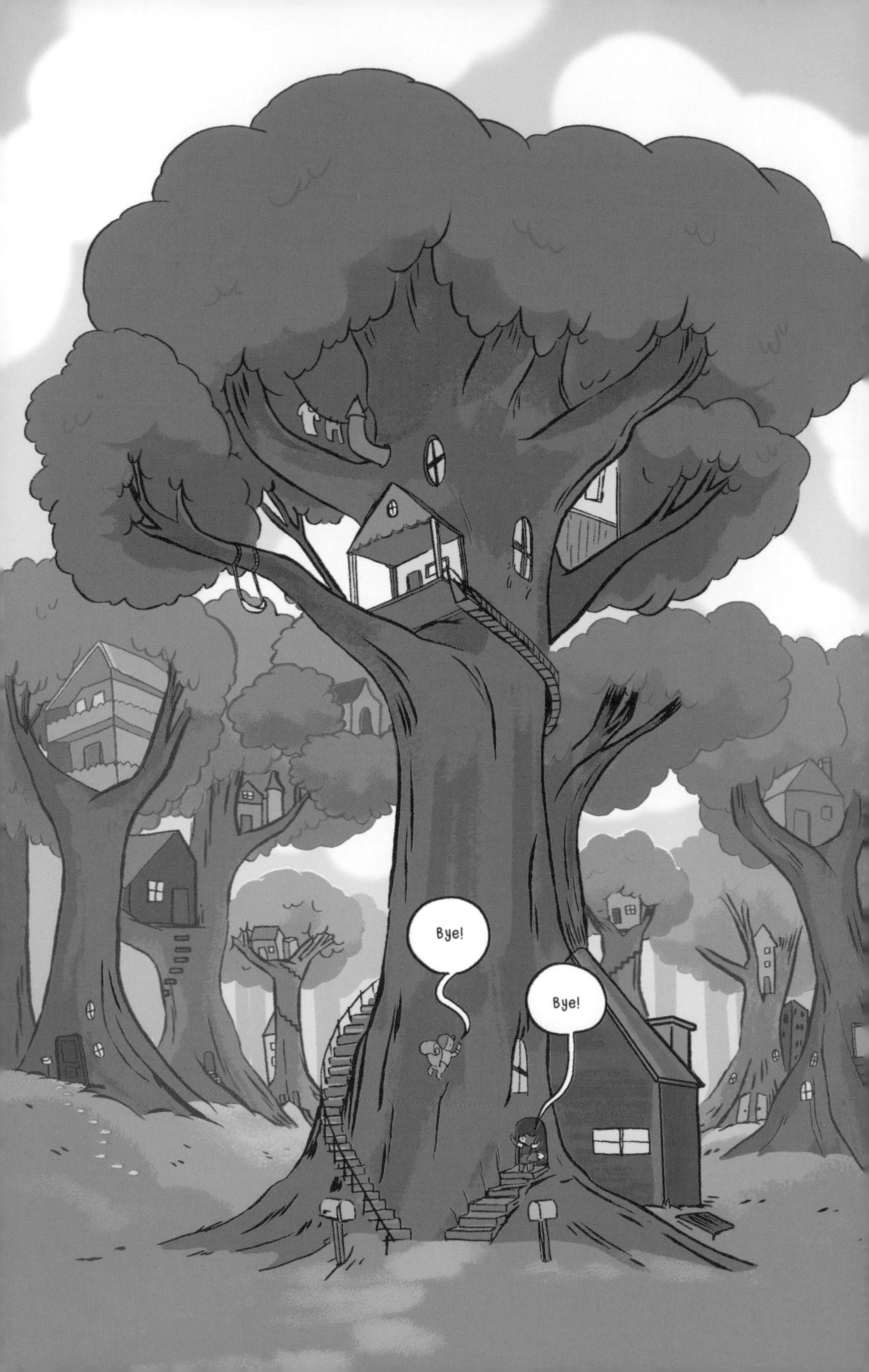
Bye!
Bye!

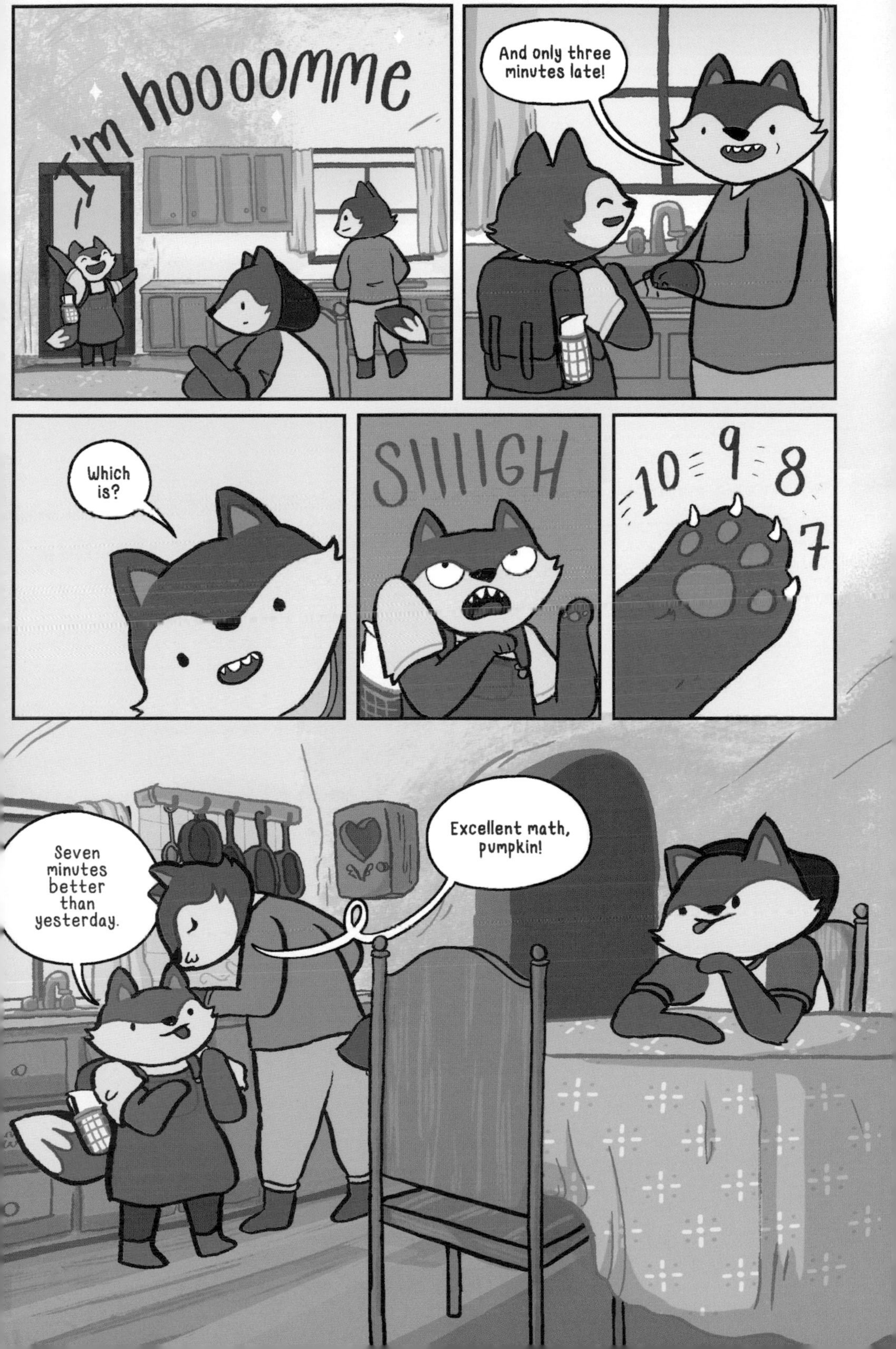
I'm hoooomme
And only three minutes late!
Which is?
SIIIIGH
10
9
8
7
Seven minutes better than yesterday.
Excellent math, pumpkin!

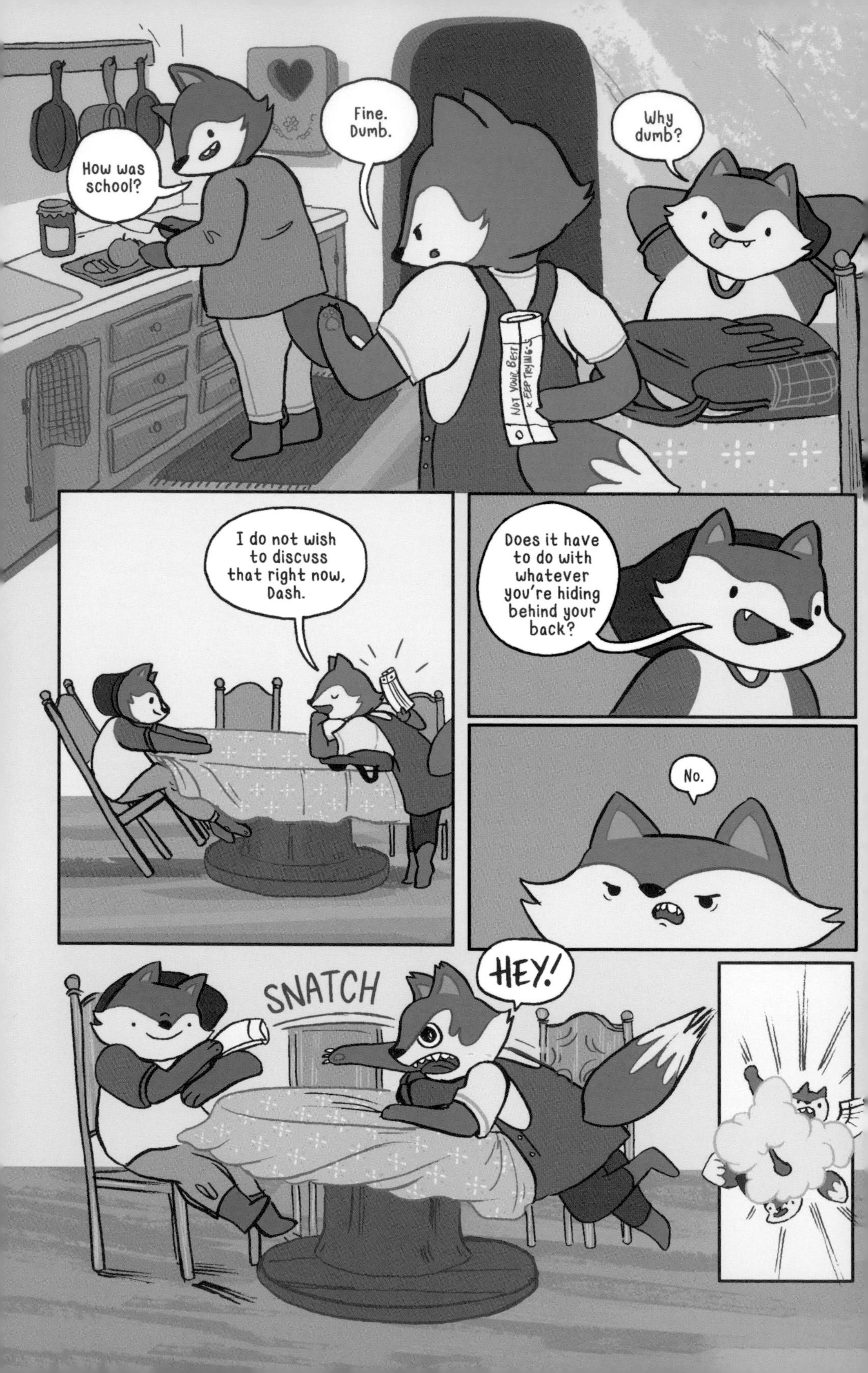
How was school?
Fine. Dumb.
Why dumb?
I do not wish to discuss that right now, Dash.
Does it have to do with whatever you're hiding behind your back?
No.
SNATCH
HEY!

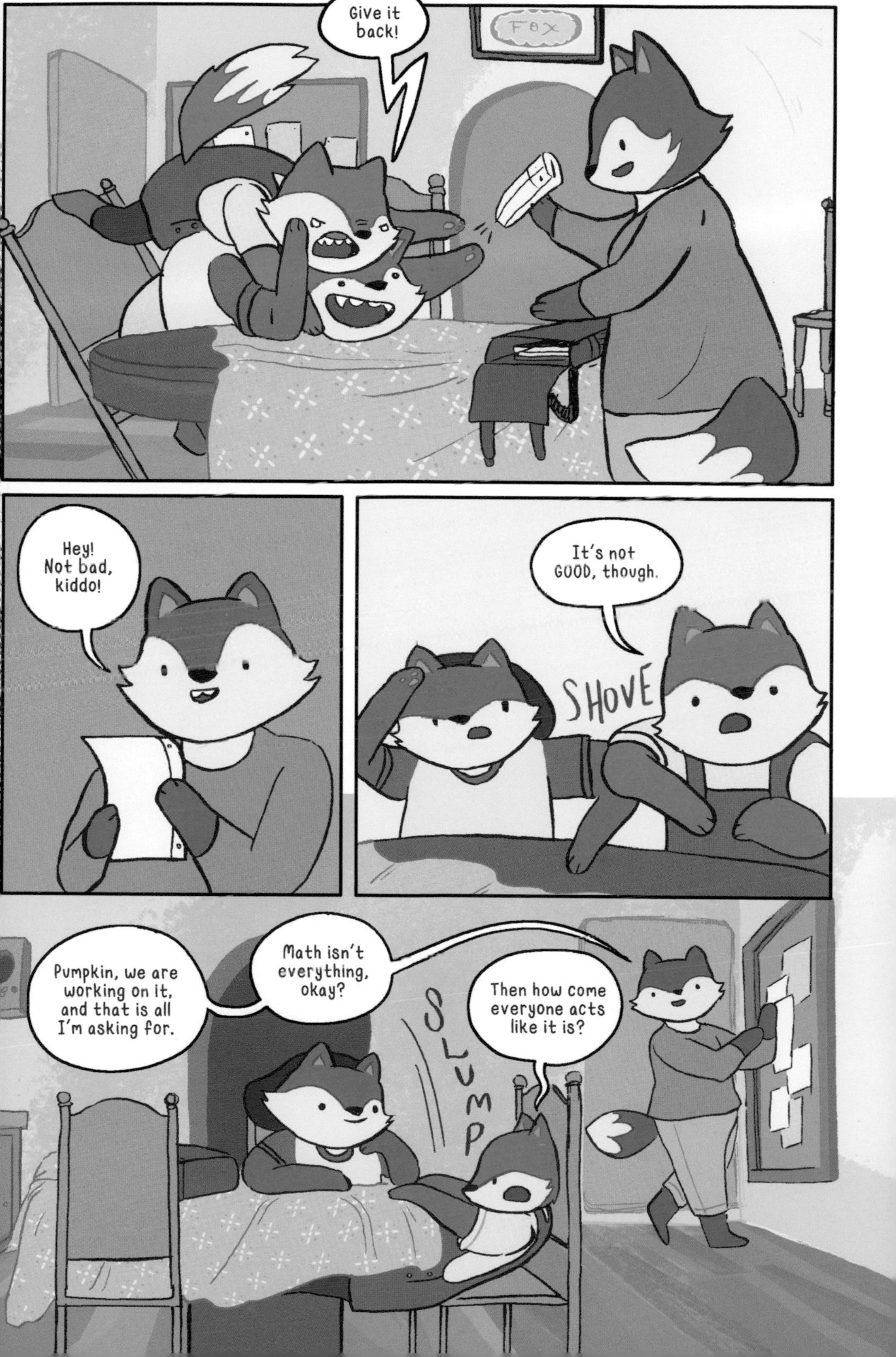

FOX
Give it back!
Hey! Not bad, kiddo!
It's not GOOD, though.
SHOVE
Pumpkin, we are working on it, and that is all I'm asking for.
Math isn't everything, okay?
SLUMP
Then how come everyone acts like it is?

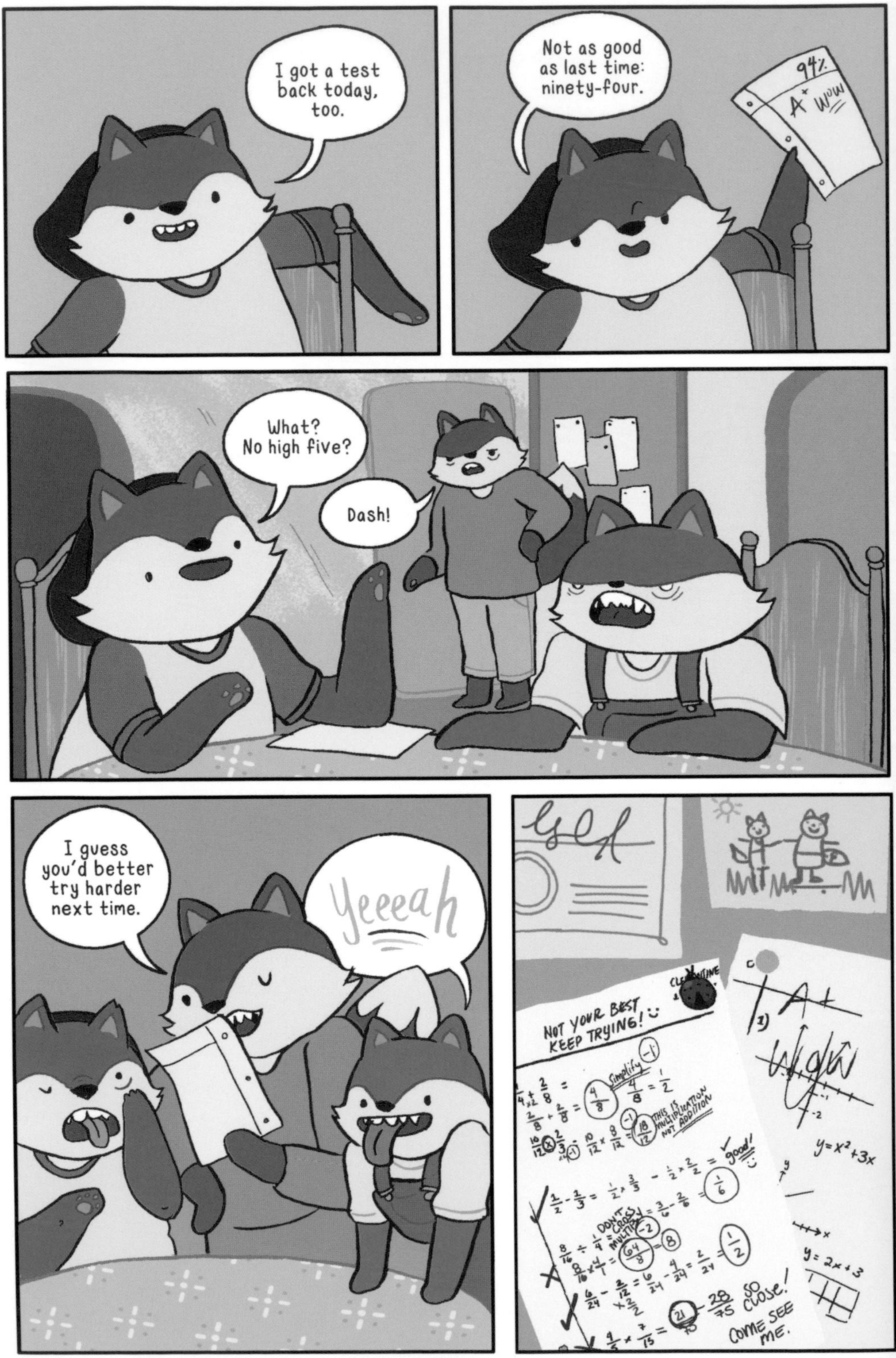

I got a test back today, too.
Not as good as last time: ninety-four.
94%
A+ wow
What? No high five?
Dash!
I guess you'd better try harder next time.
Yeeeah
NOT YOUR BEST KEEP TRYING!
Simplify
THIS IS MULTIPLICATION NOT ADDITION
good!
DON'T CROSS MULTIPLY
SO CLOSE!
COME SEE ME.
A+
WOW
$y = x^2 + 3x$
$y = 2x + 3$

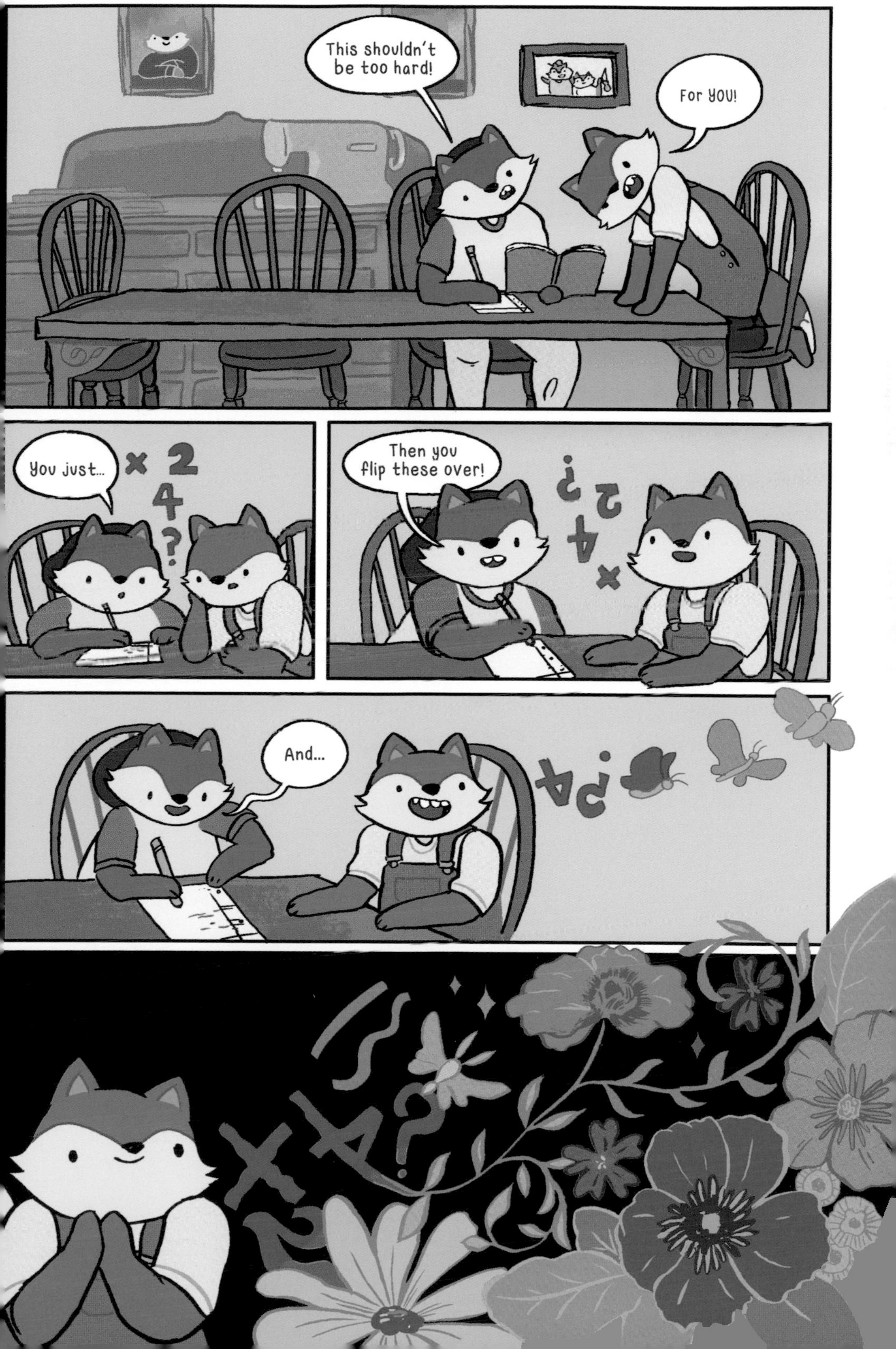
This shouldn't be too hard!
For YOU!
You just...
× 2
4
?
Then you flip these over!
And...

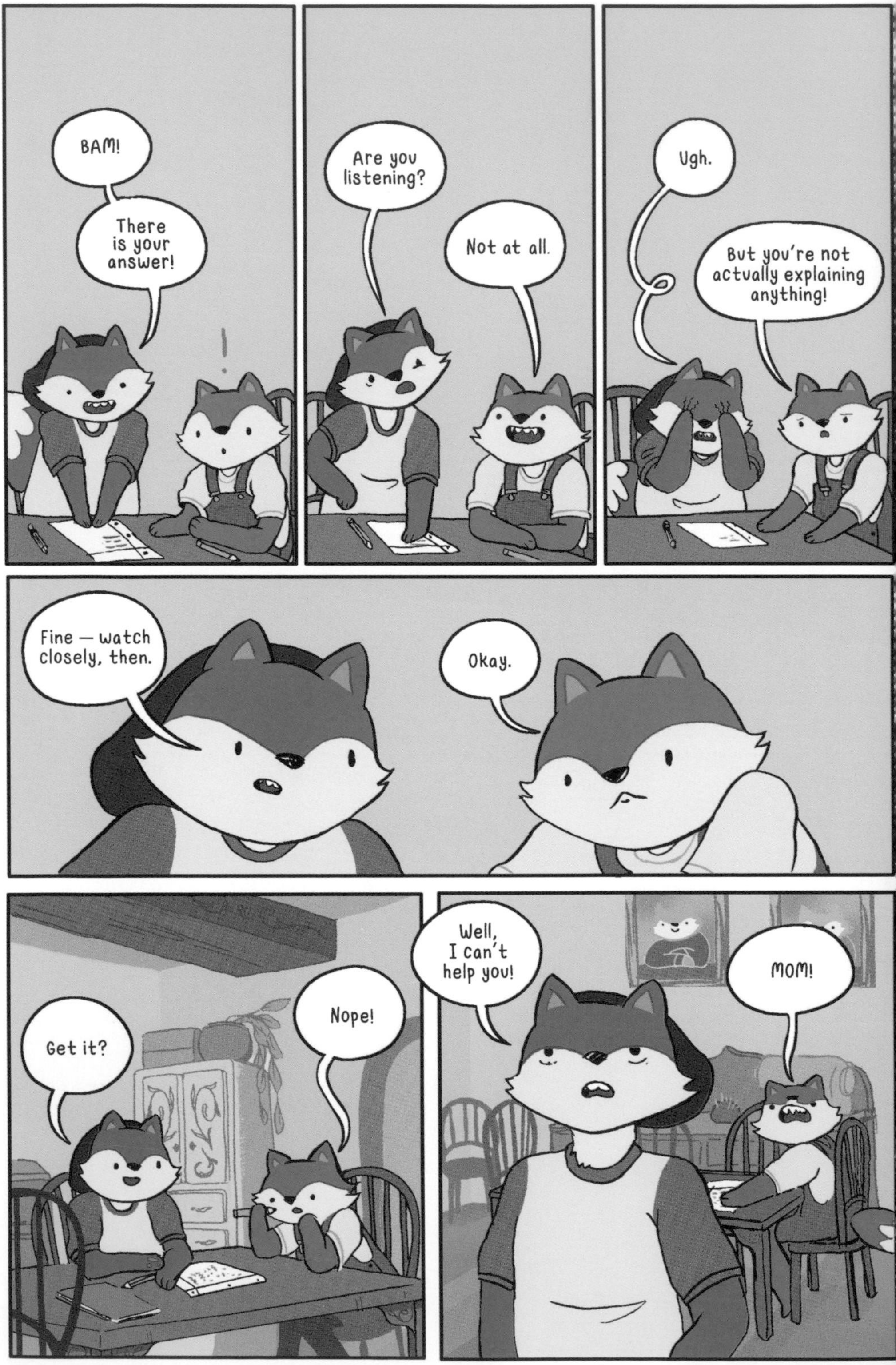
BAM!
There is your answer!
!
Are you listening?
Not at all.
Ugh.
But you're not actually explaining anything!
Fine — watch closely, then.
Okay.
Get it?
Nope!
Well, I can't help you!
MOM!

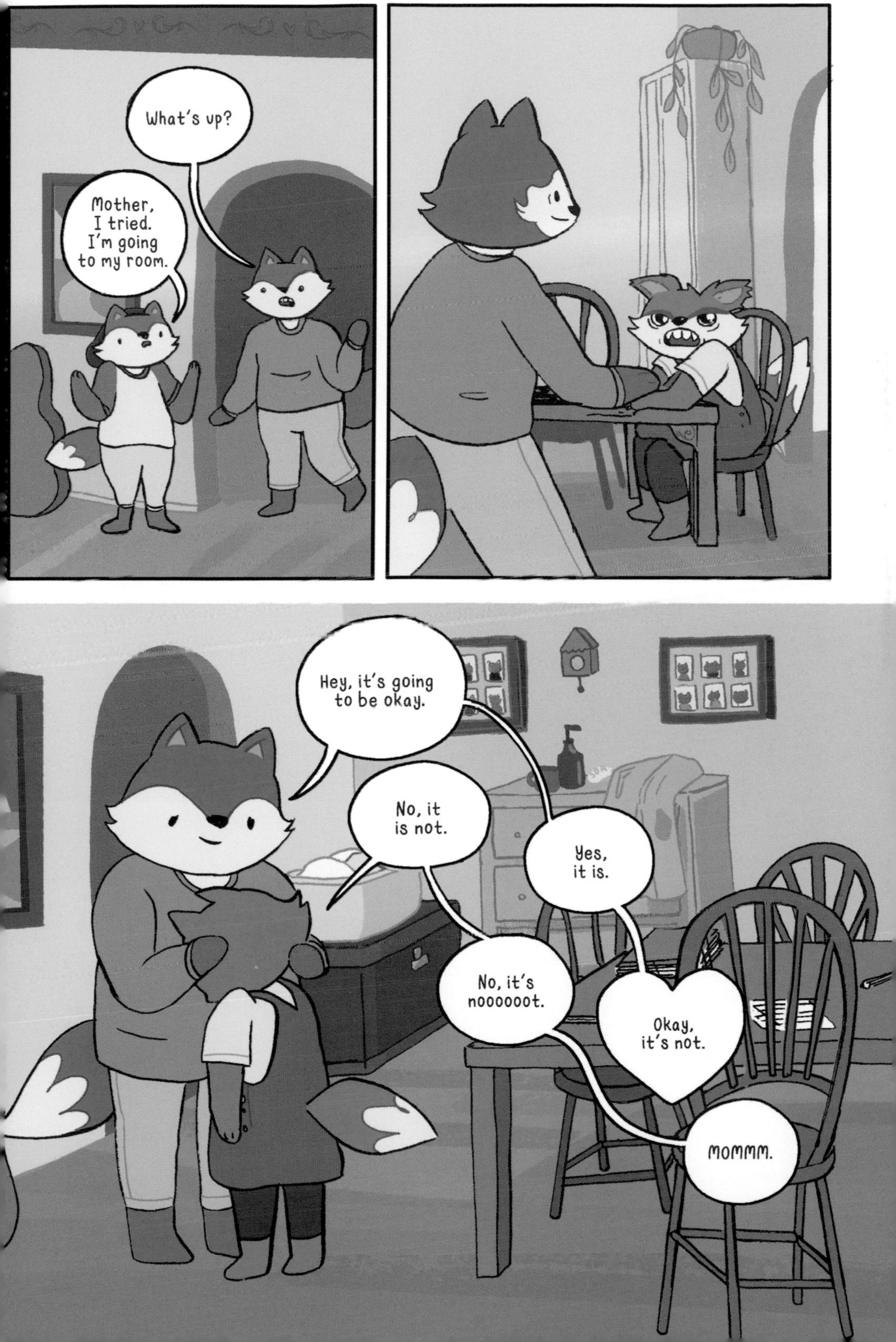
What's up?
Mother, I tried. I'm going to my room.
Hey, it's going to be okay.
No, it is not.
Yes, it is.
No, it's noooooot.
Okay, it's not.
MOMMM.

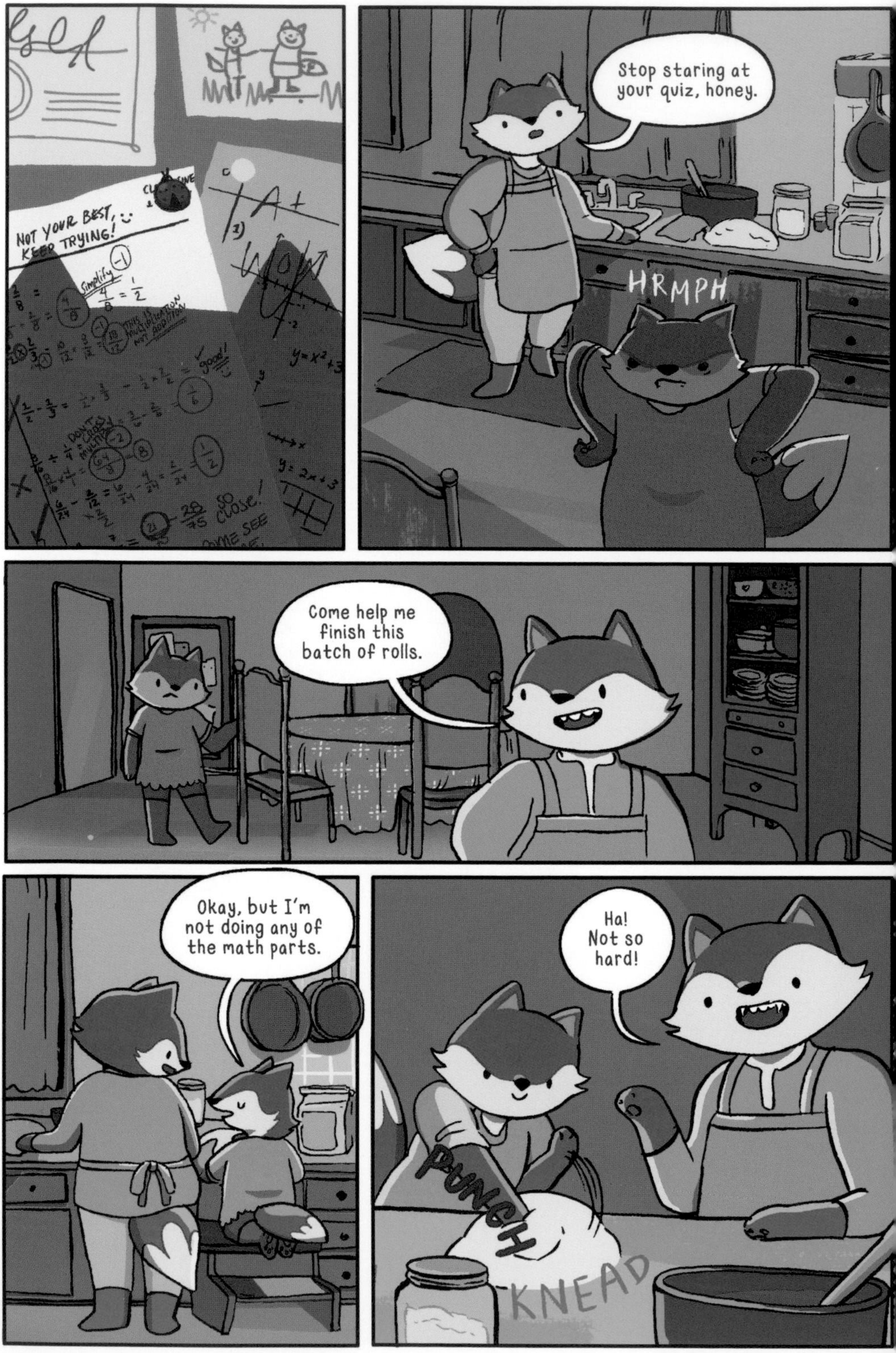
NOT YOUR BEST, KEEP TRYING!
Simplify
good!
SO CLOSE!
Stop staring at your quiz, honey.
HRMPH
Come help me finish this batch of rolls.
Okay, but I'm not doing any of the math parts.
Ha! Not so hard!
PUNCH
KNEAD

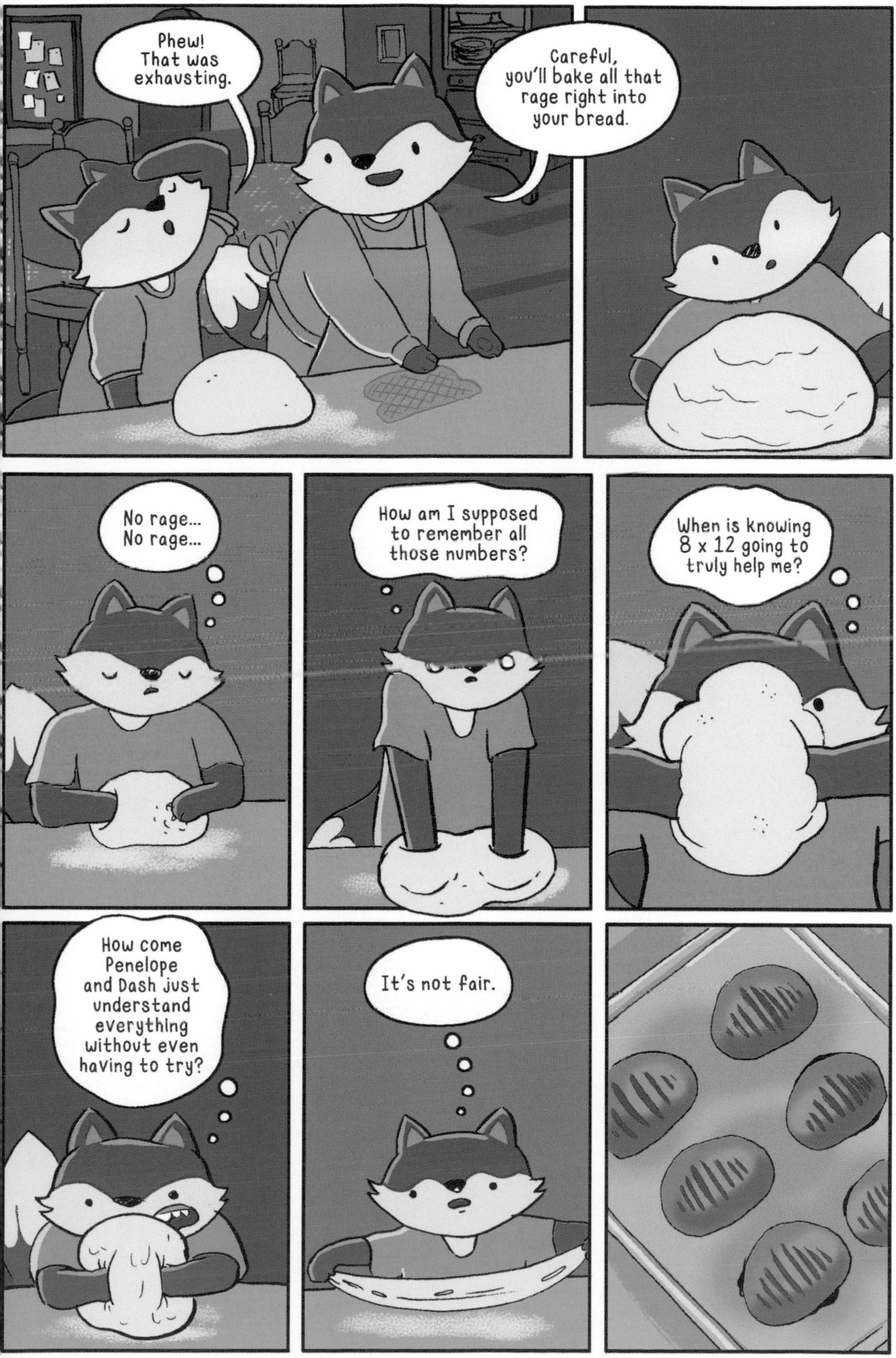
Phew! That was exhausting.
Careful, you'll bake all that rage right into your bread.
No rage... No rage...
How am I supposed to remember all those numbers?
When is knowing 8 x 12 going to truly help me?
How come Penelope and Dash just understand everything without even having to try?
It's not fair.

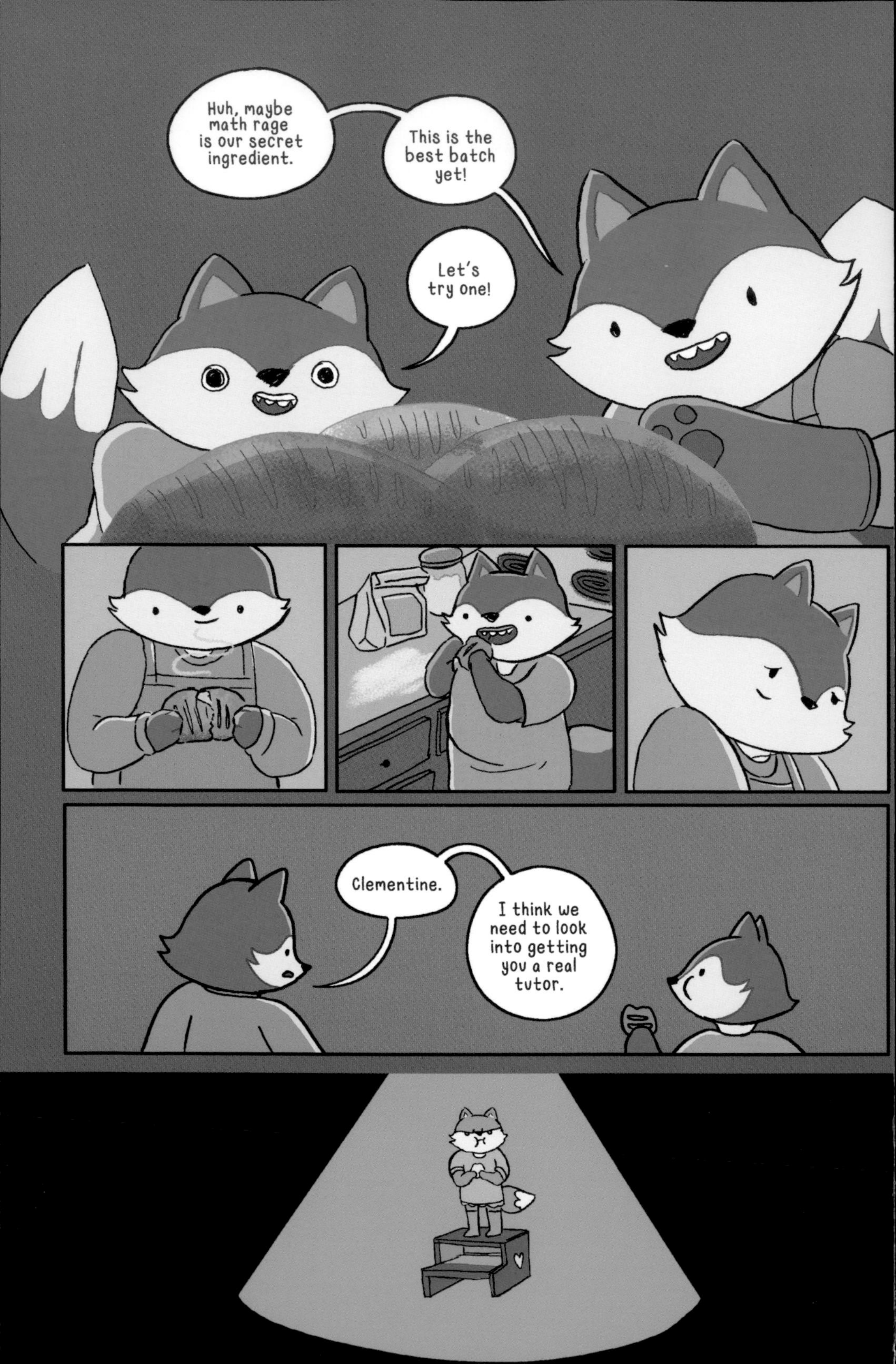
Huh, maybe math rage is our secret ingredient.
This is the best batch yet!
Let's try one!
Clementine.
I think we need to look into getting you a real tutor.

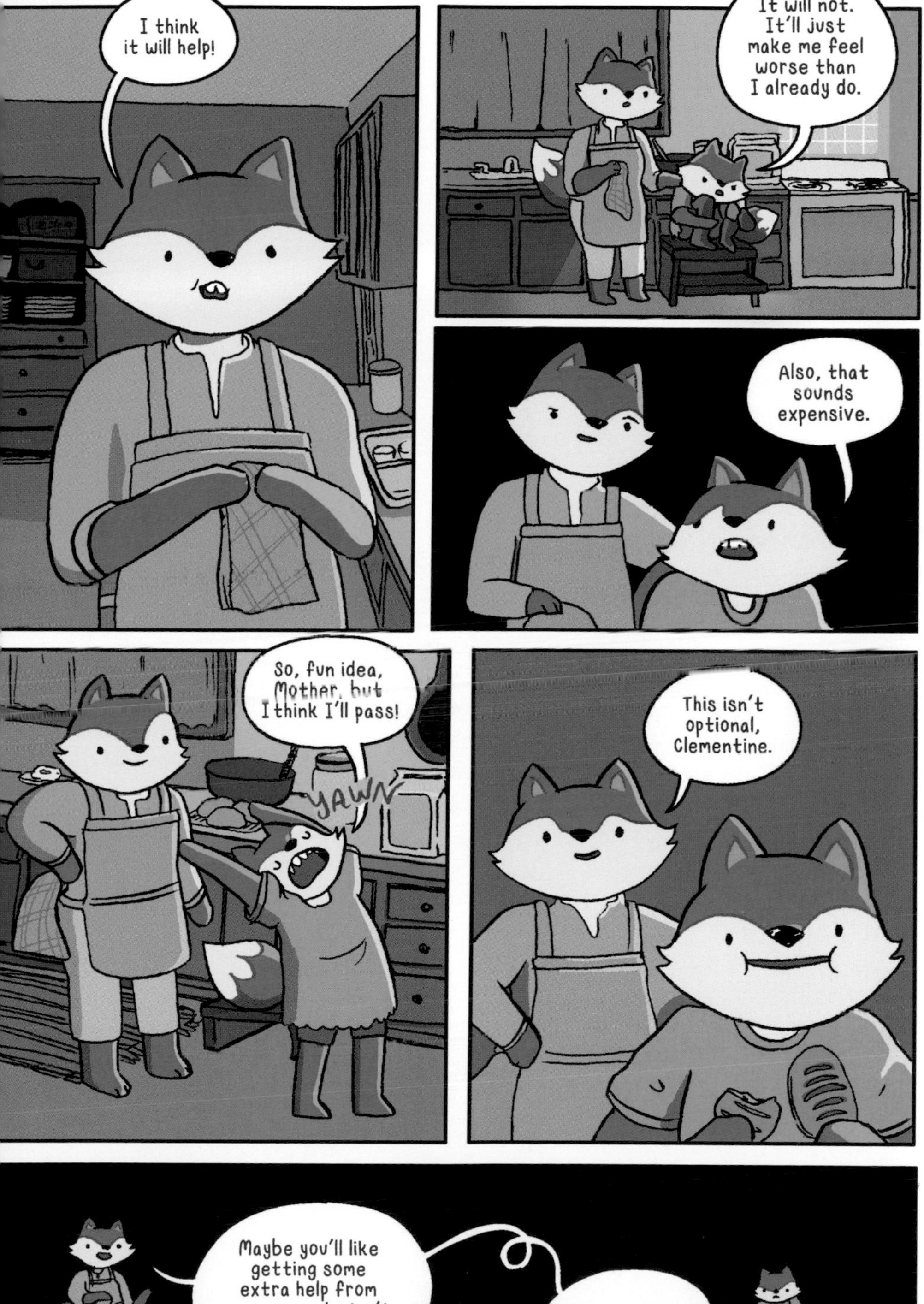
I think it will help!
It will not. It'll just make me feel worse than I already do.
Also, that sounds expensive.
So, fun idea, Mother, but I think I'll pass!
YAWN
This isn't optional, Clementine.
Maybe you'll like getting some extra help from someone who isn't your brother.
We are going to try this!

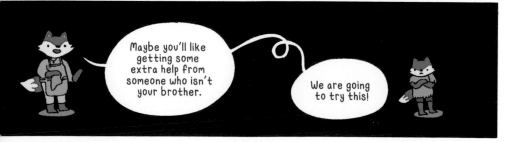

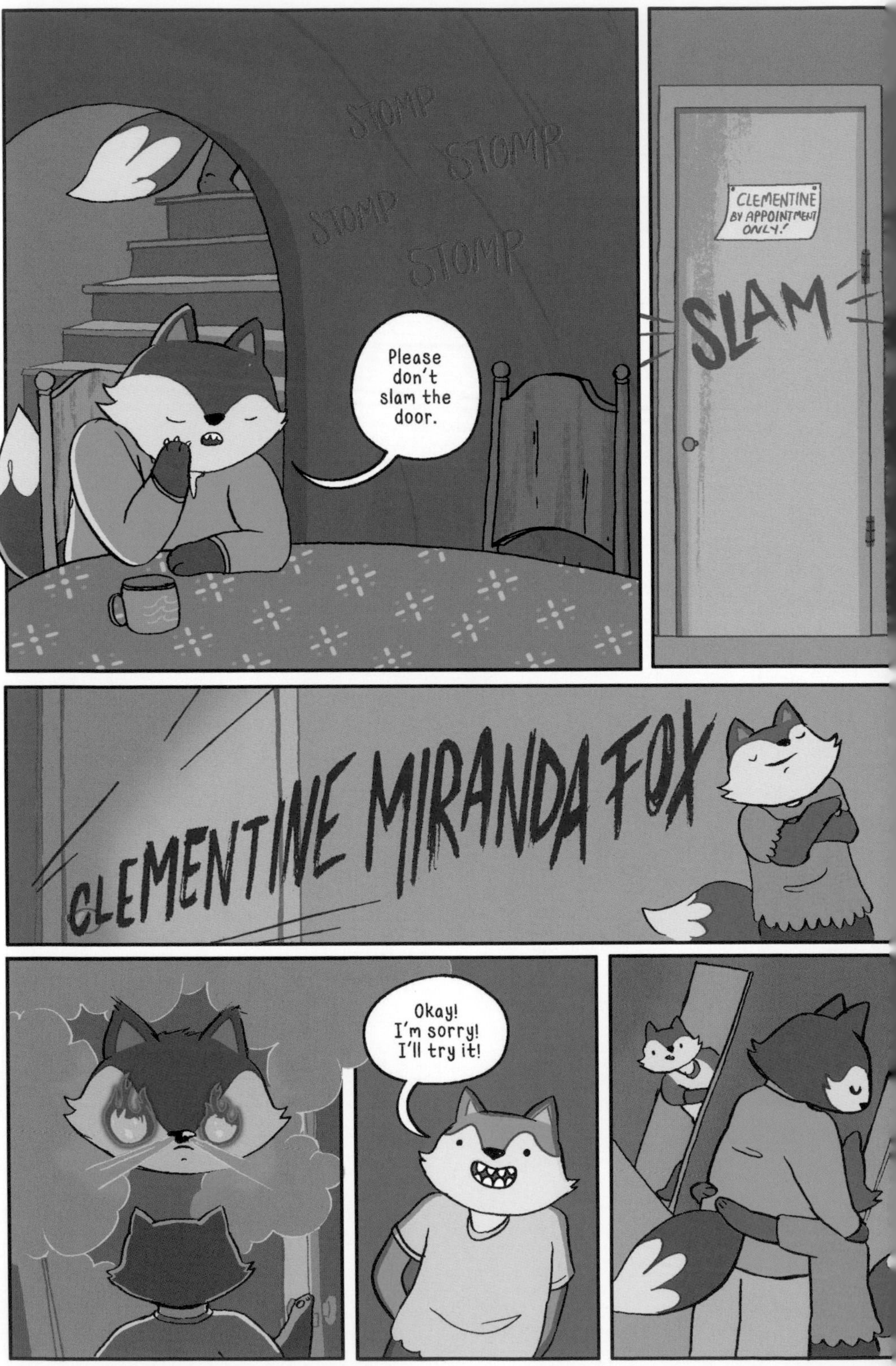
STOMP
STOMP
STOMP
STOMP
Please don't slam the door.
CLEMENTINE BY APPOINTMENT ONLY!
SLAM
CLEMENTINE MIRANDA FOX
Okay! I'm sorry! I'll try it!

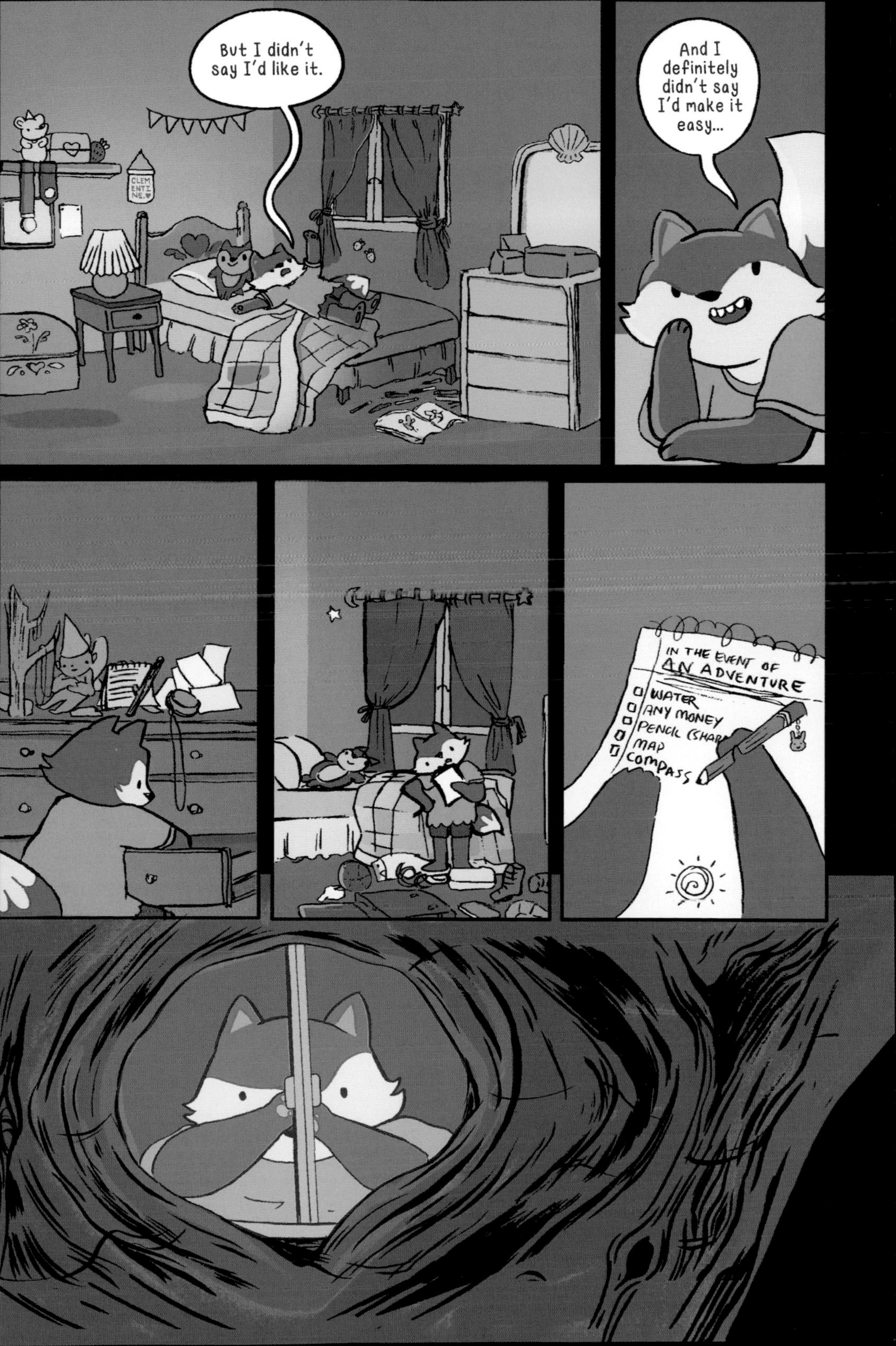
But I didn't say I'd like it.
CLEMENTINE.
And I definitely didn't say I'd make it easy...
IN THE EVENT OF AN ADVENTURE
WATER
ANY MONEY
PENCIL (SHAR
MAP
COMPASS

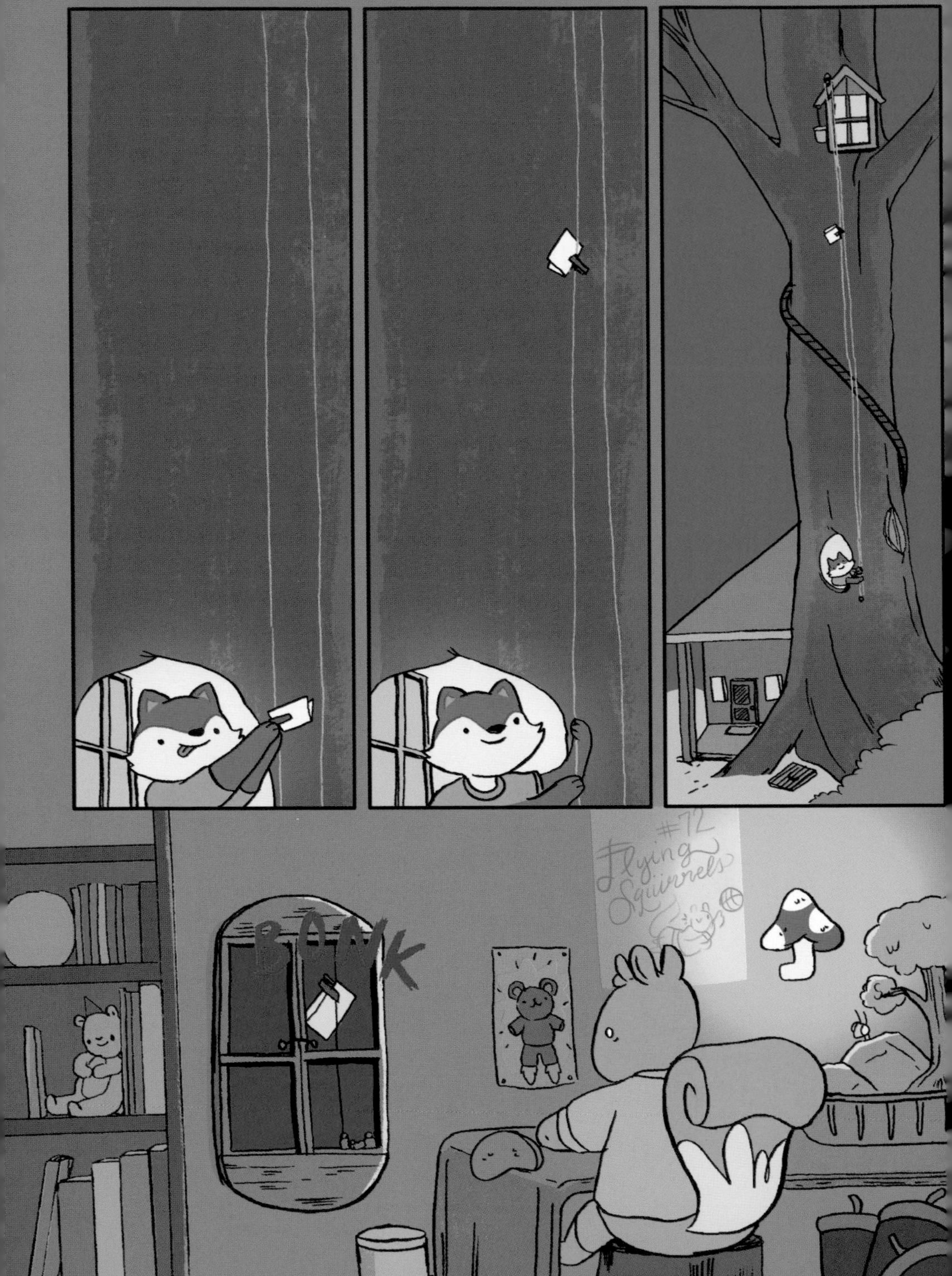
BONK
#72
Flying Squirrels

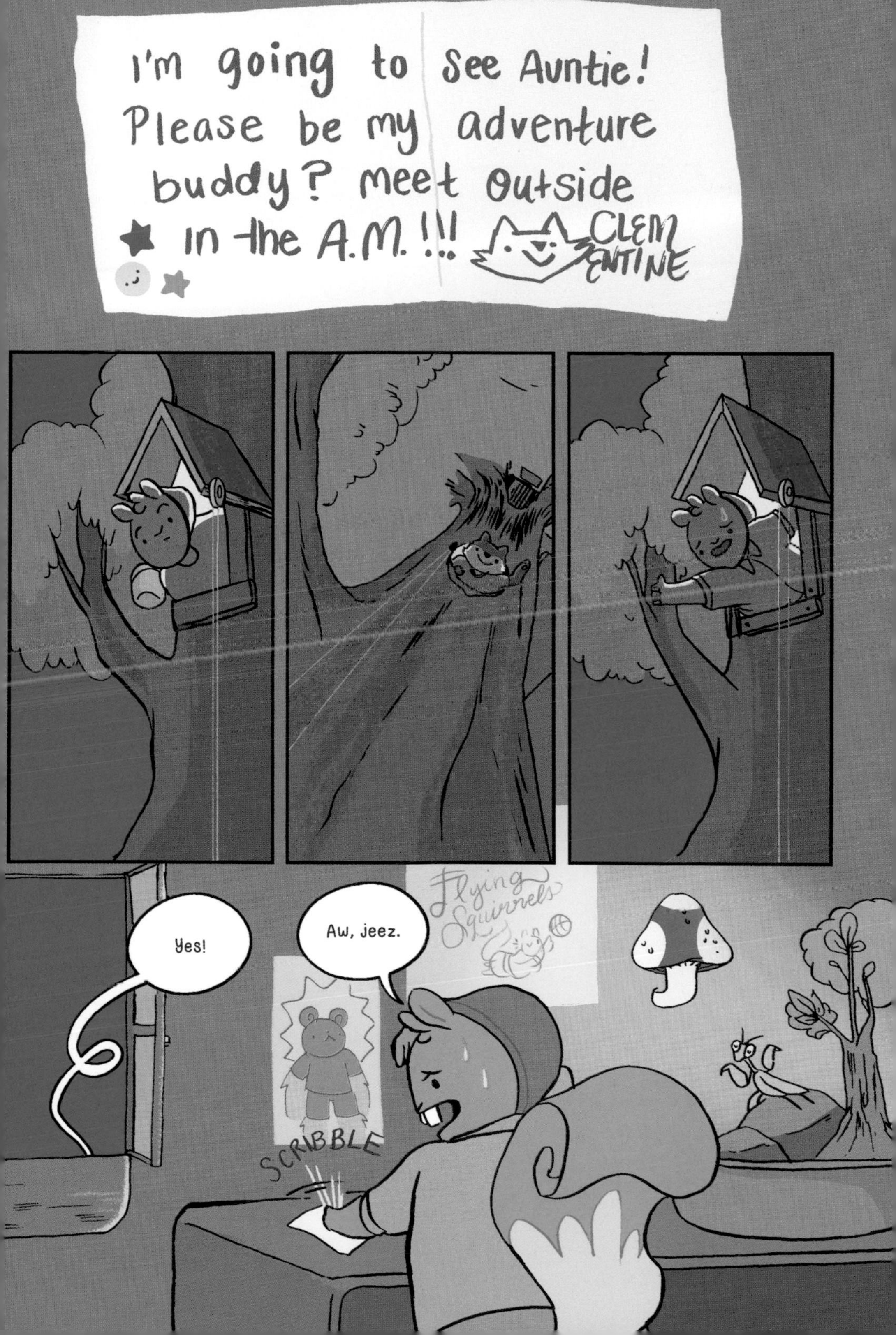
I'm going to see Auntie! Please be my adventure buddy? meet Outside in the A.M. !!! CLEMENTINE
Yes!
Aw, jeez.
Flying Squirrels
SCRIBBLE

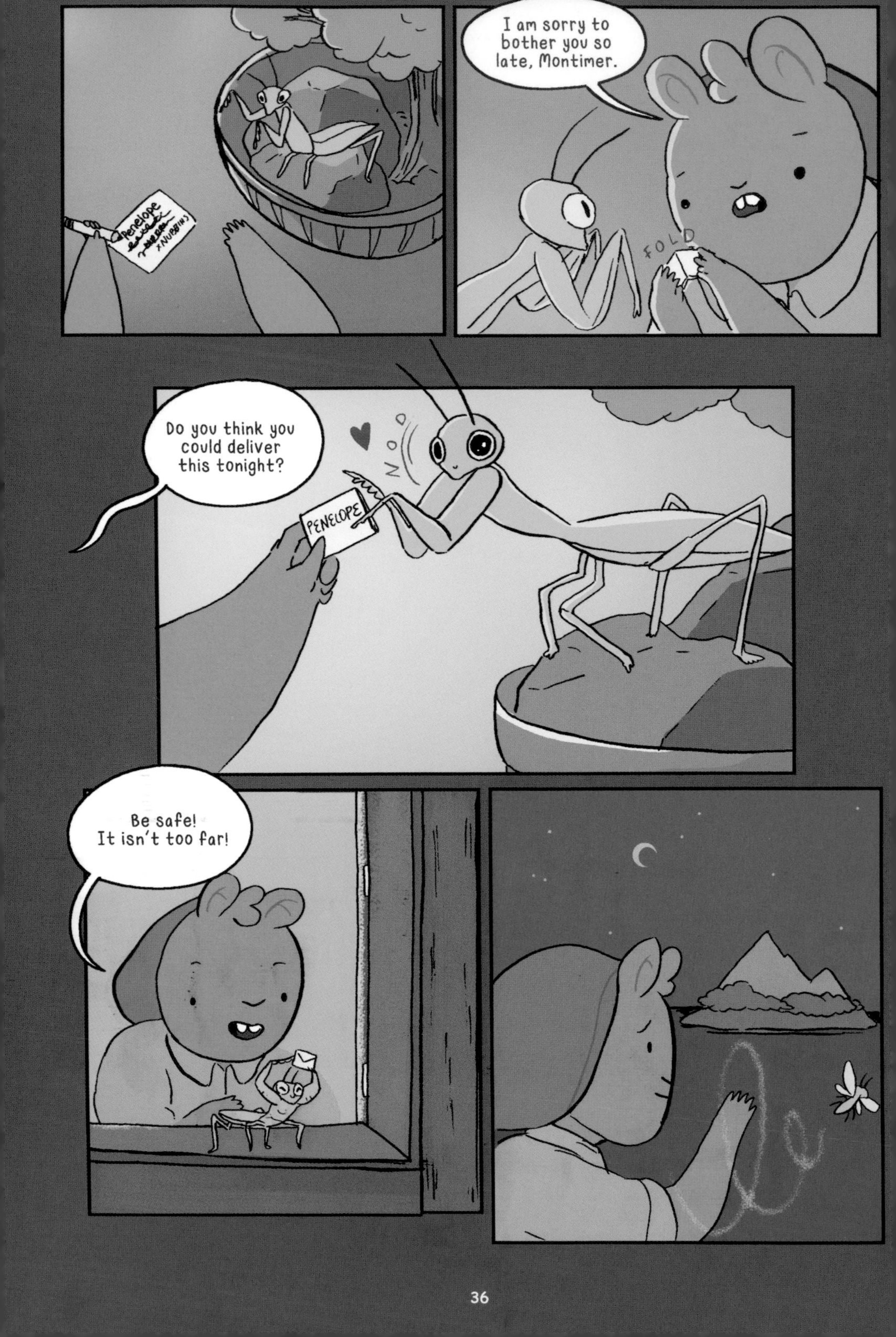
Penelope
xNUBBINS
I am sorry to bother you so late, Montimer.
FOLD
Do you think you could deliver this tonight?
NOD
PENELOPE
Be safe! It isn't too far!

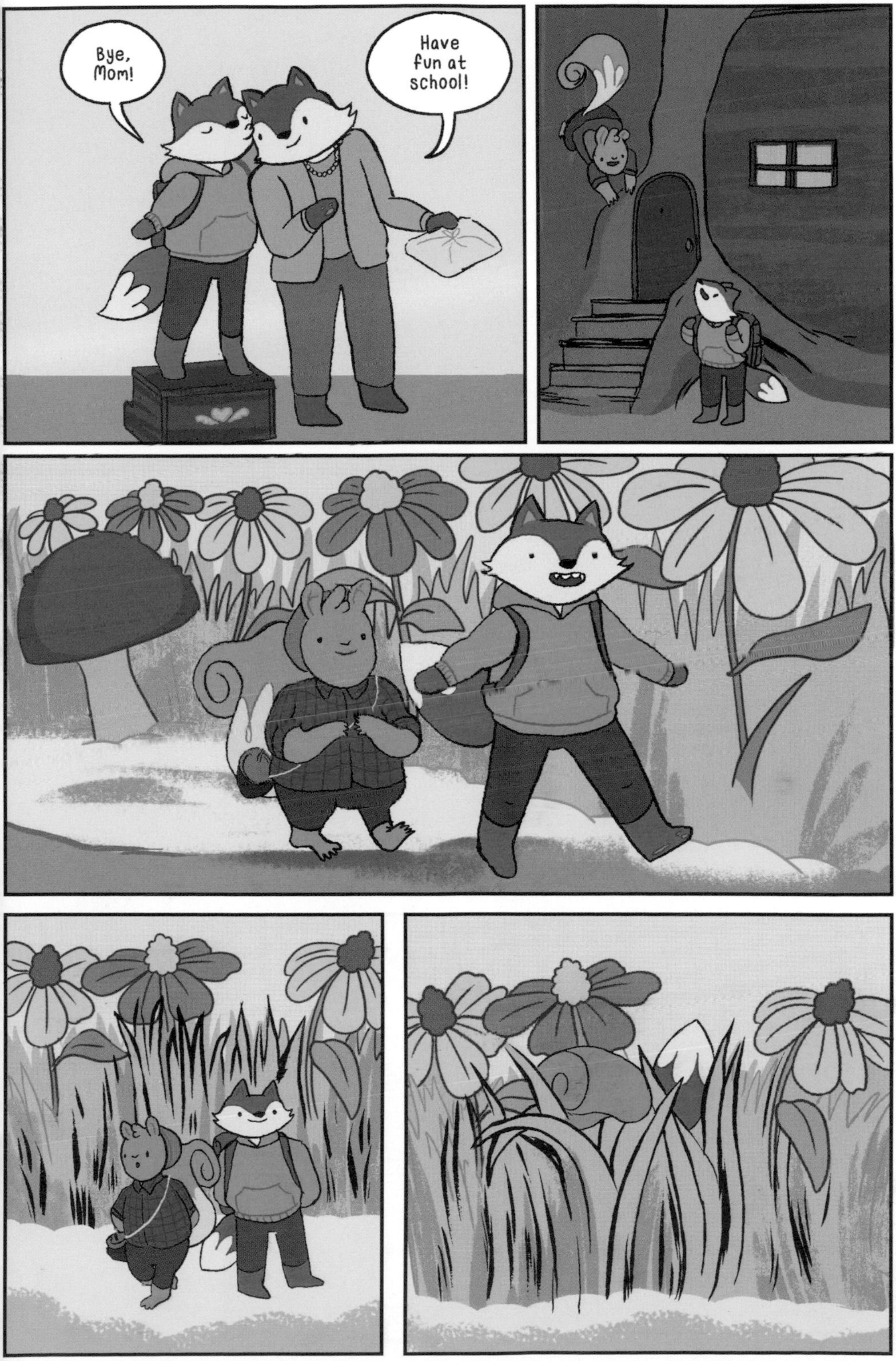
Bye, Mom!
Have fun at school!

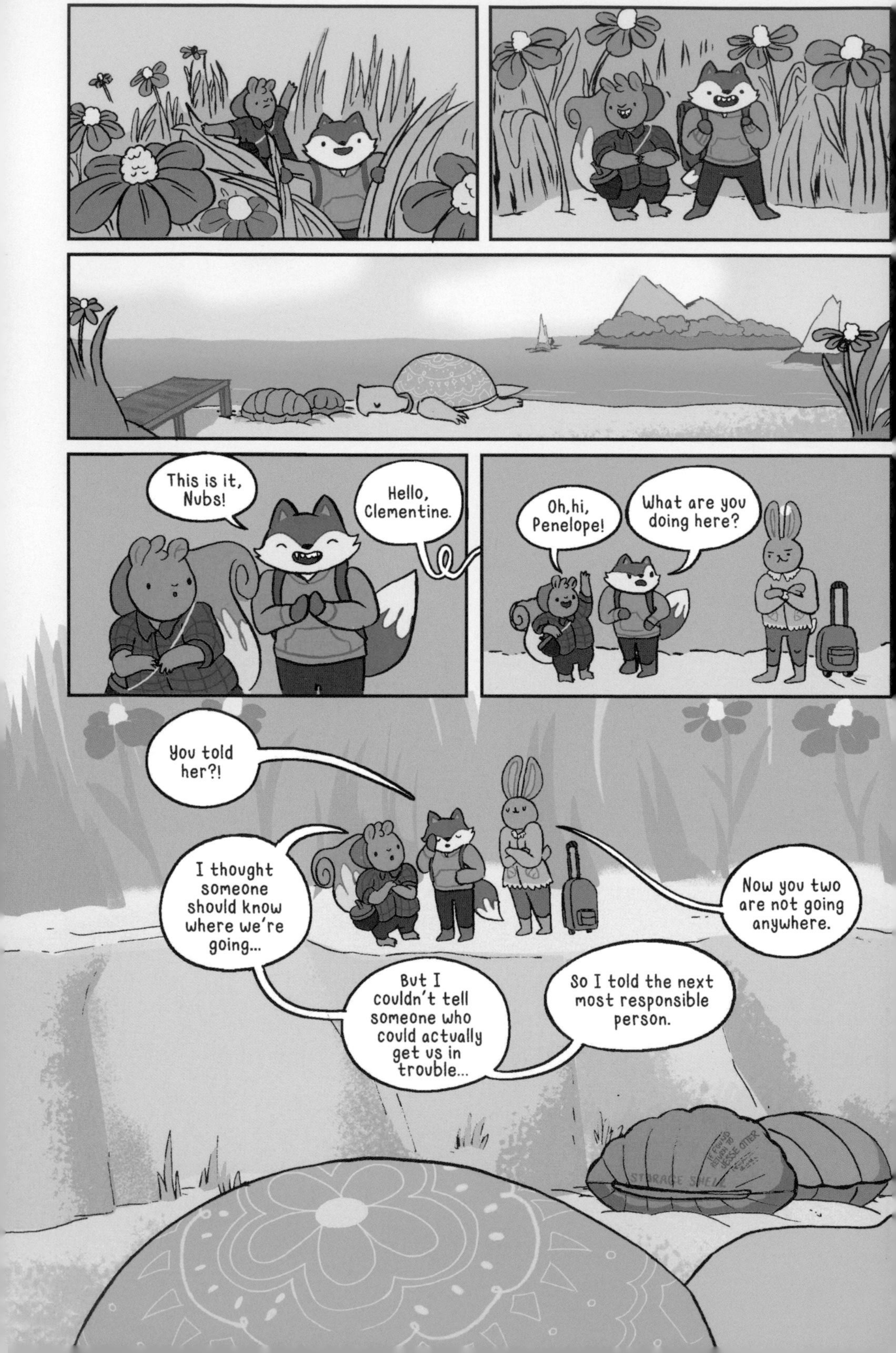

This is it, Nubs!
Hello, Clementine.
Oh, hi, Penelope!
What are you doing here?
You told her?!
I thought someone should know where we're going...
But I couldn't tell someone who could actually get us in trouble...
So I told the next most responsible person.
Now you two are not going anywhere.
IF FOUND RETURN TO JESSE OTTER

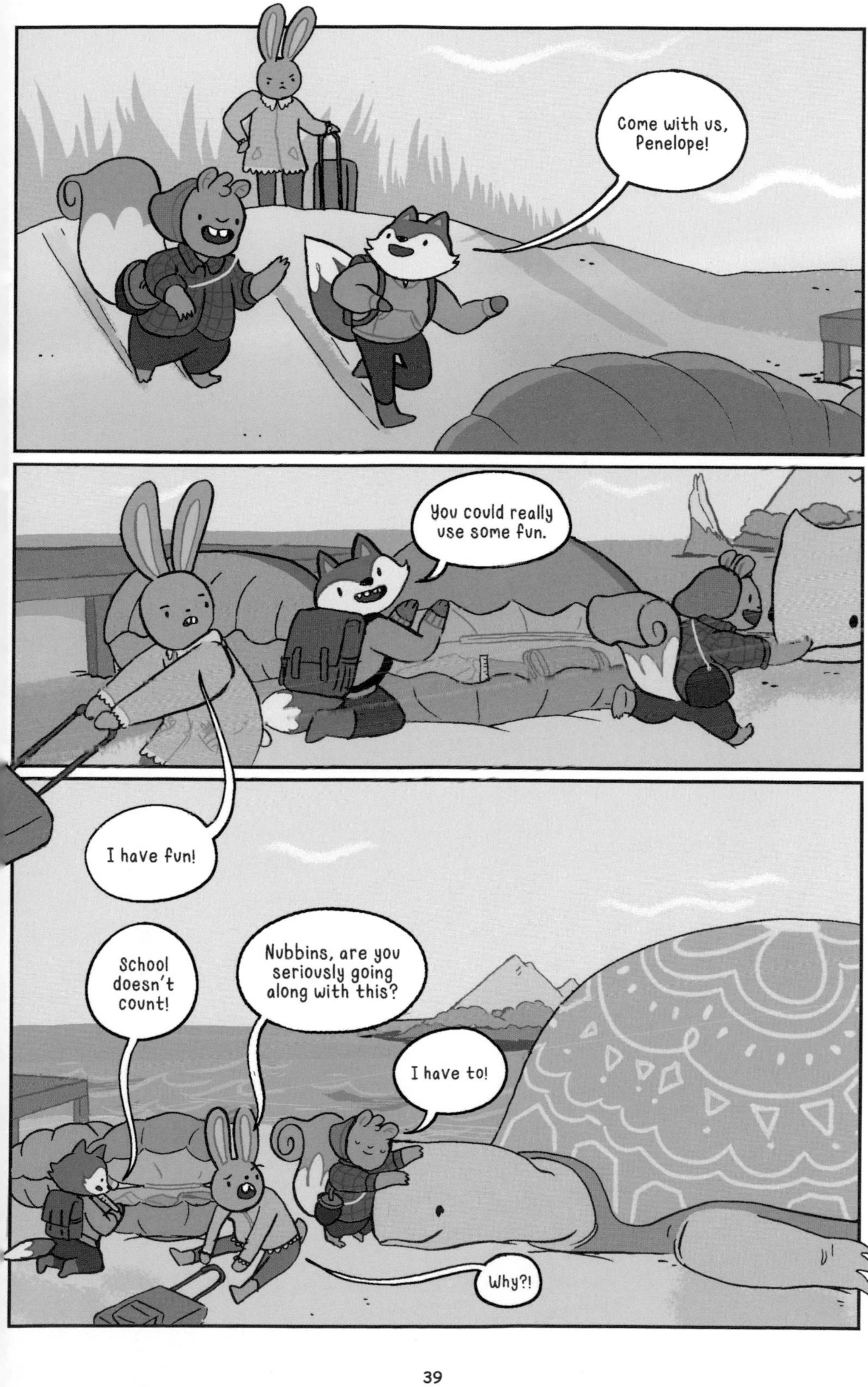
Come with us, Penelope!
You could really use some fun.
I have fun!
School doesn't count!
Nubbins, are you seriously going along with this?
I have to!
Why?!

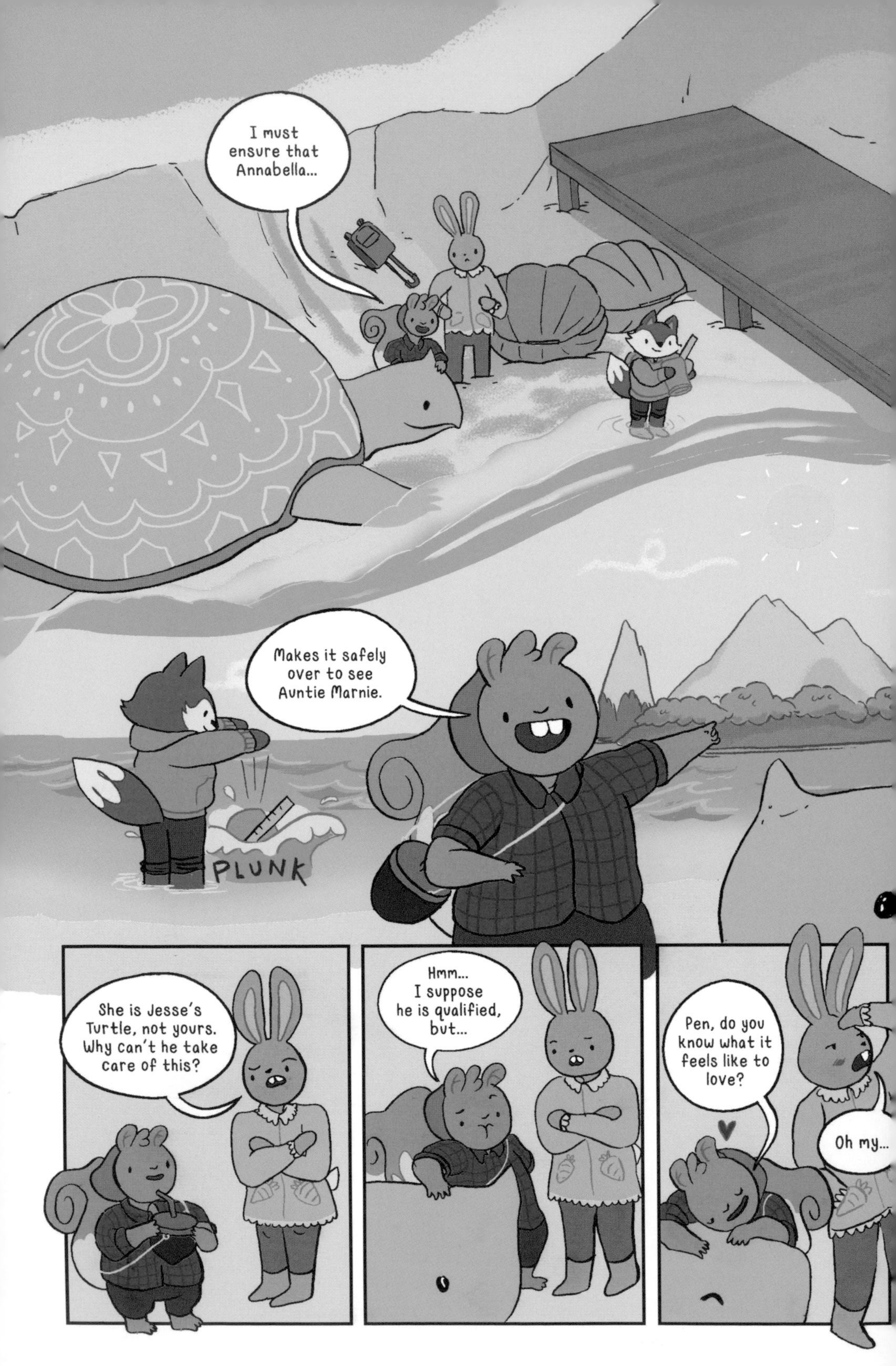
I must ensure that Annabella...
Makes it safely over to see Auntie Marnie.
PLUNK
She is Jesse's Turtle, not yours. Why can't he take care of this?
Hmm... I suppose he is qualified, but...
Pen, do you know what it feels like to love?
Oh my...

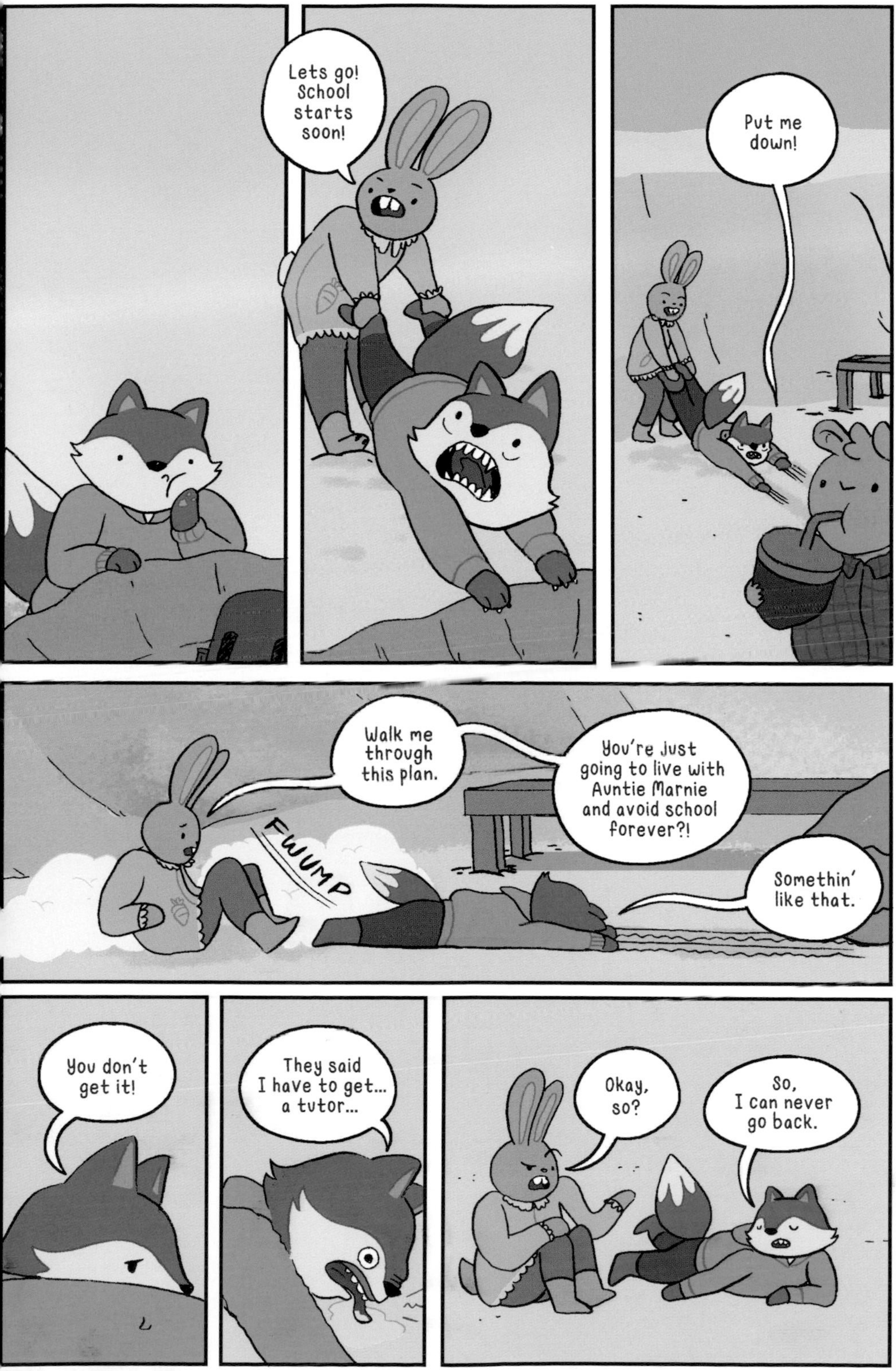
Lets go! School starts soon!
Put me down!
Walk me through this plan.
You're just going to live with Auntie Marnie and avoid school forever?!
FWUMP
Somethin' like that.
You don't get it!
They said I have to get... a tutor...
Okay, so?
So, I can never go back.

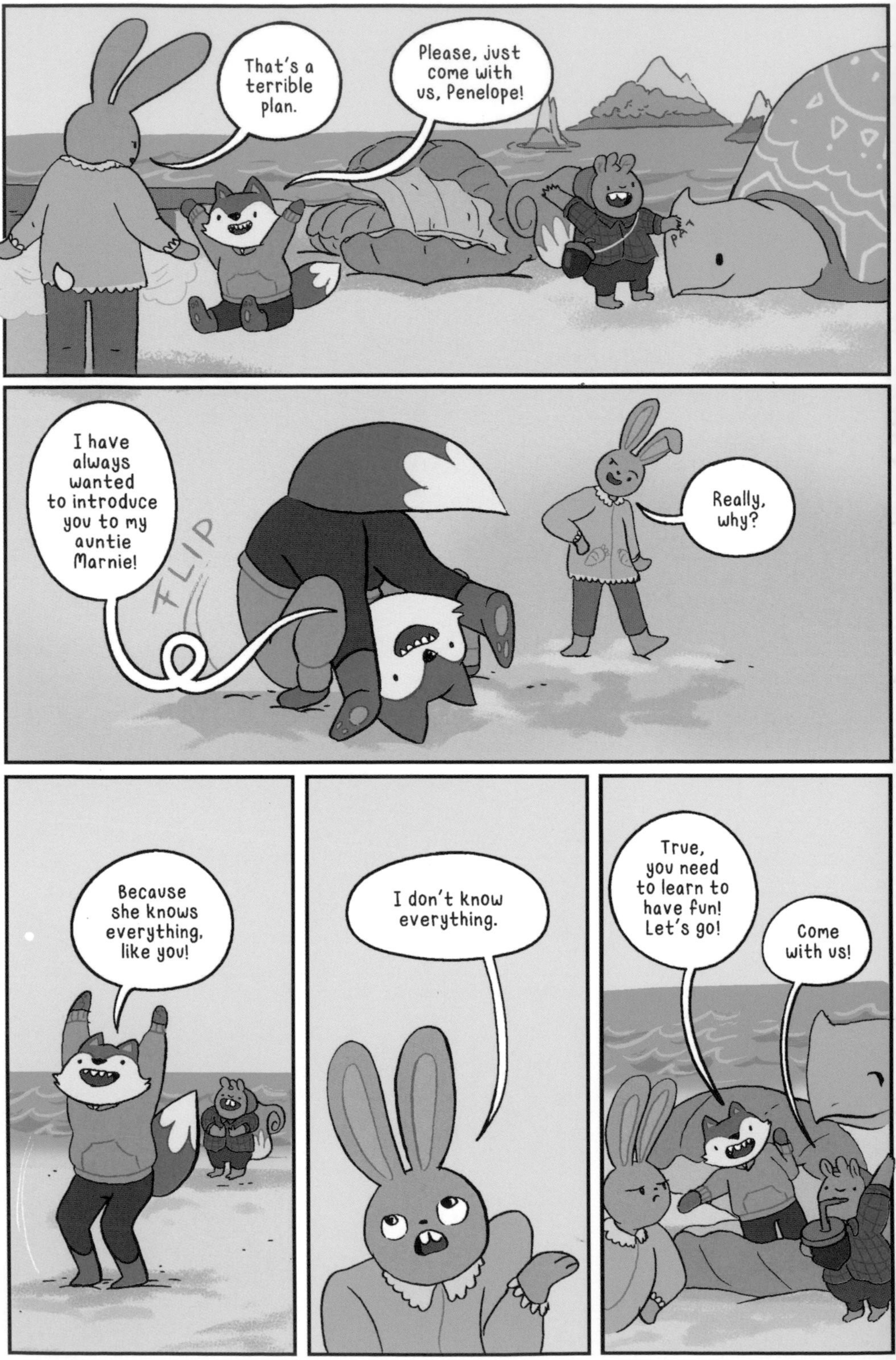
That's a terrible plan.
Please, just come with us, Penelope!
PAT
I have always wanted to introduce you to my auntie Marnie!
FLIP
Really, why?
Because she knows everything, like you!
I don't know everything.
True, you need to learn to have fun! Let's go!
Come with us!

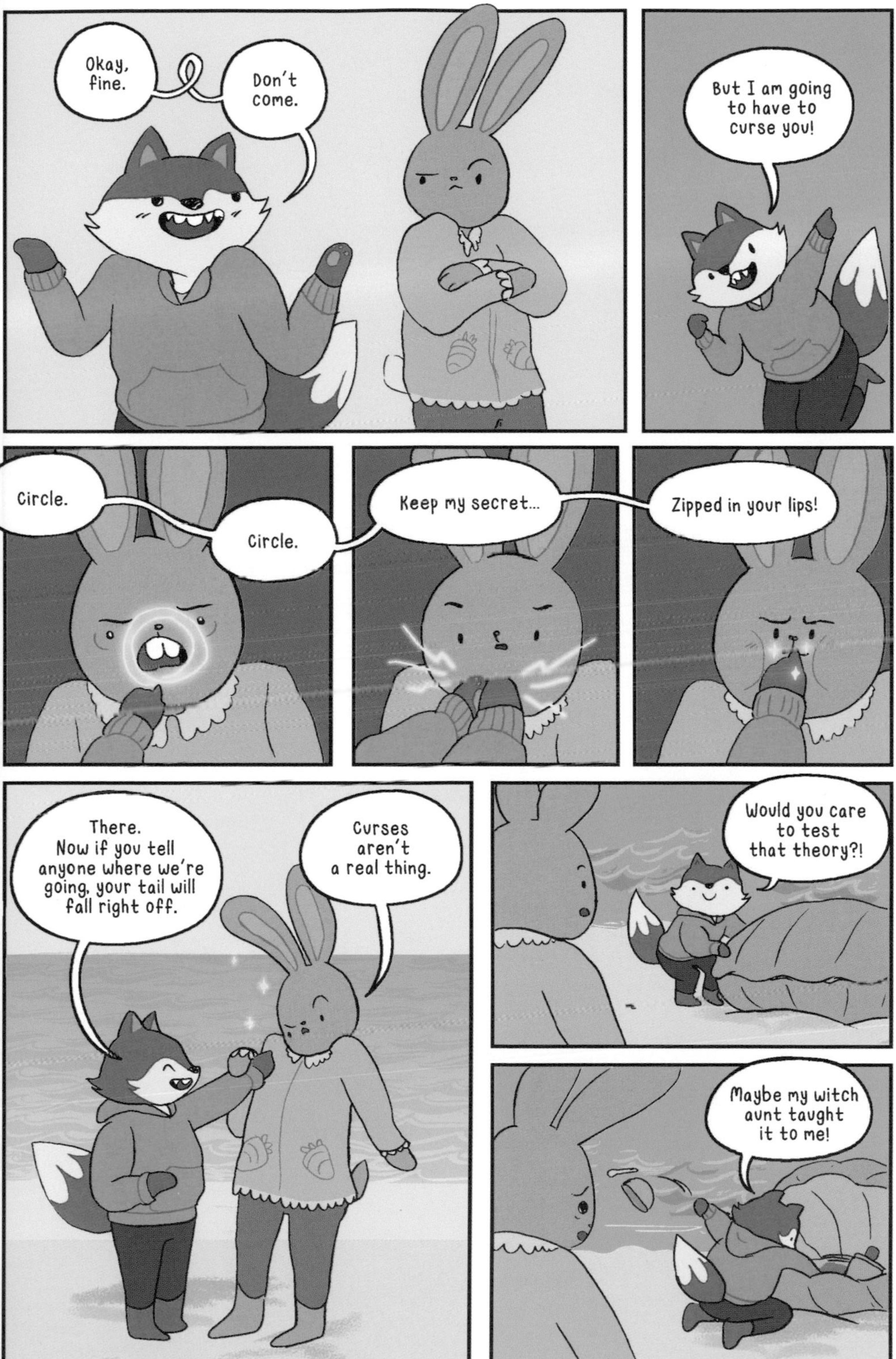
Okay, fine.
Don't come.
But I am going to have to curse you!
Circle.
Circle.
Keep my secret...
Zipped in your lips!
There. Now if you tell anyone where we're going, your tail will fall right off.
Curses aren't a real thing.
Would you care to test that theory?!
Maybe my witch aunt taught it to me!

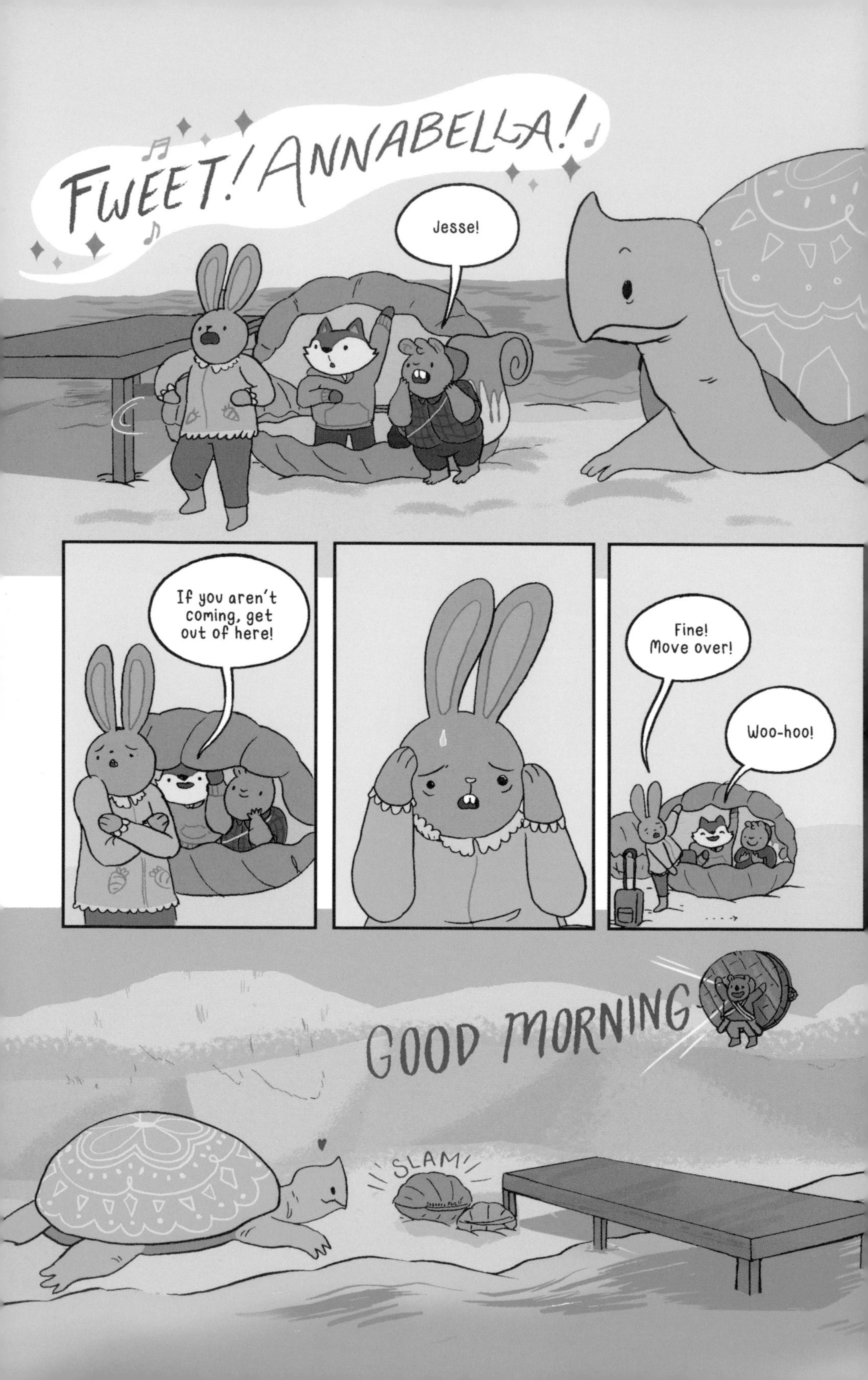
FWEET! ANNABELLA!
Jesse!
If you aren't coming, get out of here!
Fine! Move over!
Woo-hoo!
GOOD MORNING
SLAM

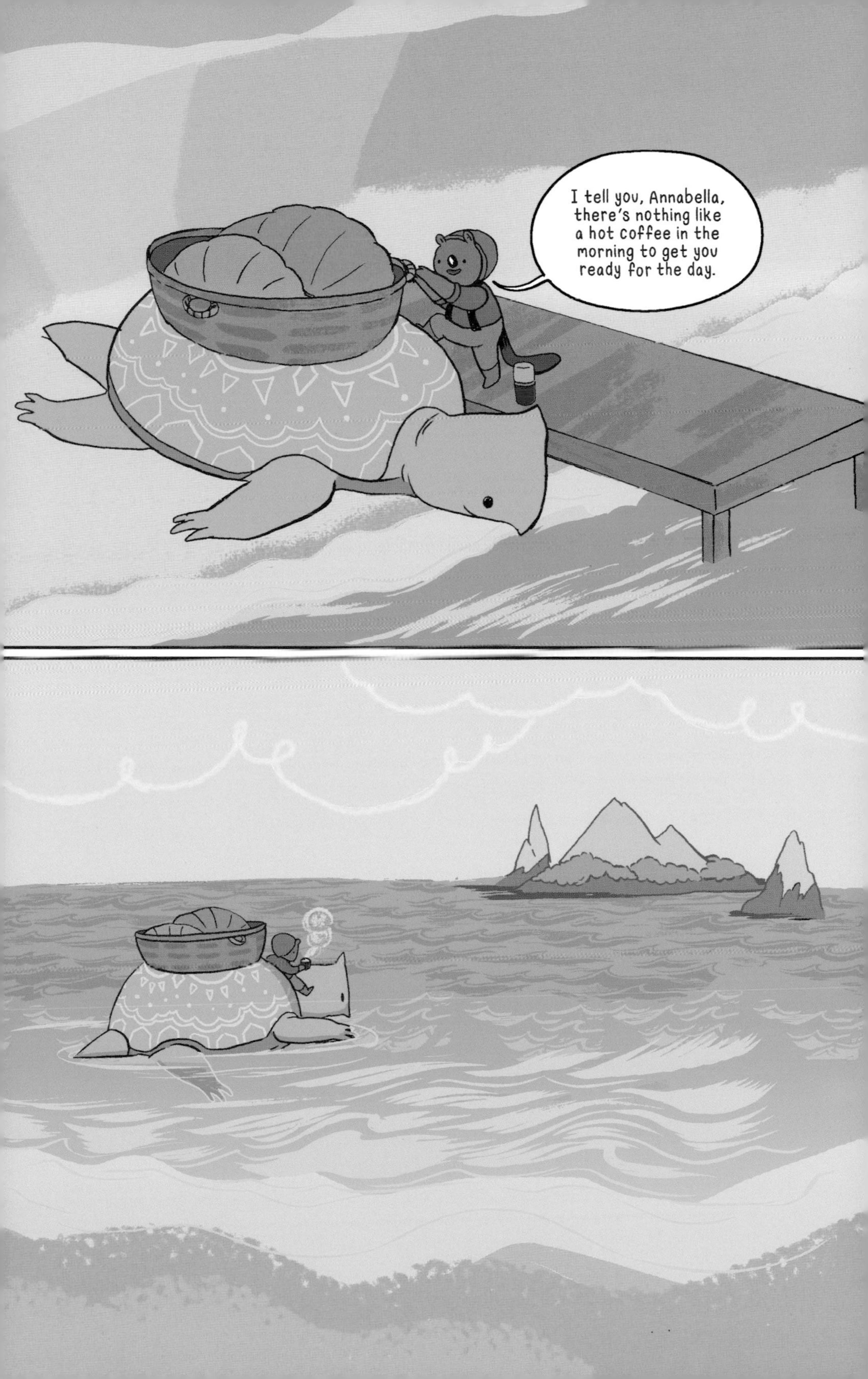
I tell you, Annabella, there's nothing like a hot coffee in the morning to get you ready for the day.

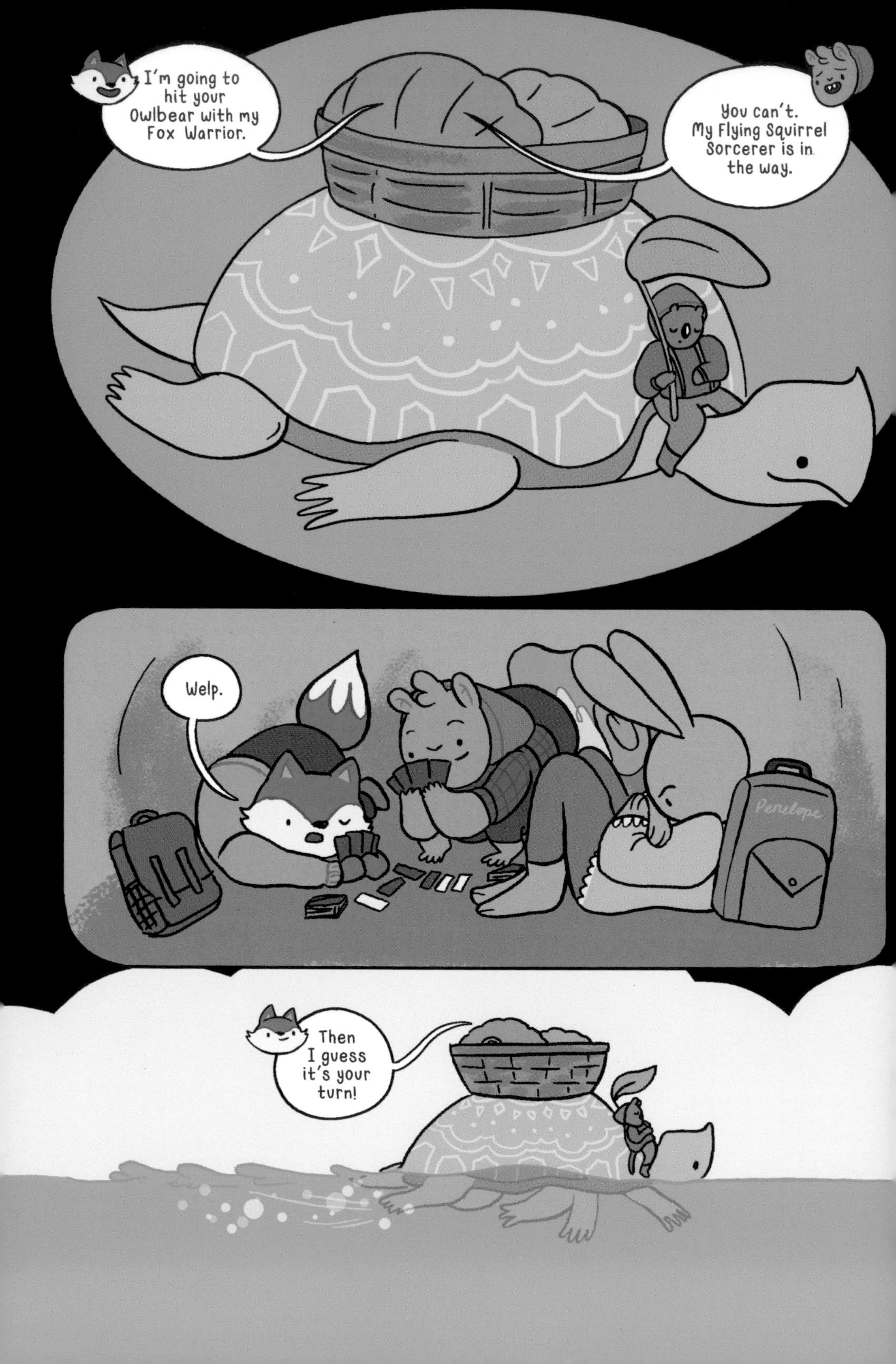

I'm going to hit your Owlbear with my Fox Warrior.
You can't. My Flying Squirrel Sorcerer is in the way.
Welp.
Penelope
Then I guess it's your turn!

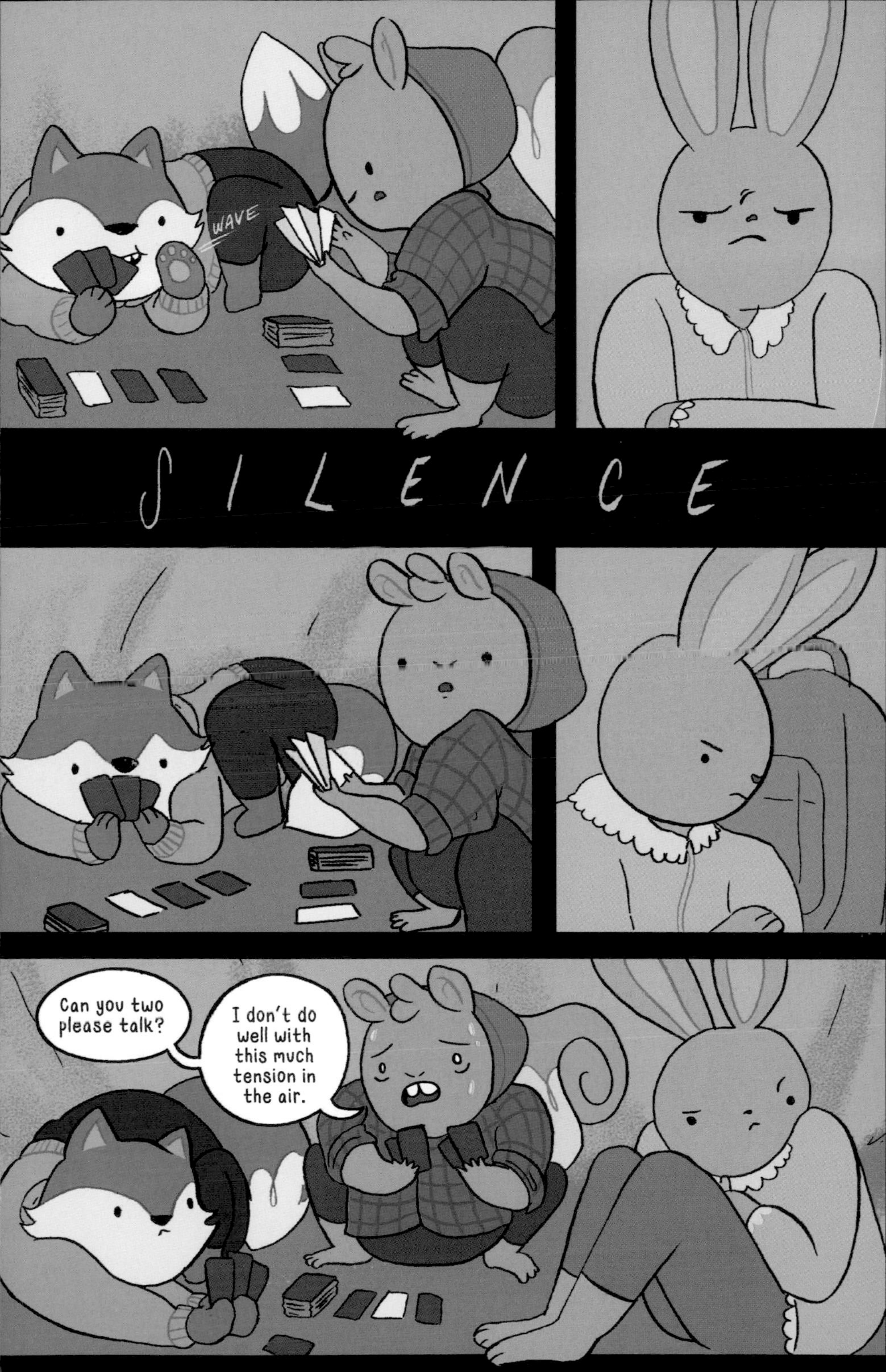
WAVE
SILENCE
Can you two please talk?
I don't do well with this much tension in the air.

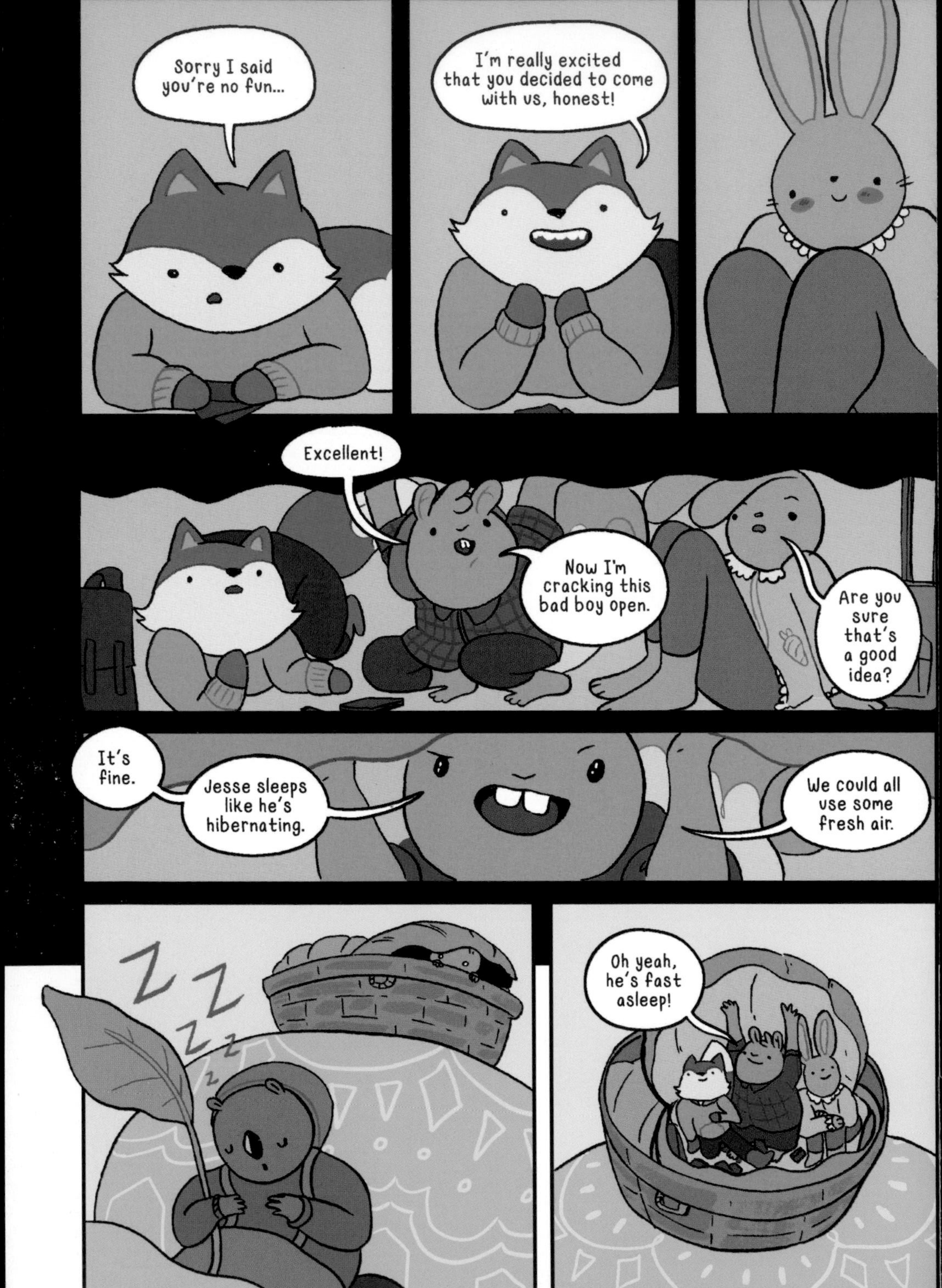
Sorry I said you're no fun...
I'm really excited that you decided to come with us, honest!
Excellent!
Now I'm cracking this bad boy open.
Are you sure that's a good idea?
It's fine.
Jesse sleeps like he's hibernating.
We could all use some fresh air.
Oh yeah, he's fast asleep!

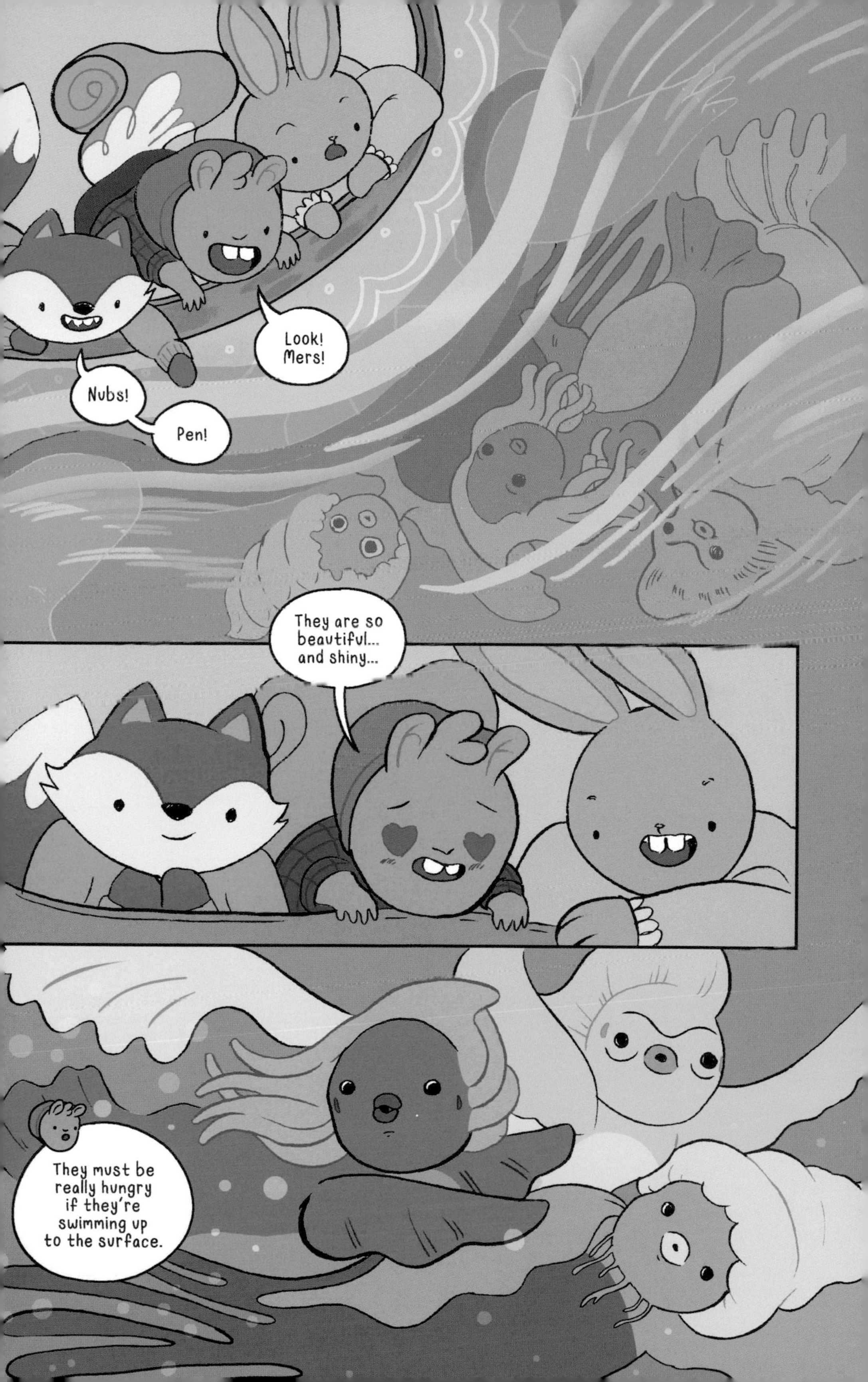
Look! Mers!
Nubs!
Pen!
They are so beautiful... and shiny...
They must be really hungry if they're swimming up to the surface.

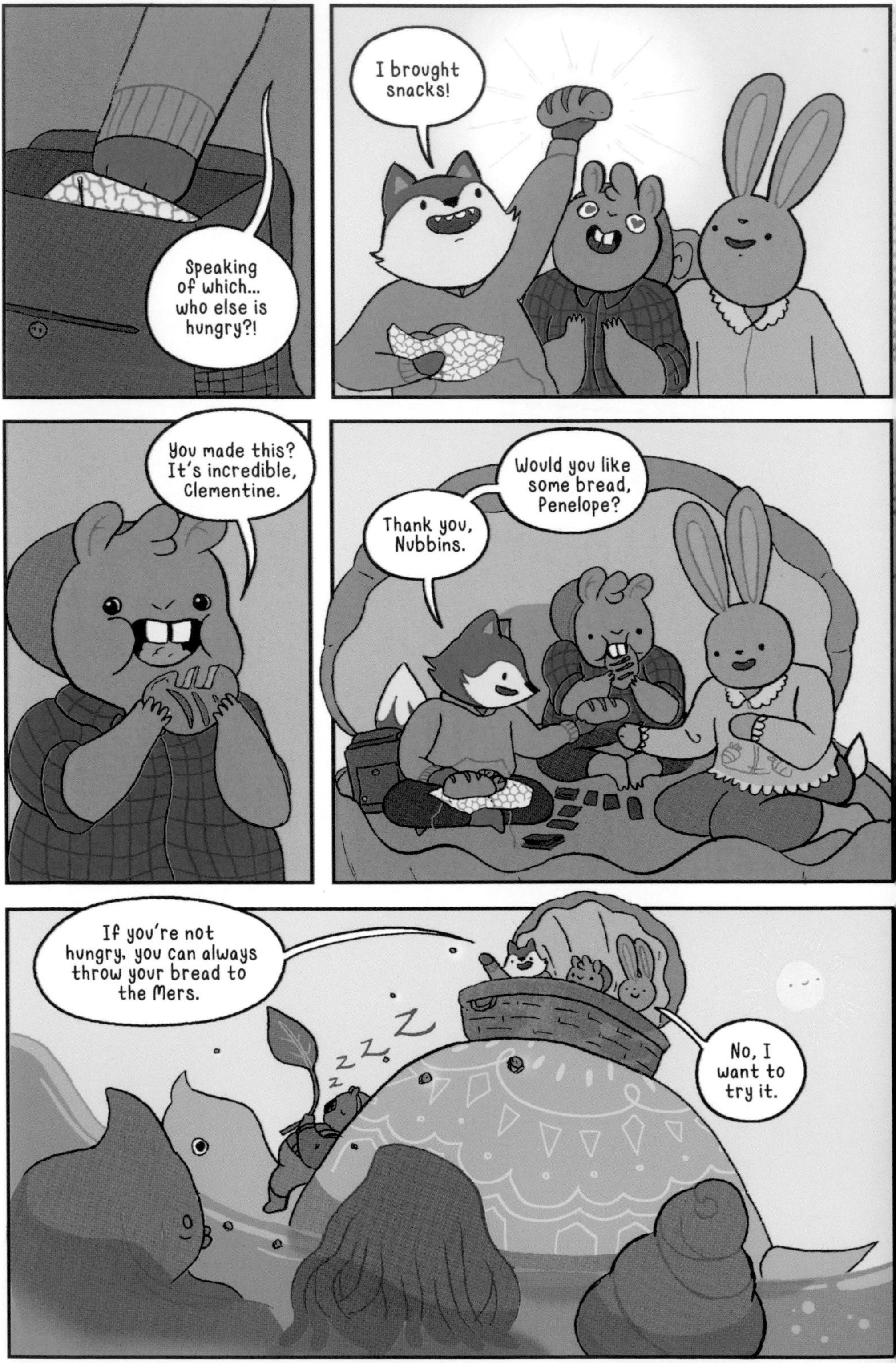
Speaking of which... who else is hungry?!
I brought snacks!
You made this? It's incredible, Clementine.
Thank you, Nubbins.
Would you like some bread, Penelope?
If you're not hungry, you can always throw your bread to the Mers.
Z Z Z Z
No, I want to try it.

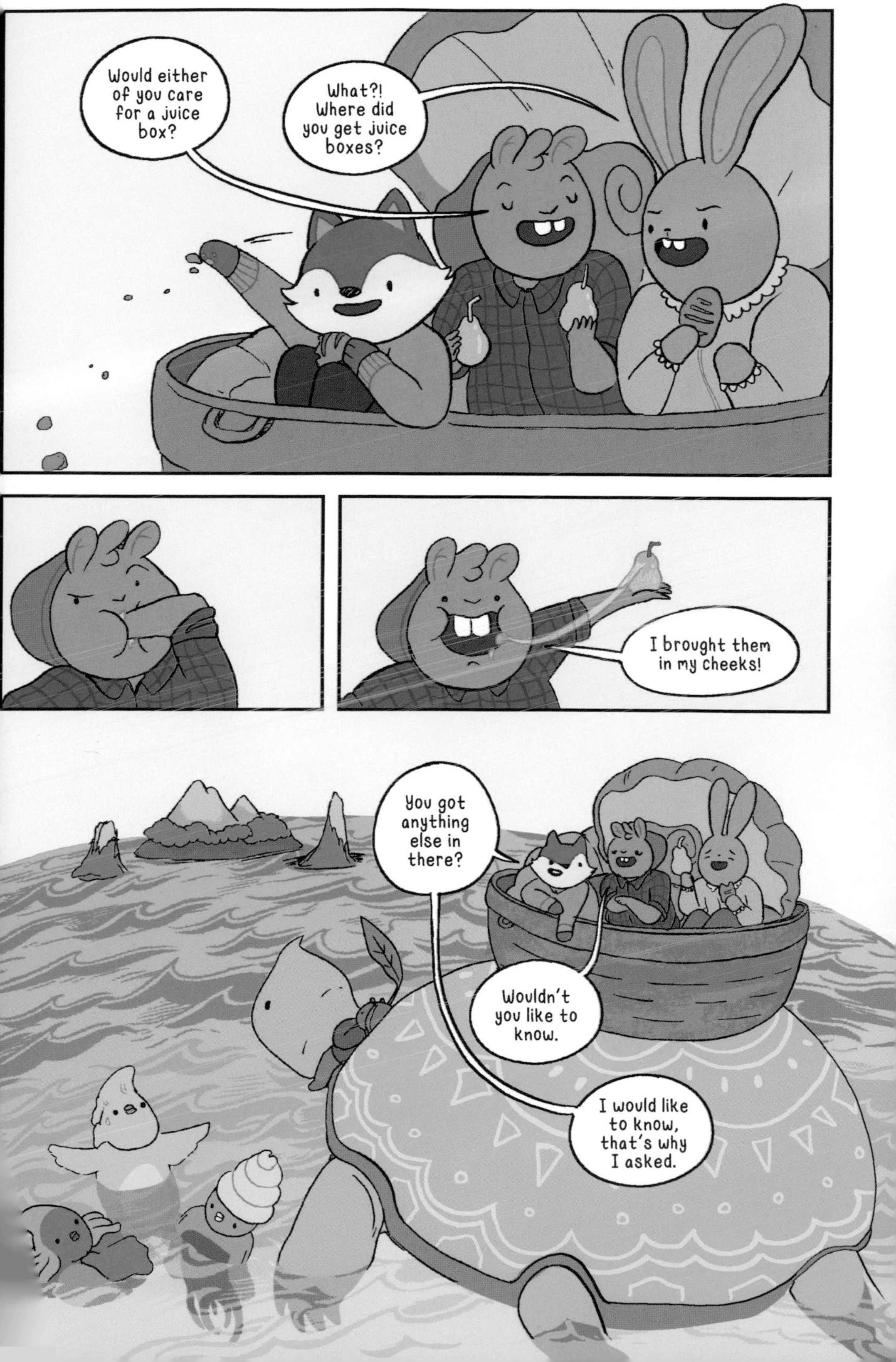

Would either of you care for a juice box?
What?! Where did you get juice boxes?
I brought them in my cheeks!
You got anything else in there?
Wouldn't you like to know.
I would like to know, that's why I asked.

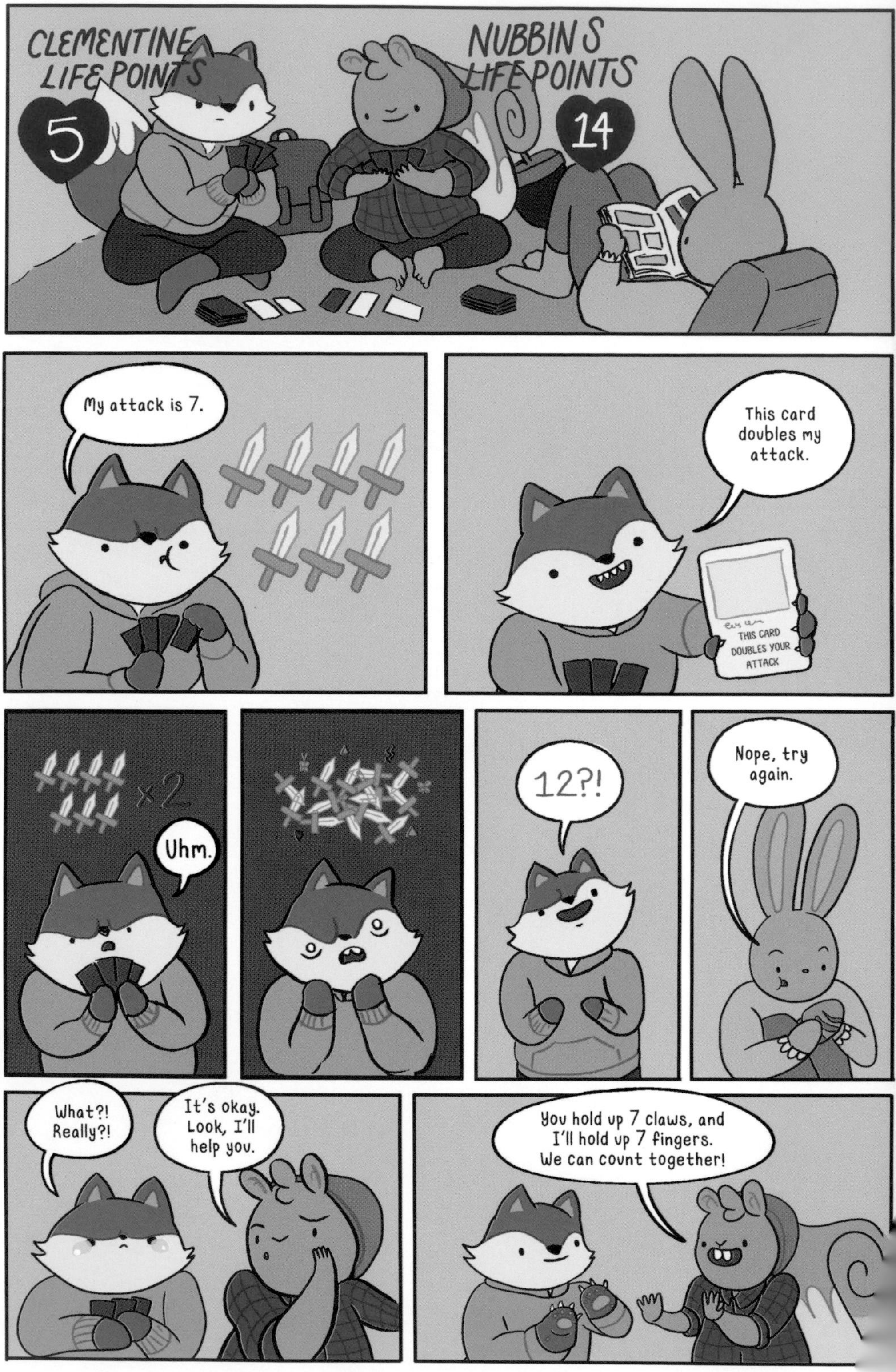
CLEMENTINE LIFE POINTS
5
NUBBINS LIFE POINTS
14
My attack is 7.
This card doubles my attack.
THIS CARD DOUBLES YOUR ATTACK
x2
Uhm.
12?!
Nope, try again.
What?! Really?!
It's okay. Look, I'll help you.
You hold up 7 claws, and I'll hold up 7 fingers. We can count together!

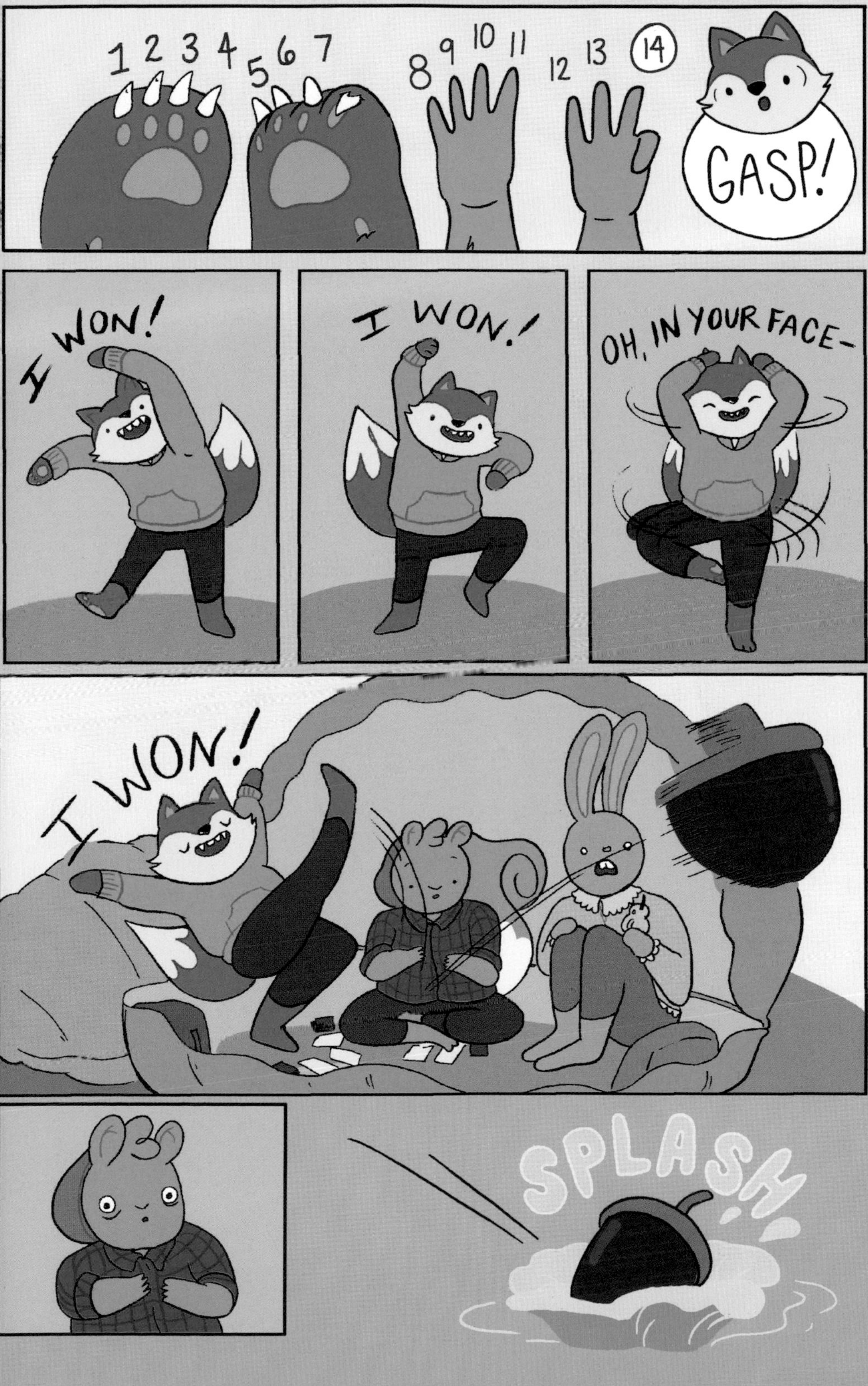
1 2 3 4 5 6 7
8 9 10 11
12 13 14
GASP!
I WON!
I WON!
OH, IN YOUR FACE-
I WON!
SPLASH

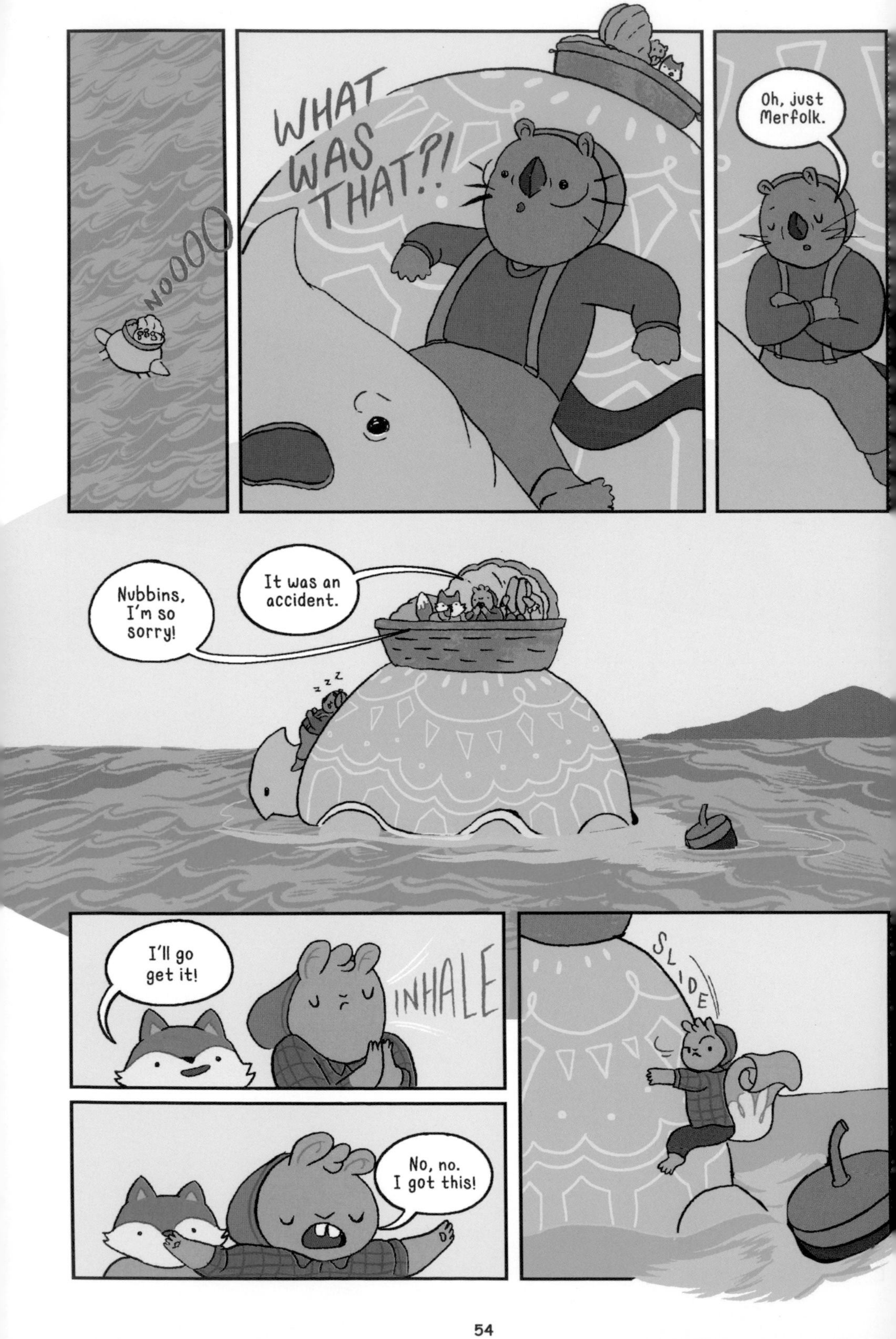
NOOOO
WHAT WAS THAT?!
Oh, just Merfolk.
Nubbins, I'm so sorry!
It was an accident.
I'll go get it!
INHALE
No, no. I got this!
SLIDE

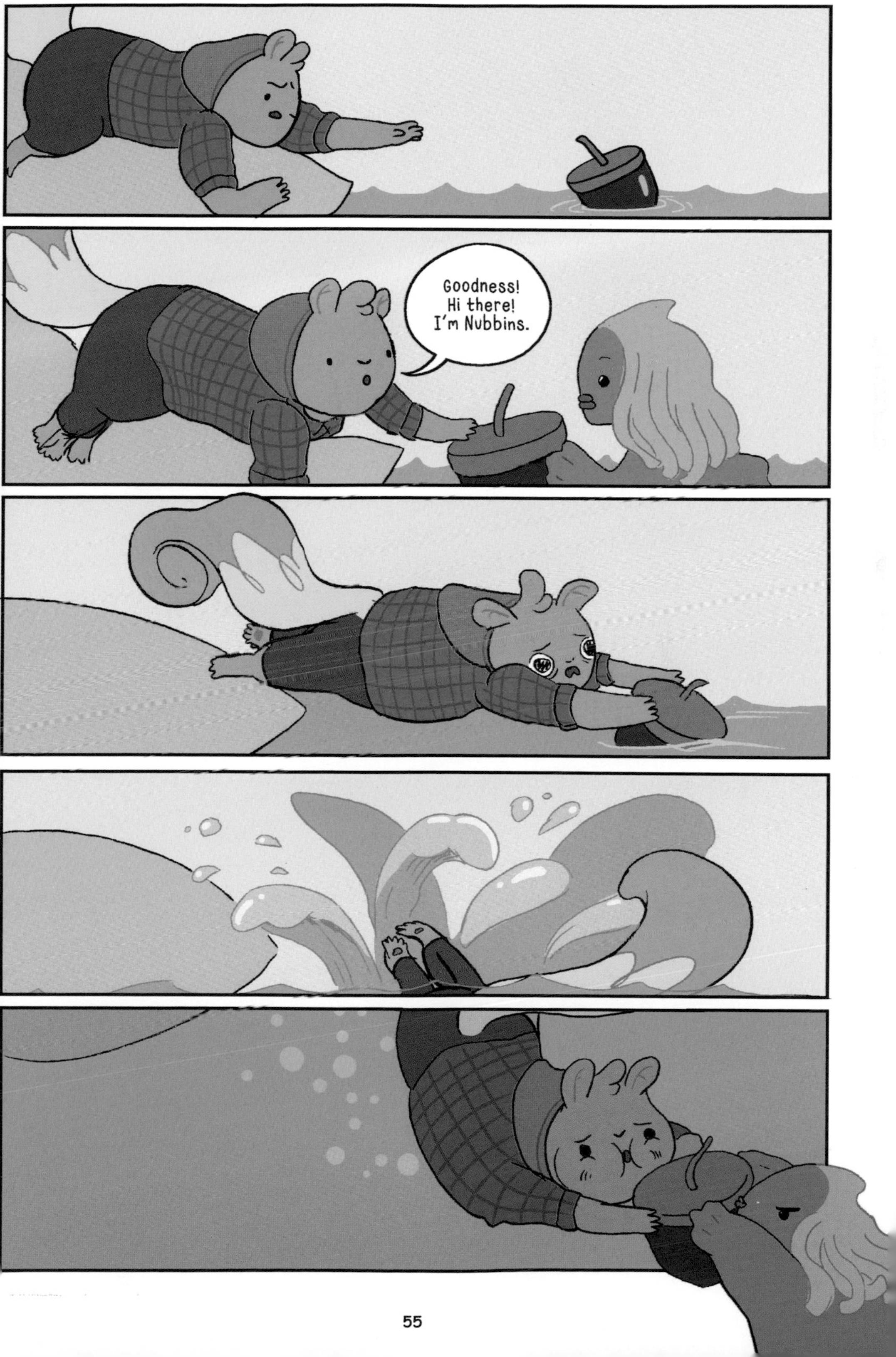
Goodness!
Hi there!
I'm Nubbins.

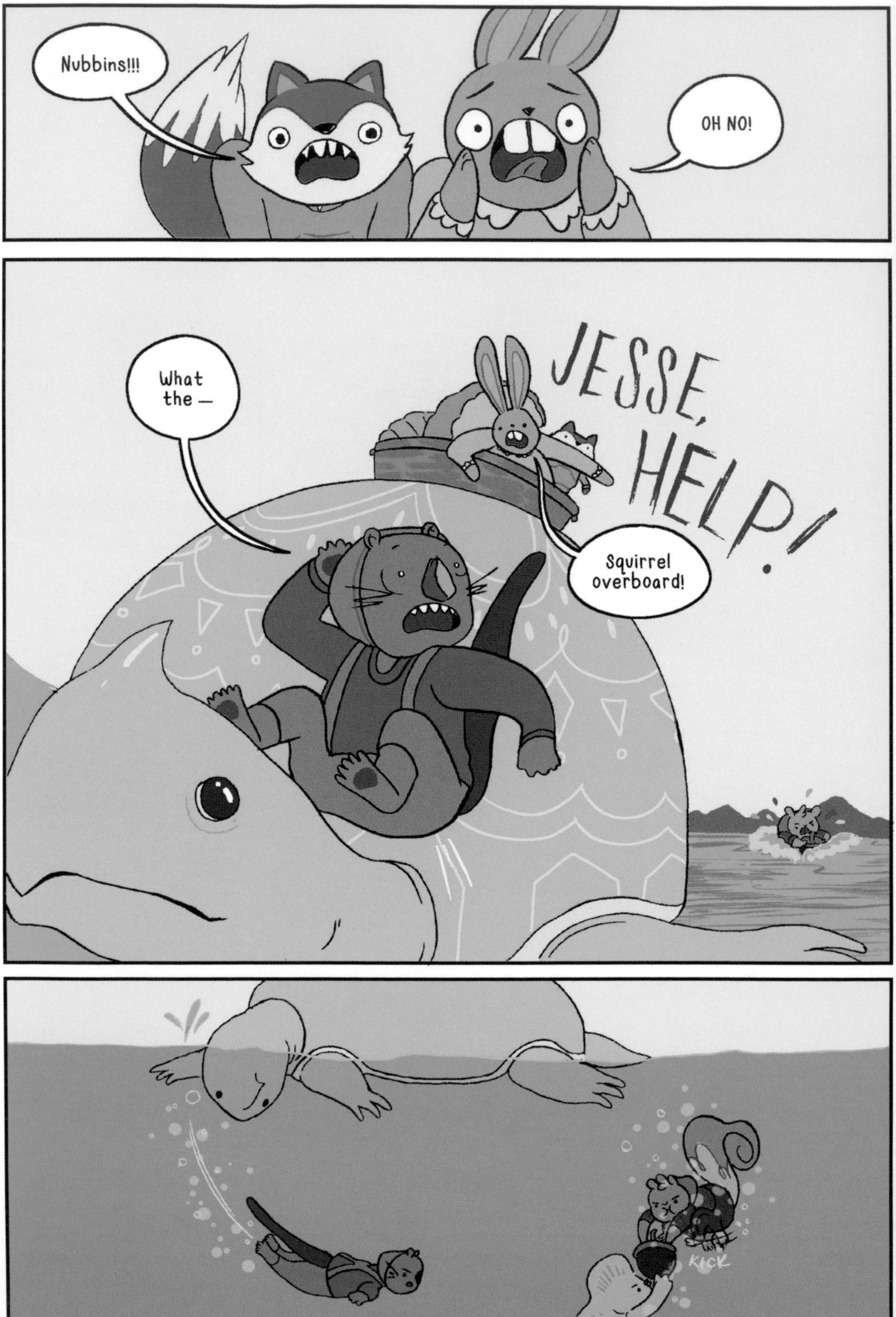
Nubbins!!!
OH NO!
What the —
JESSE, HELP!
Squirrel overboard!
KICK

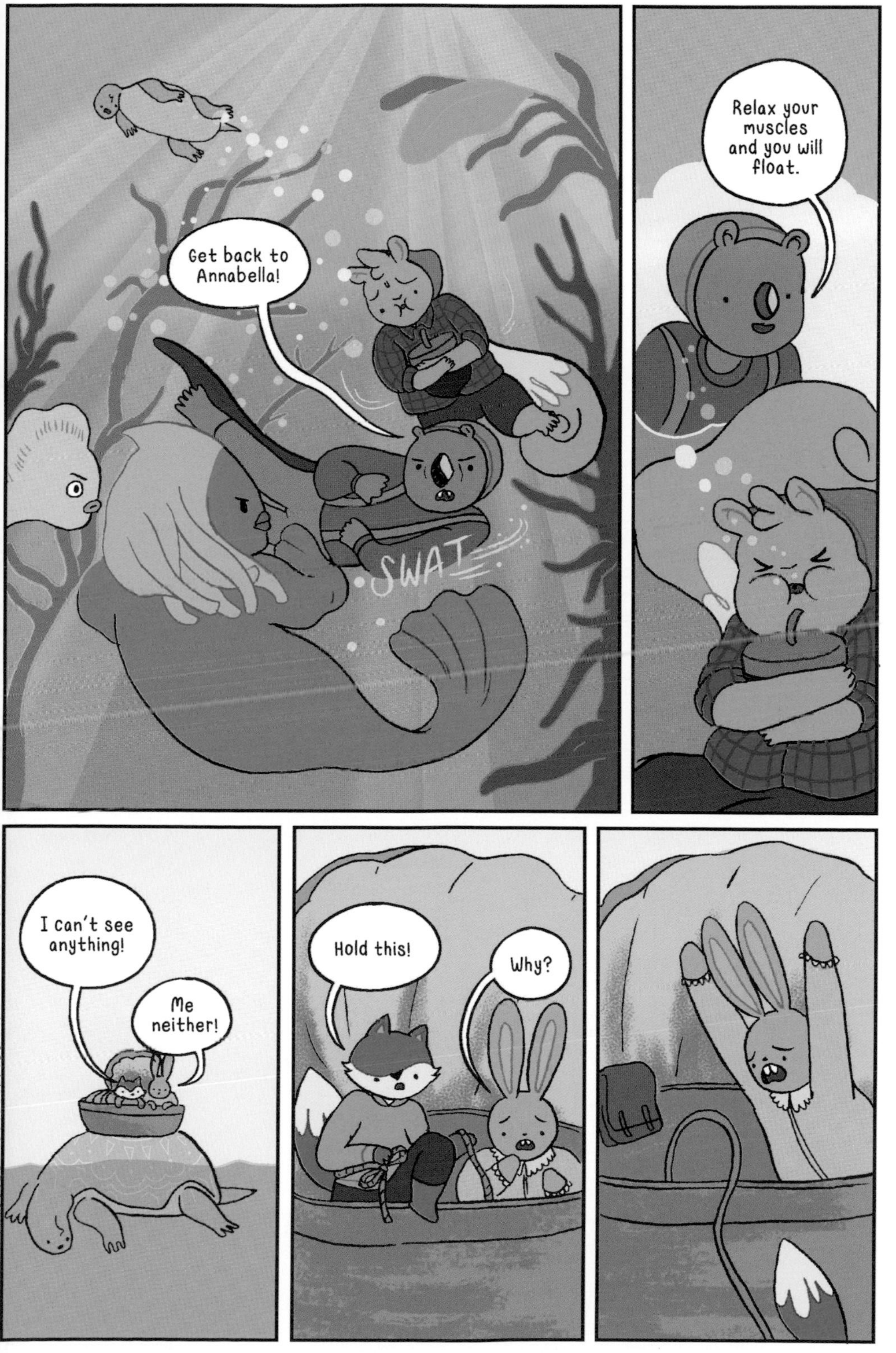
Get back to Annabella!
SWAT
Relax your muscles and you will float.
I can't see anything!
Me neither!
Hold this!
Why?

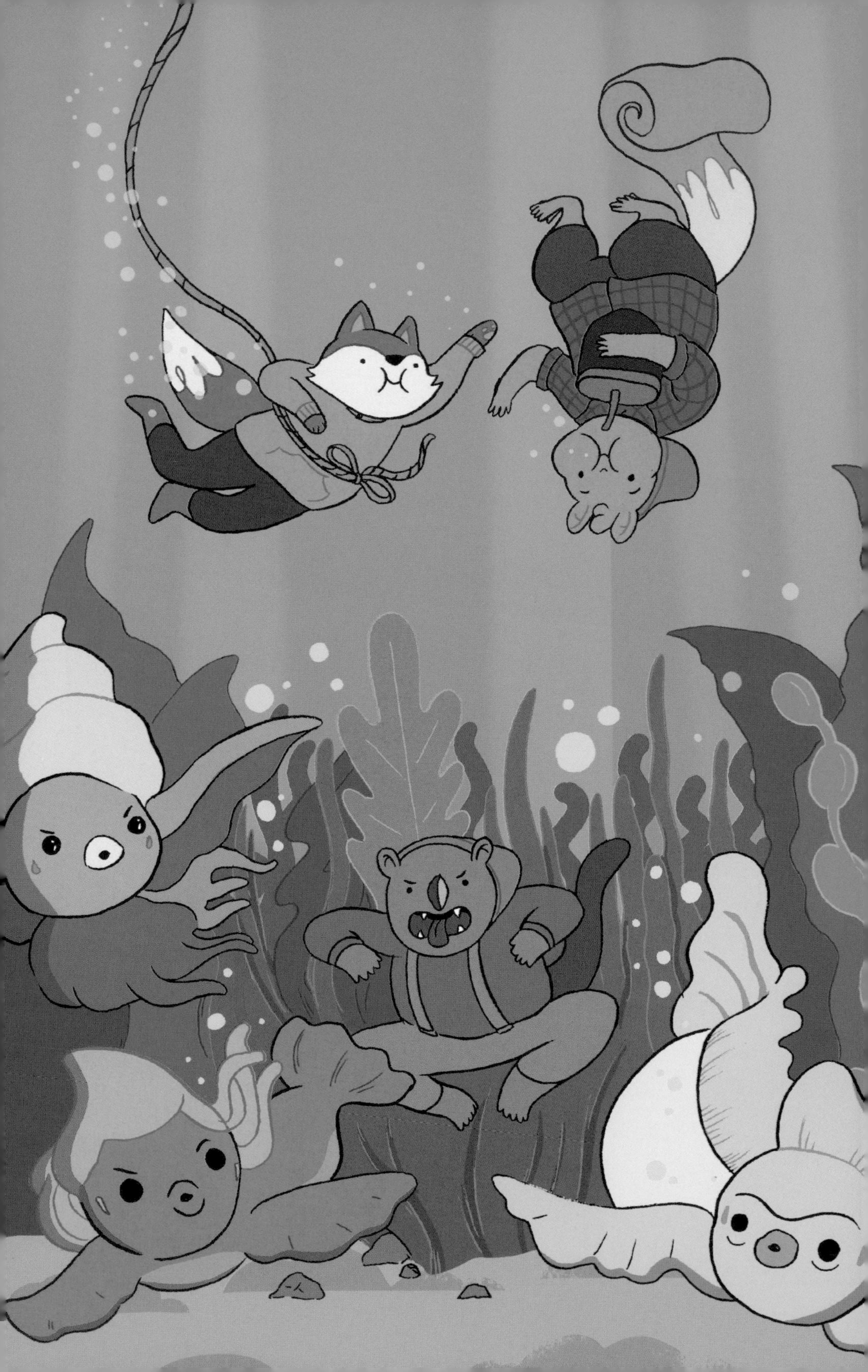

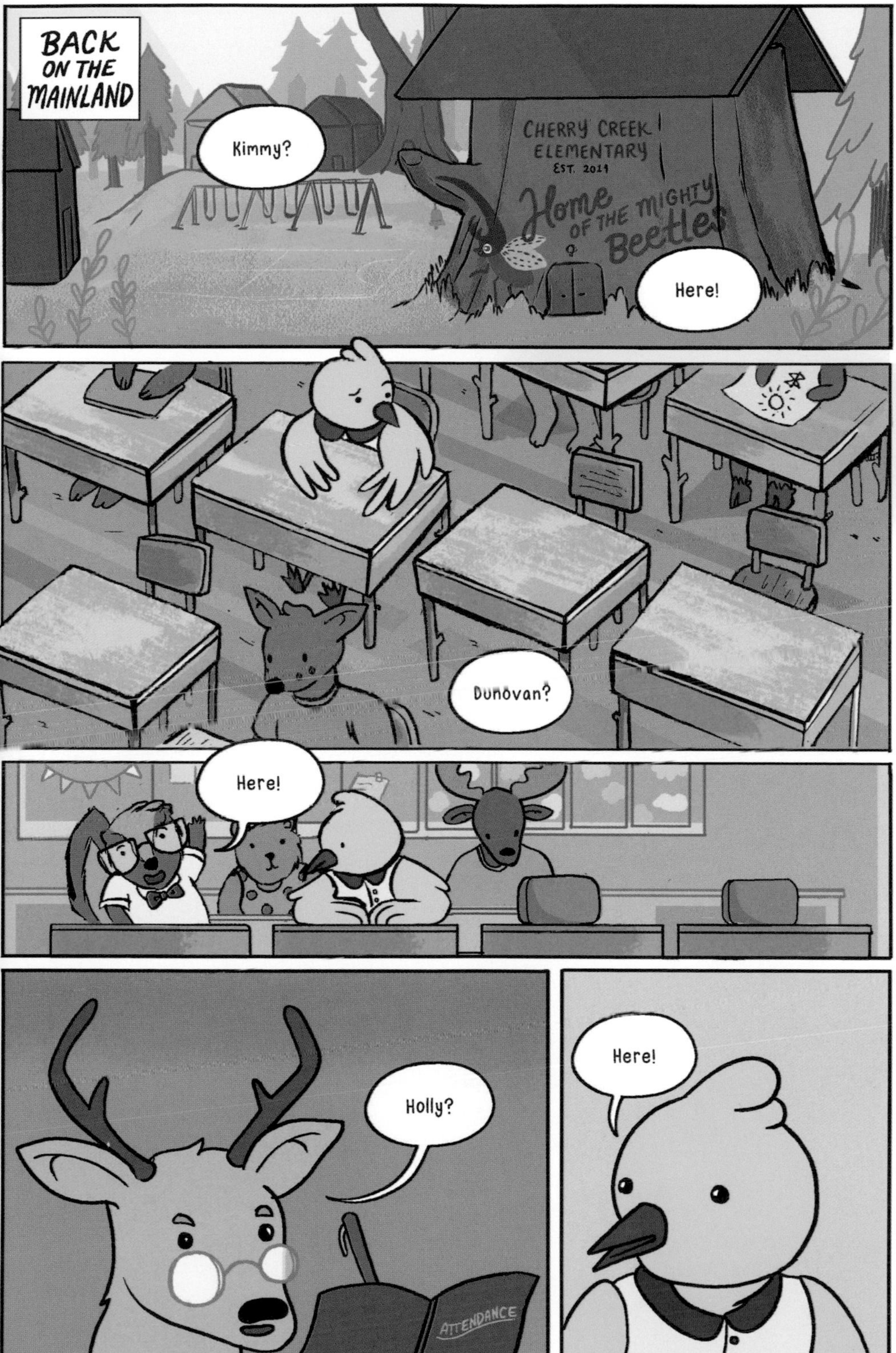
BACK ON THE MAINLAND
Kimmy?
CHERRY CREEK ELEMENTARY EST. 2019 Home OF THE MIGHTY Beetles
Here!
Dunovan?
Here!
Holly?
ATTENDANCE
Here!

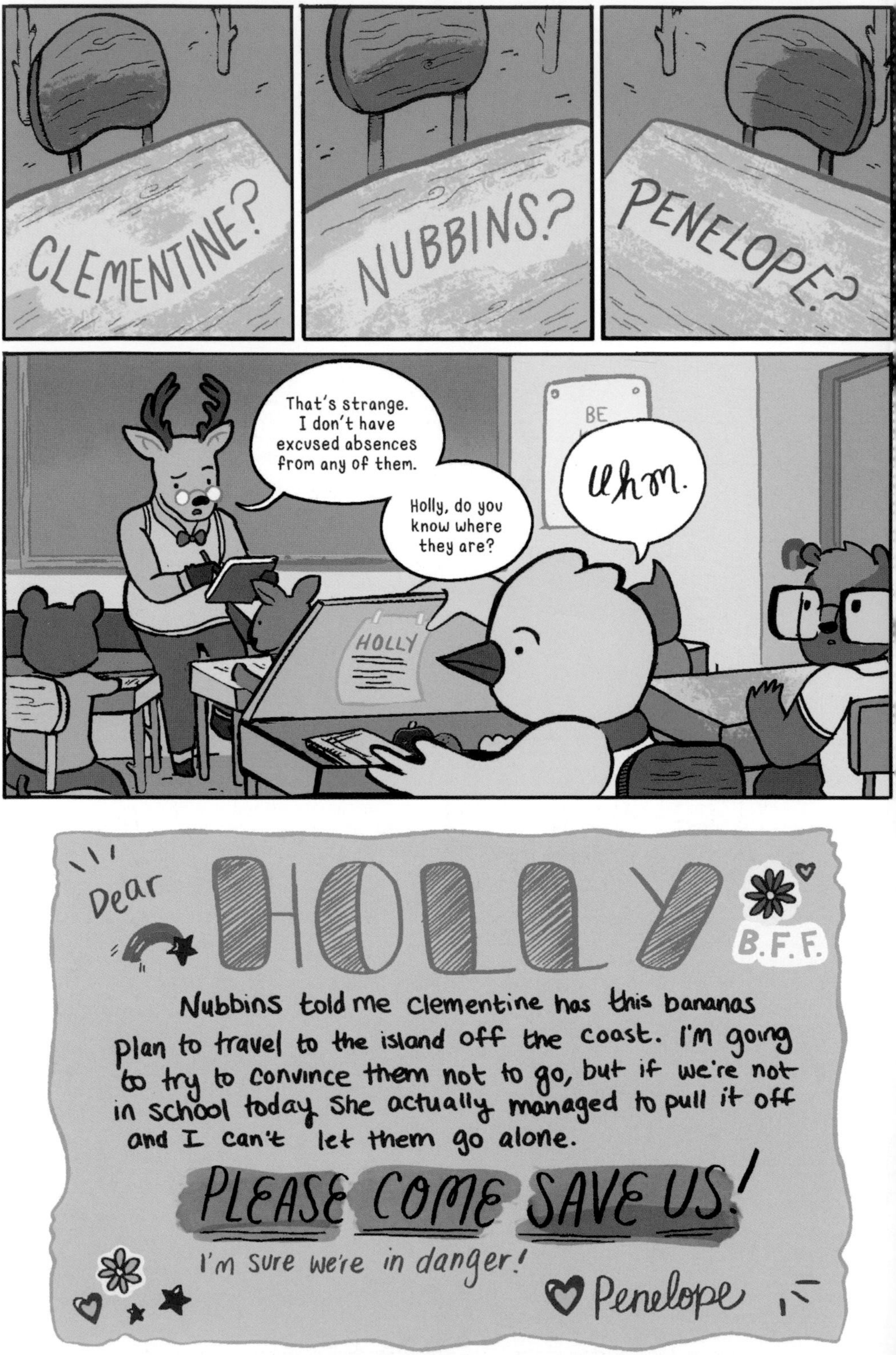
CLEMENTINE?
NUBBINS?
PENELOPE?
That's strange. I don't have excused absences from any of them.
Holly, do you know where they are?
BE
Uhm.
HOLLY
Dear HOLLY
B.F.F.
Nubbins told me Clementine has this bananas plan to travel to the island off the coast. I'm going to try to convince them not to go, but if we're not in school today she actually managed to pull it off and I can't let them go alone.
PLEASE COME SAVE US!
I'm sure we're in danger!
Penelope

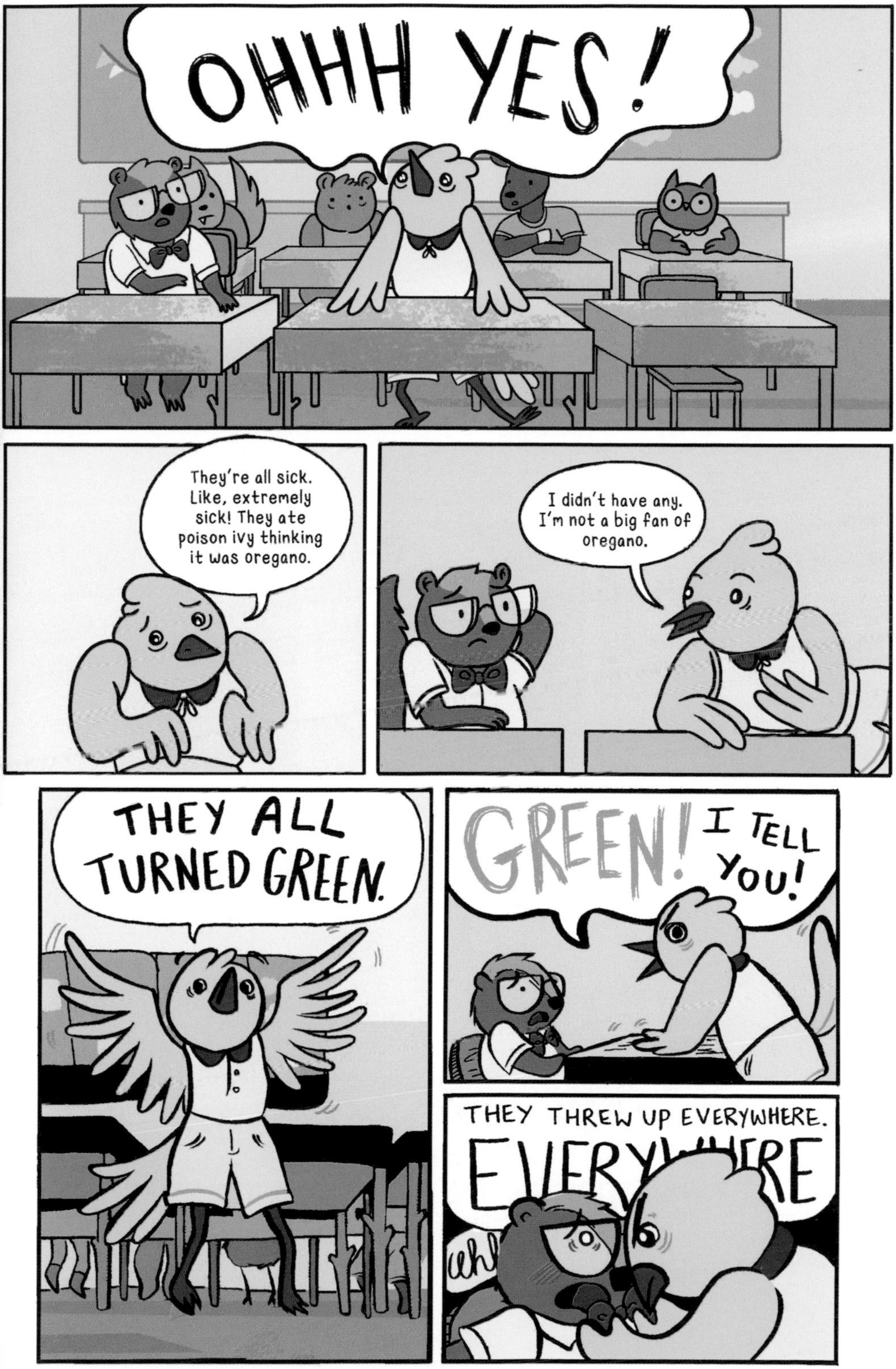
OHHH YES!
They're all sick. Like, extremely sick! They ate poison ivy thinking it was oregano.
I didn't have any. I'm not a big fan of oregano.
THEY ALL TURNED GREEN.
GREEN! I TELL YOU!
THEY THREW UP EVERYWHERE.
EVERY RE
uh

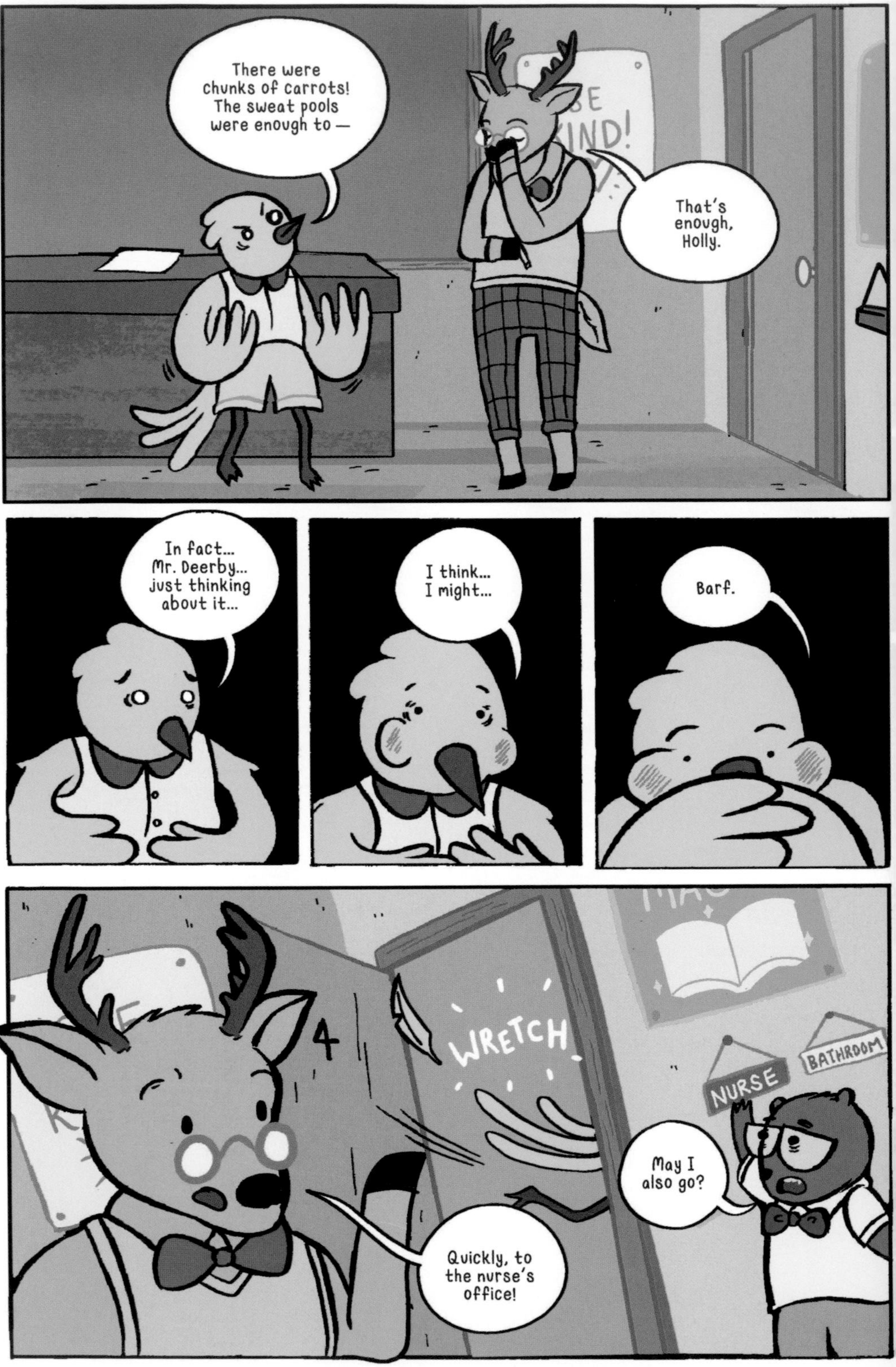

There were chunks of carrots! The sweat pools were enough to —
That's enough, Holly.
In fact... Mr. Deerby... just thinking about it...
I think... I might...
Barf.
WRETCH
Quickly, to the nurse's office!
NURSE
BATHROOM
May I also go?

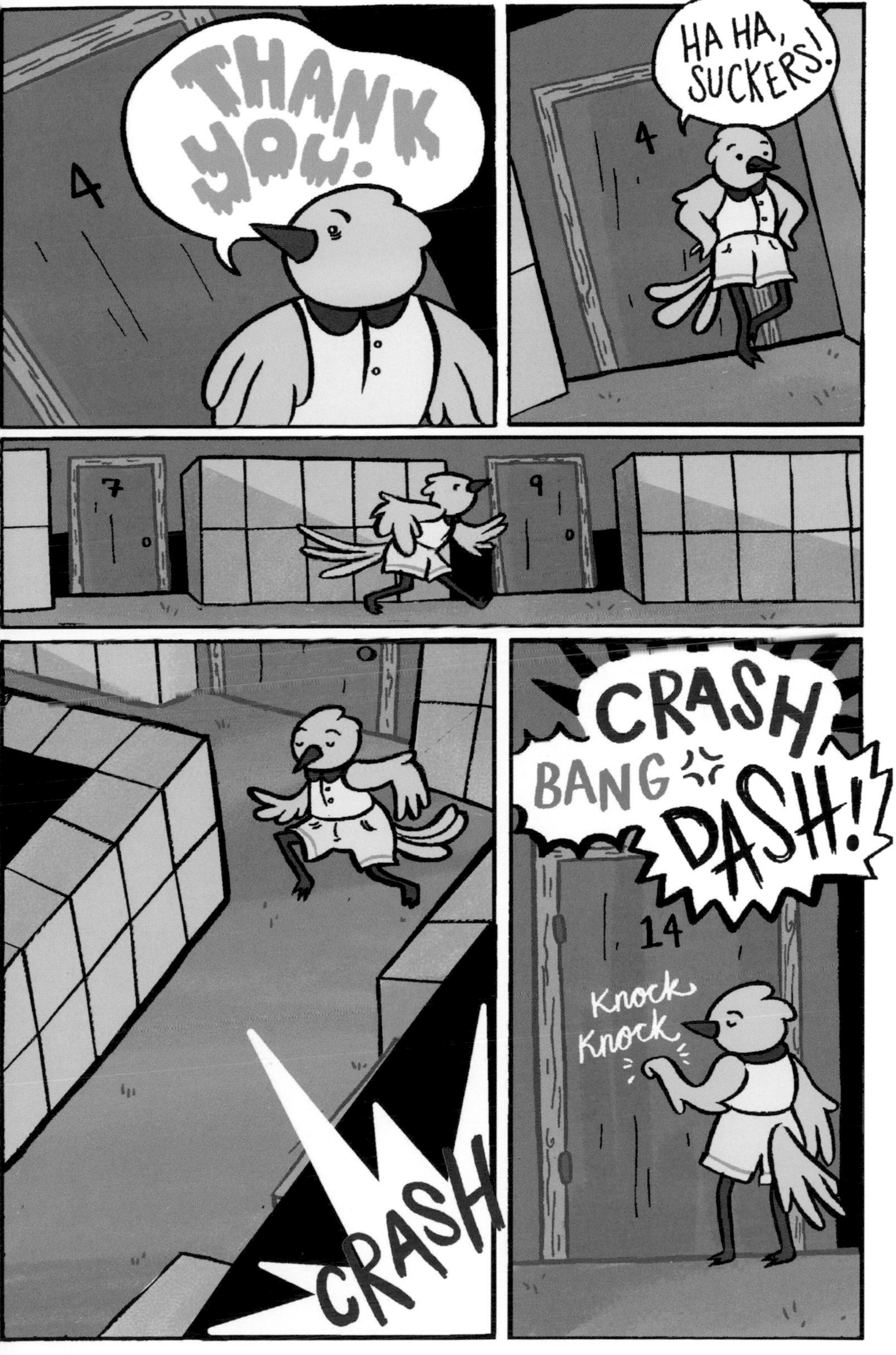
THANK YOU!
4
HA HA, SUCKERS!
4
7
9
CRASH
CRASH BANG DASH!
14
Knock Knock

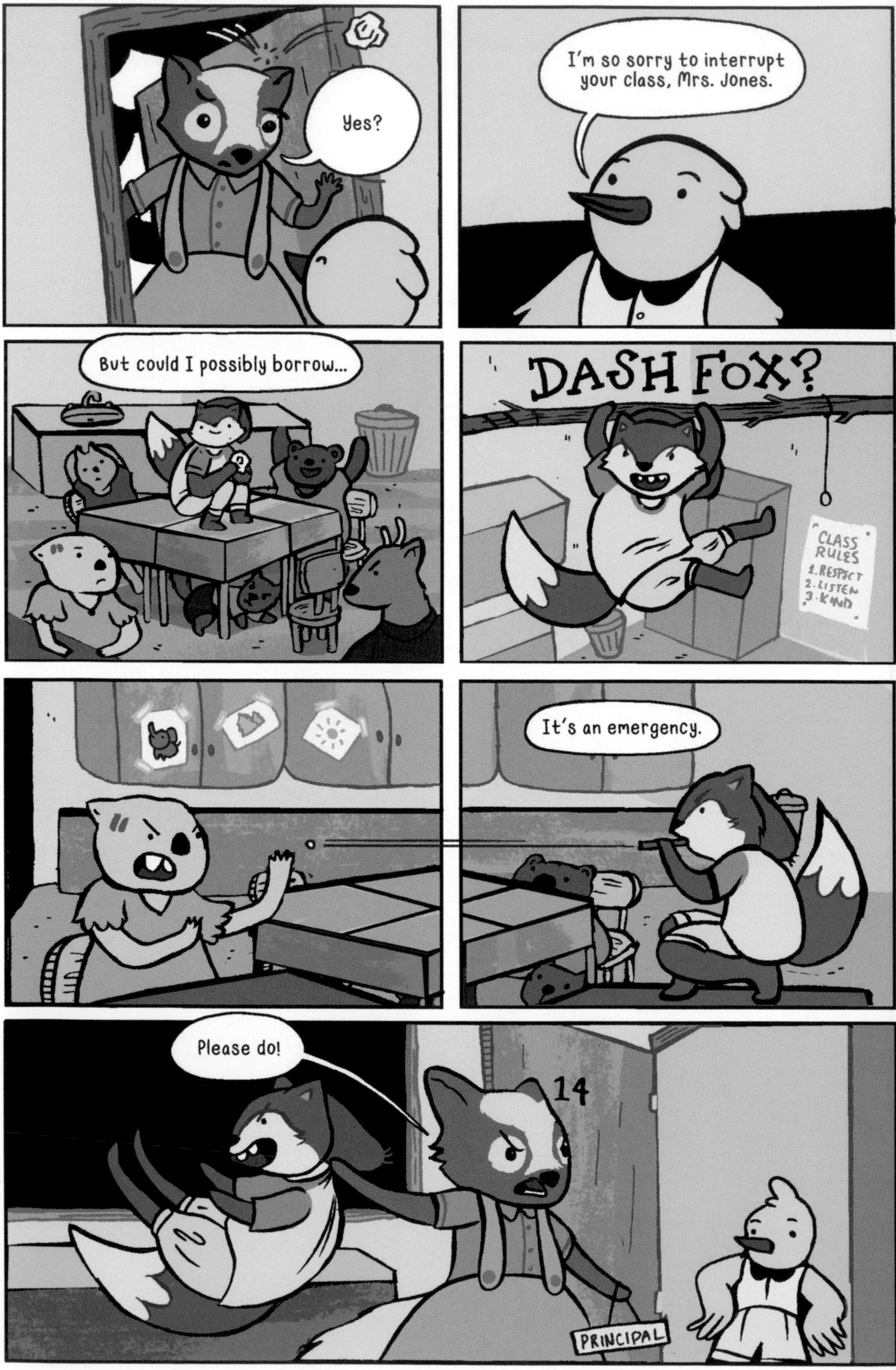
Yes?
I'm so sorry to interrupt your class, Mrs. Jones.
But could I possibly borrow...
DASH FOX?
CLASS RULES
1. RESPECT
2. LISTEN
3. KIND
It's an emergency.
Please do!
14
PRINCIPAL

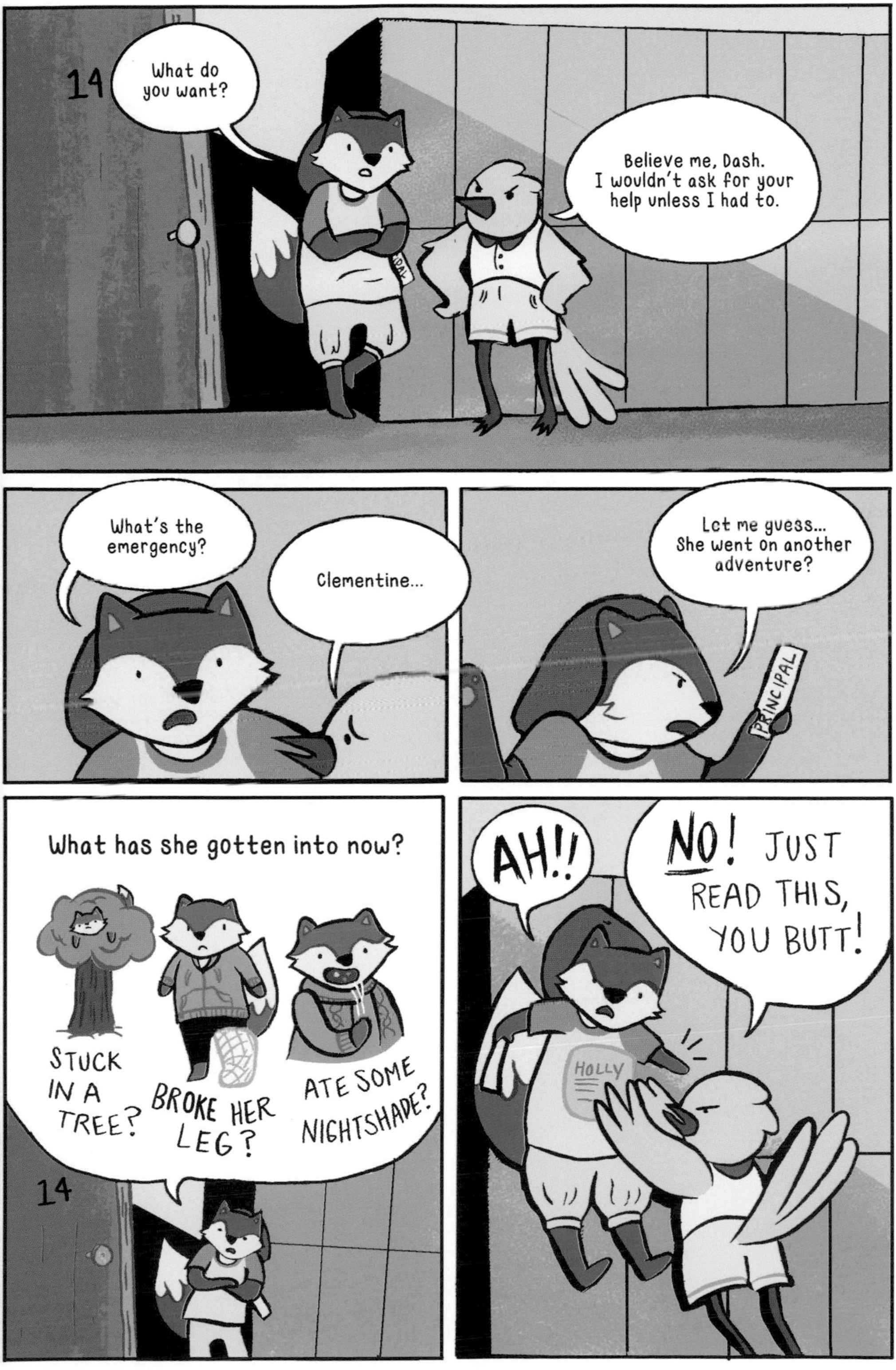
14
What do you want?
Believe me, Dash. I wouldn't ask for your help unless I had to.
What's the emergency?
Clementine...
Let me guess... She went on another adventure?
PRINCIPAL
What has she gotten into now?
STUCK IN A TREE?
BROKE HER LEG?
ATE SOME NIGHTSHADE?
14
AH!!
NO! JUST READ THIS, YOU BUTT!
HOLLY

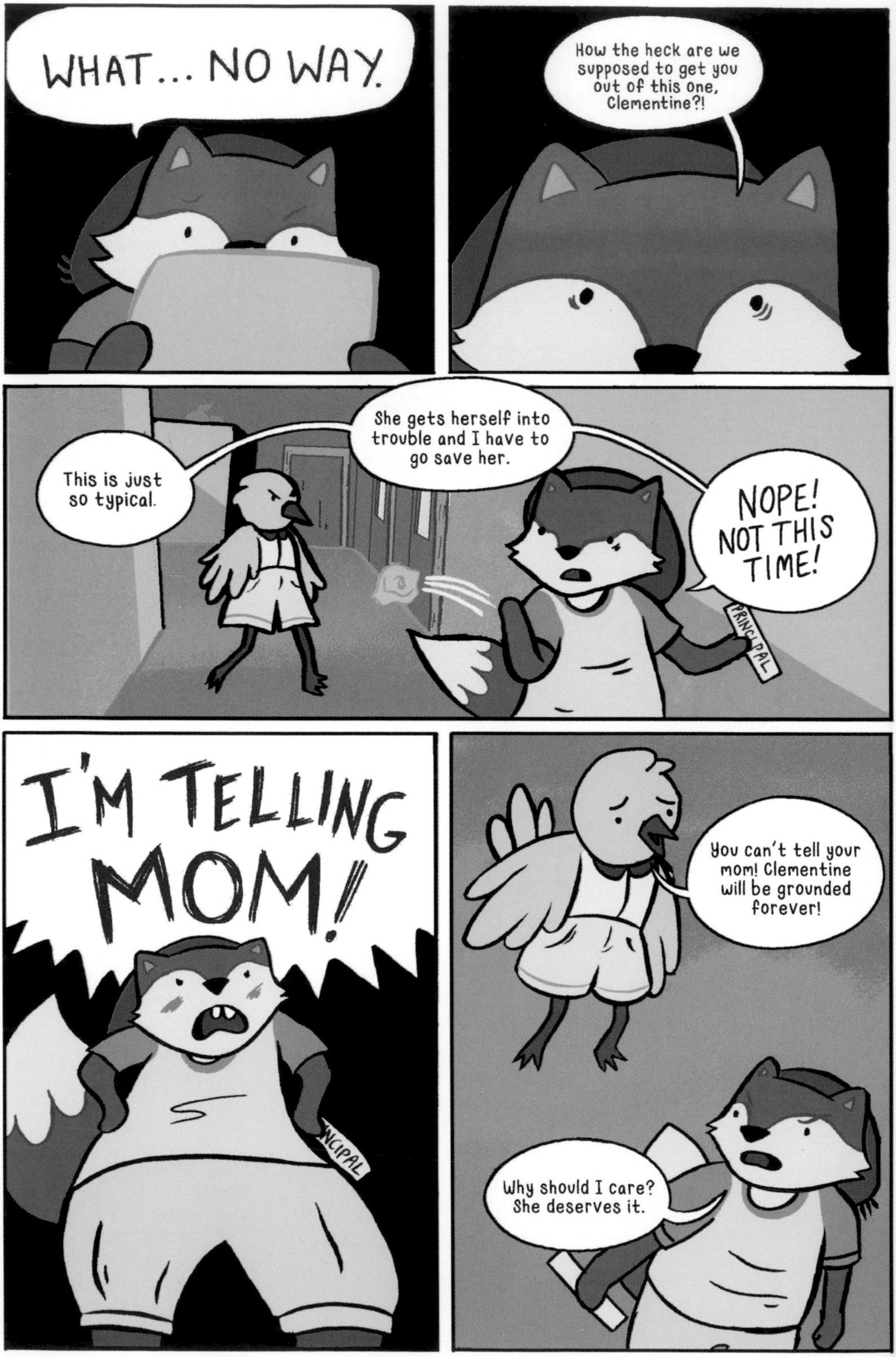
WHAT... NO WAY.
How the heck are we supposed to get you out of this one, Clementine?!
This is just so typical.
She gets herself into trouble and I have to go save her.
NOPE! NOT THIS TIME!
PRINCIPAL
I'M TELLING MOM!
NCIPAL
You can't tell your mom! Clementine will be grounded forever!
Why should I care? She deserves it.

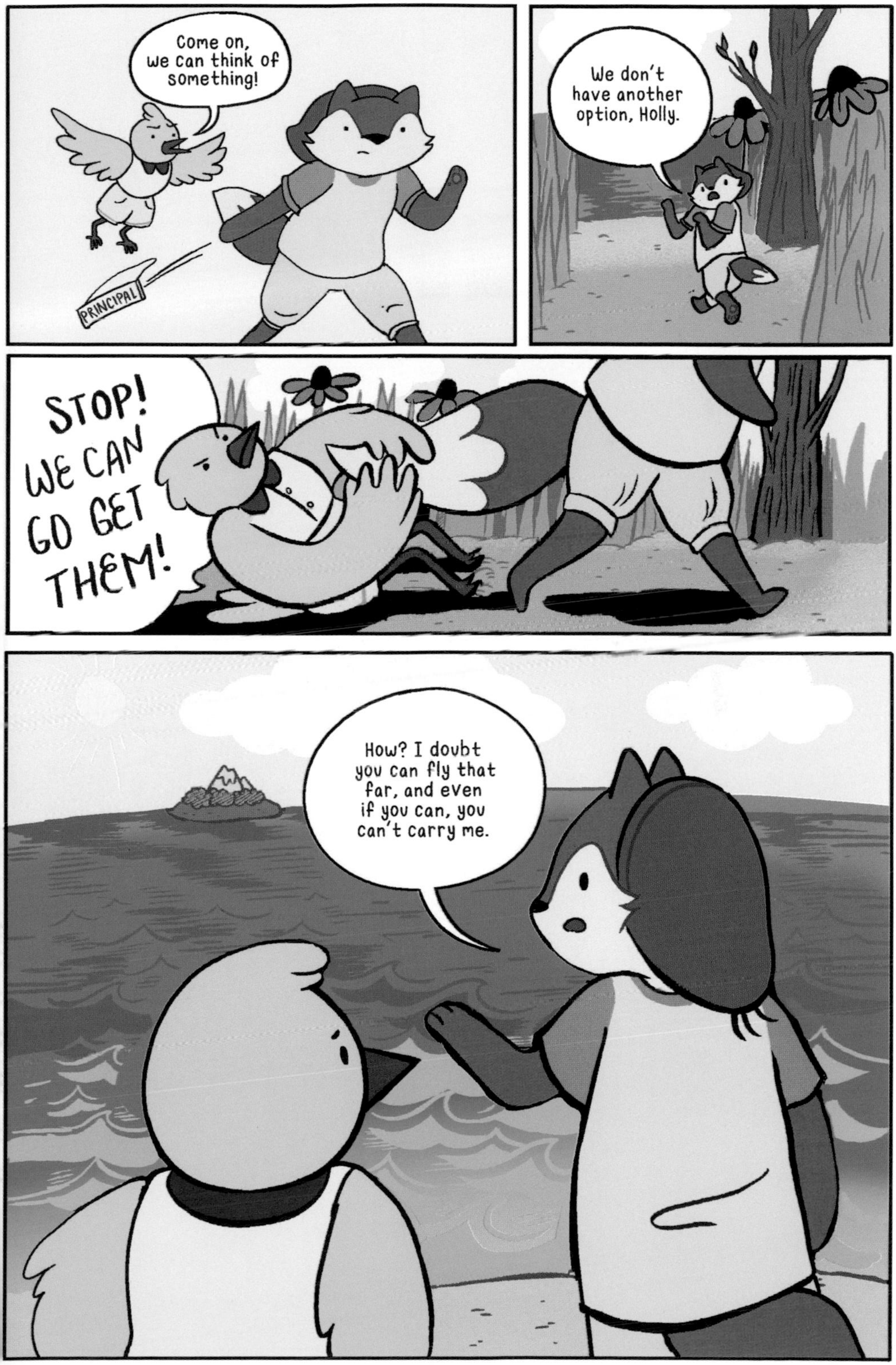

Come on, we can think of something!
PRINCIPAL
We don't have another option, Holly.
STOP! WE CAN GO GET THEM!
How? I doubt you can fly that far, and even if you can, you can't carry me.

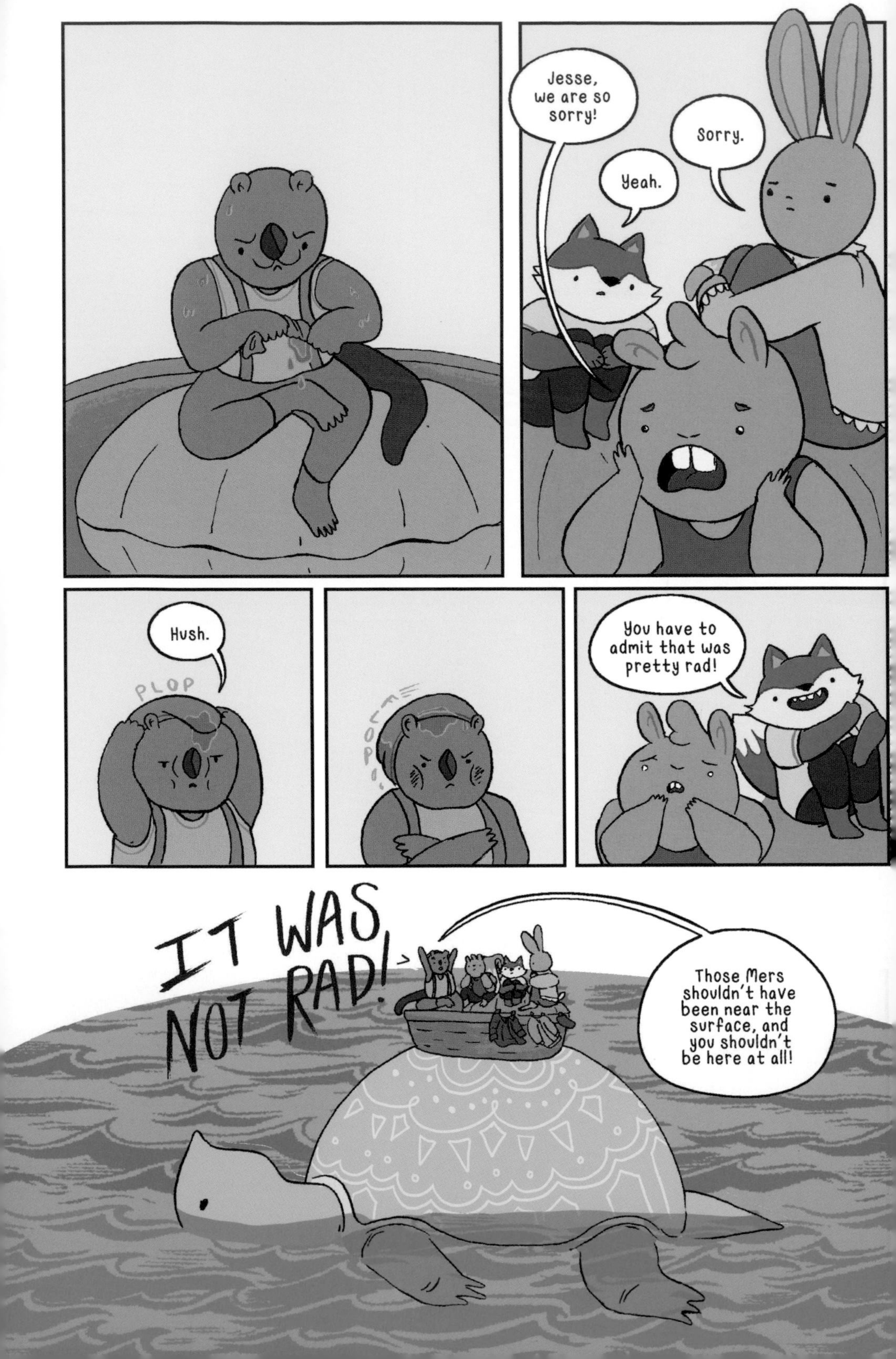
Jesse, we are so sorry!
Yeah.
Sorry.
Hush.
PLOP
PLOP
You have to admit that was pretty rad!
IT WAS NOT RAD!
Those Mers shouldn't have been near the surface, and you shouldn't be here at all!

Jesse, this is my fault —

Annabella! Turn around! We have some stowaways to return home.

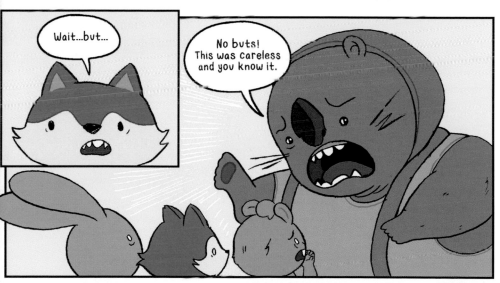

Wait...but...

No buts! This was careless and you know it.

I'm disappointed in all of you.

disappointed

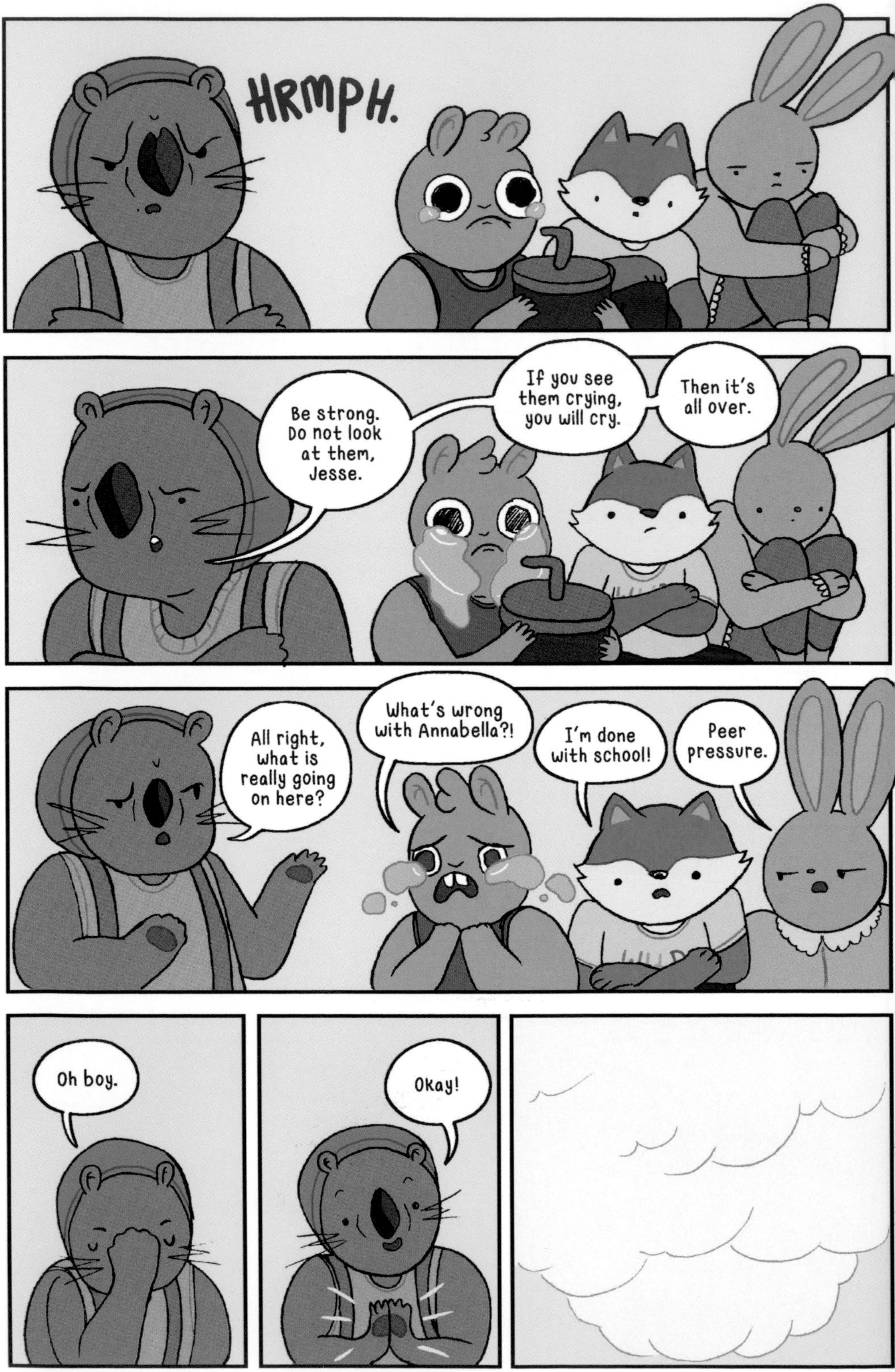
HRMPH.
Be strong. Do not look at them, Jesse.
If you see them crying, you will cry.
Then it's all over.
All right, what is really going on here?
What's wrong with Annabella?!
I'm done with school!
Peer pressure.
Oh boy.
Okay!

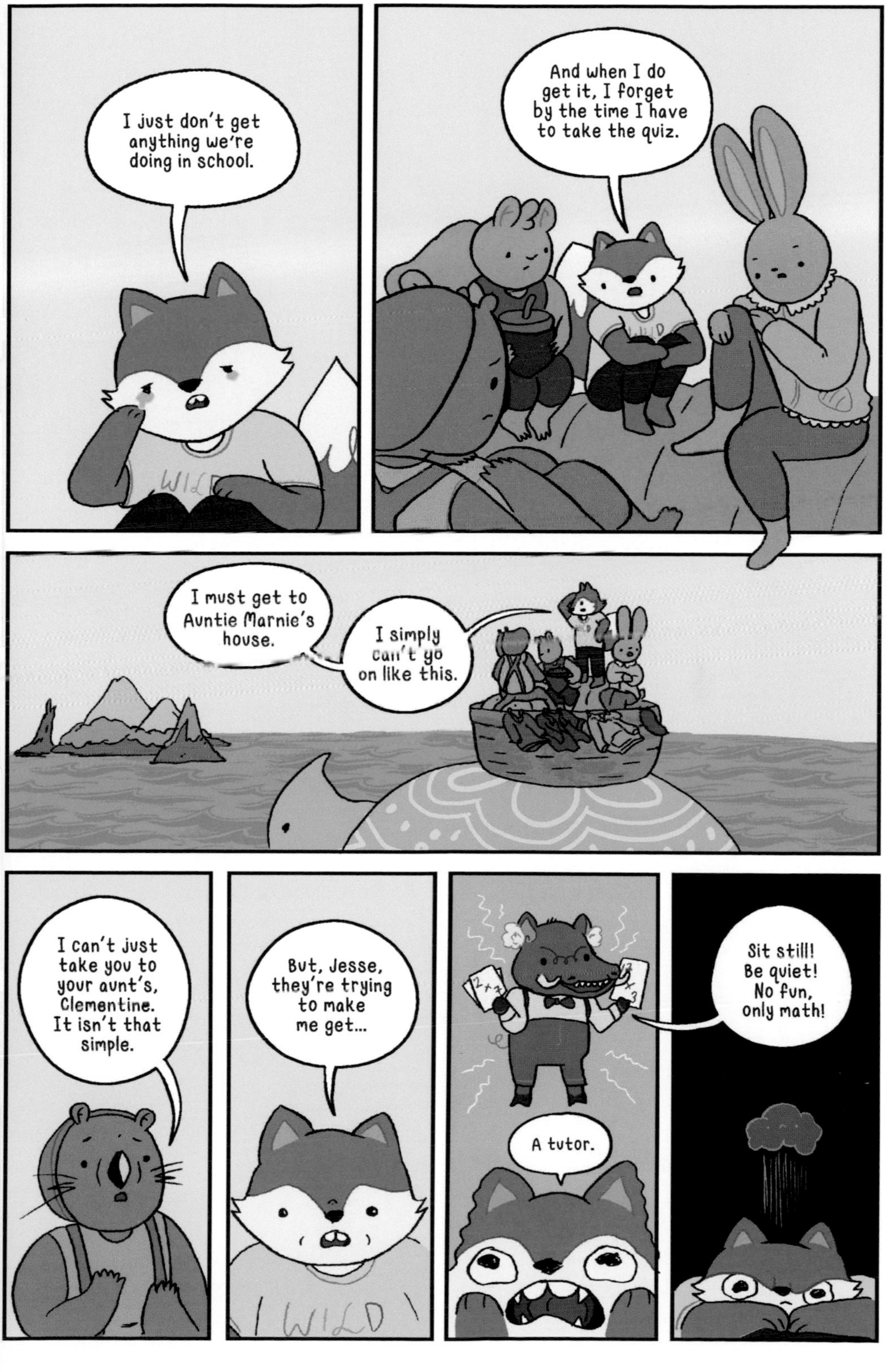
I just don't get anything we're doing in school.
And when I do get it, I forget by the time I have to take the quiz.
I must get to Auntie Marnie's house.
I simply can't go on like this.
I can't just take you to your aunt's, Clementine. It isn't that simple.
But, Jesse, they're trying to make me get...
A tutor.
Sit still! Be quiet! No fun, only math!

What?! That rules!

Really?

I wish my mom had gotten me a tutor when I was younger!

I was awful at school!

It wasn't until I found Annabella that I discovered what I was good at.

I have some classmates who tutor after school.

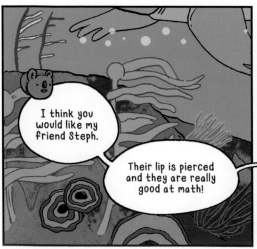

I think you would like my friend Steph.

Their lip is pierced and they are really good at math!

I'll give your mom their contact info.

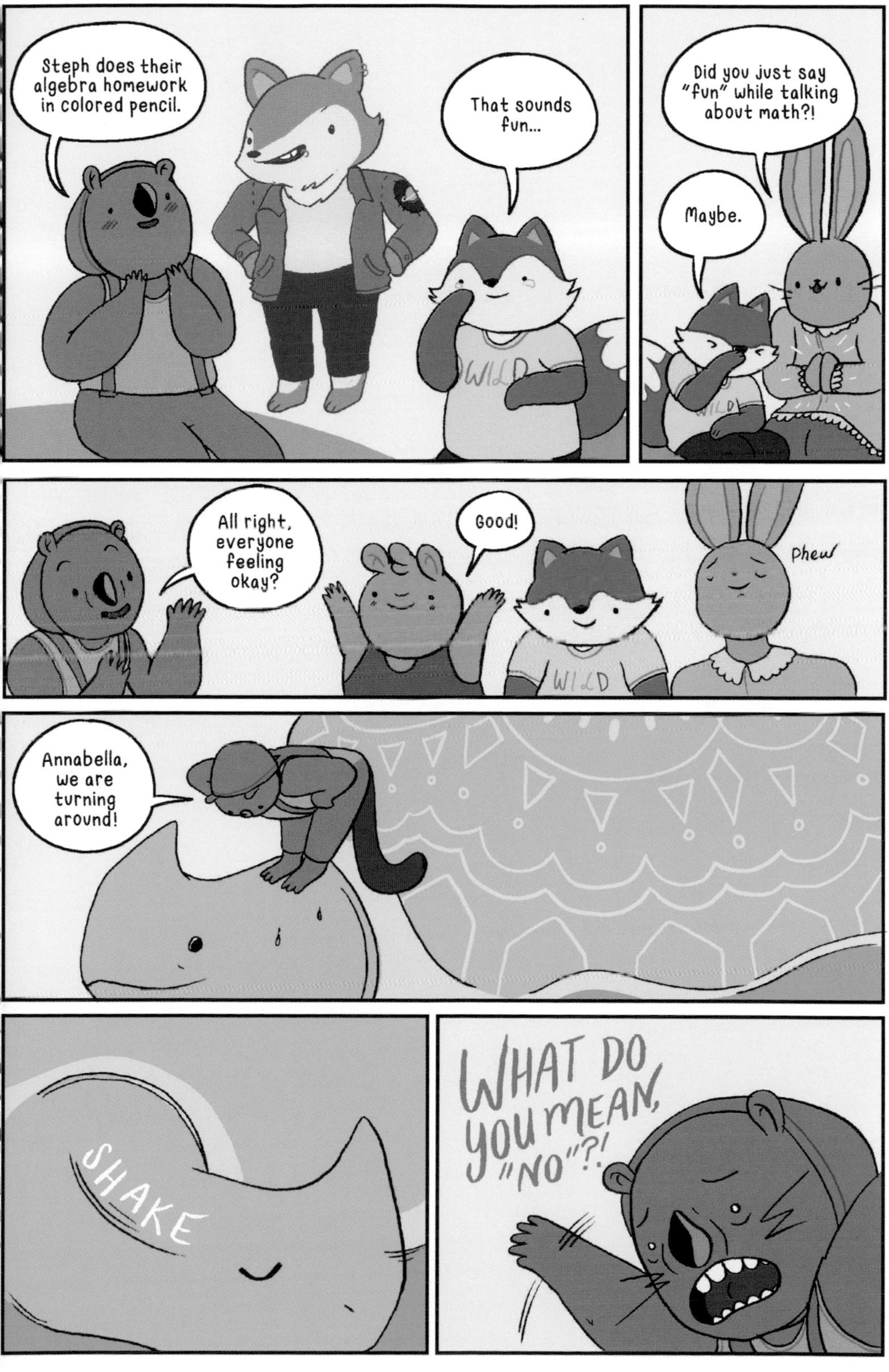
Steph does their algebra homework in colored pencil.
That sounds fun...
WILD
Did you just say "fun" while talking about math?!
Maybe.
WILD
All right, everyone feeling okay?
Good!
Phew
WILD
Annabella, we are turning around!
SHAKE
WHAT DO YOU MEAN, "NO"?!

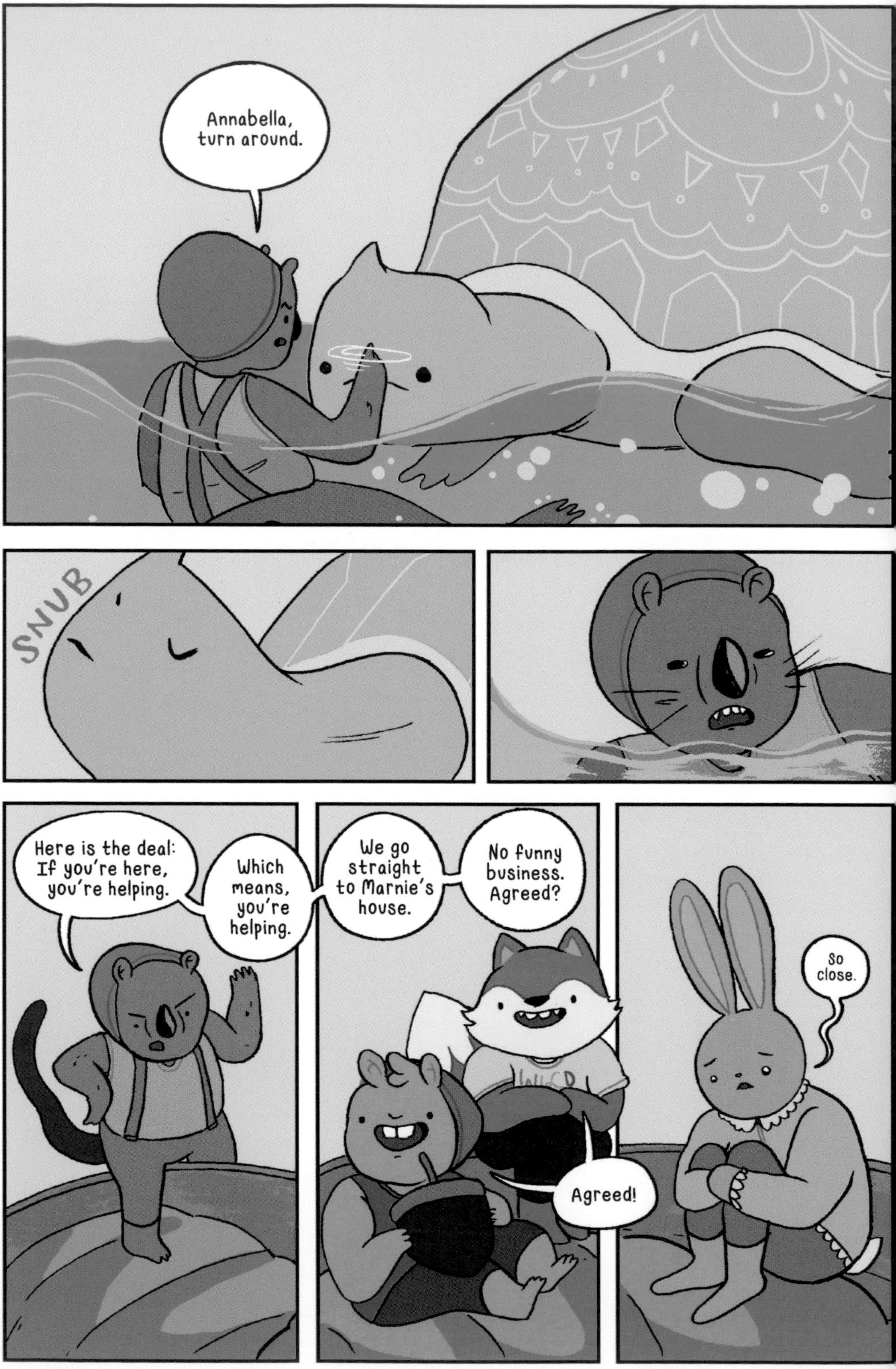
Annabella, turn around.
SNUB
Here is the deal: If you're here, you're helping.
Which means, you're helping.
We go straight to Marnie's house.
No funny business. Agreed?
Agreed!
So close.

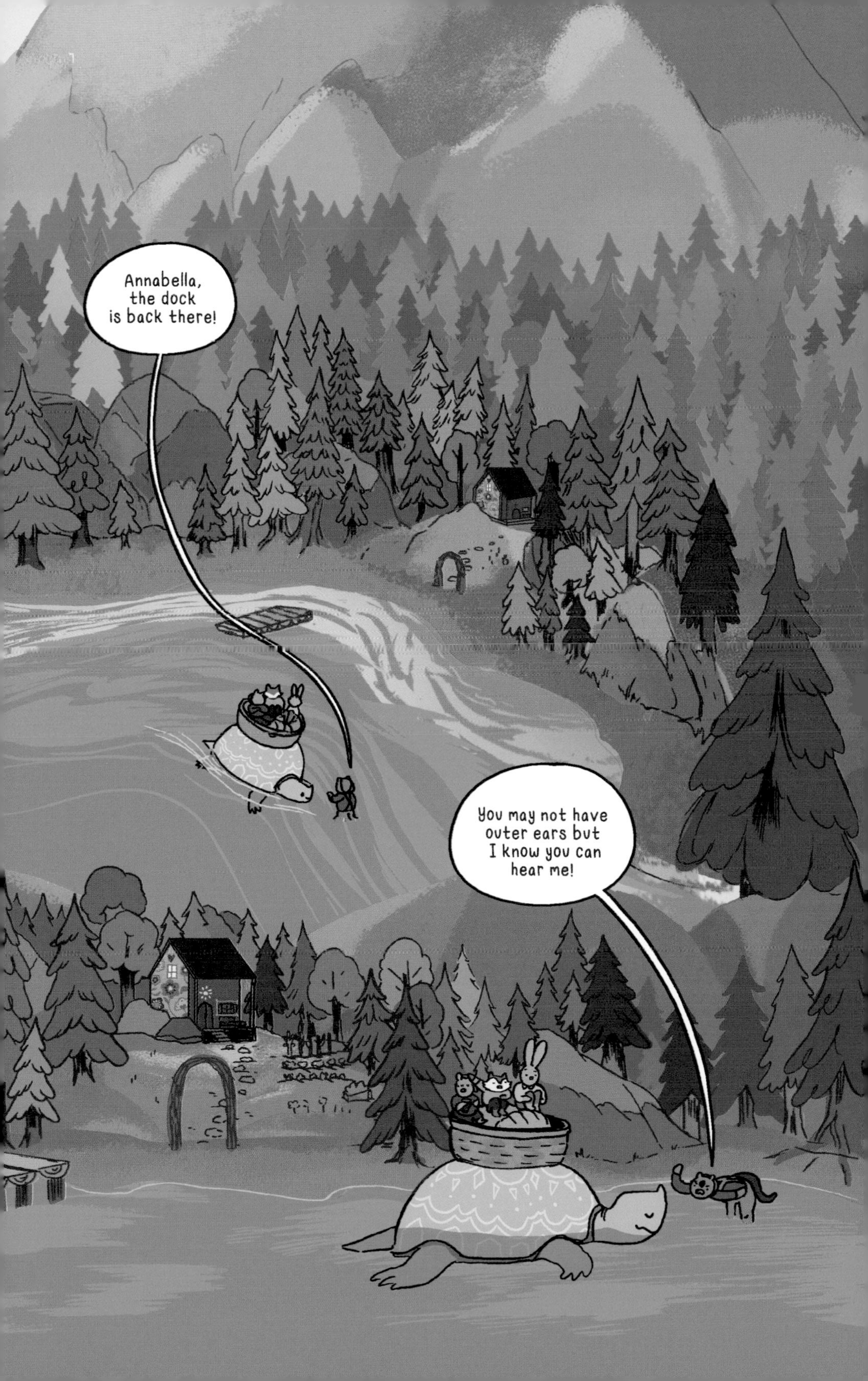

Annabella, the dock is back there!
You may not have outer ears but I know you can hear me!

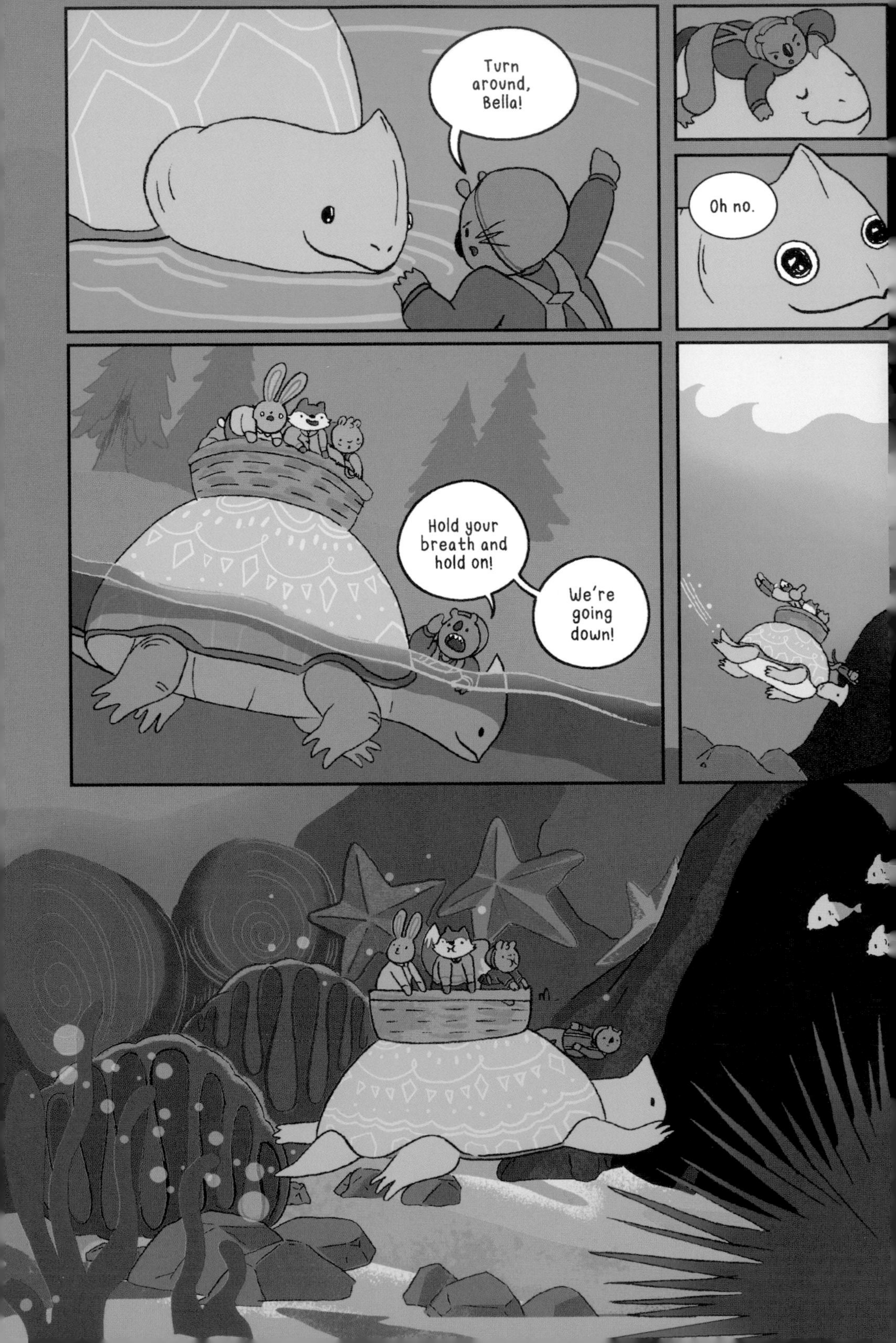
Turn around, Bella!
Oh no.
Hold your breath and hold on!
We're going down!

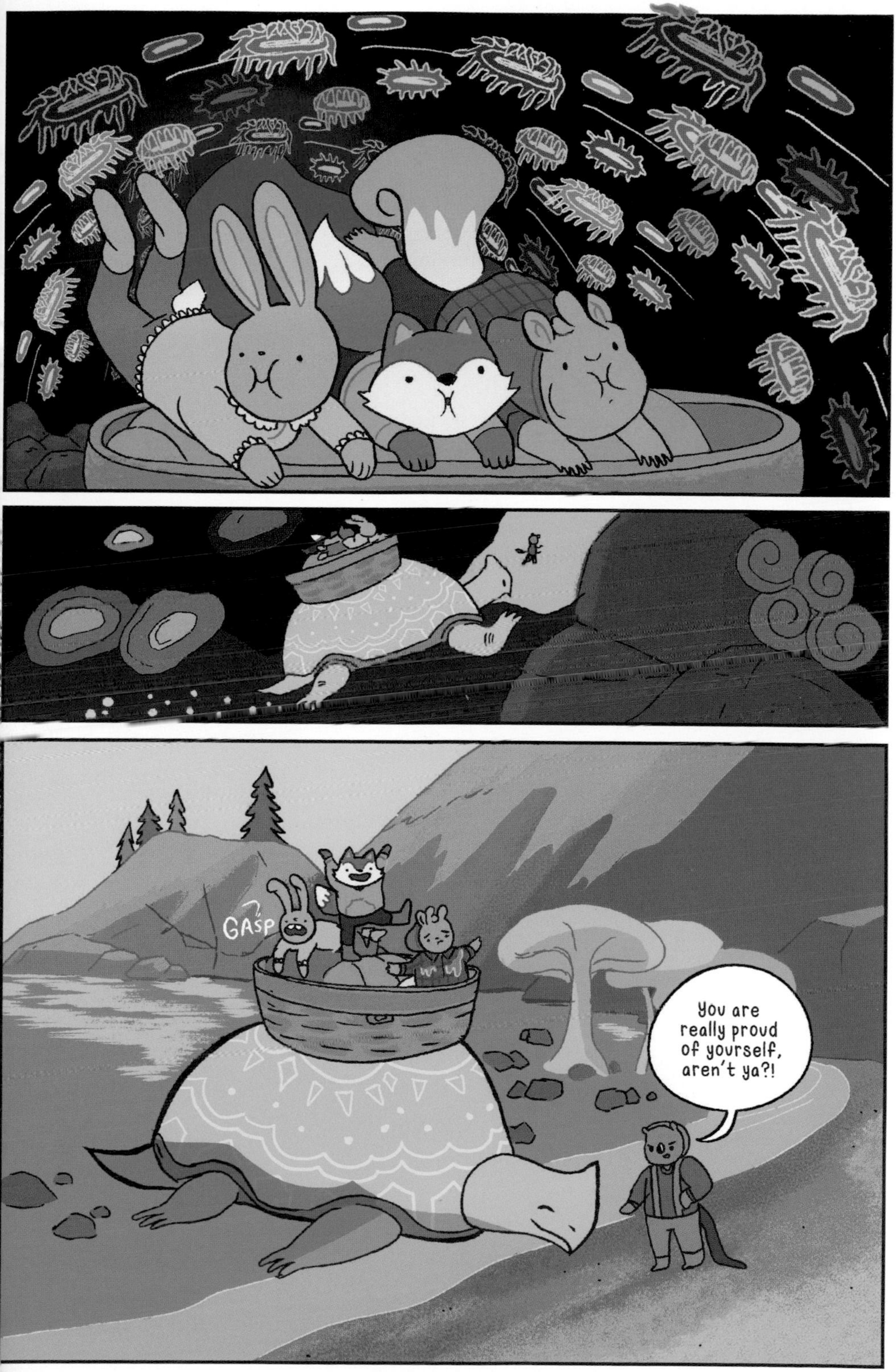
GASP
You are really proud of yourself, aren't ya?!

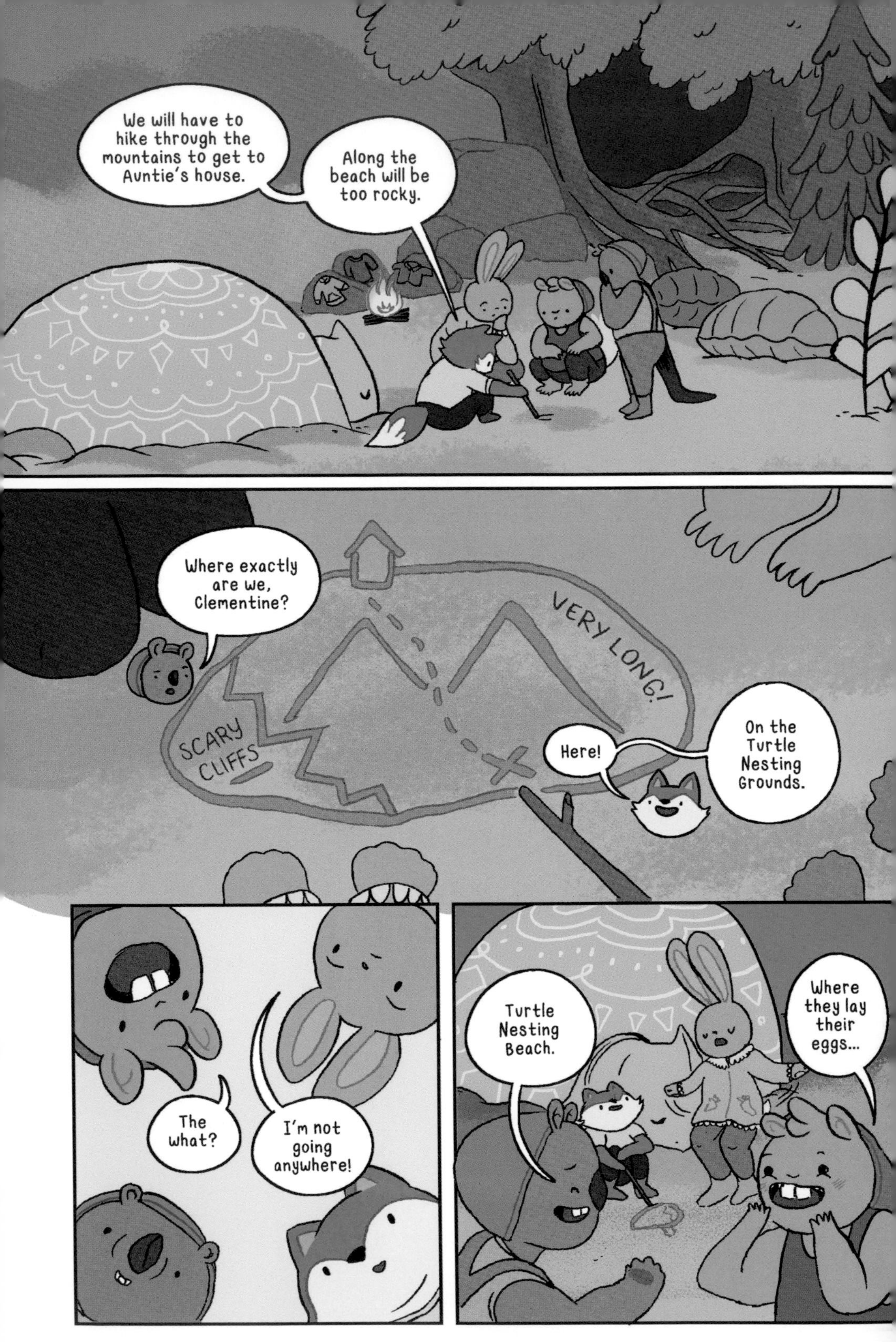

We will have to hike through the mountains to get to Auntie's house.
Along the beach will be too rocky.
Where exactly are we, Clementine?
VERY LONG!
SCARY CLIFFS
Here!
On the Turtle Nesting Grounds.
The what?
I'm not going anywhere!
Turtle Nesting Beach.
Where they lay their eggs...

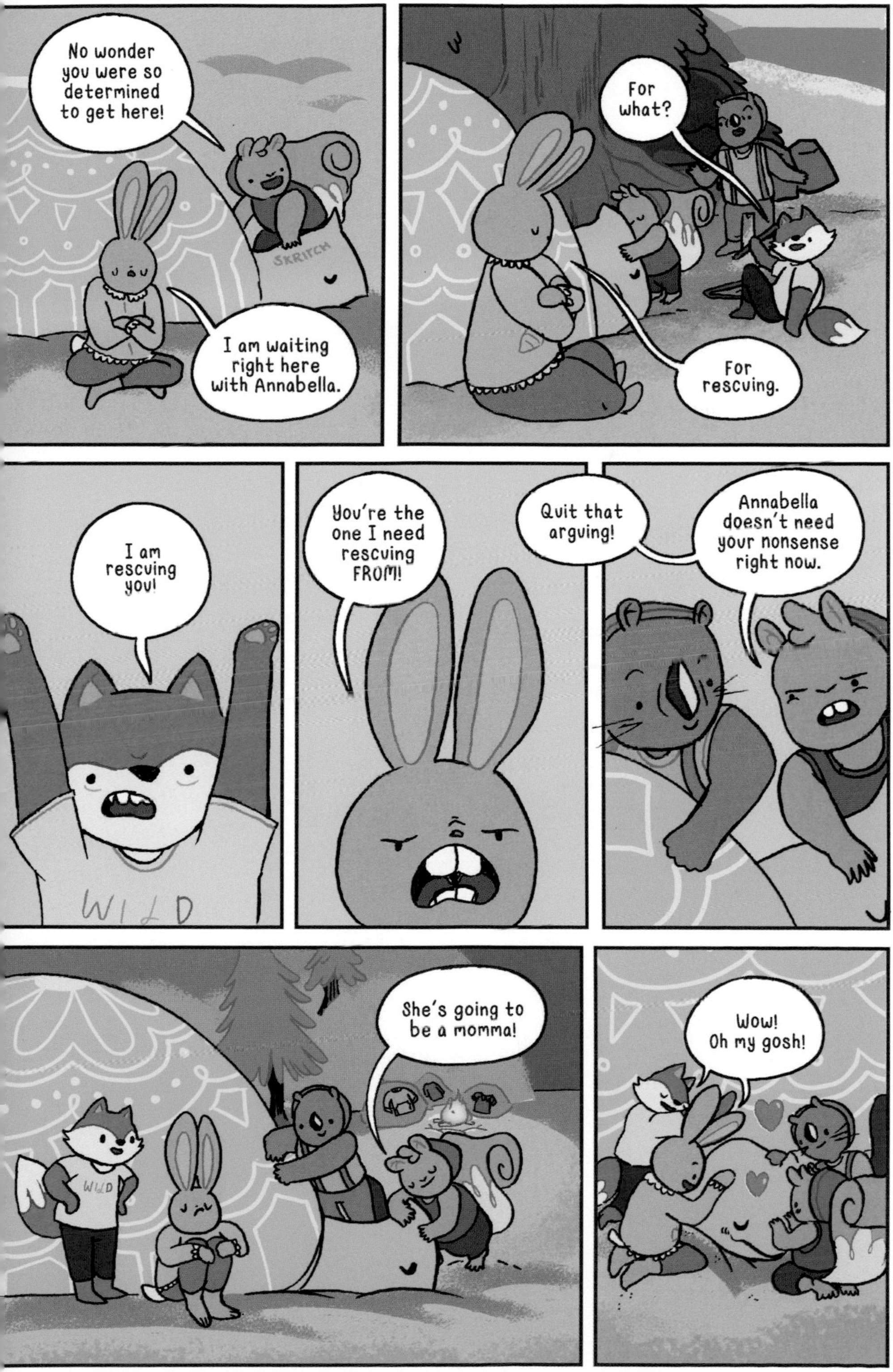
No wonder you were so determined to get here!
SKRITCH
I am waiting right here with Annabella.
For what?
For rescuing.
I am rescuing you!
WILD
You're the one I need rescuing FROM!
Quit that arguing!
Annabella doesn't need your nonsense right now.
She's going to be a momma!
WILD
Wow! Oh my gosh!

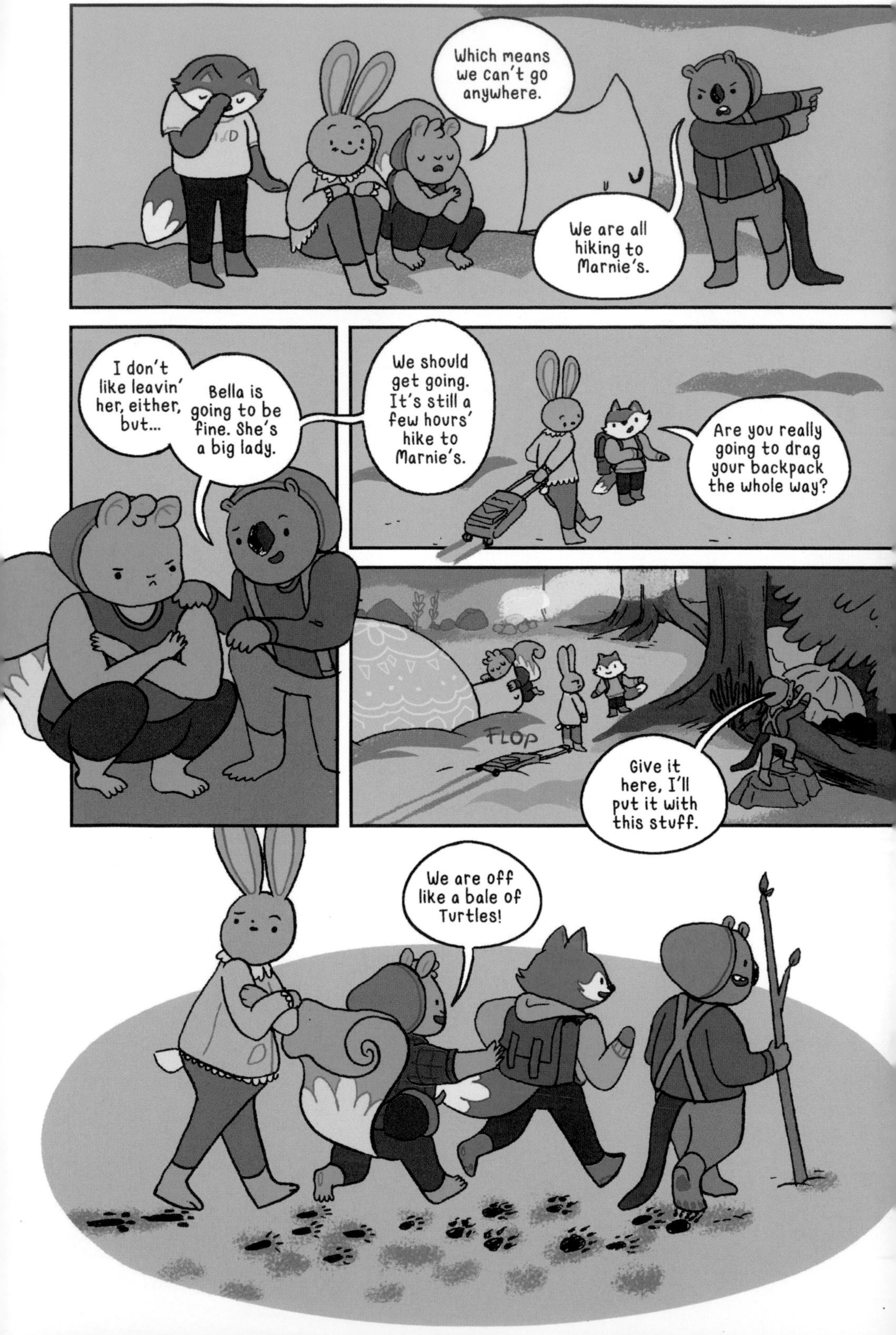
Which means we can't go anywhere.
We are all hiking to Marnie's.
I don't like leavin' her, either, but...
Bella is going to be fine. She's a big lady.
We should get going. It's still a few hours' hike to Marnie's.
Are you really going to drag your backpack the whole way?
FLOP
Give it here, I'll put it with this stuff.
We are off like a bale of Turtles!

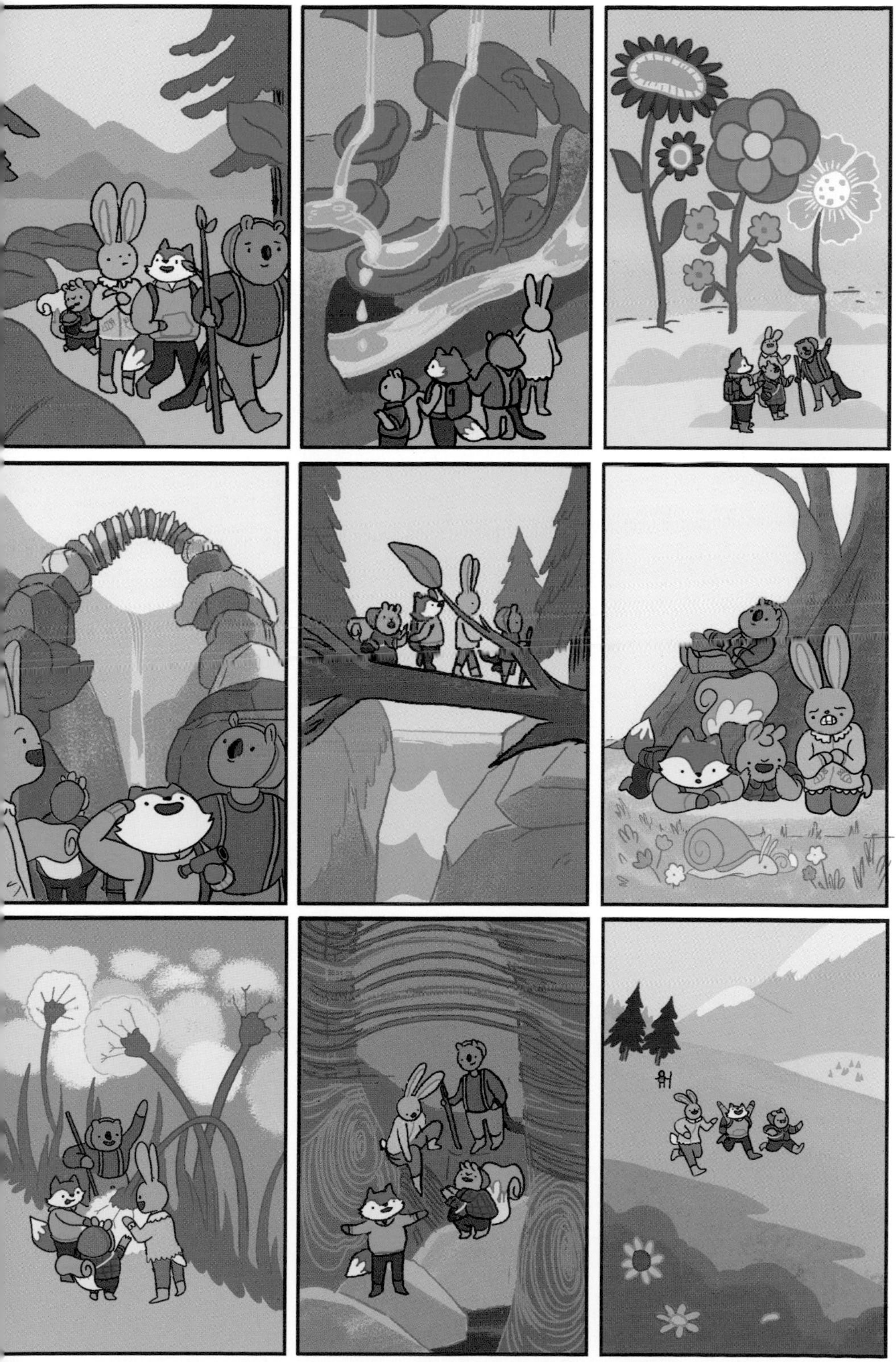

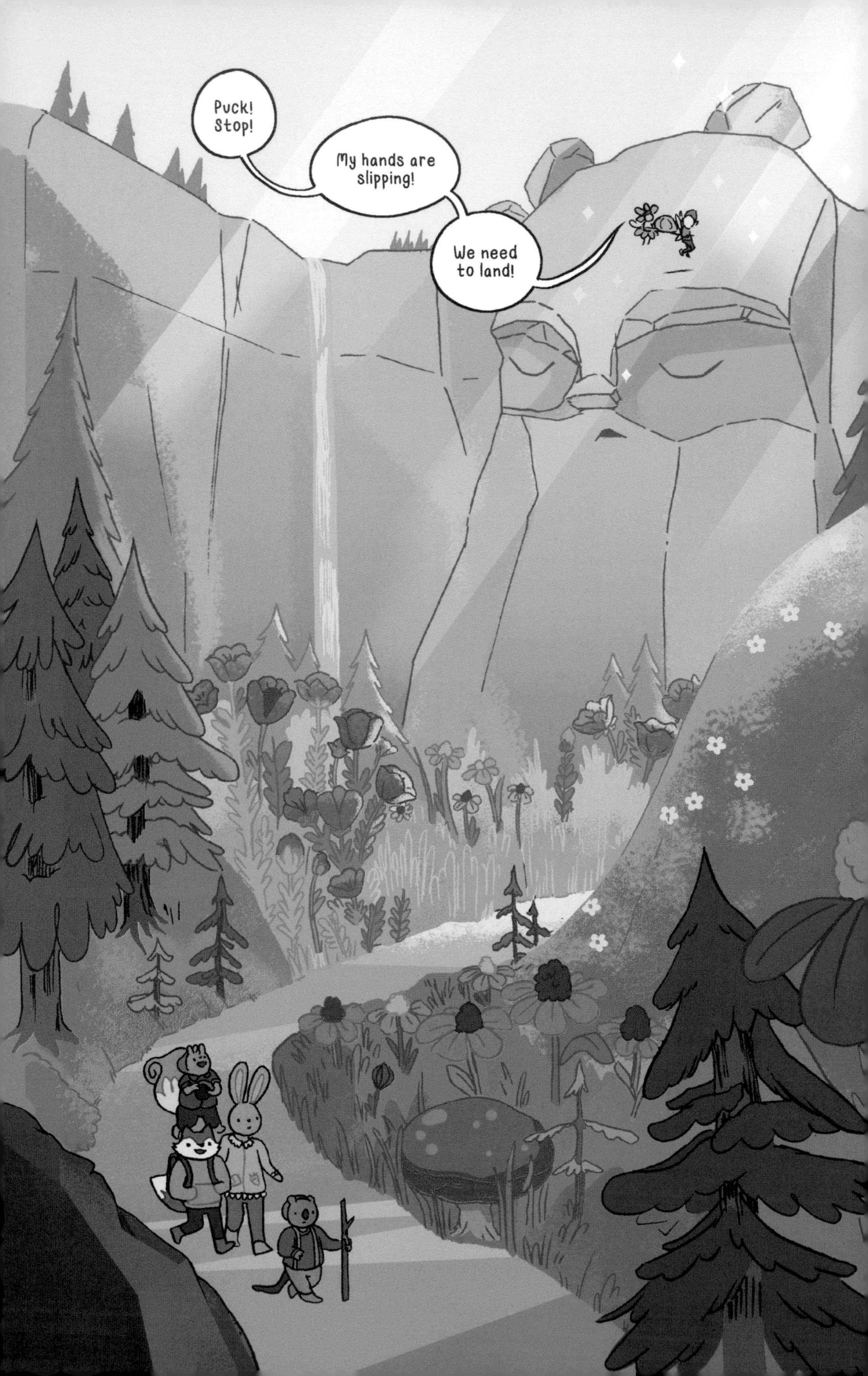
Puck! Stop!
My hands are slipping!
We need to land!

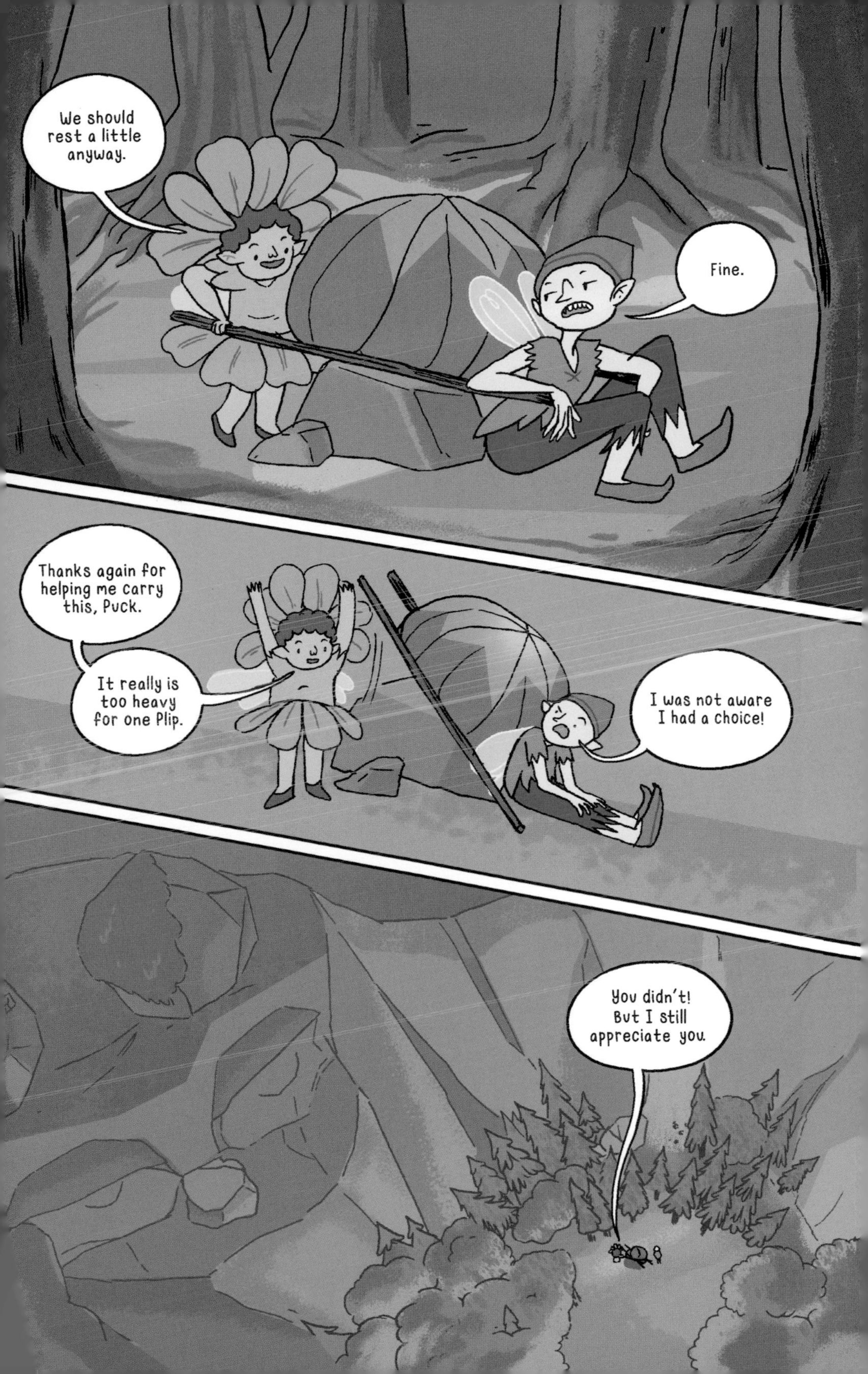
We should rest a little anyway.
Fine.
Thanks again for helping me carry this, Puck.
It really is too heavy for one Plip.
I was not aware I had a choice!
You didn't! But I still appreciate you.

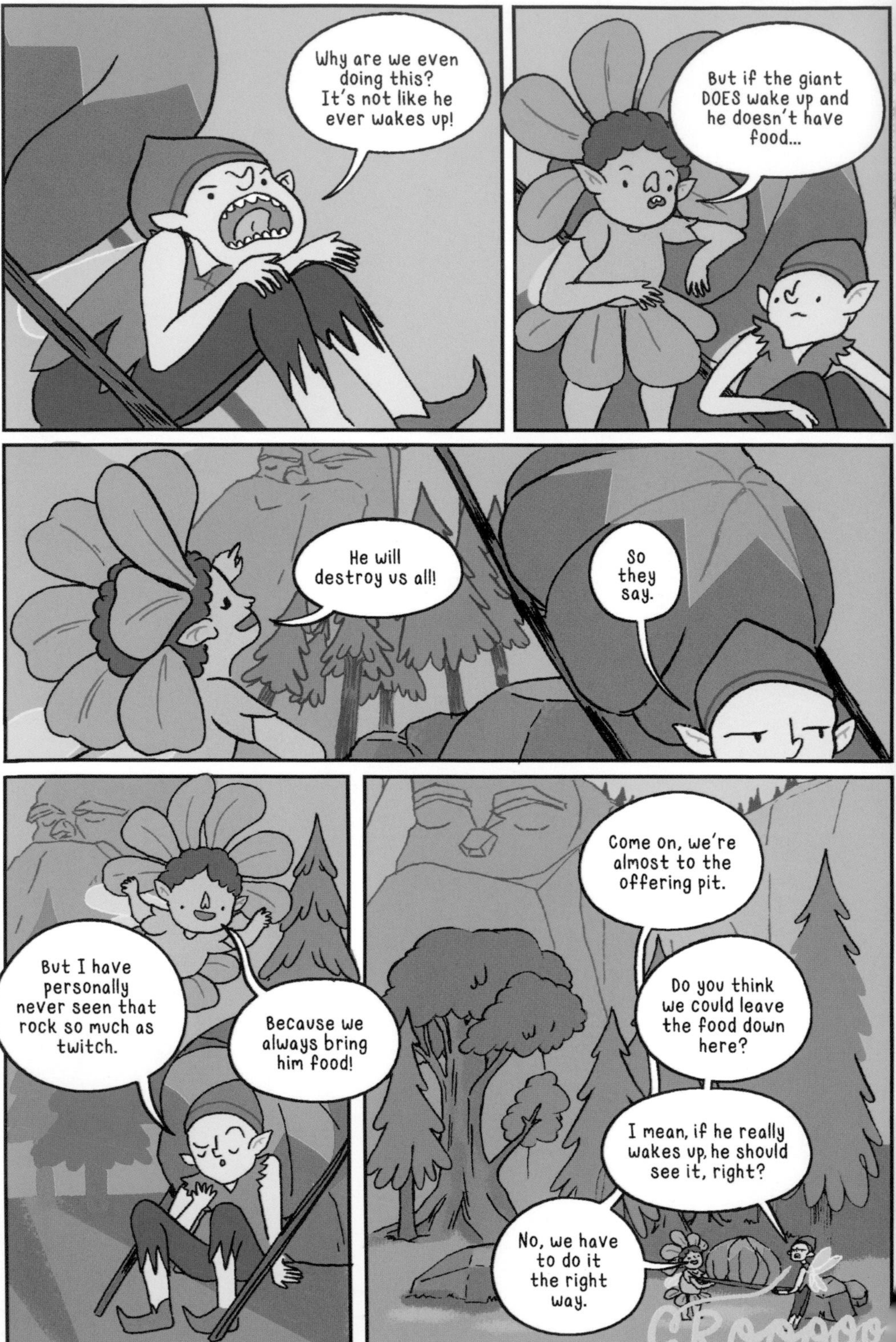
Why are we even doing this? It's not like he ever wakes up!
But if the giant DOES wake up and he doesn't have food...
He will destroy us all!
So they say.
But I have personally never seen that rock so much as twitch.
Because we always bring him food!
Come on, we're almost to the offering pit.
Do you think we could leave the food down here?
I mean, if he really wakes up, he should see it, right?
No, we have to do it the right way.
GROoooo

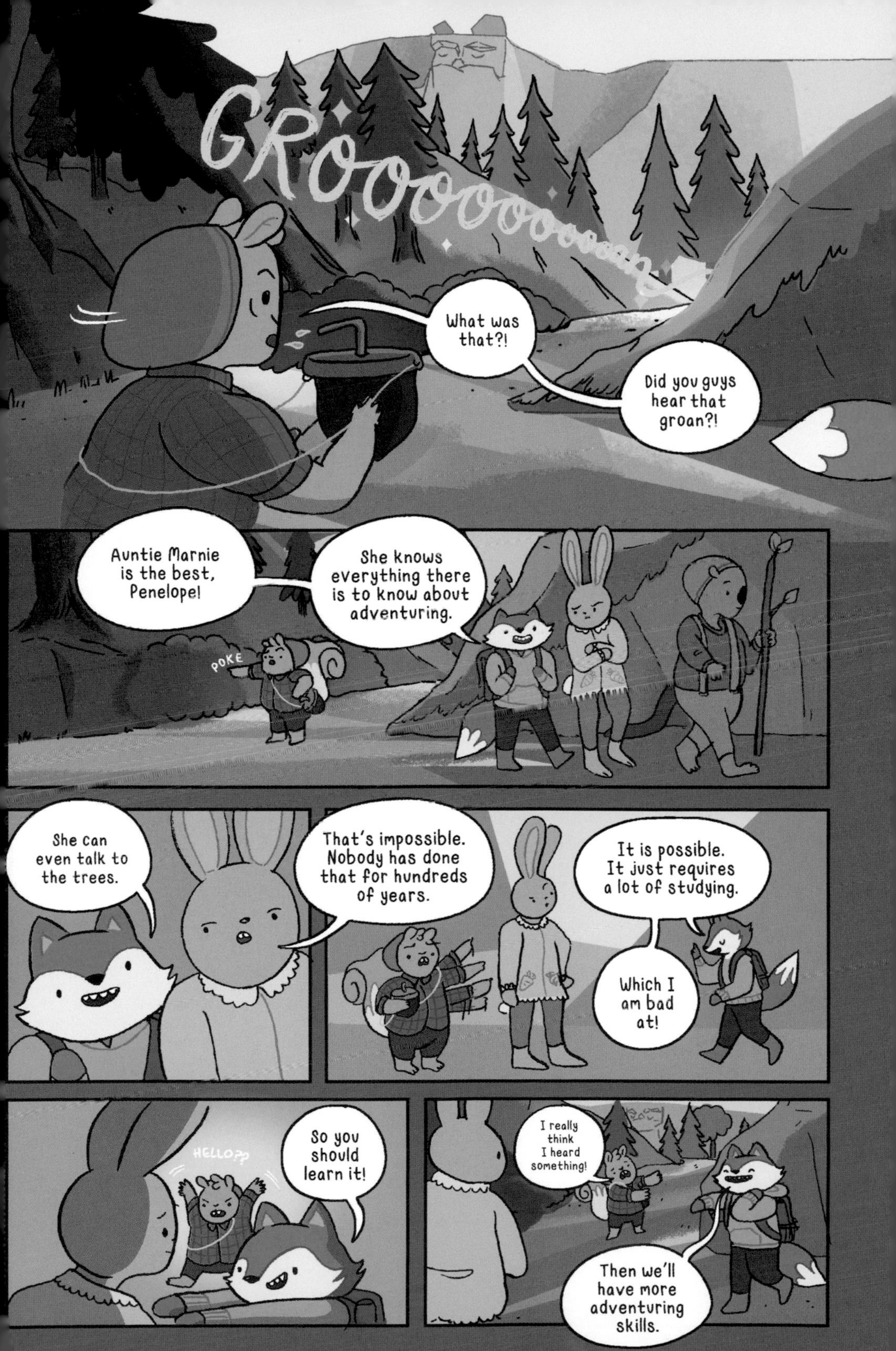
GROOOOOOOAN
What was that?!
Did you guys hear that groan?!
Auntie Marnie is the best, Penelope!
She knows everything there is to know about adventuring.
POKE
She can even talk to the trees.
That's impossible. Nobody has done that for hundreds of years.
It is possible. It just requires a lot of studying.
Which I am bad at!
HELLO??
So you should learn it!
I really think I heard something!
Then we'll have more adventuring skills.

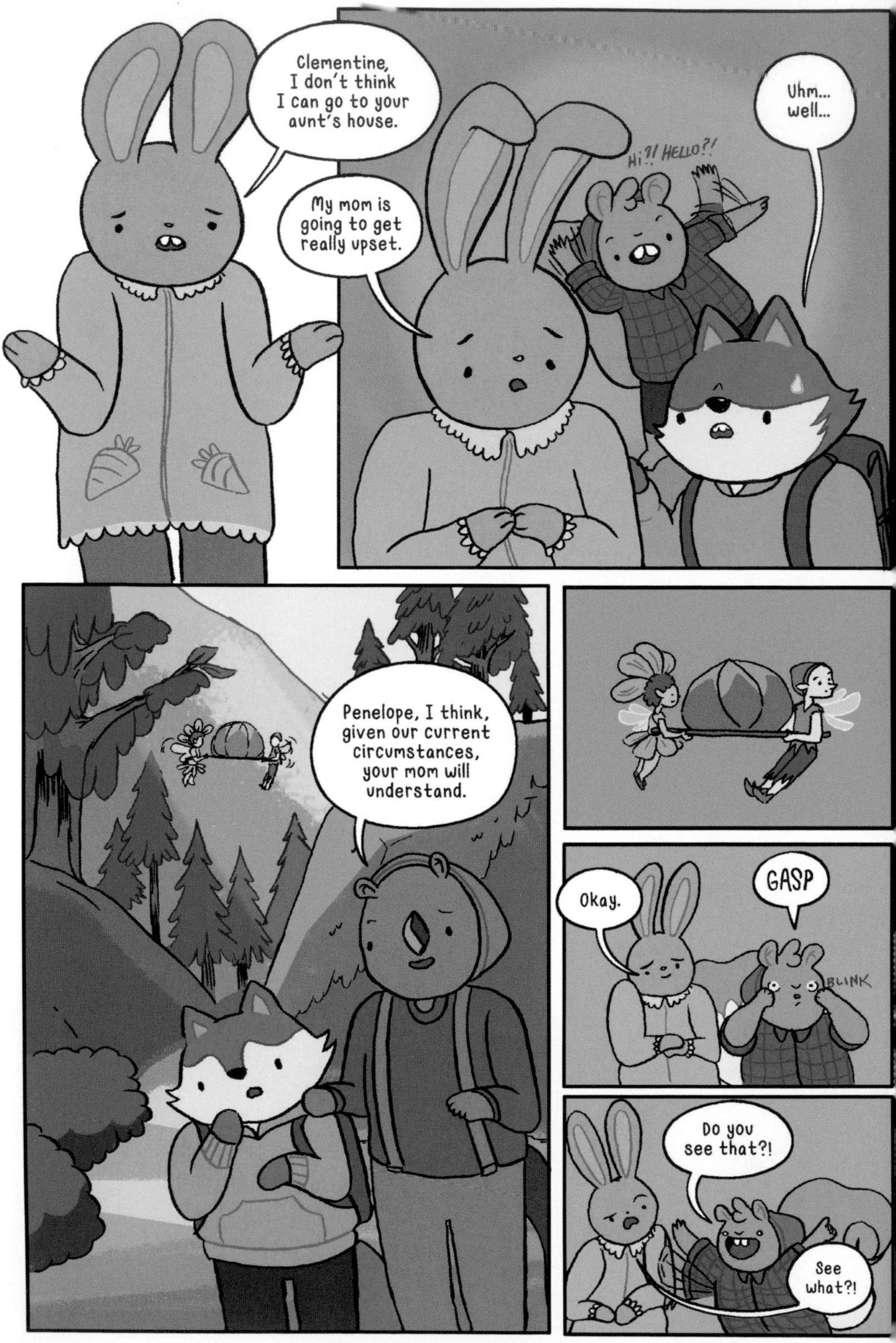

Clementine, I don't think I can go to your aunt's house.
My mom is going to get really upset.
HI?! HELLO?!
Uhm... well...
Penelope, I think, given our current circumstances, your mom will understand.
Okay.
GASP
BLINK
Do you see that?!
See what?!

Up there!

I think they're Plips!

Flora, do you get the feeling we're being watched?

Ohh...

No way!

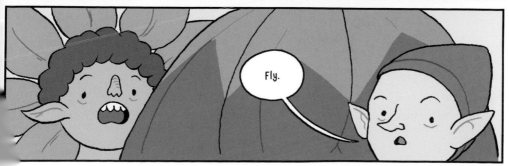

Fly.

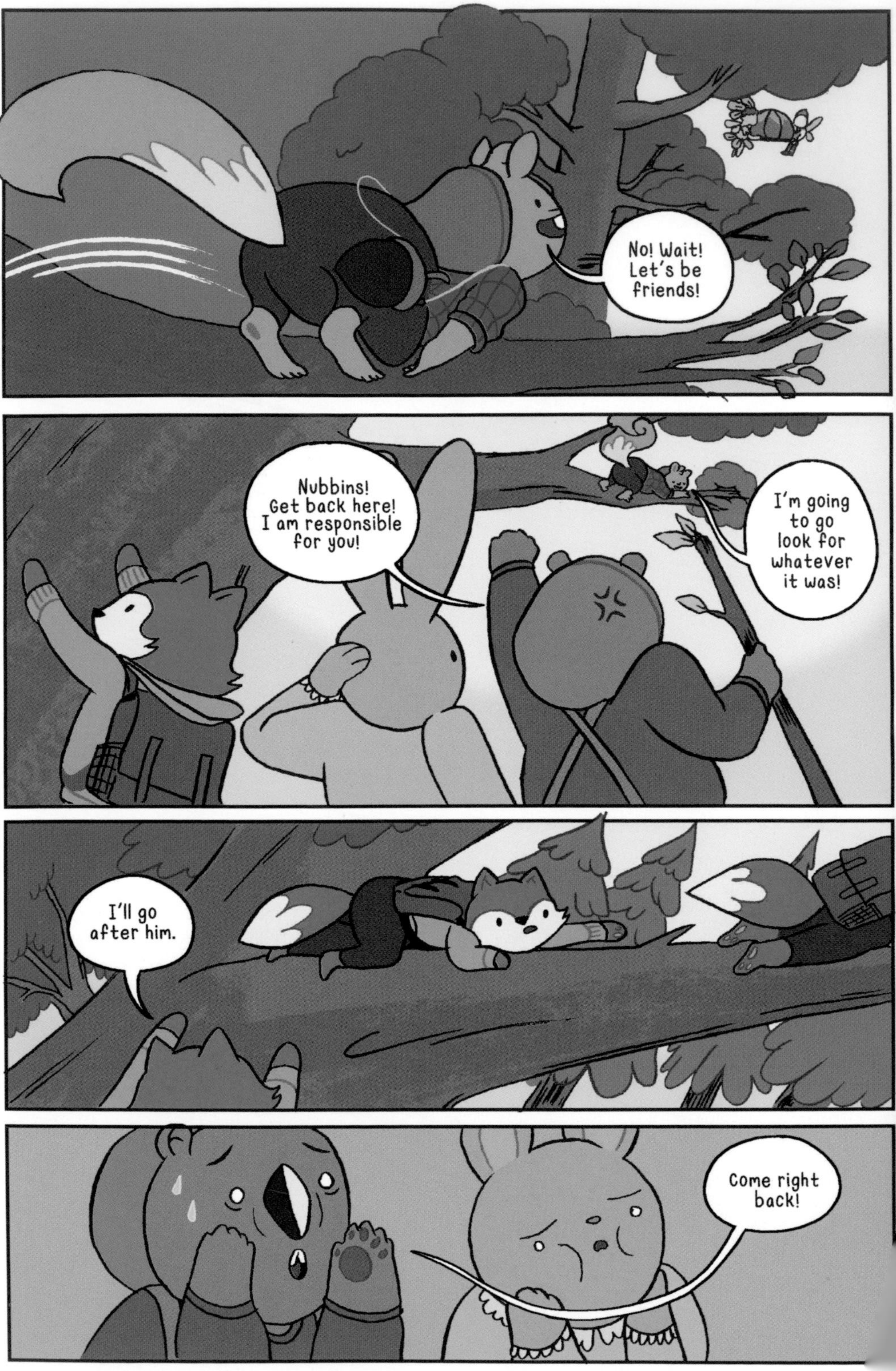
No! Wait! Let's be friends!
Nubbins! Get back here! I am responsible for you!
I'm going to go look for whatever it was!
I'll go after him.
Come right back!

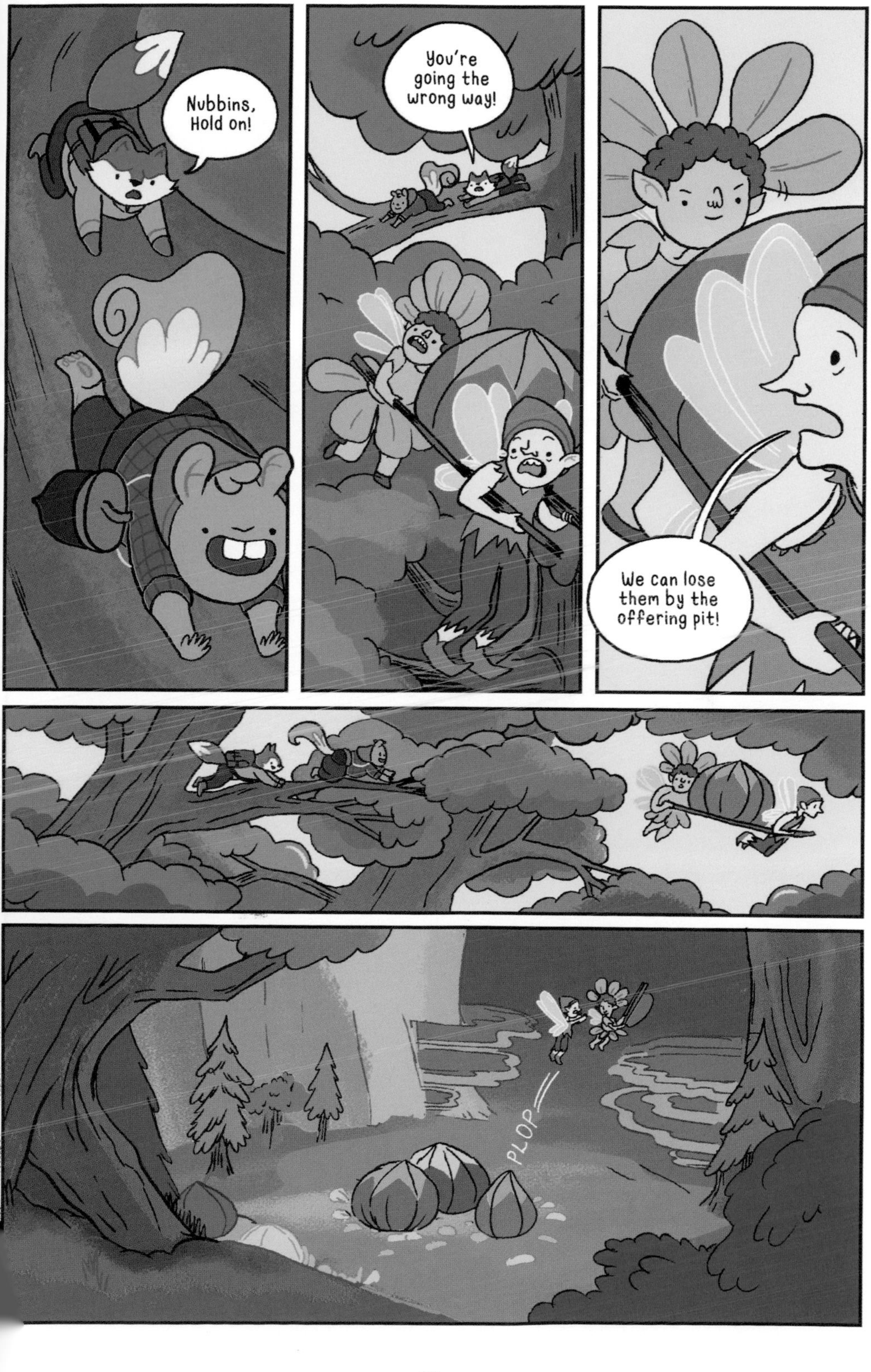
Nubbins, Hold on!
You're going the wrong way!
We can lose them by the offering pit!
PLOP

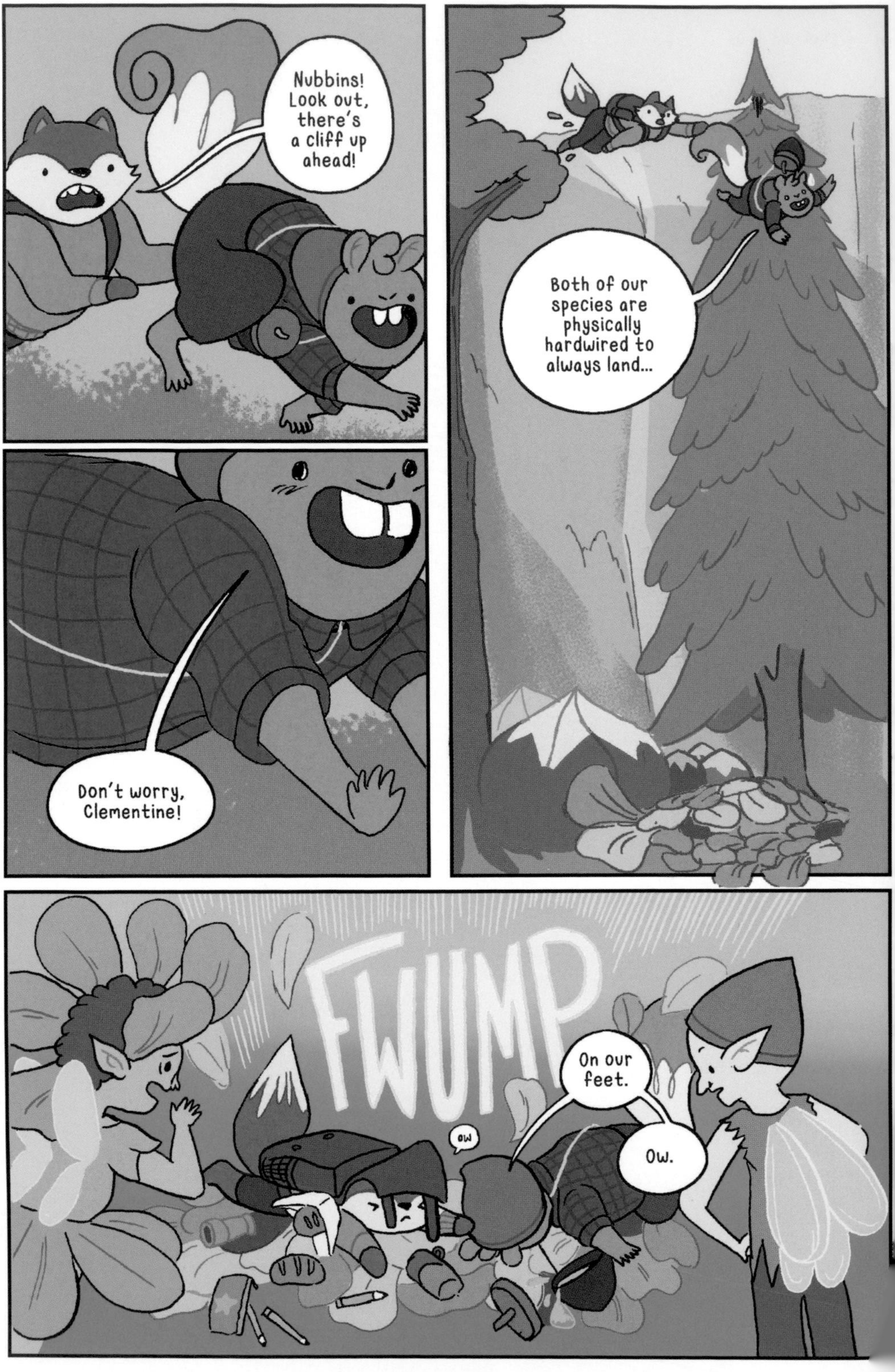
Nubbins! Look out, there's a cliff up ahead!
Don't worry, Clementine!
Both of our species are physically hardwired to always land...
FWUMP
OW
On our feet.
Ow.

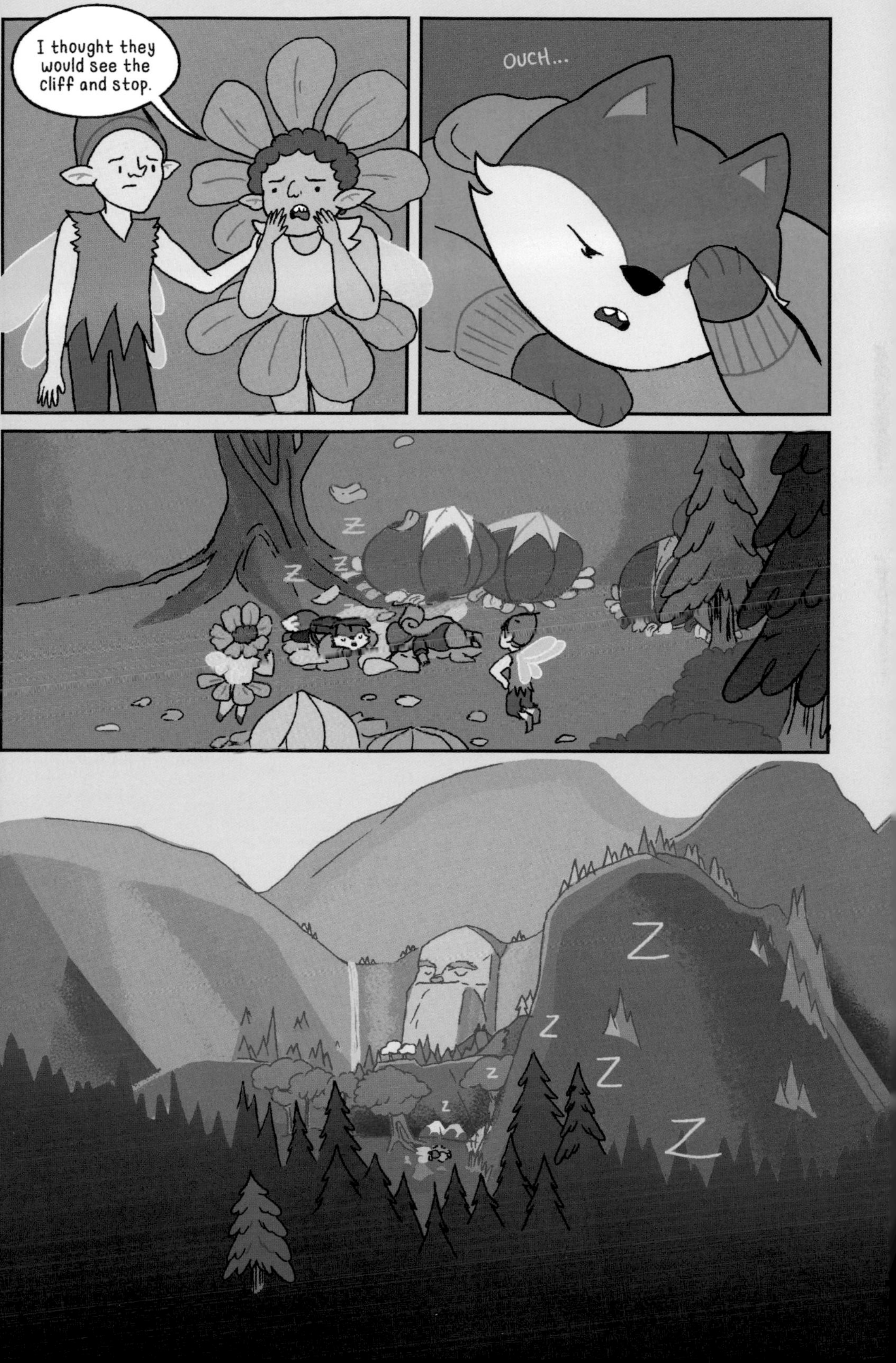

I thought they would see the cliff and stop.
OUCH...
Z
Z
Z
Z
Z
Z
Z

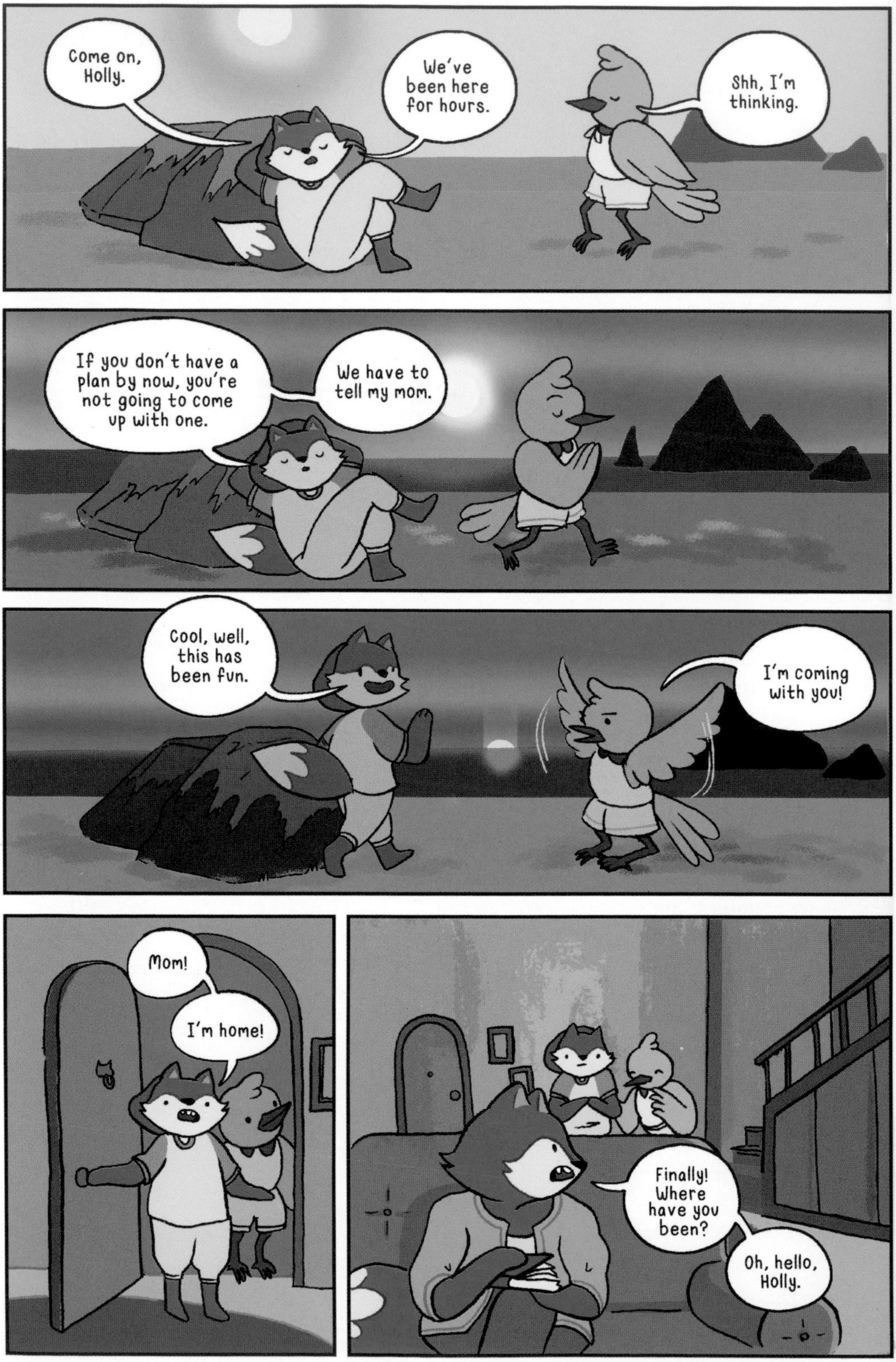
Come on, Holly.
We've been here for hours.
Shh, I'm thinking.
If you don't have a plan by now, you're not going to come up with one.
We have to tell my mom.
Cool, well, this has been fun.
I'm coming with you!
Mom!
I'm home!
Finally! Where have you been?
Oh, hello, Holly.

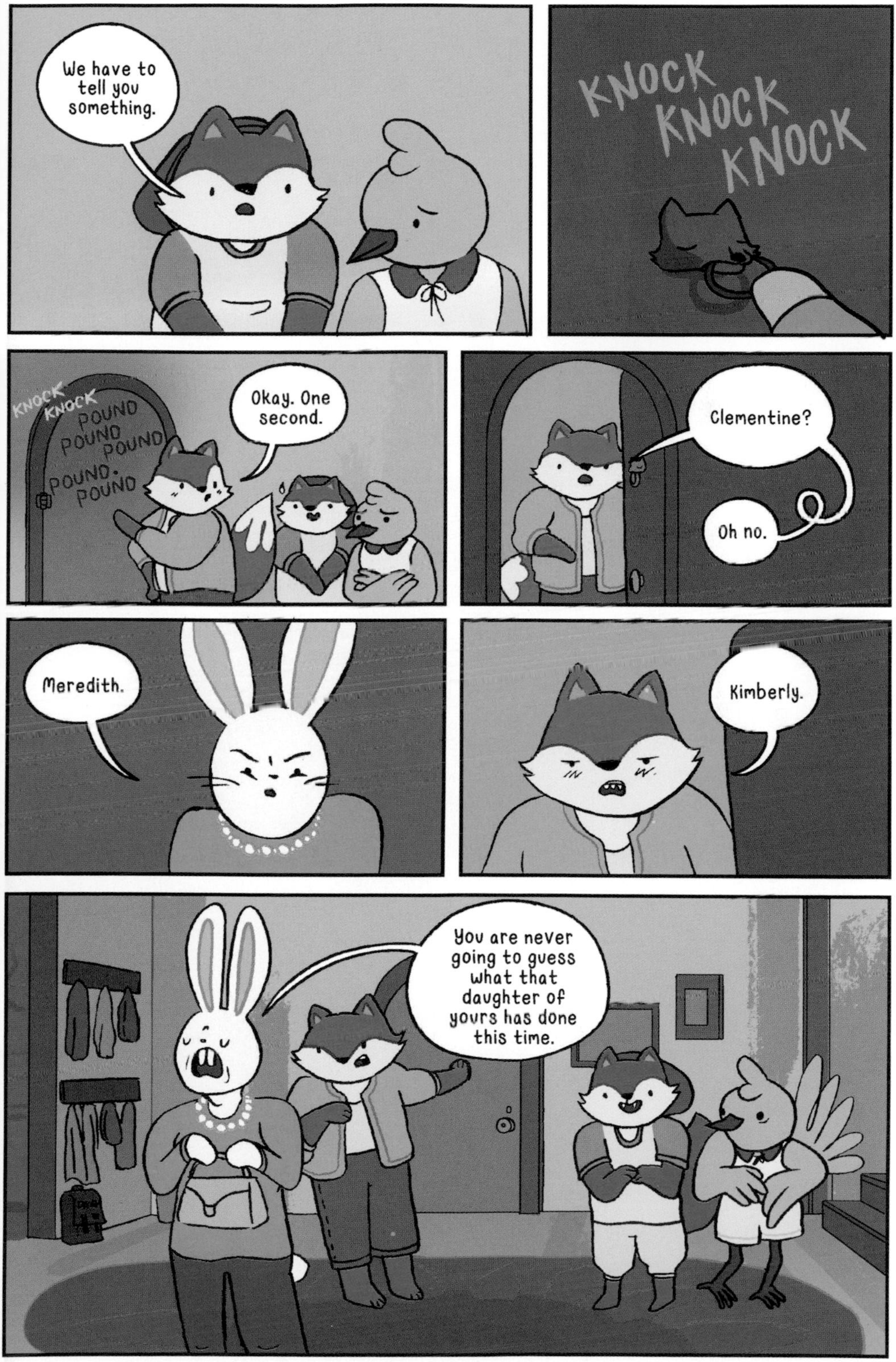

We have to tell you something.
KNOCK KNOCK KNOCK
KNOCK KNOCK
POUND POUND POUND POUND POUND
Okay. One second.
Clementine?
Oh no.
Meredith.
Kimberly.
You are never going to guess what that daughter of yours has done this time.

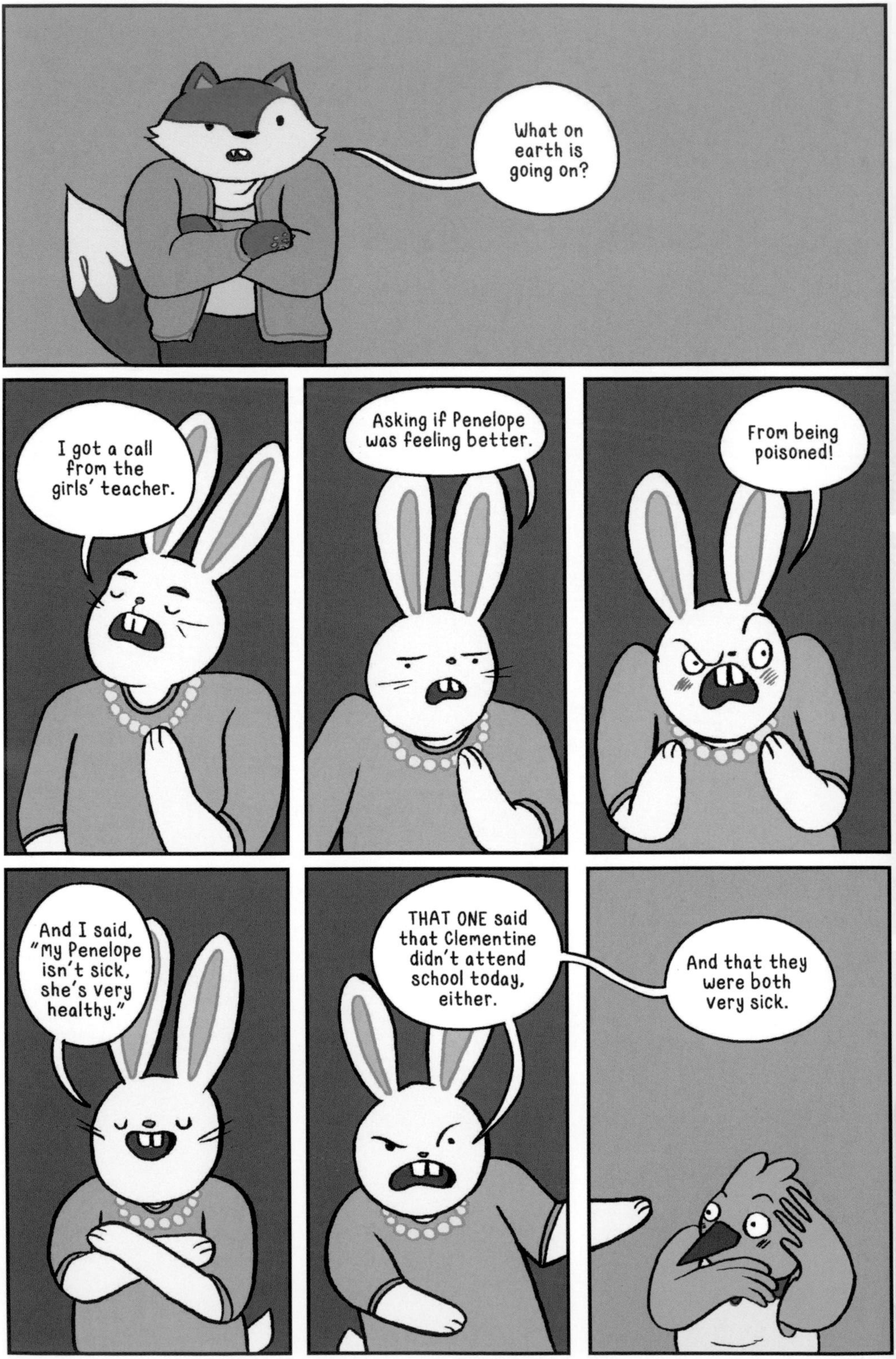
What on earth is going on?
I got a call from the girls' teacher.
Asking if Penelope was feeling better.
From being poisoned!
And I said, "My Penelope isn't sick, she's very healthy."
THAT ONE said that Clementine didn't attend school today, either.
And that they were both very sick.

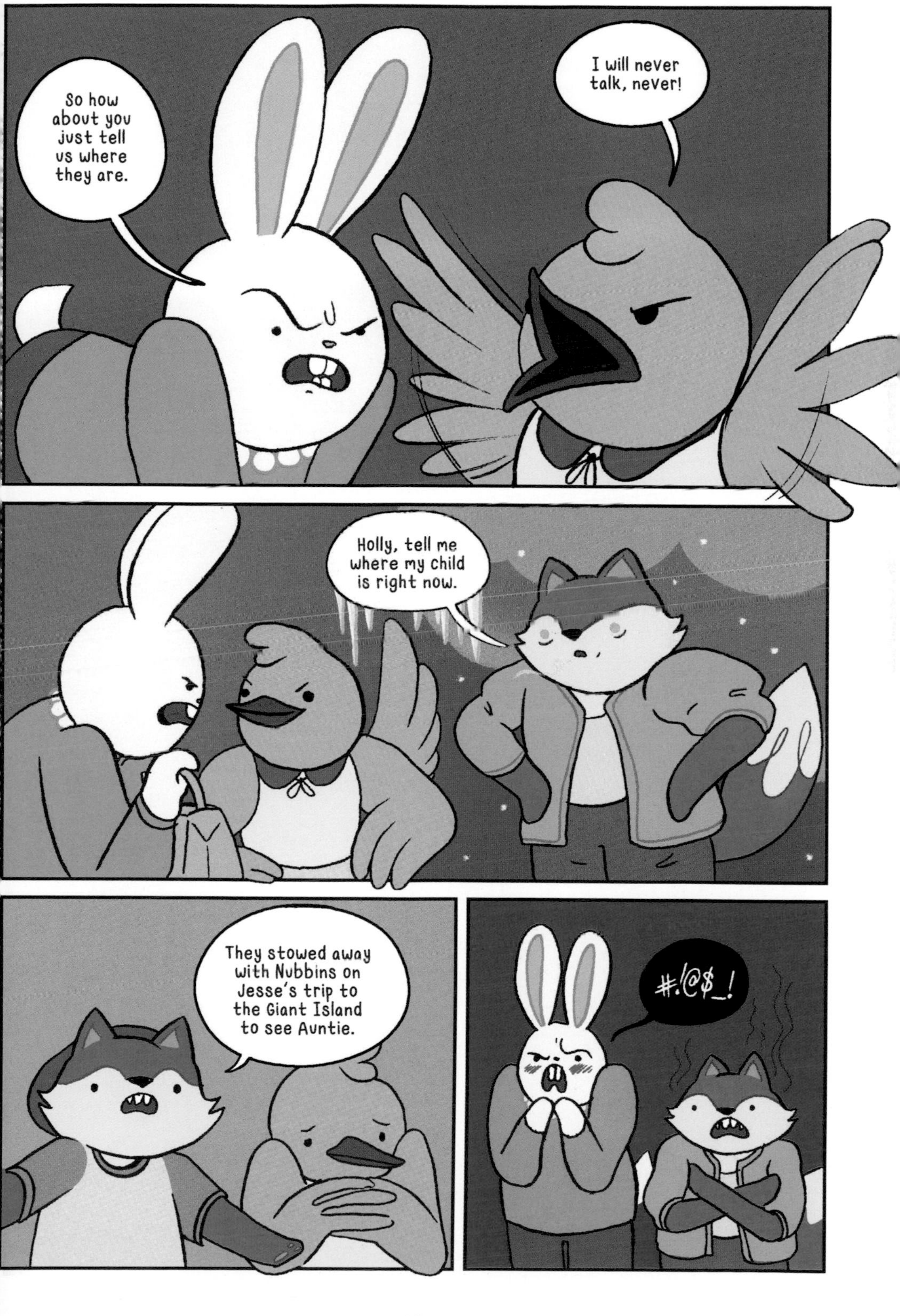
So how about you just tell us where they are.
I will never talk, never!
Holly, tell me where my child is right now.
They stowed away with Nubbins on Jesse's trip to the Giant Island to see Auntie.
#!@$_!

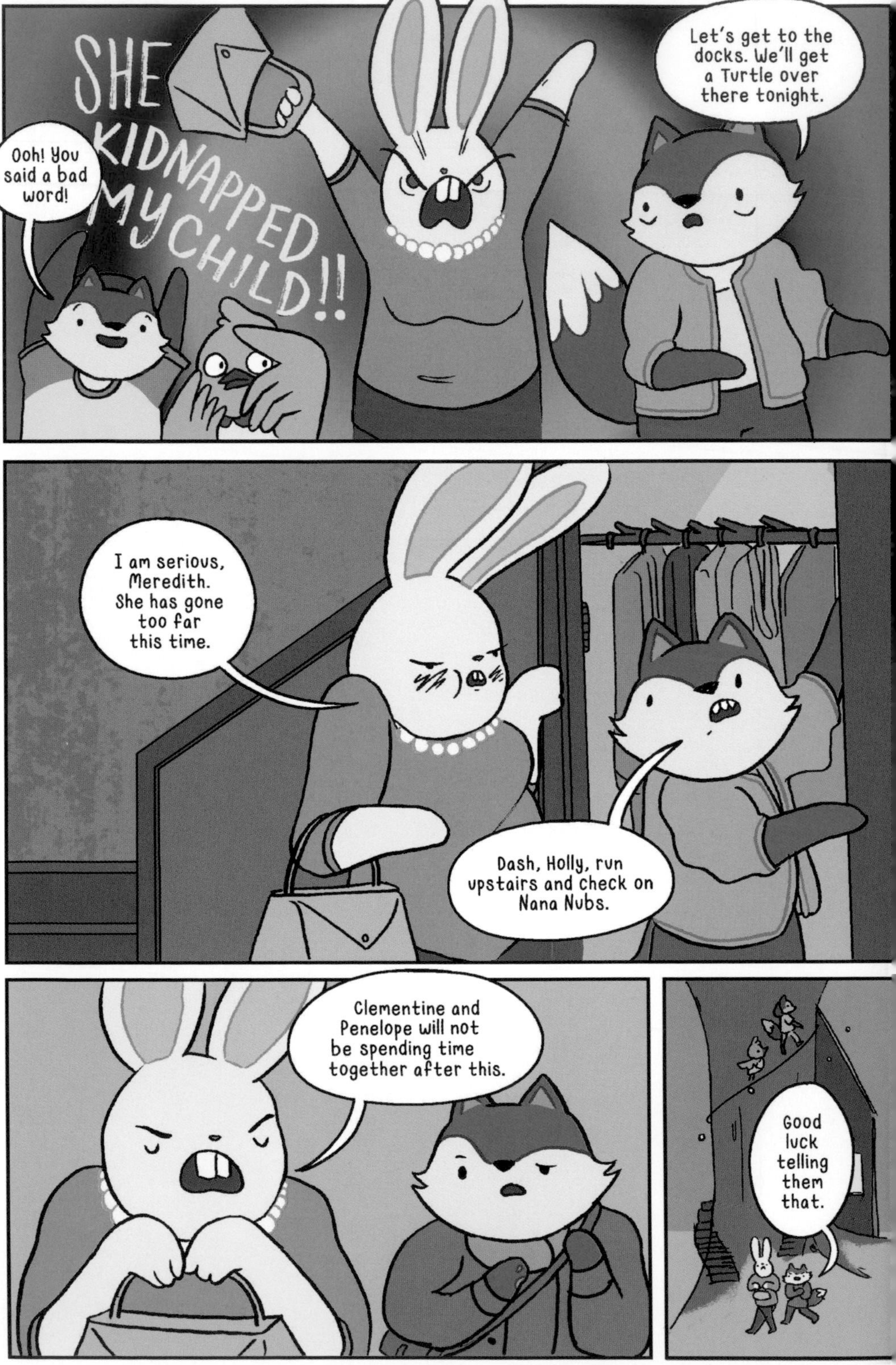
Ooh! You said a bad word!
SHE KIDNAPPED MY CHILD!!
Let's get to the docks. We'll get a Turtle over there tonight.
I am serious, Meredith. She has gone too far this time.
Dash, Holly, run upstairs and check on Nana Nubs.
Clementine and Penelope will not be spending time together after this.
Good luck telling them that.

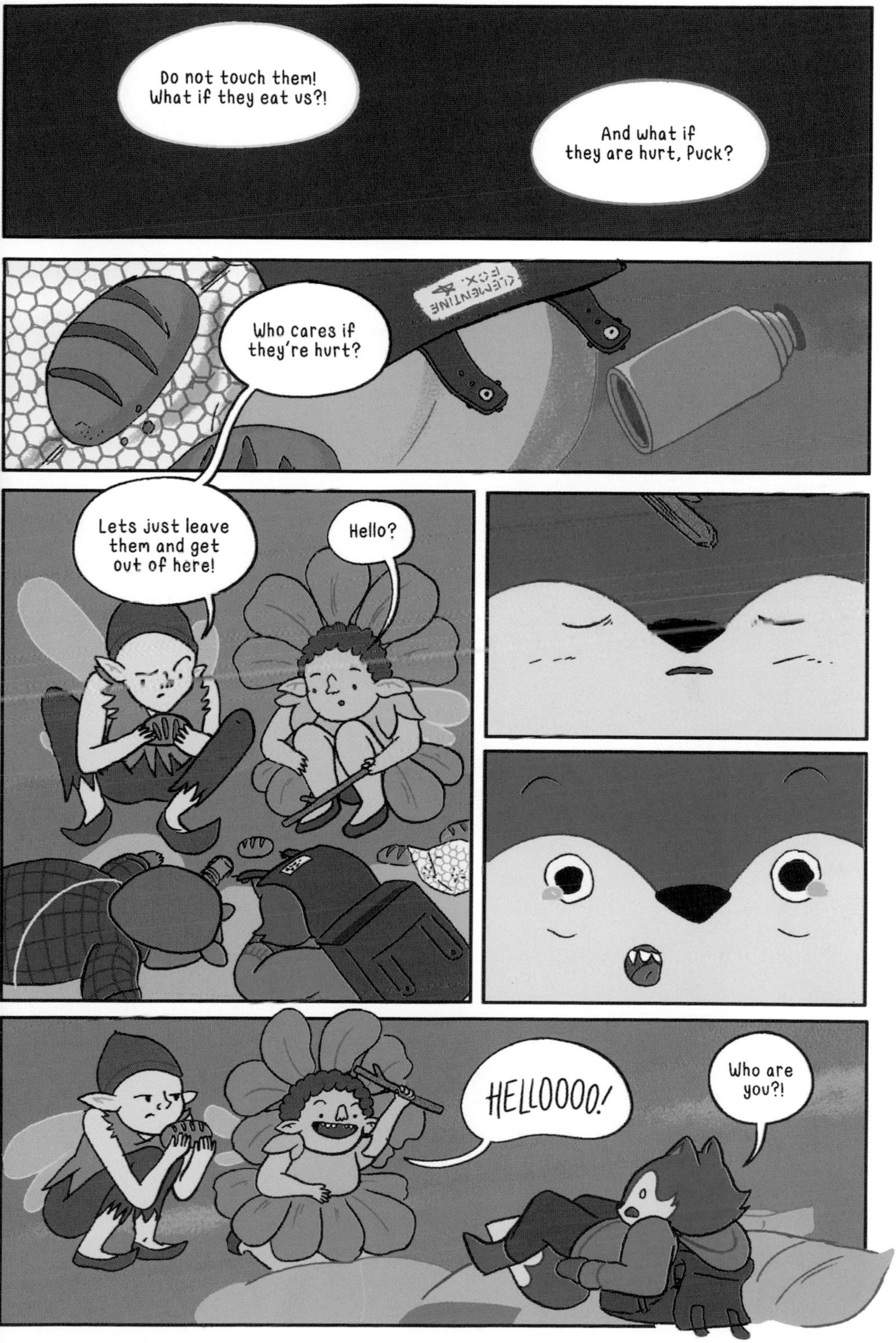
Do not touch them! What if they eat us?!
And what if they are hurt, Puck?
Who cares if they're hurt?
Lets just leave them and get out of here!
Hello?
HELLOOOO!
Who are you?!

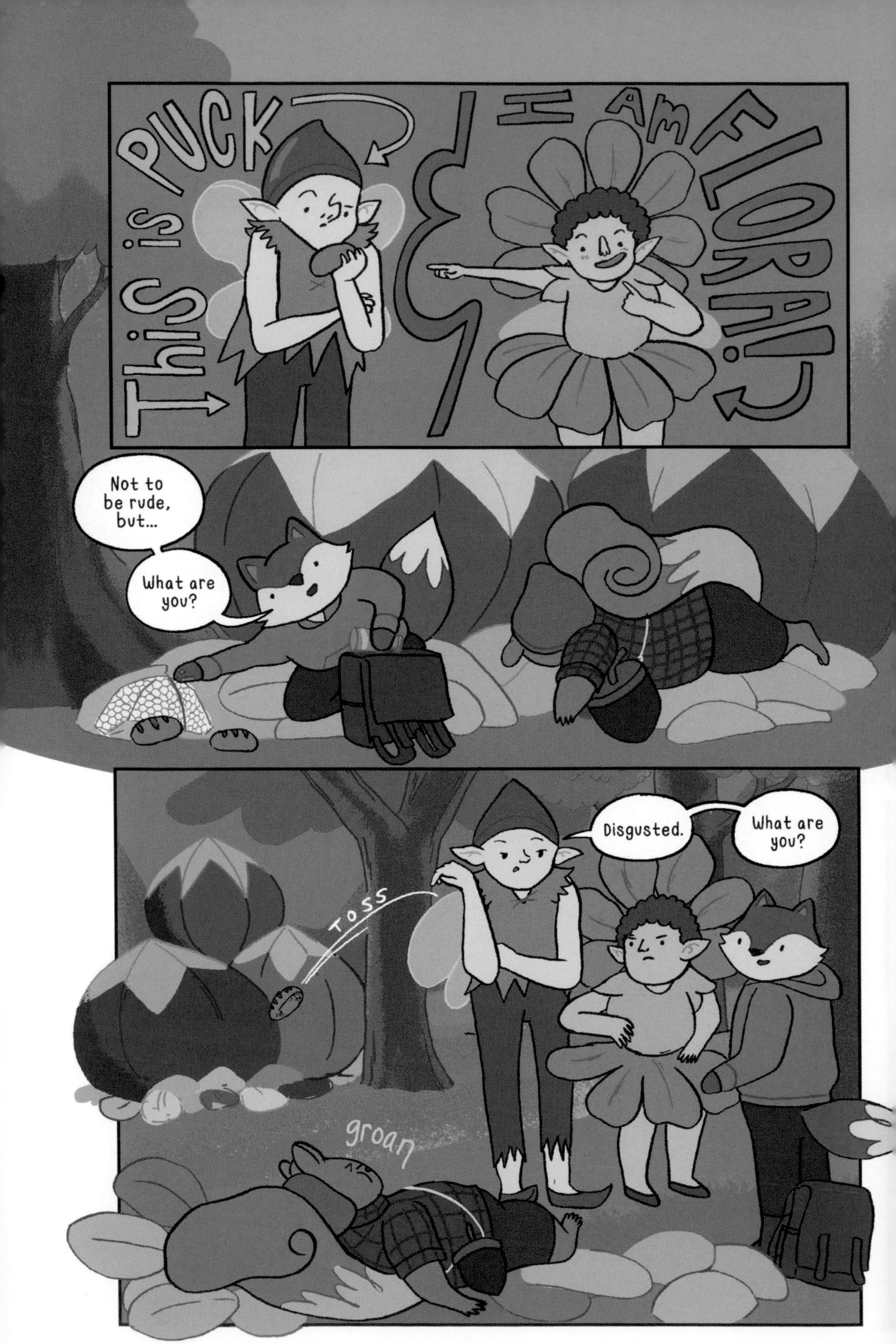
This is PUCK
I Am FLORA!
Not to be rude, but...
What are you?
Disgusted.
What are you?
TOSS
groan

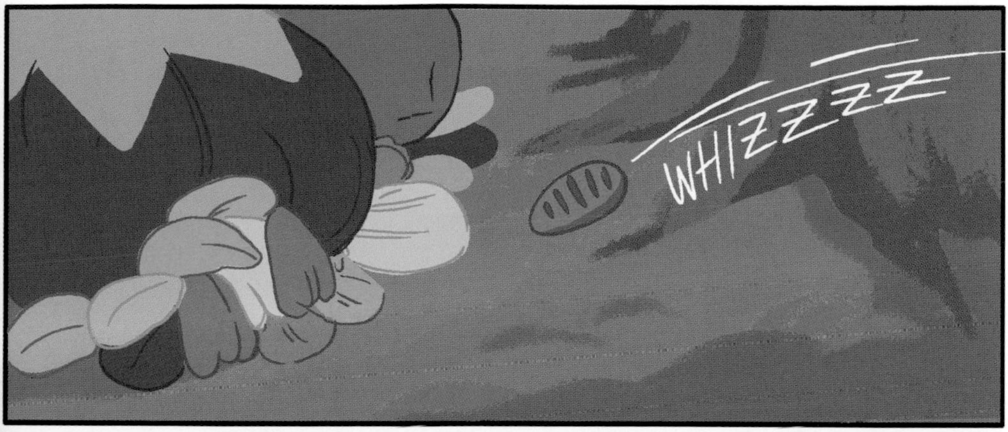
WHIZZZZZ

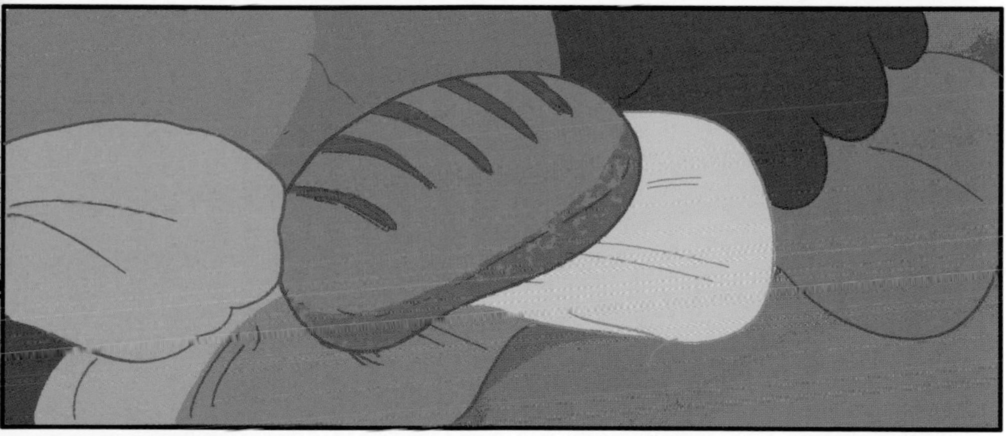

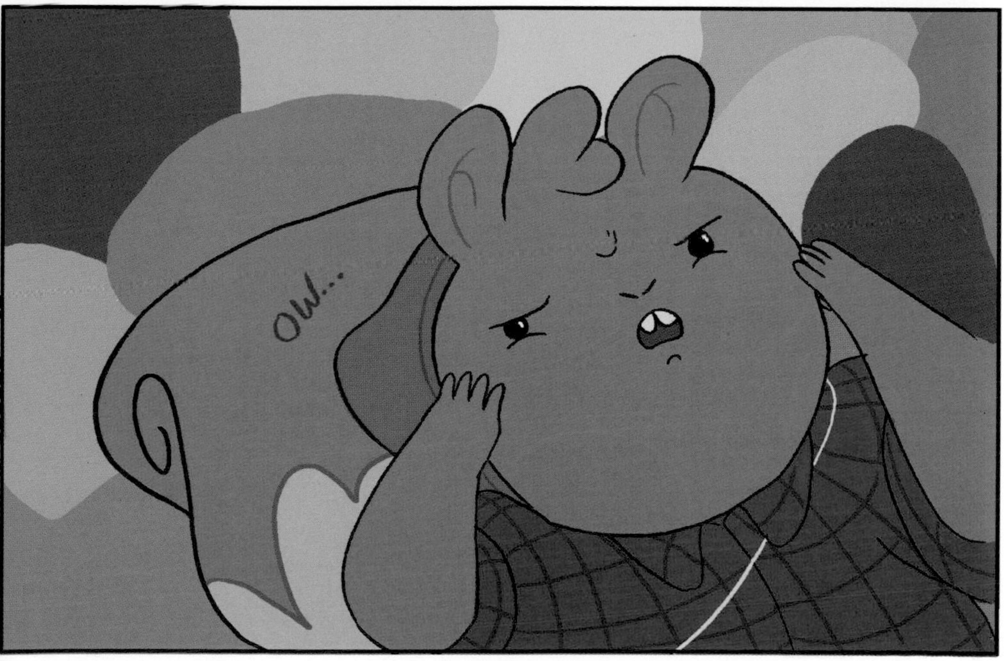
OW...

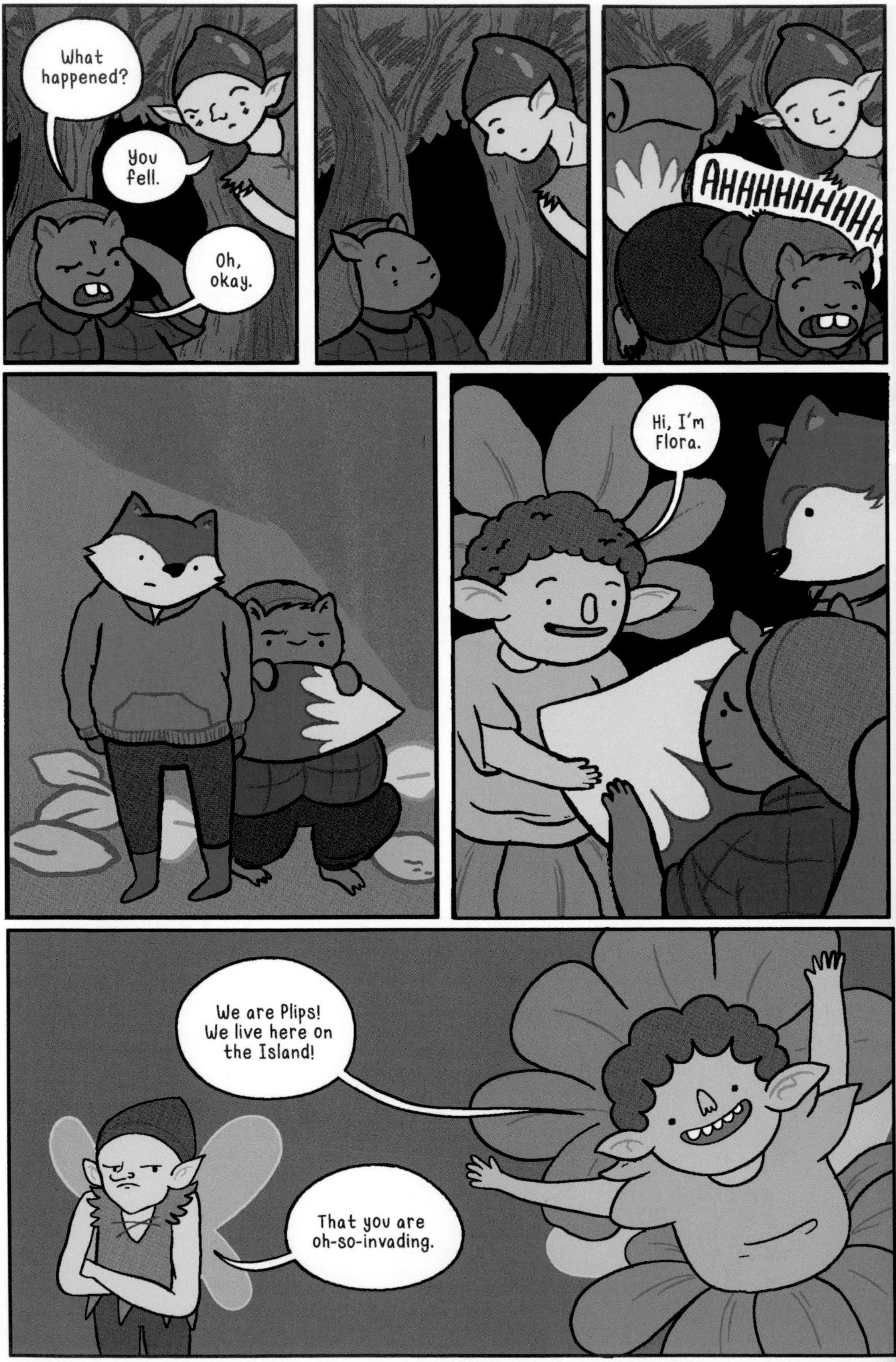
What happened?
You fell.
Oh, okay.
AHHHHHHHHH
Hi, I'm Flora.
We are Plips! We live here on the Island!
That you are oh-so-invading.

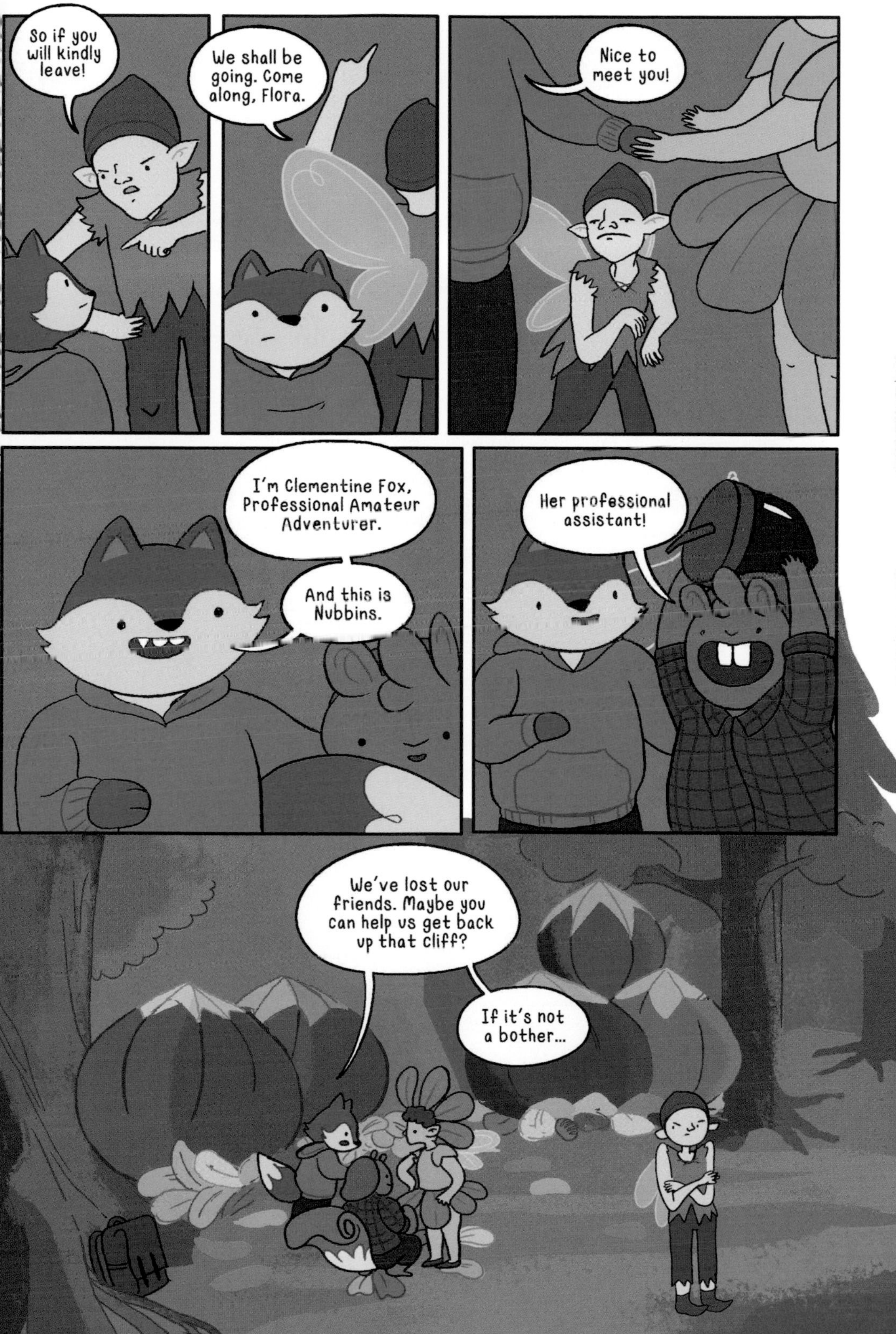
So if you will kindly leave!
We shall be going. Come along, Flora.
Nice to meet you!
I'm Clementine Fox, Professional Amateur Adventurer.
And this is Nubbins.
Her professional assistant!
We've lost our friends. Maybe you can help us get back up that cliff?
If it's not a bother...

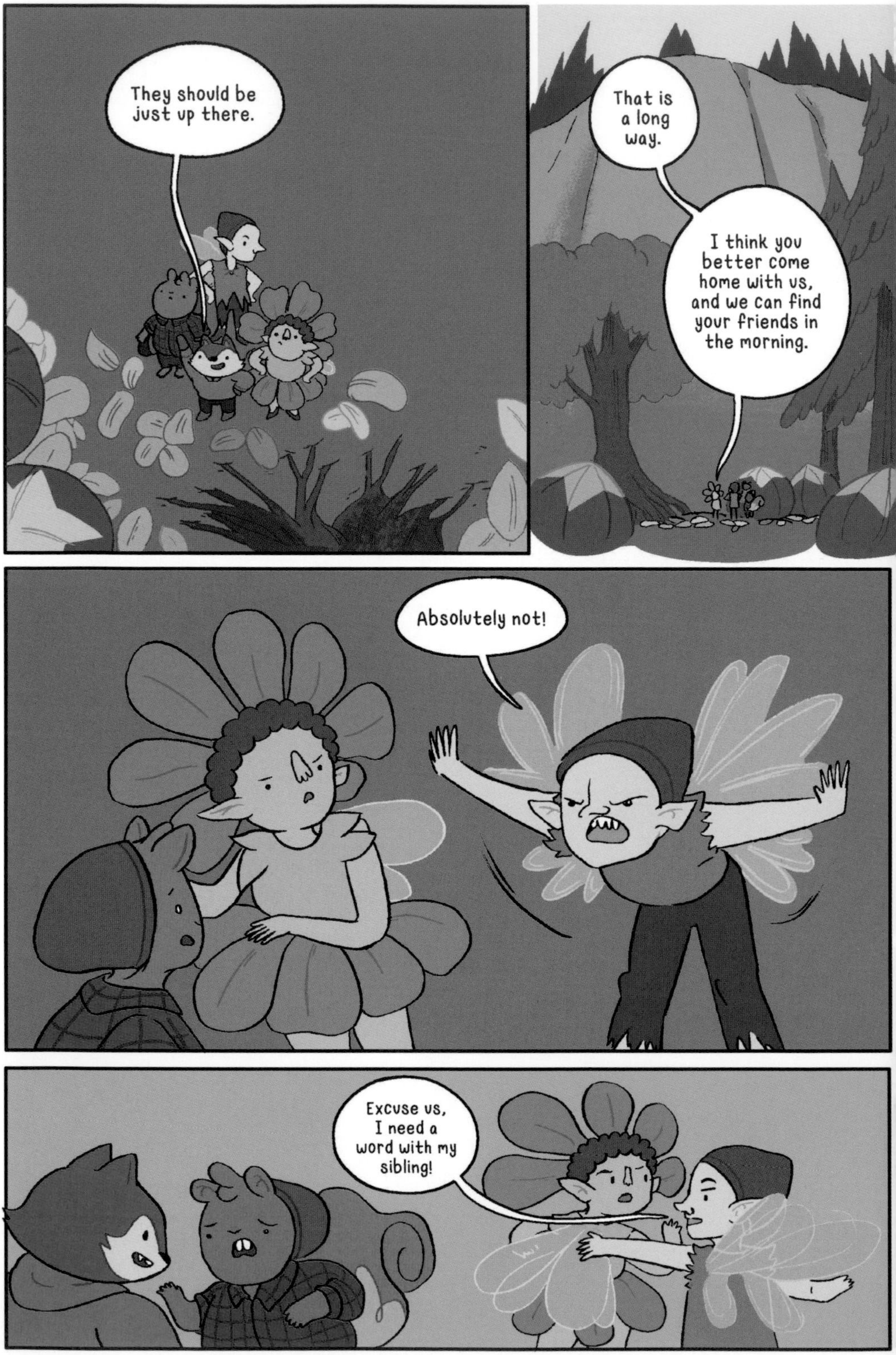
They should be just up there.
That is a long way.
I think you better come home with us, and we can find your friends in the morning.
Absolutely not!
Excuse us, I need a word with my sibling!

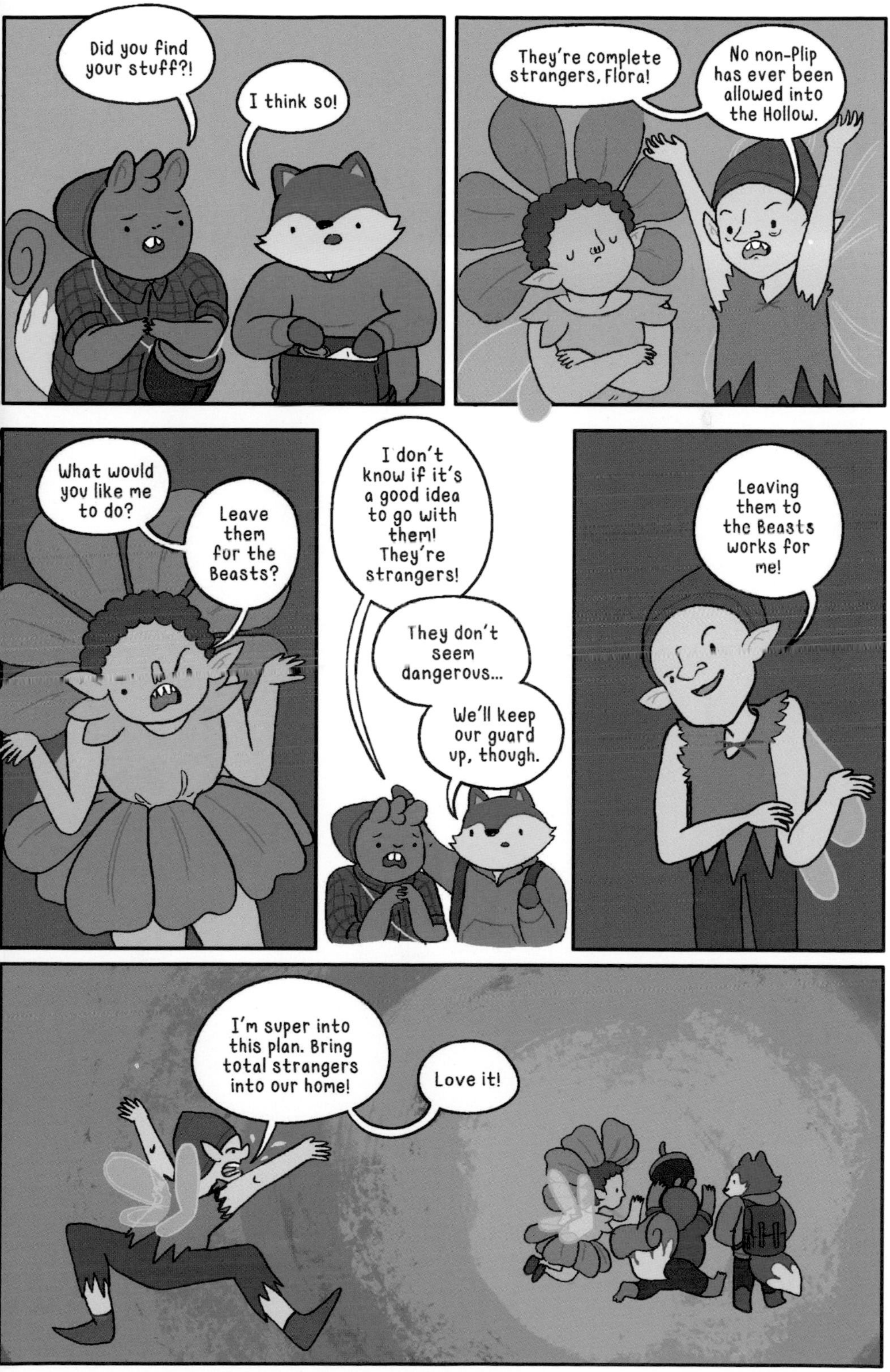
Did you find your stuff?!
I think so!
They're complete strangers, Flora!
No non-Plip has ever been allowed into the Hollow.
What would you like me to do?
Leave them for the Beasts?
I don't know if it's a good idea to go with them! They're strangers!
They don't seem dangerous...
We'll keep our guard up, though.
Leaving them to the Beasts works for me!
I'm super into this plan. Bring total strangers into our home!
Love it!

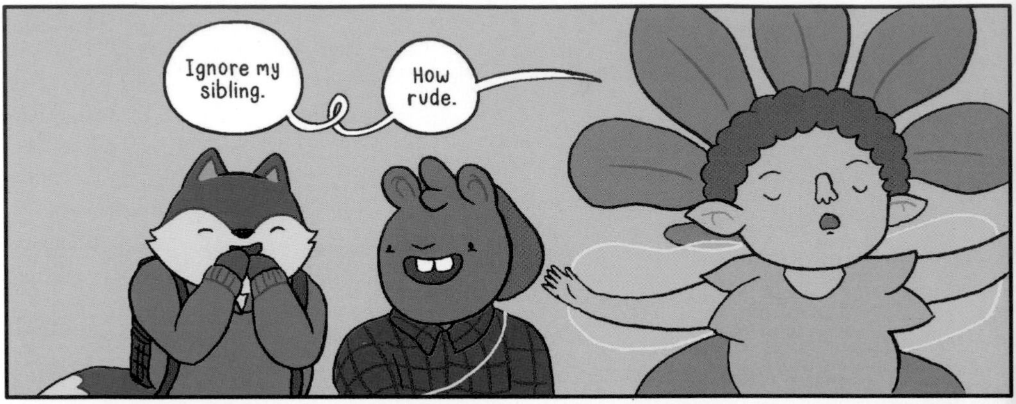
Ignore my sibling.
How rude.

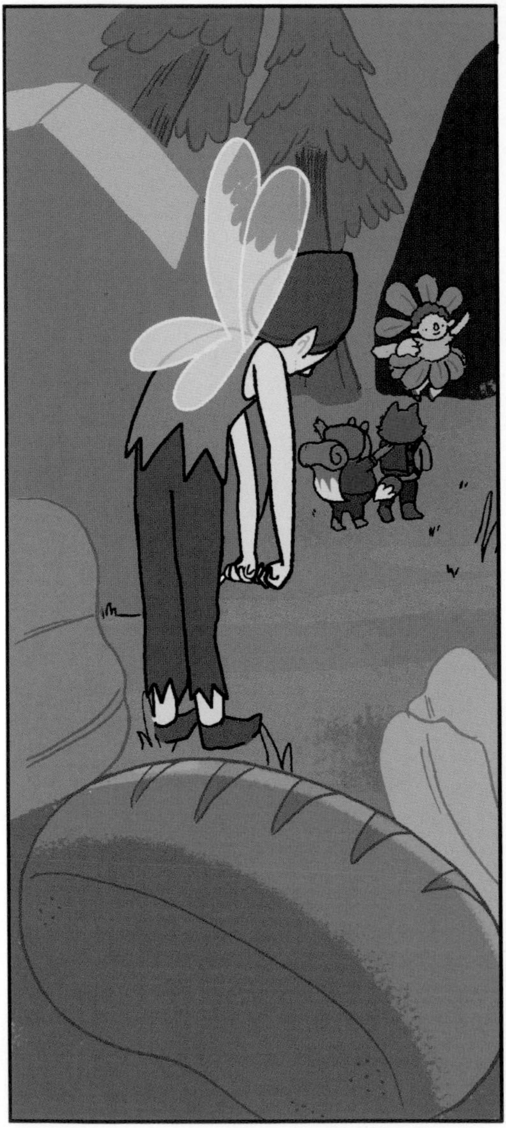

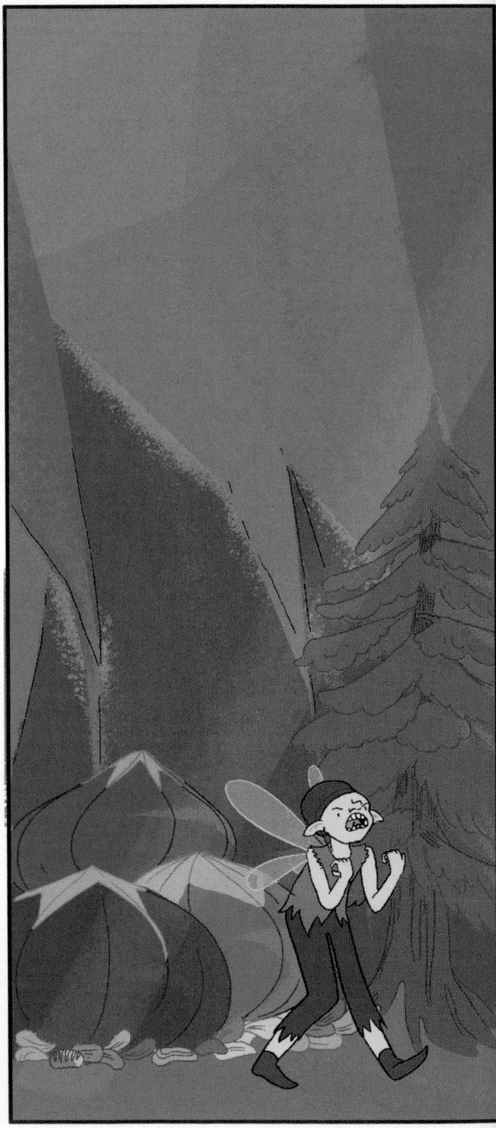

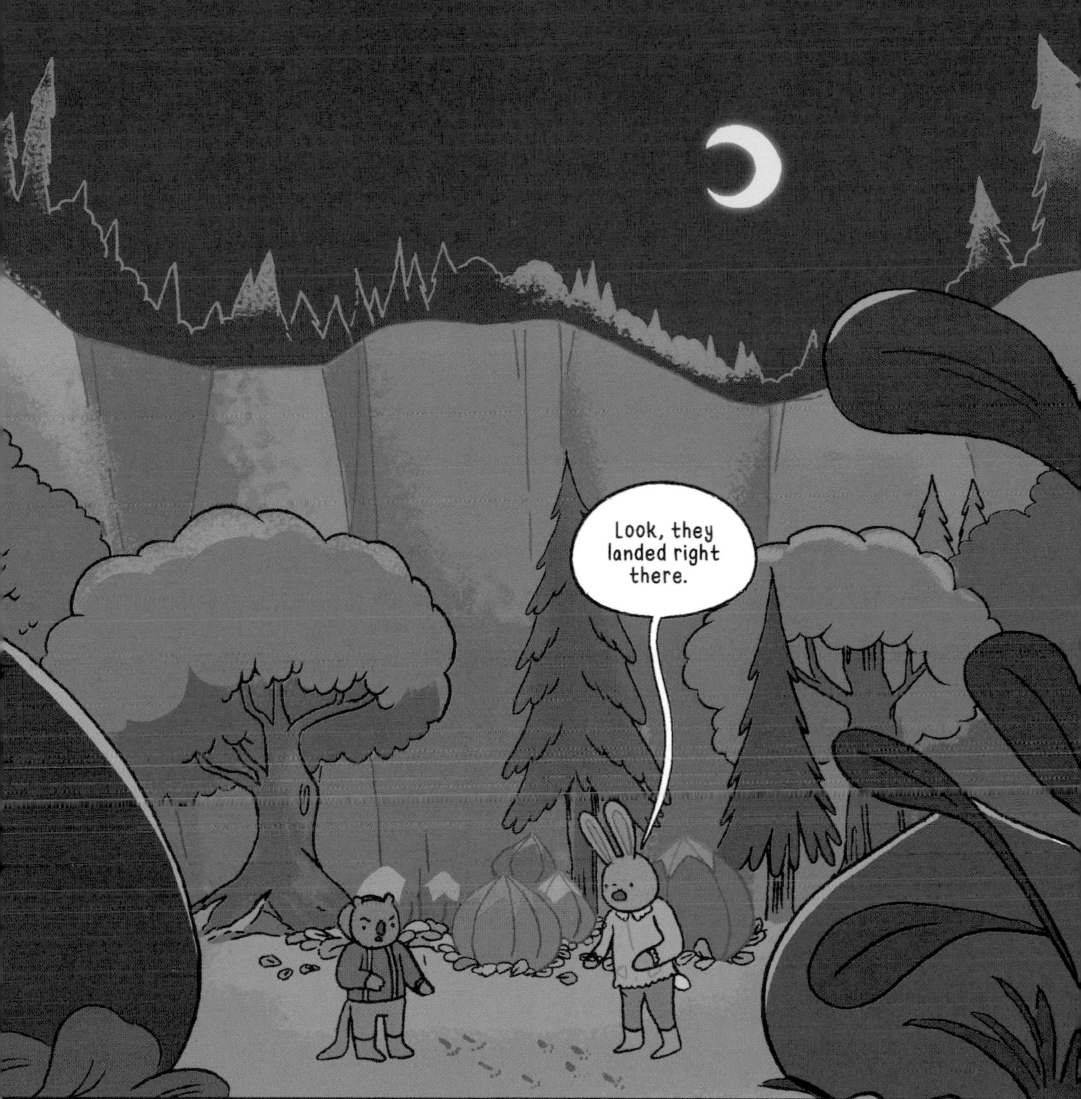
Look, they landed right there.
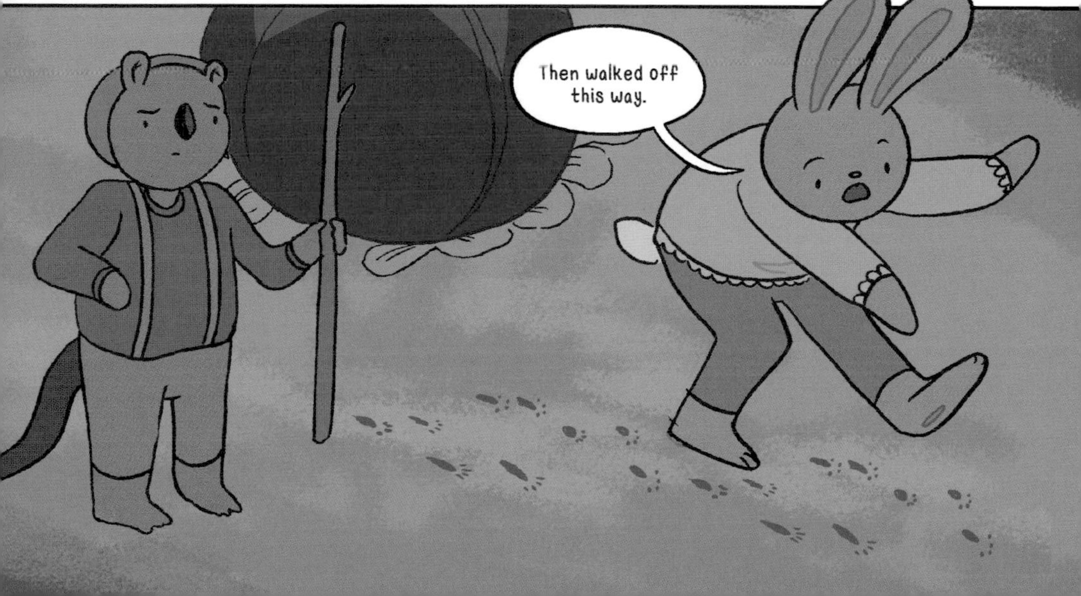
Then walked off this way.

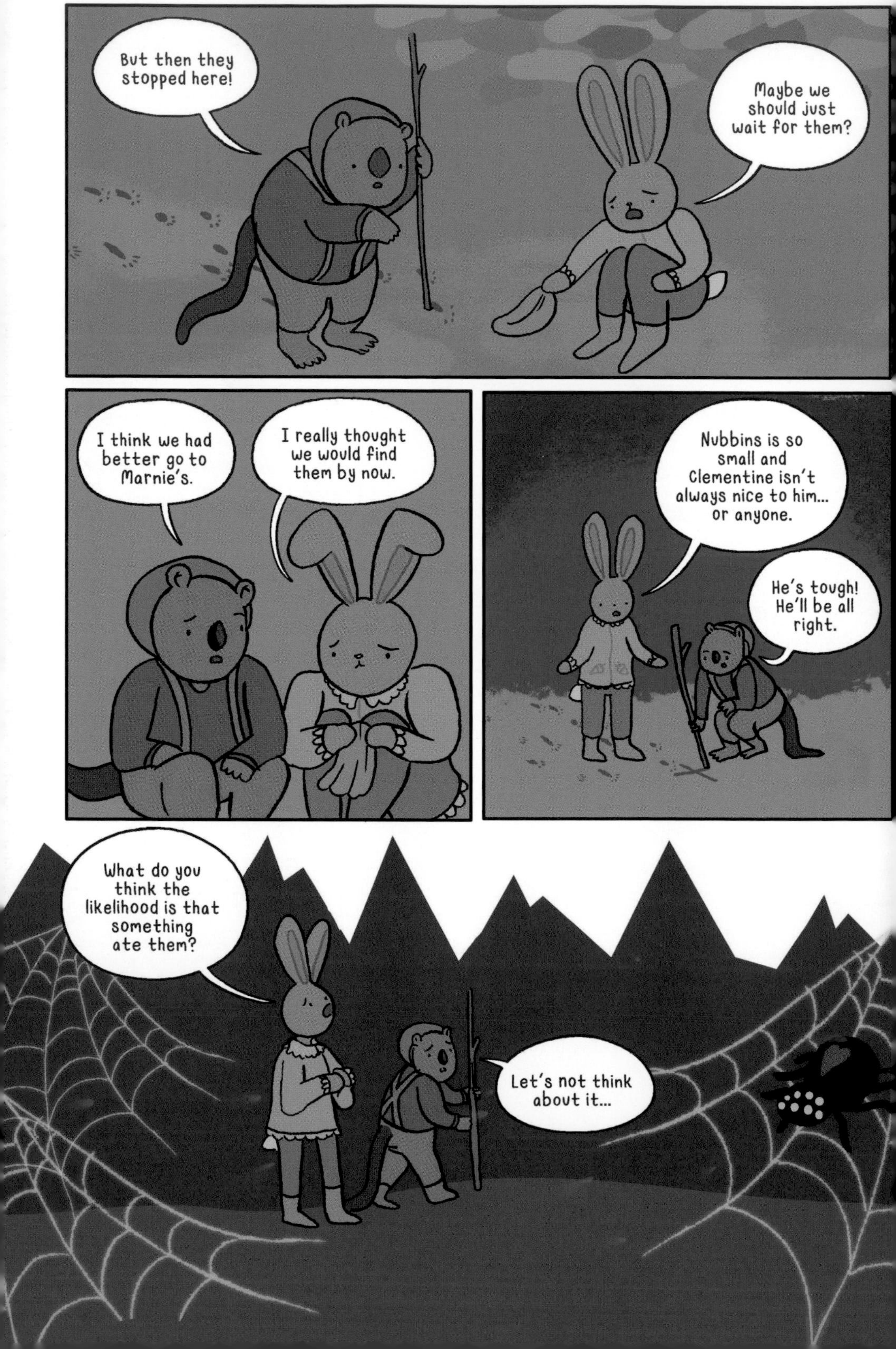
But then they stopped here!
Maybe we should just wait for them?
I think we had better go to Marnie's.
I really thought we would find them by now.
Nubbins is so small and Clementine isn't always nice to him... or anyone.
He's tough! He'll be all right.
What do you think the likelihood is that something ate them?
Let's not think about it...

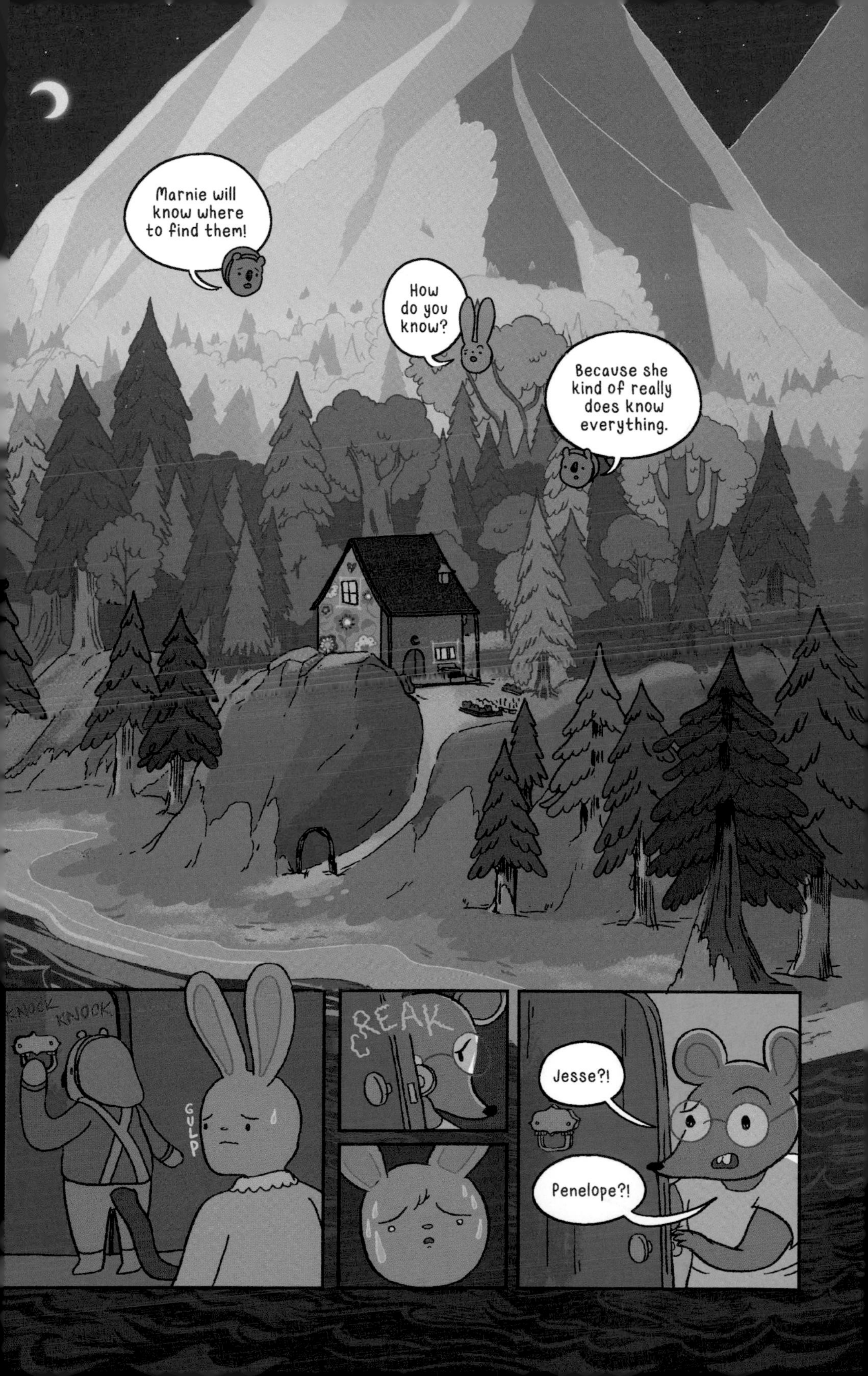
Marnie will know where to find them!
How do you know?
Because she kind of really does know everything.
KNOCK
KNOCK
GULP
CREAK
Jesse?!
Penelope?!

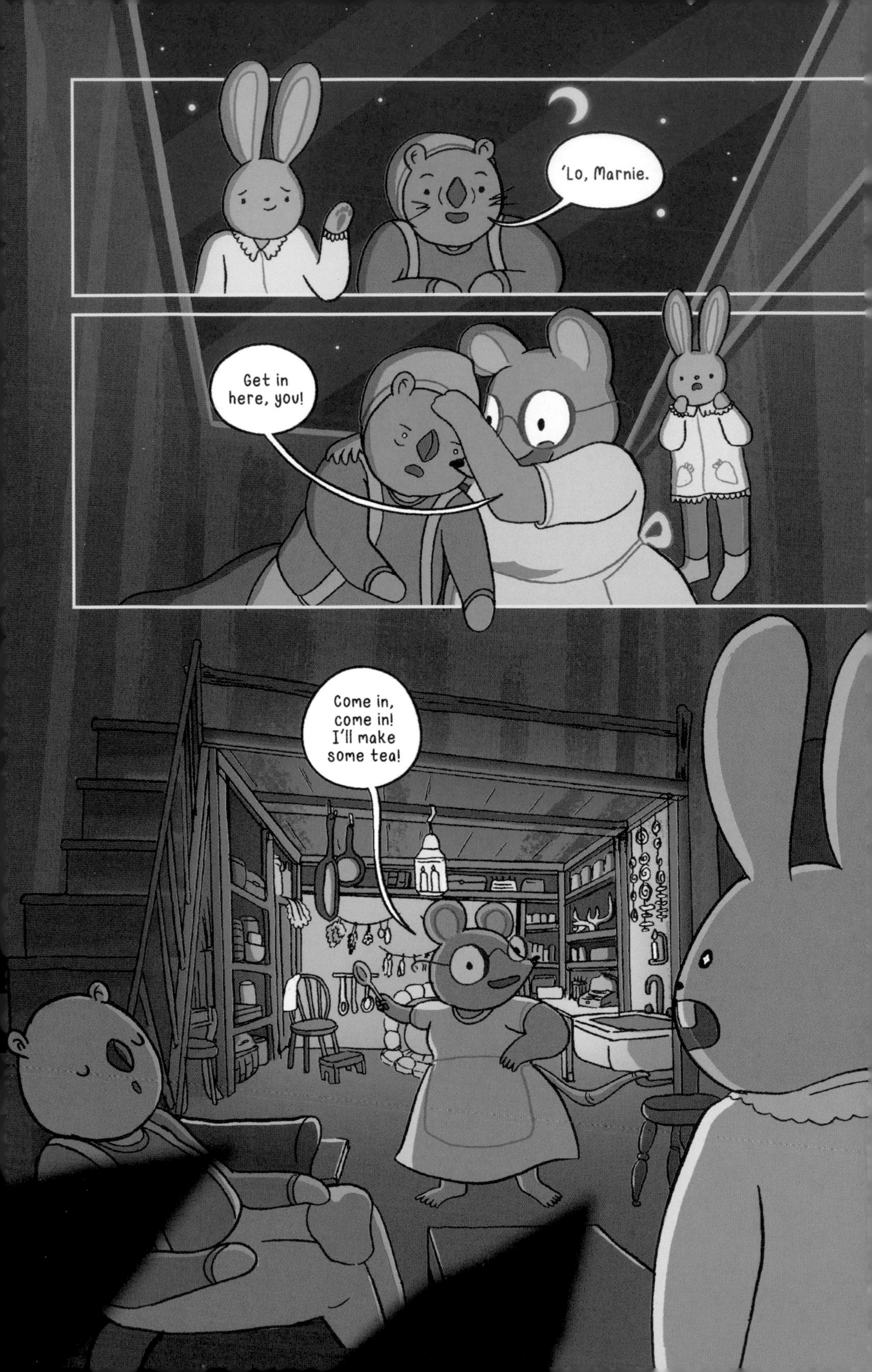
'Lo, Marnie.
Get in here, you!
Come in, come in! I'll make some tea!

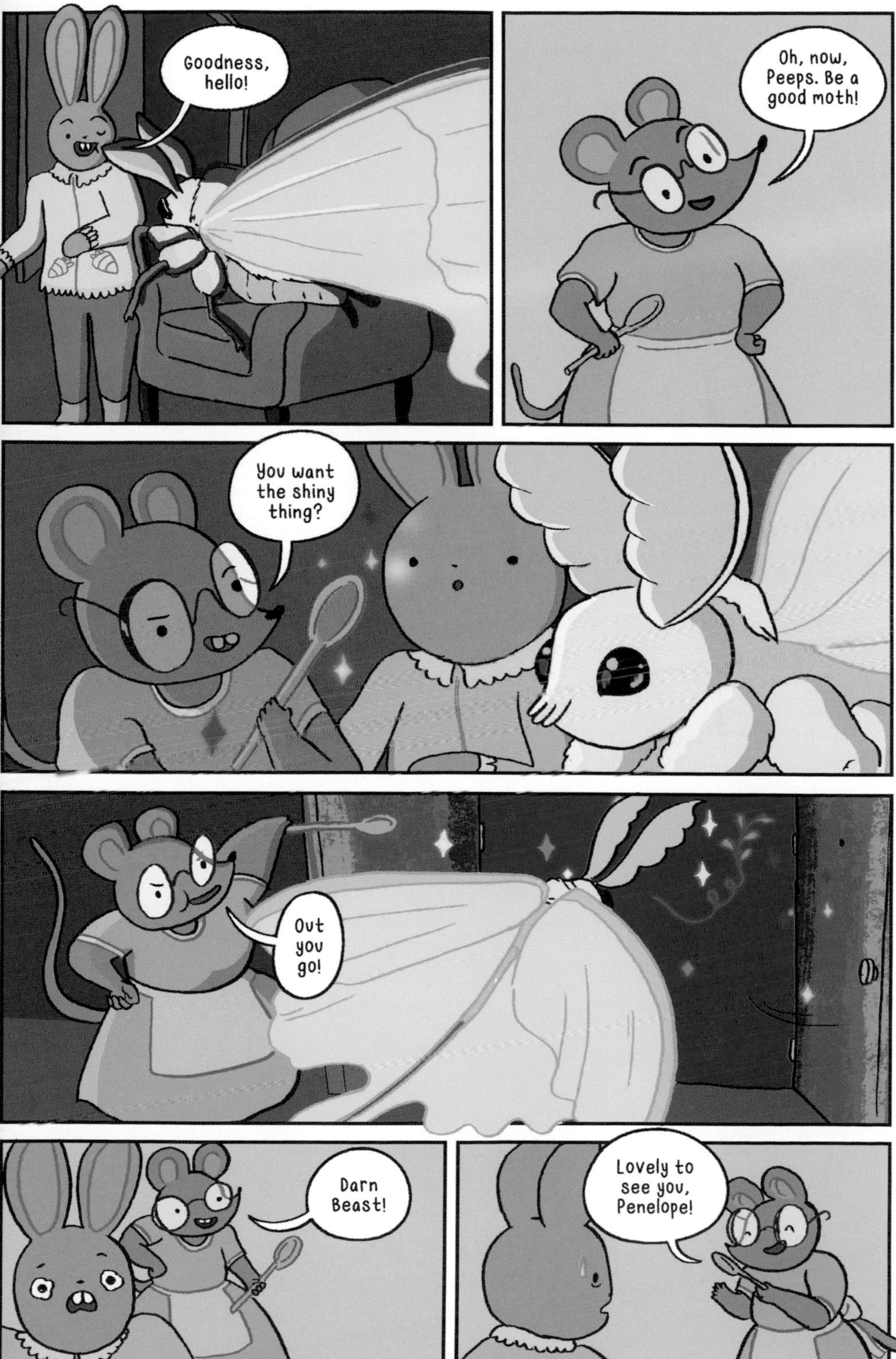
Goodness, hello!
Oh, now, Peeps. Be a good moth!
You want the shiny thing?
Out you go!
Darn Beast!
Lovely to see you, Penelope!

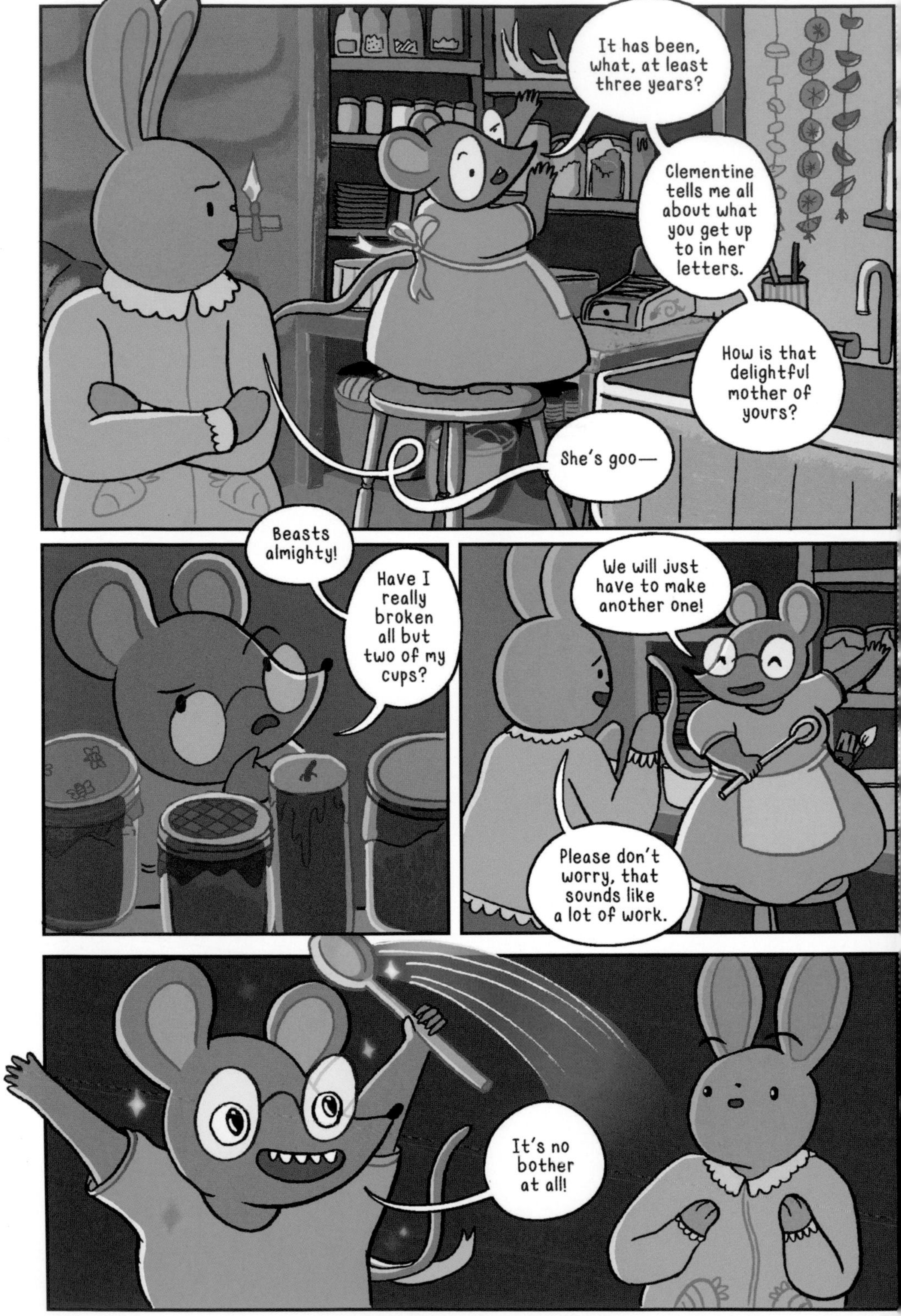
It has been, what, at least three years?
Clementine tells me all about what you get up to in her letters.
How is that delightful mother of yours?
She's goo—
Beasts almighty!
Have I really broken all but two of my cups?
We will just have to make another one!
Please don't worry, that sounds like a lot of work.
It's no bother at all!

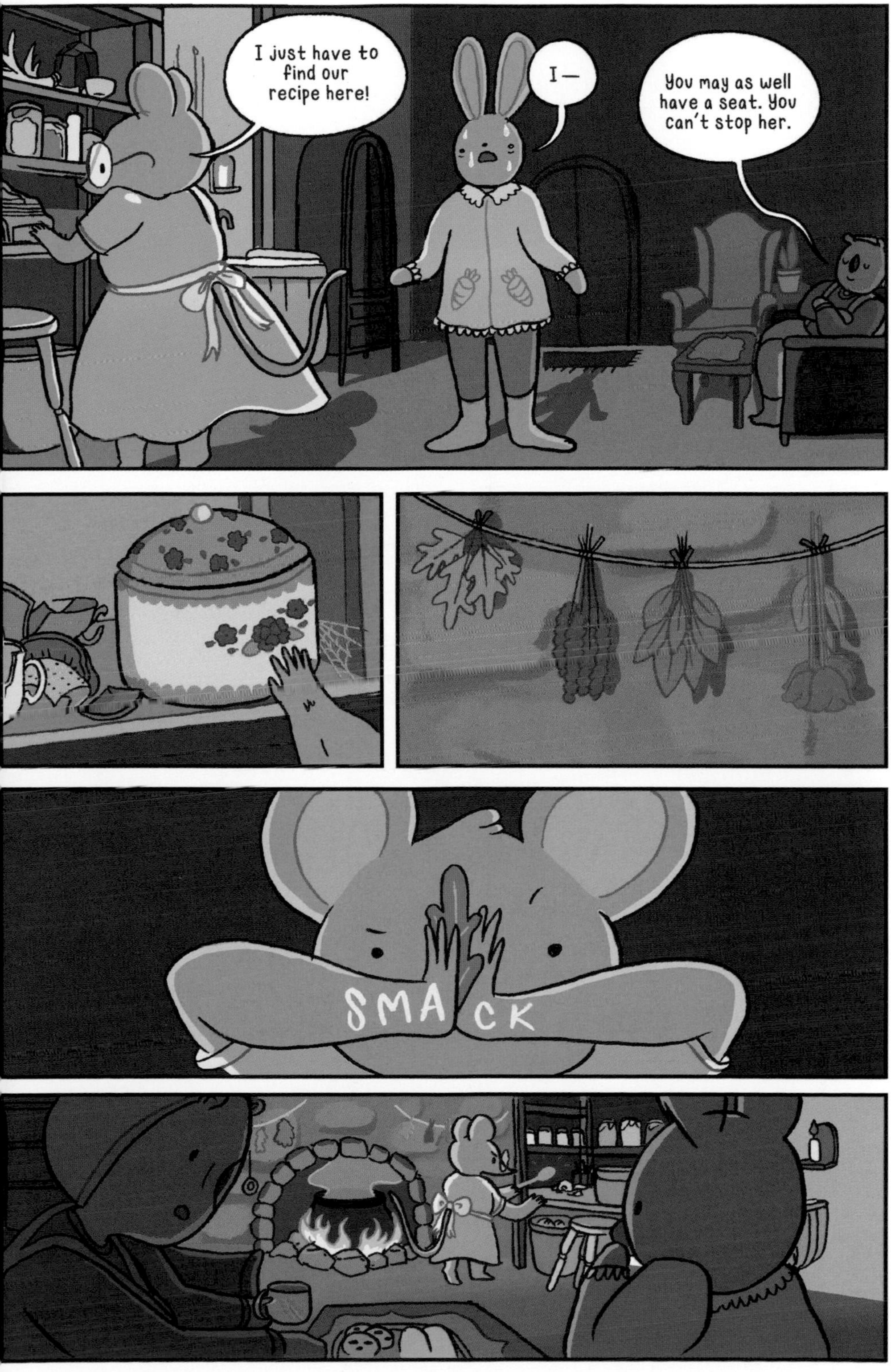
I just have to find our recipe here!
I—
You may as well have a seat. You can't stop her.
SMACK

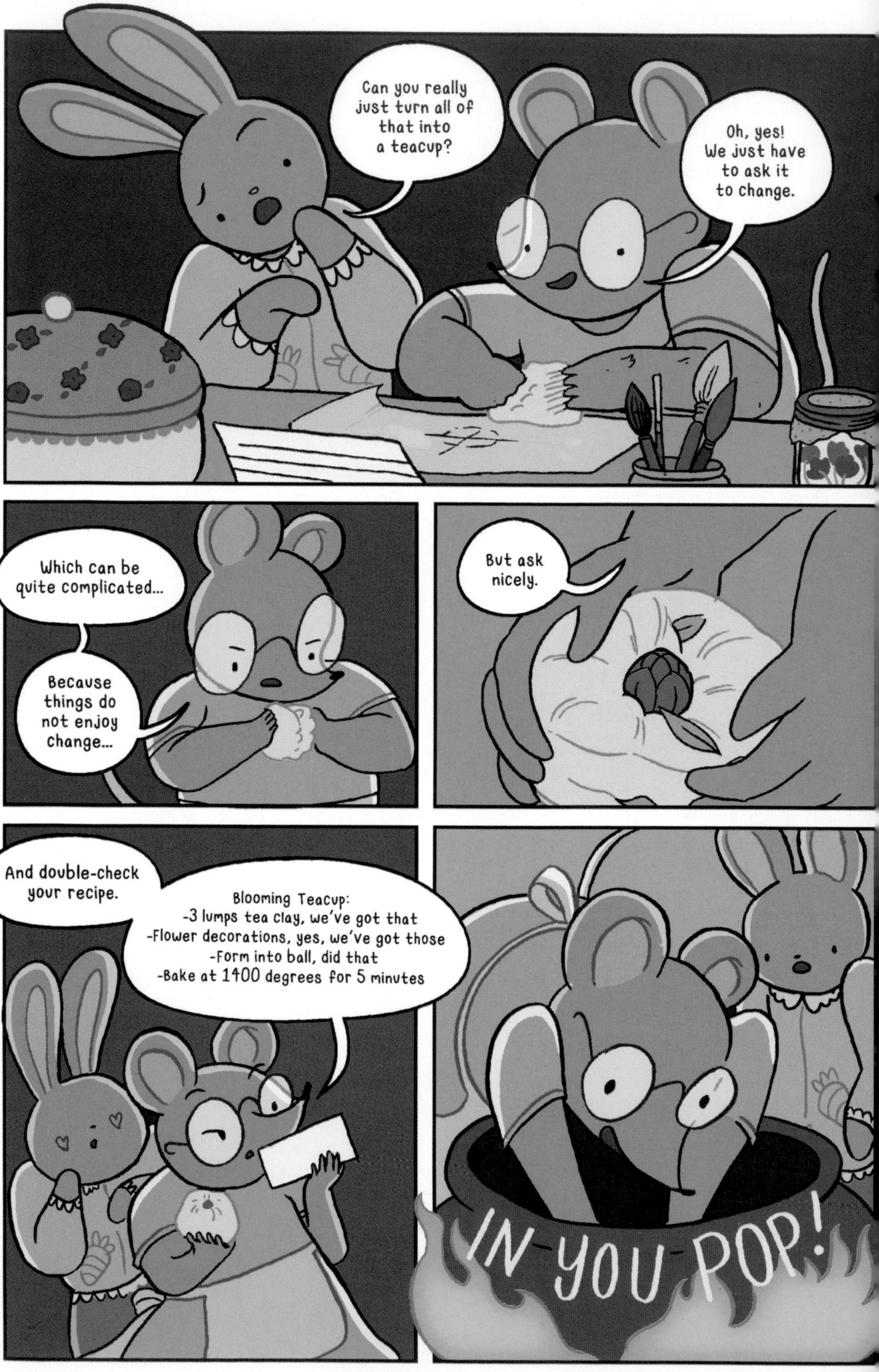

Can you really just turn all of that into a teacup?
Oh, yes! We just have to ask it to change.
Which can be quite complicated...
Because things do not enjoy change...
But ask nicely.
And double-check your recipe.
Blooming Teacup:
-3 lumps tea clay, we've got that
-Flower decorations, yes, we've got those
-Form into ball, did that
-Bake at 1400 degrees for 5 minutes
IN YOU POP!

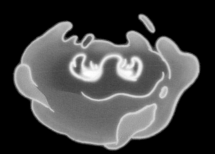

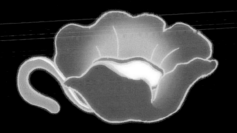

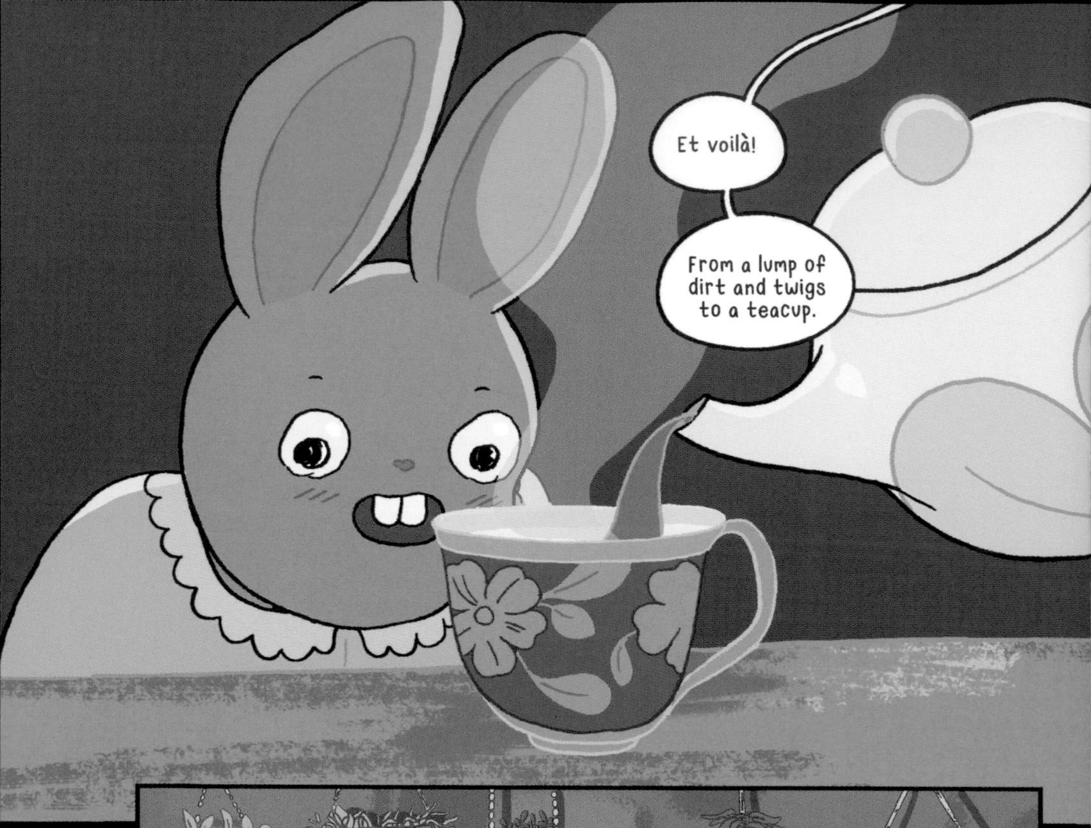
Et voilà!
From a lump of dirt and twigs to a teacup.
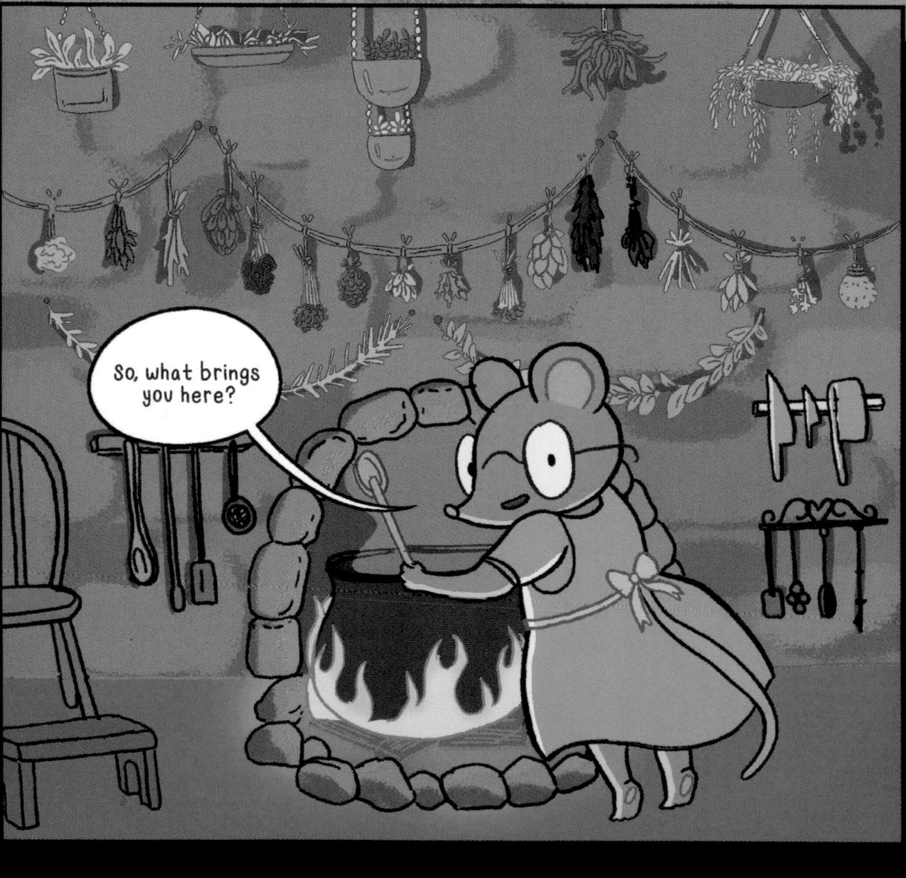
So, what brings you here?

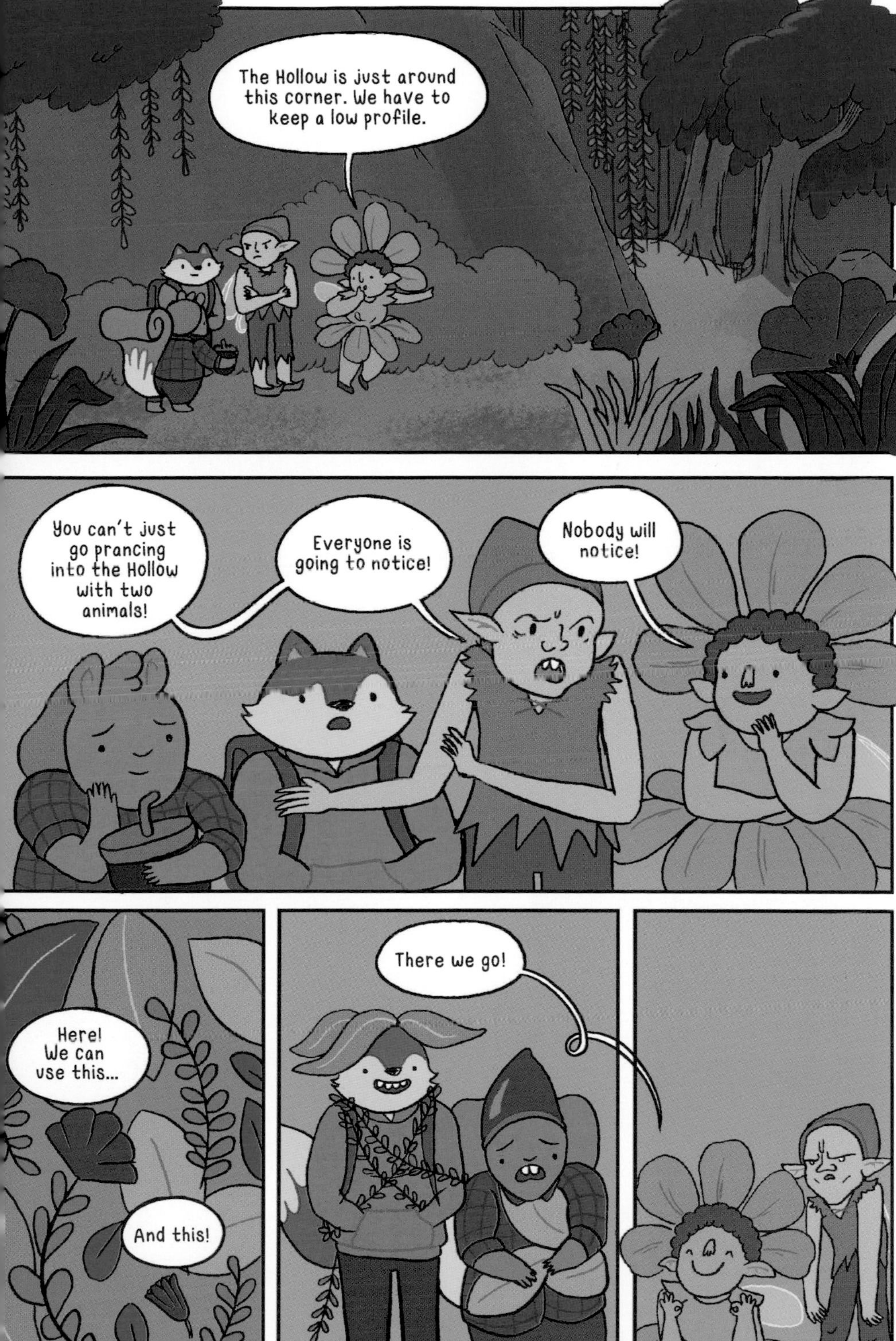
The Hollow is just around this corner. We have to keep a low profile.
You can't just go prancing into the Hollow with two animals!
Everyone is going to notice!
Nobody will notice!
Here! We can use this...
And this!
There we go!

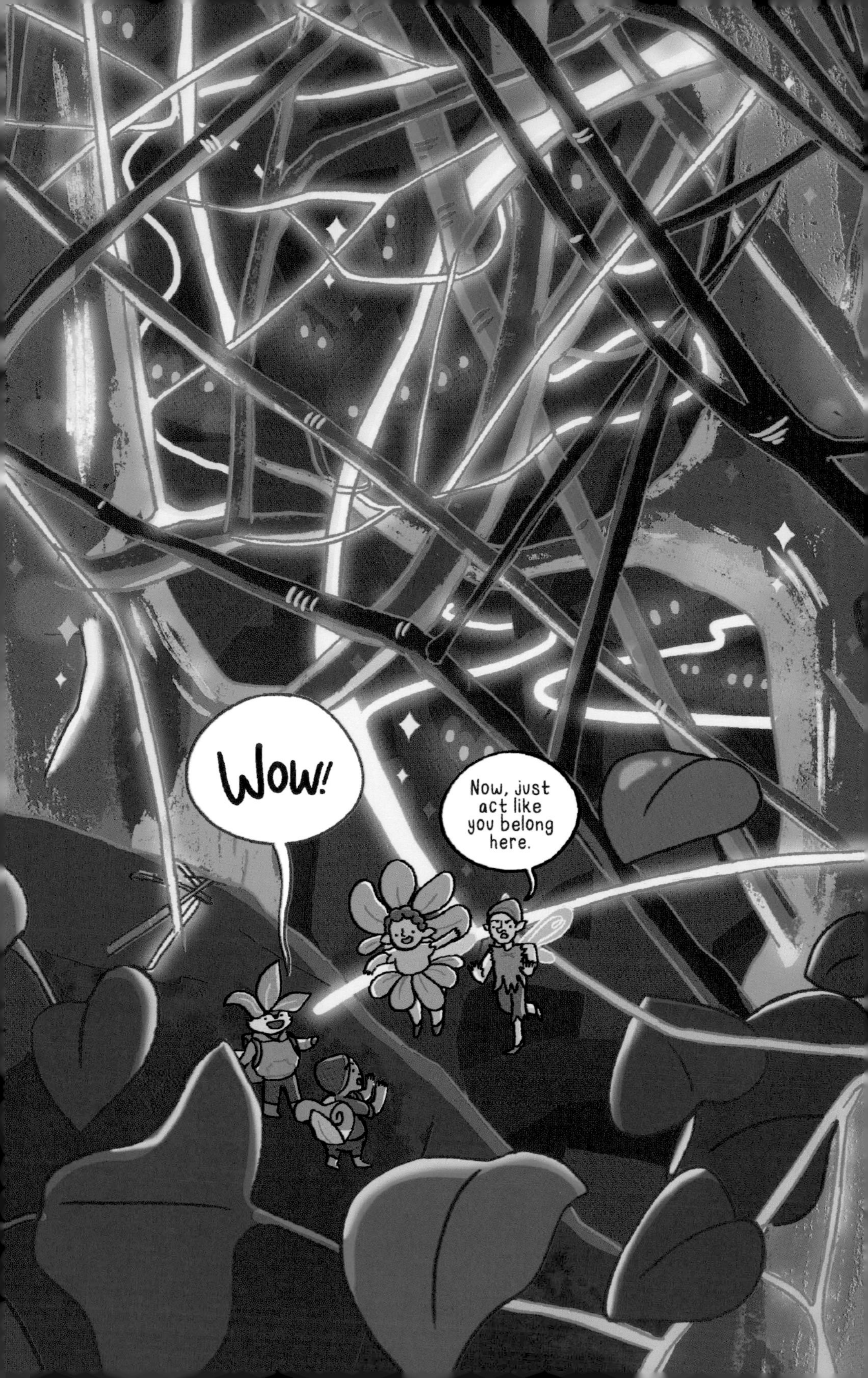
WOW!
Now, just act like you belong here.

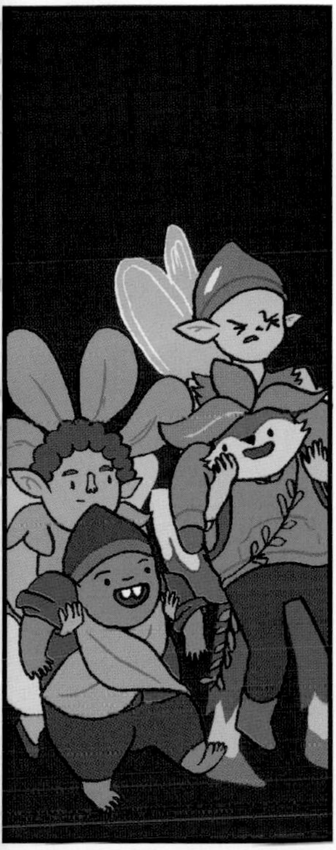

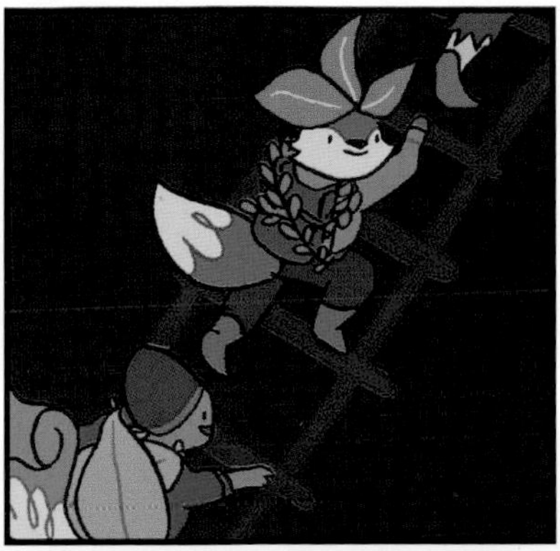

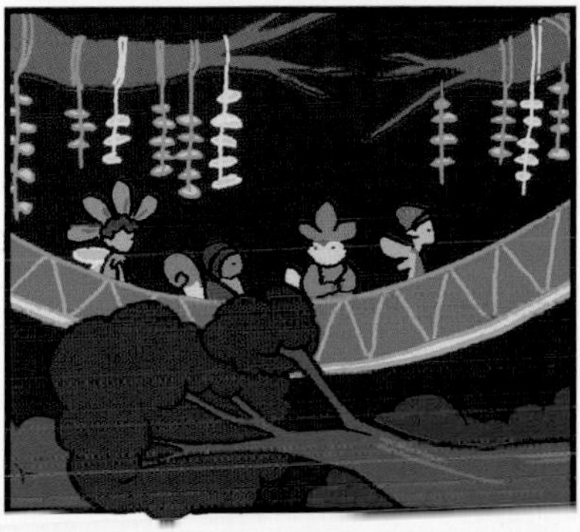

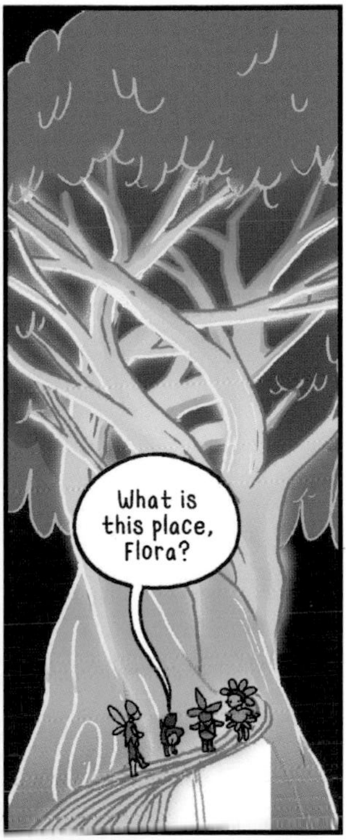
What is this place, Flora?

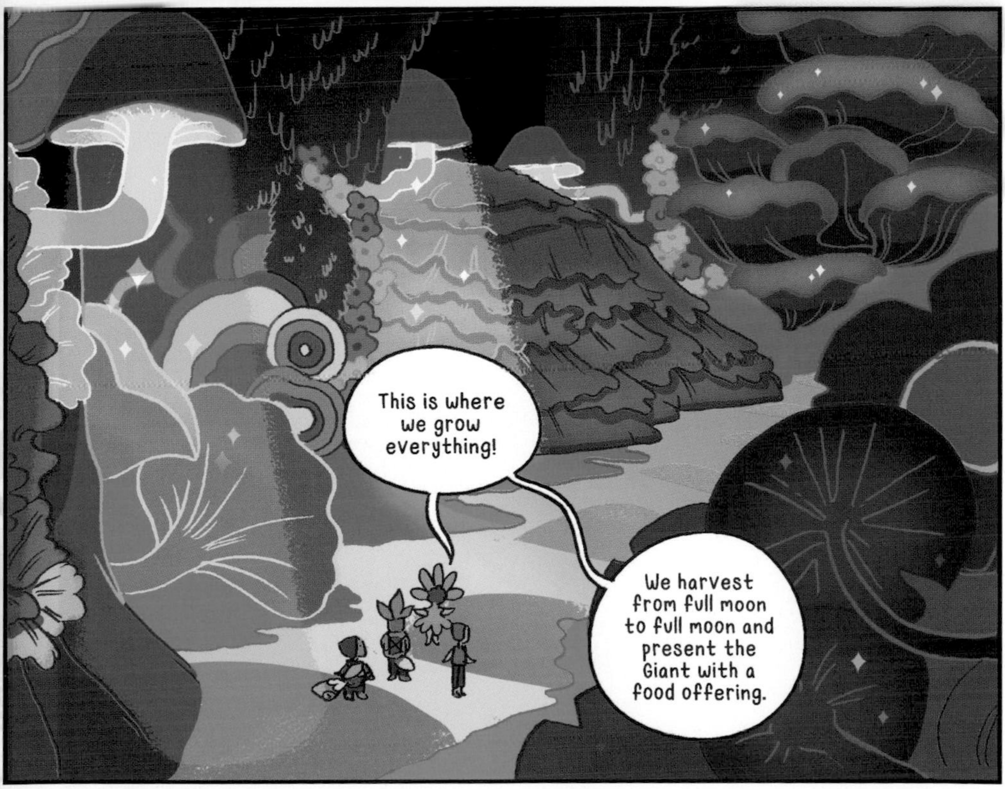
This is where we grow everything!
We harvest from full moon to full moon and present the Giant with a food offering.

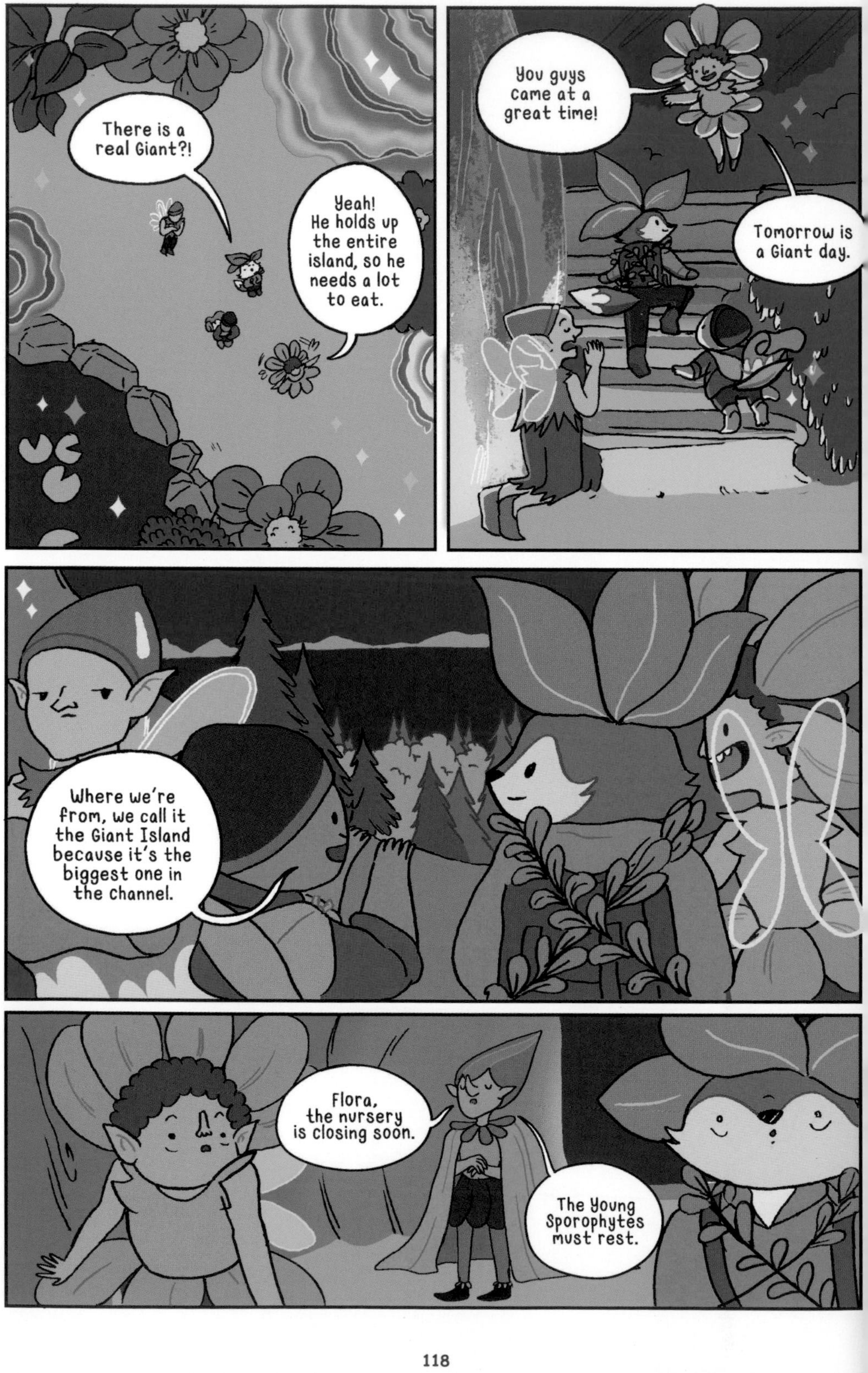
There is a real Giant?!
Yeah! He holds up the entire island, so he needs a lot to eat.
You guys came at a great time!
Tomorrow is a Giant day.
Where we're from, we call it the Giant Island because it's the biggest one in the channel.
Flora, the nursery is closing soon.
The Young Sporophytes must rest.

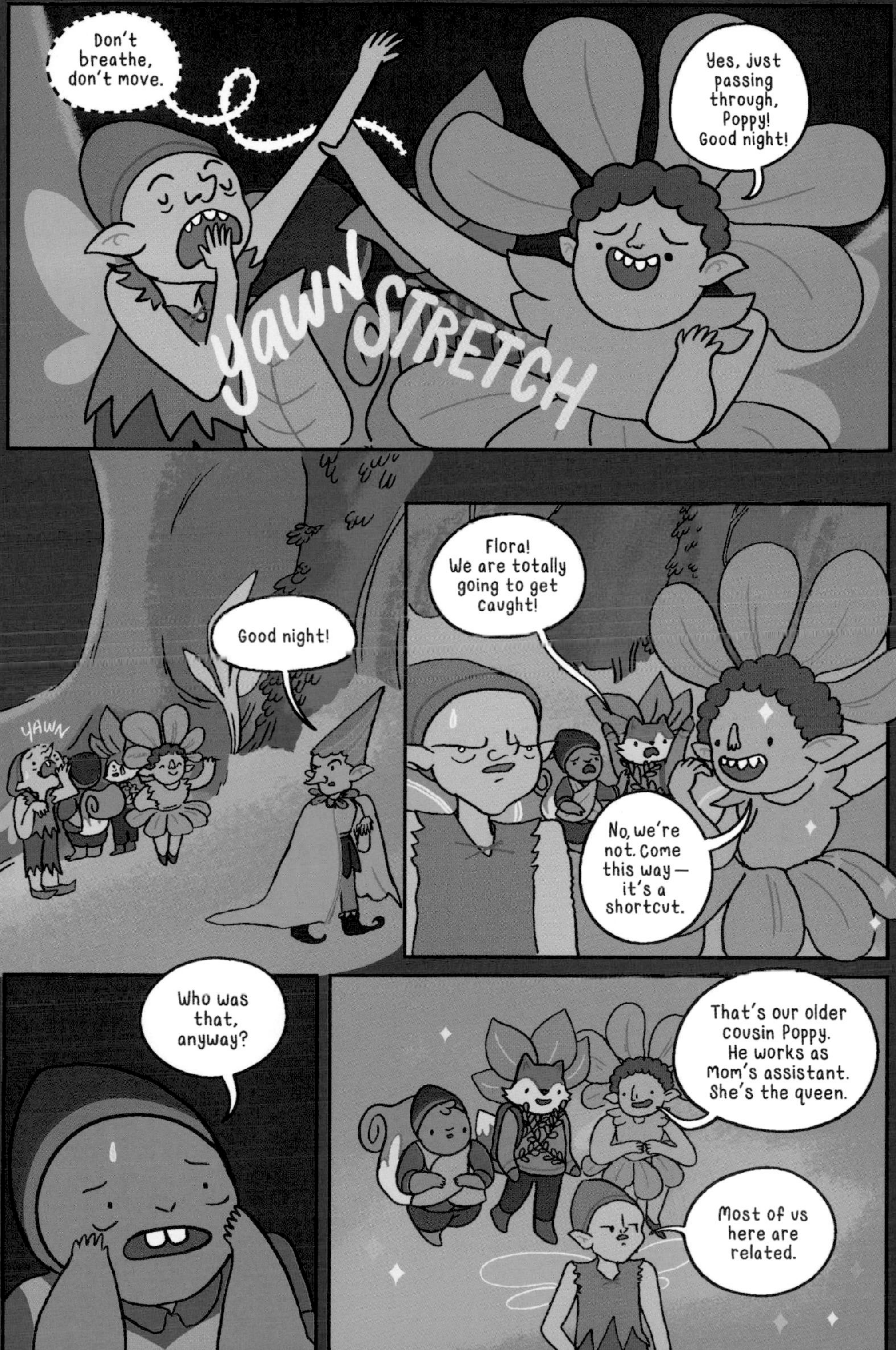
Don't breathe, don't move.
Yes, just passing through, Poppy! Good night!
YAWN
STRETCH
YAWN
Good night!
Flora! We are totally going to get caught!
No, we're not. Come this way— it's a shortcut.
Who was that, anyway?
That's our older cousin Poppy. He works as Mom's assistant. She's the queen.
Most of us here are related.

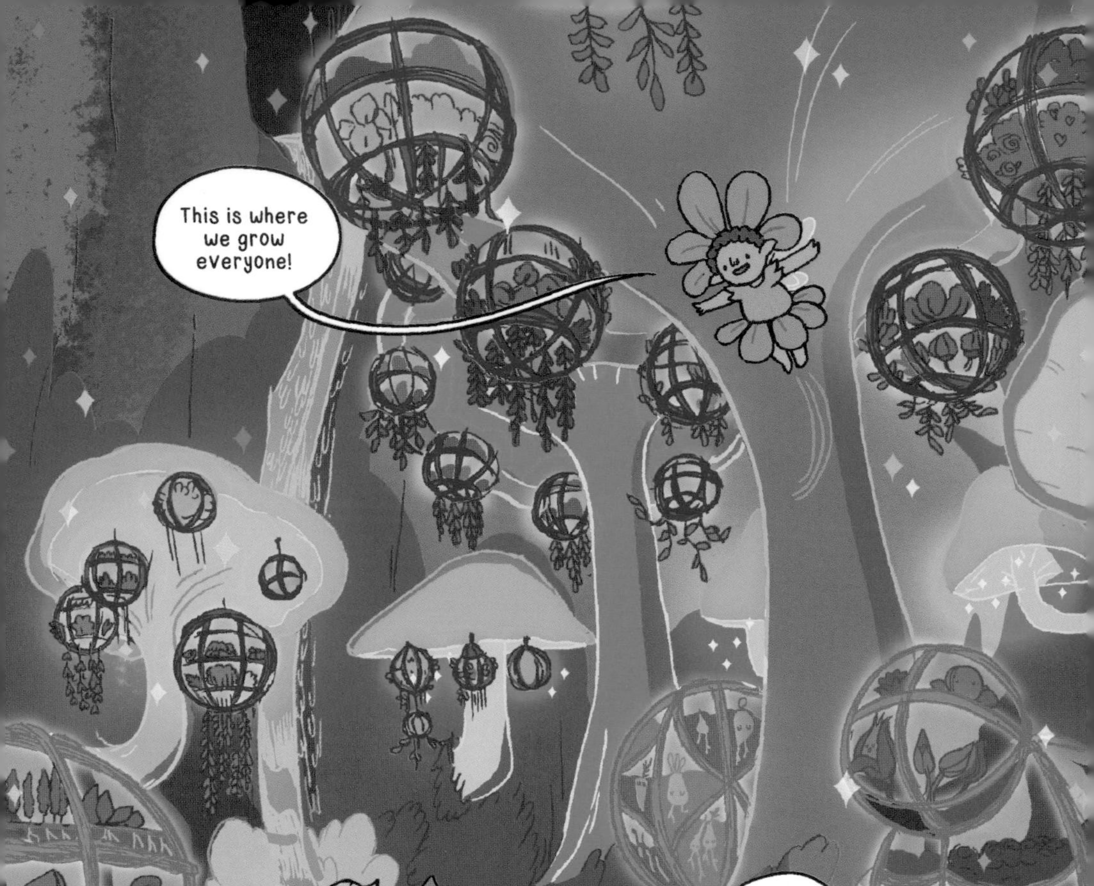
This is where we grow everyone!
Whoa. I thought having one sibling was bad enough.
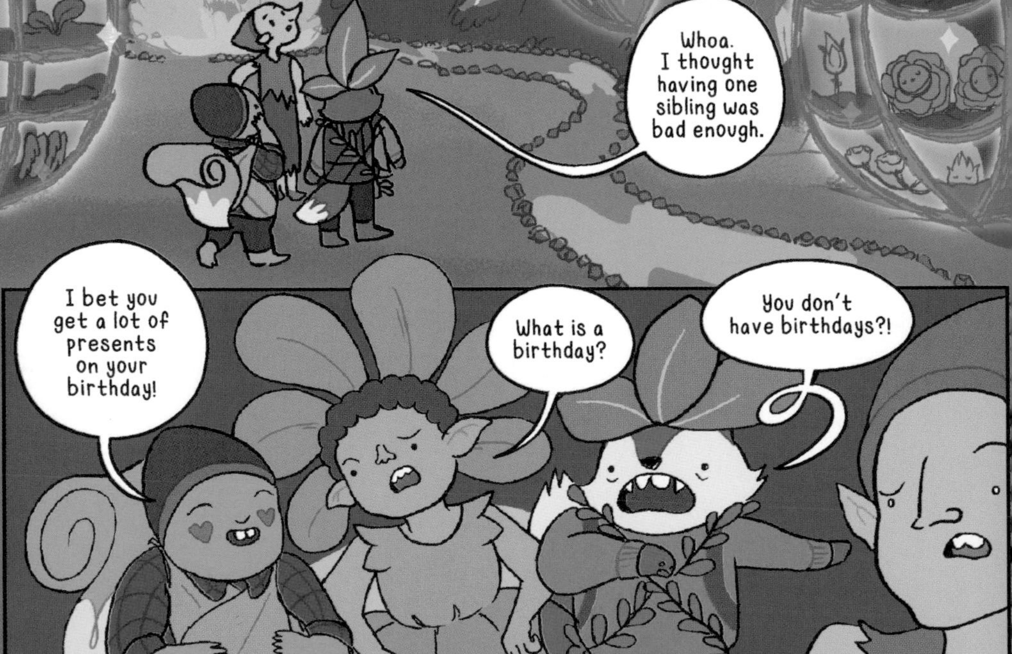
I bet you get a lot of presents on your birthday!
What is a birthday?
You don't have birthdays?!

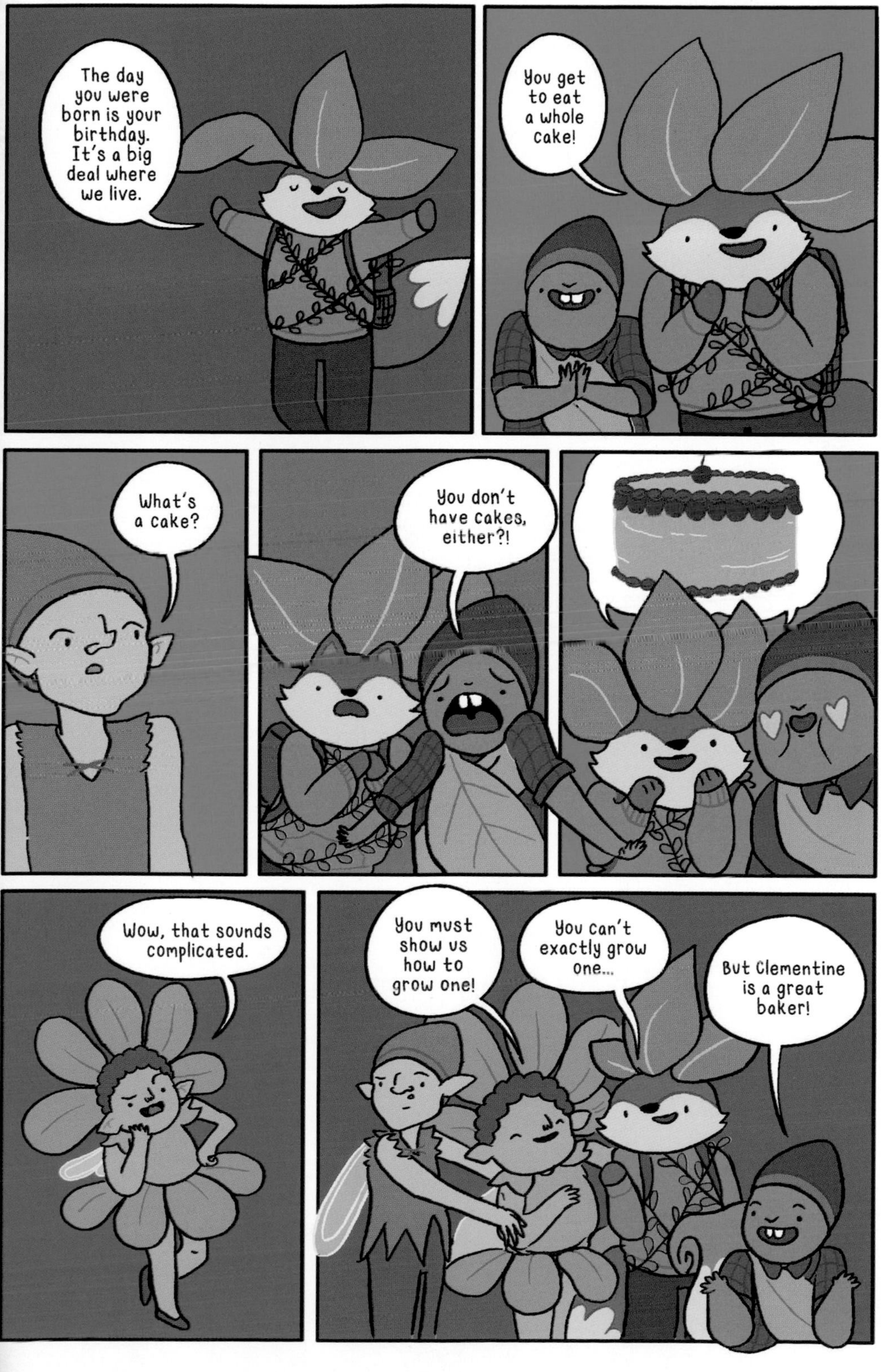
The day you were born is your birthday. It's a big deal where we live.
You get to eat a whole cake!
What's a cake?
You don't have cakes, either?!
Wow, that sounds complicated.
You must show us how to grow one!
You can't exactly grow one...
But Clementine is a great baker!

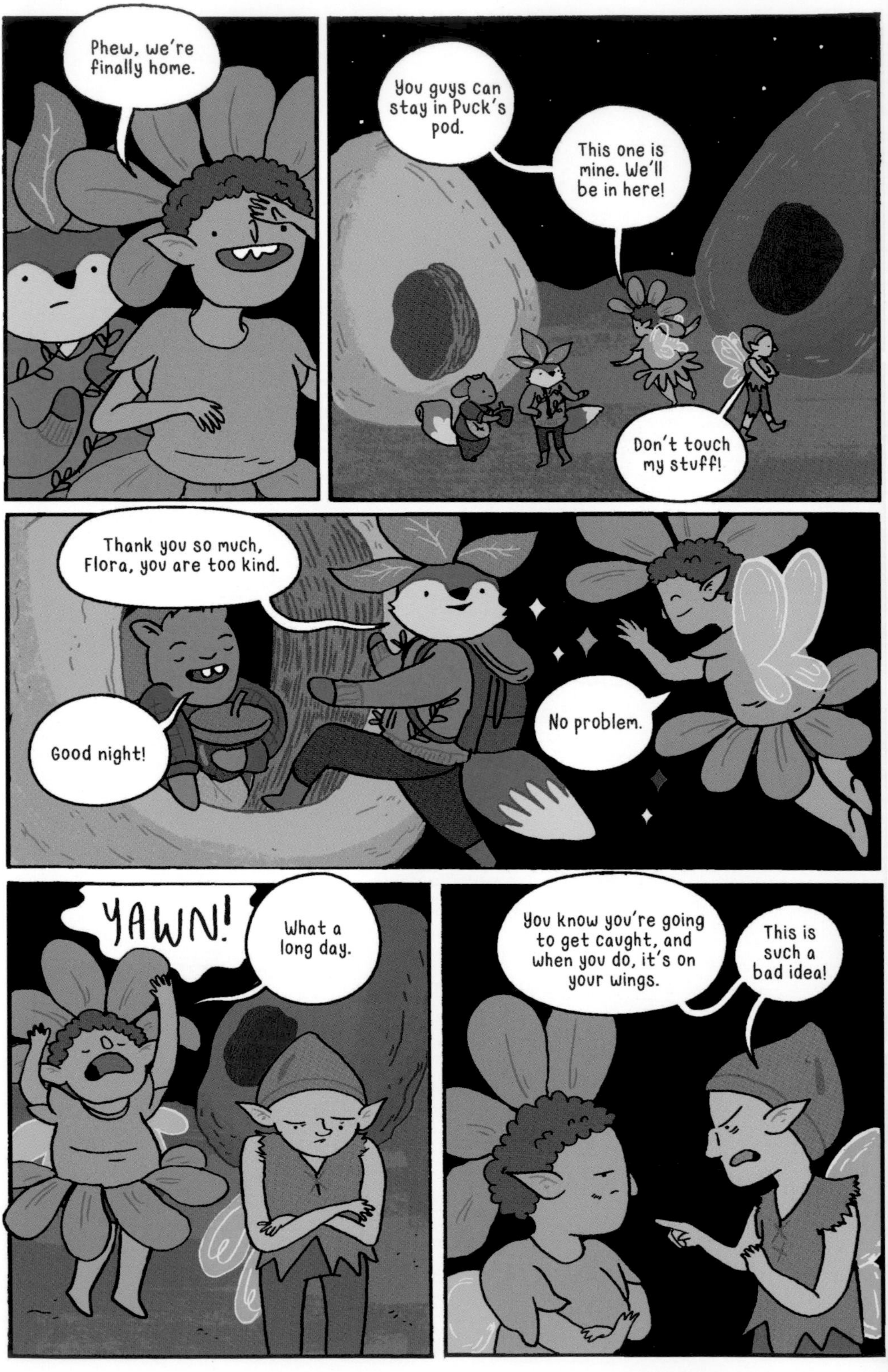
Phew, we're finally home.
You guys can stay in Puck's pod.
This one is mine. We'll be in here!
Don't touch my stuff!
Thank you so much, Flora, you are too kind.
Good night!
No problem.
YAWN!
What a long day.
You know you're going to get caught, and when you do, it's on your wings.
This is such a bad idea!

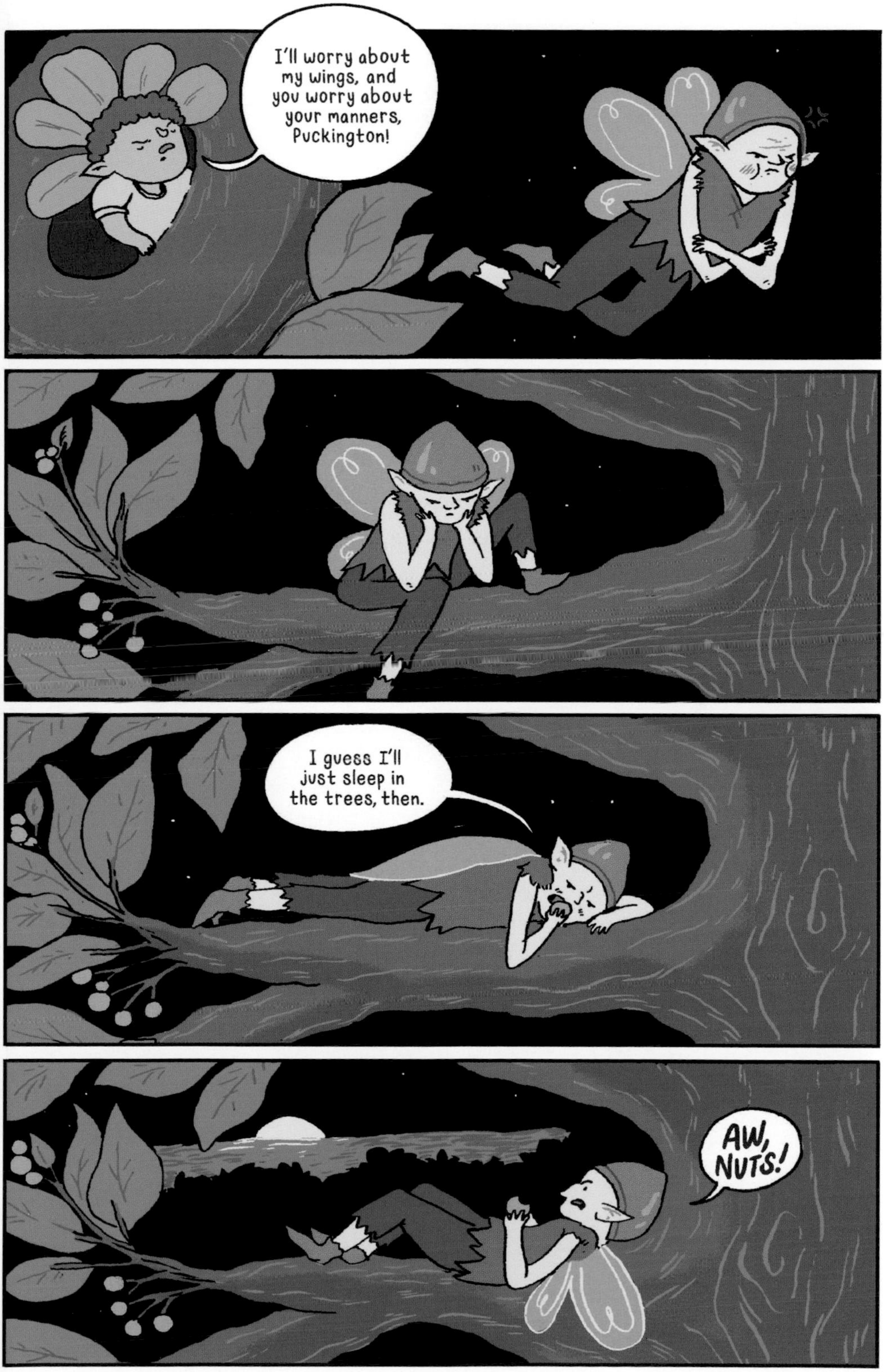
I'll worry about my wings, and you worry about your manners, Puckington!
I guess I'll just sleep in the trees, then.
AW, NUTS!

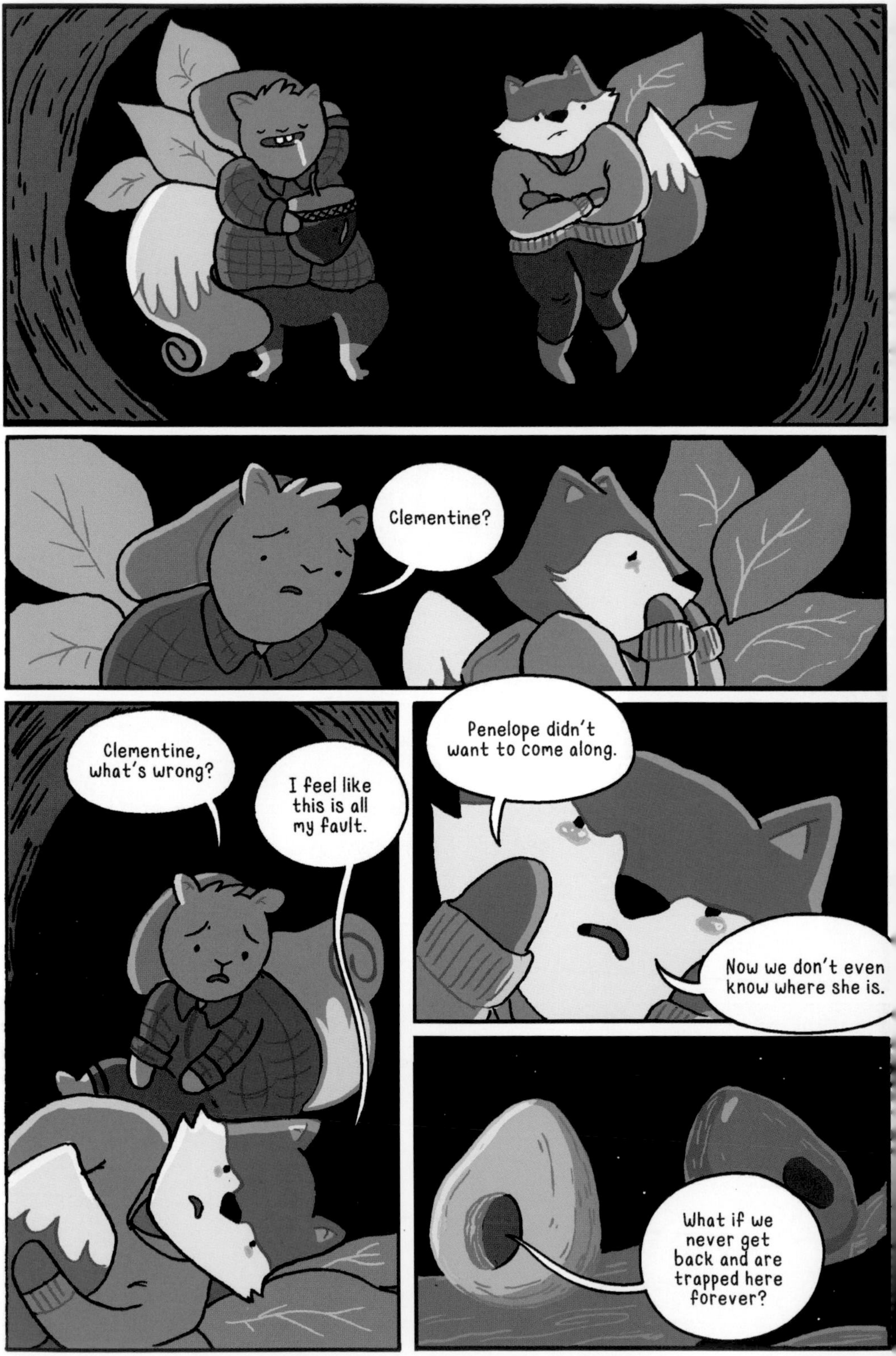

Clementine?
Clementine, what's wrong?
I feel like this is all my fault.
Penelope didn't want to come along.
Now we don't even know where she is.
What if we never get back and are trapped here forever?

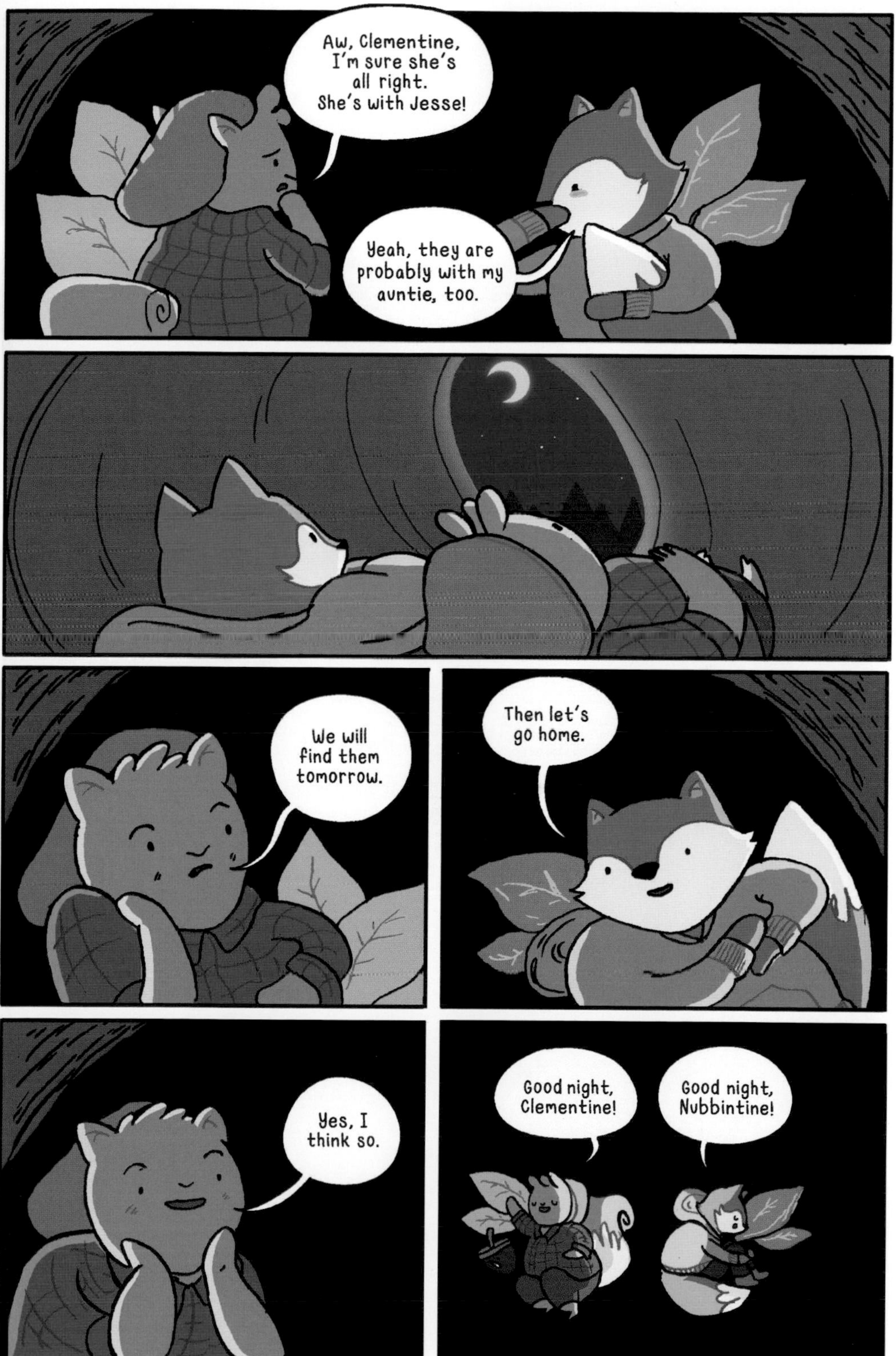
Aw, Clementine, I'm sure she's all right. She's with Jesse!
Yeah, they are probably with my auntie, too.
We will find them tomorrow.
Then let's go home.
Yes, I think so.
Good night, Clementine!
Good night, Nubbintine!

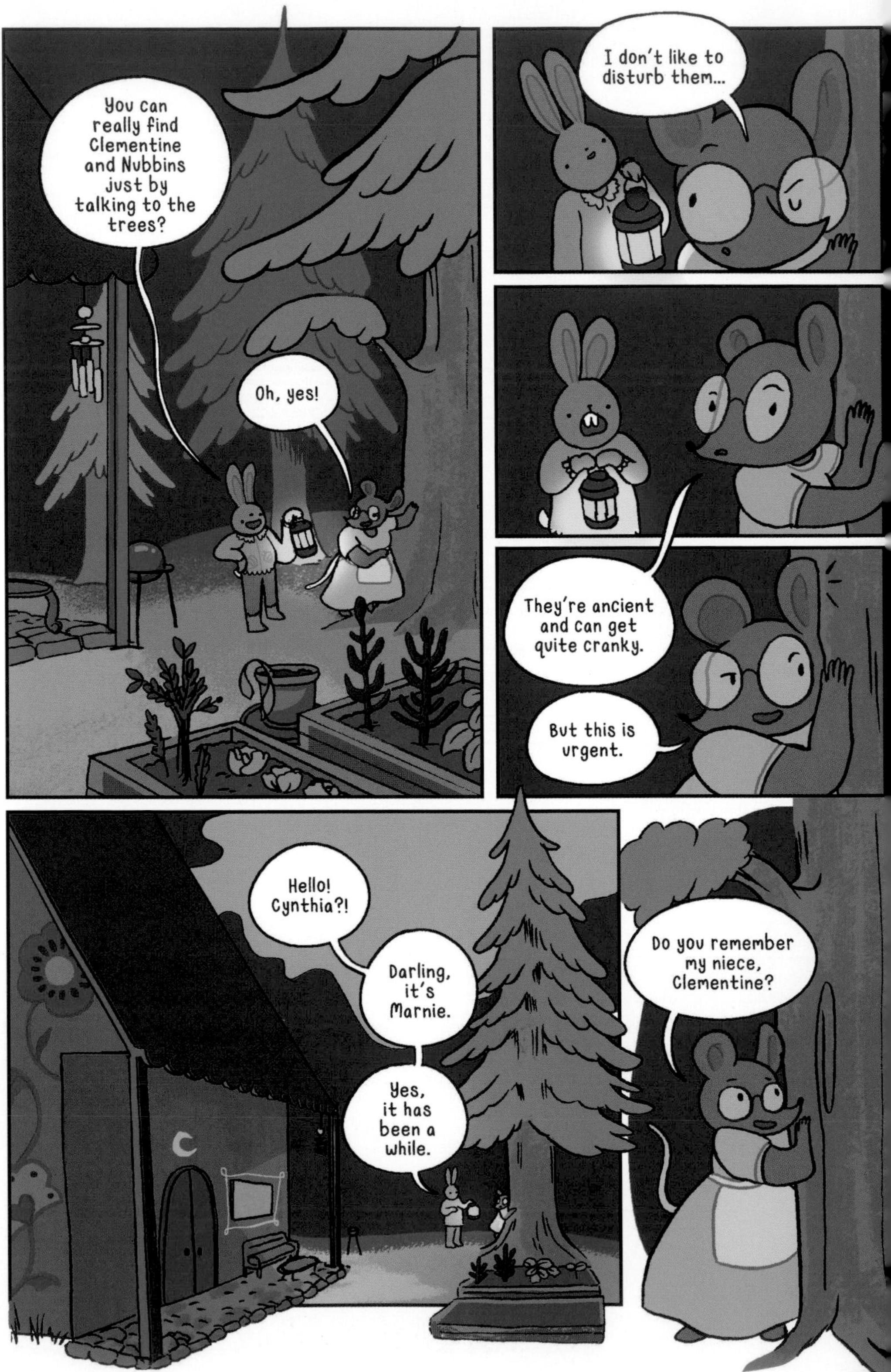
You can really find Clementine and Nubbins just by talking to the trees?
Oh, yes!
I don't like to disturb them...
They're ancient and can get quite cranky.
But this is urgent.
Hello! Cynthia?!
Darling, it's Marnie.
Yes, it has been a while.
Do you remember my niece, Clementine?

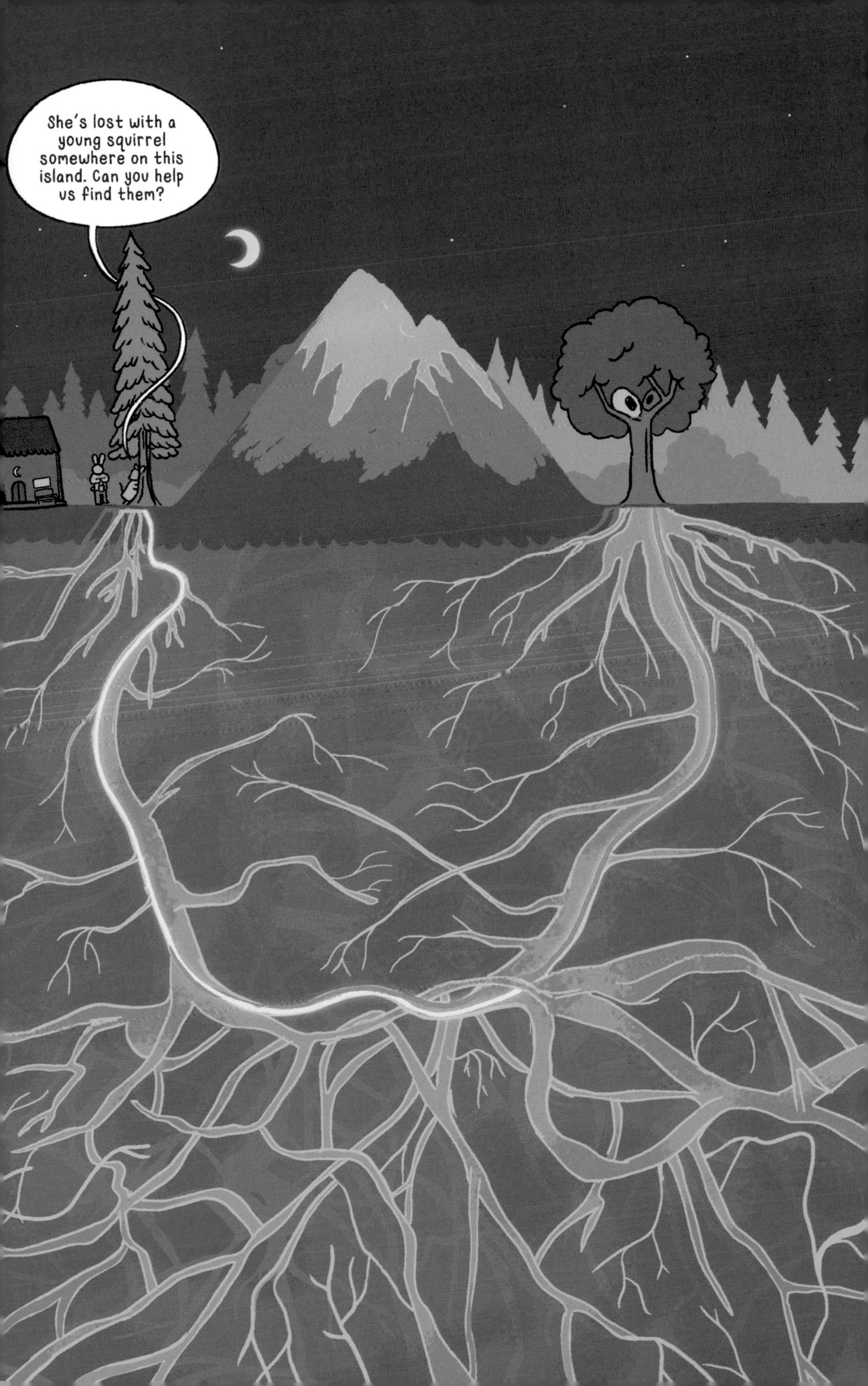
She's lost with a young squirrel somewhere on this island. Can you help us find them?

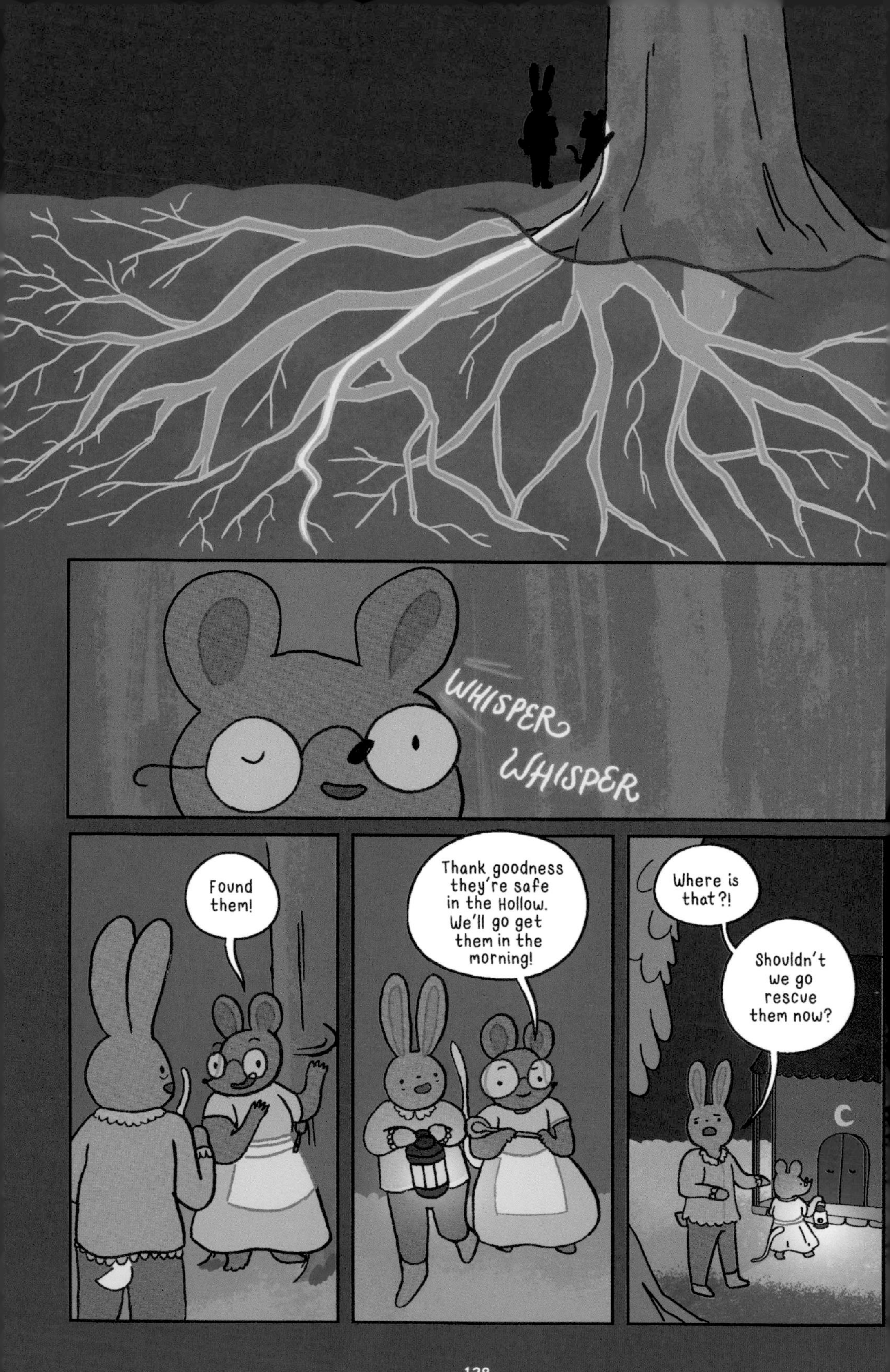

WHISPER
WHISPER
Found them!
Thank goodness they're safe in the Hollow. We'll go get them in the morning!
Where is that?!
Shouldn't we go rescue them now?

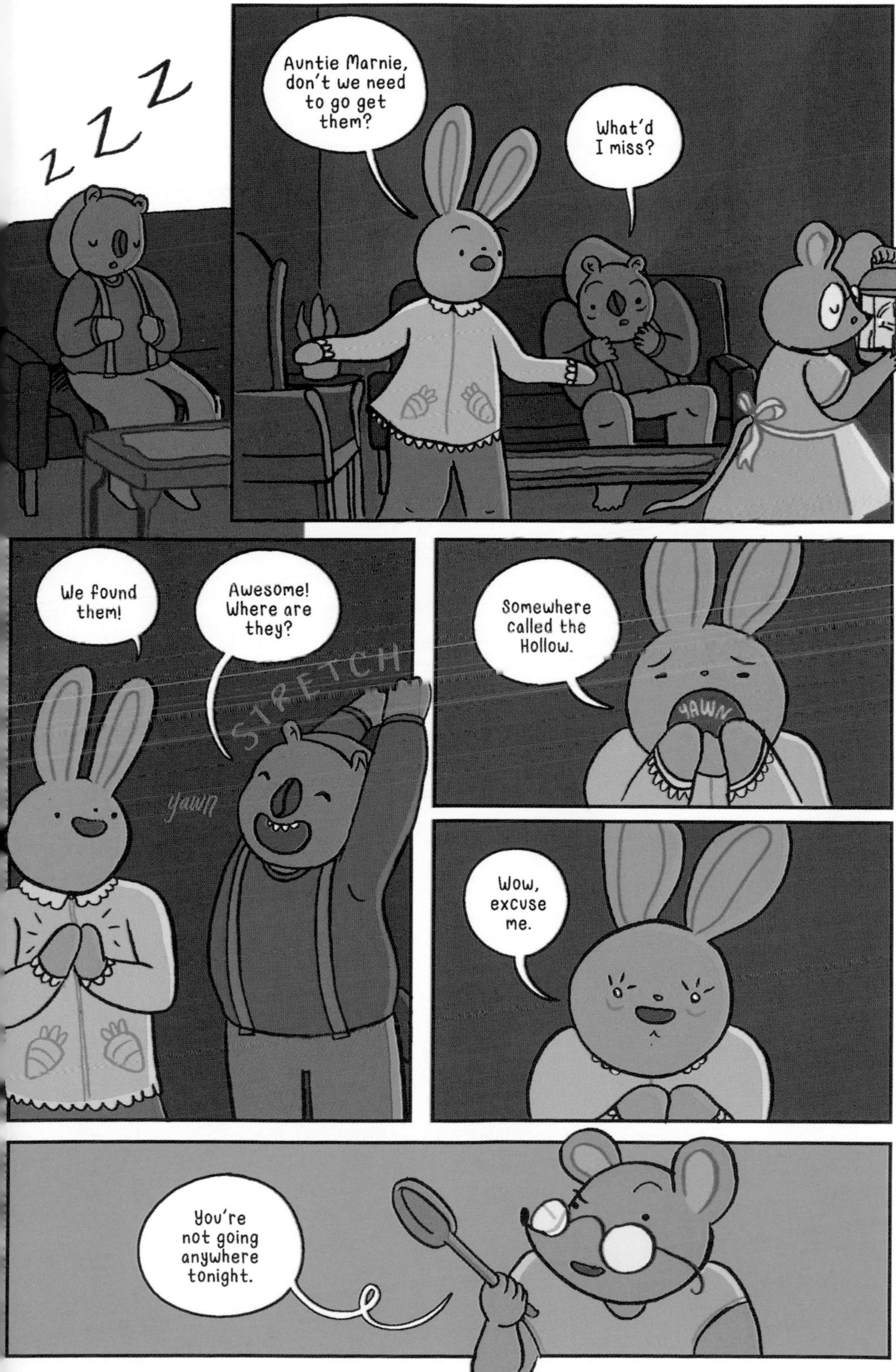
Z Z Z
Auntie Marnie, don't we need to go get them?
What'd I miss?
We found them!
Awesome! Where are they?
STRETCH
yawn
Somewhere called the Hollow.
YAWN
Wow, excuse me.
You're not going anywhere tonight.

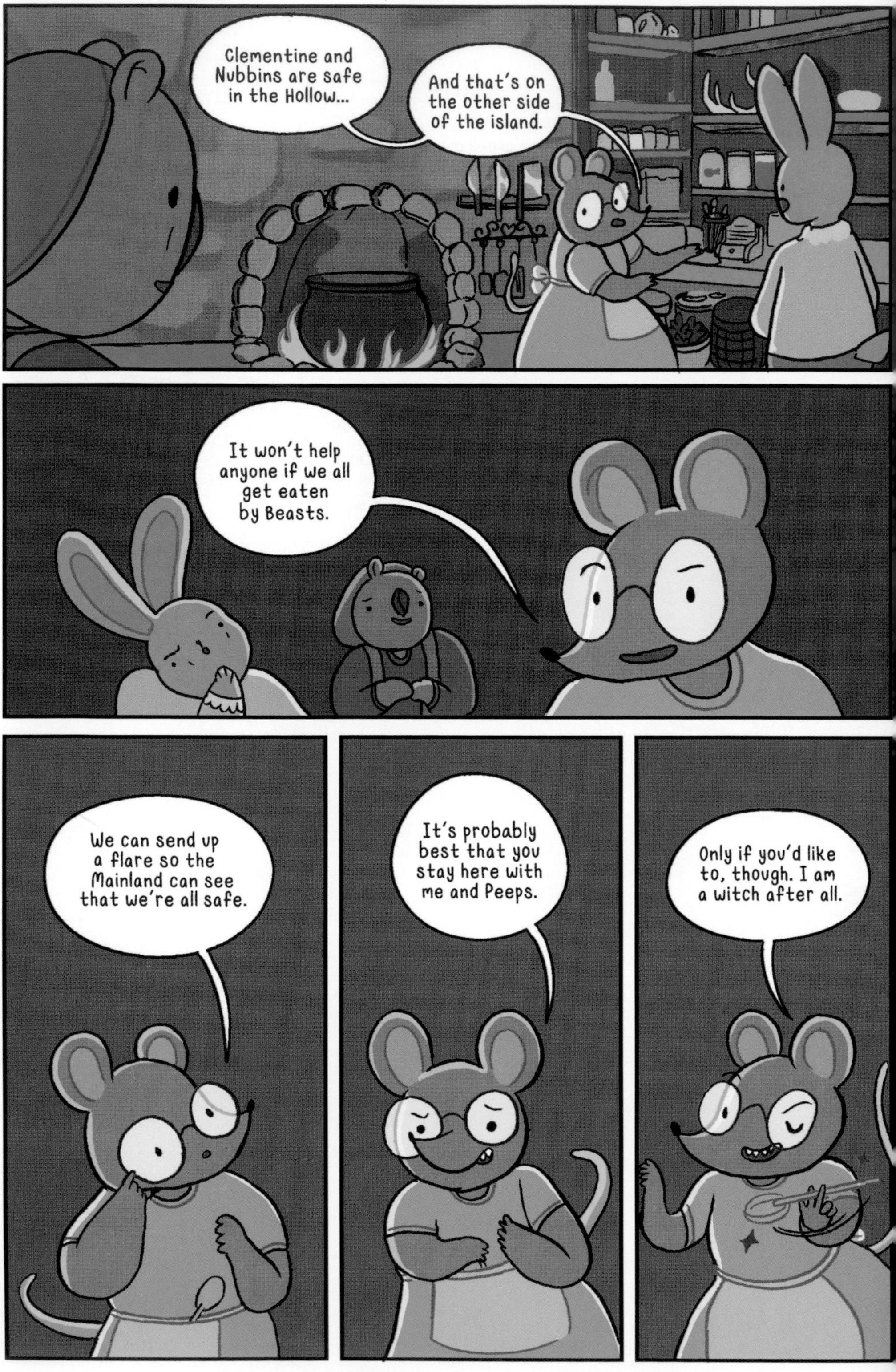
Clementine and Nubbins are safe in the Hollow...
And that's on the other side of the island.
It won't help anyone if we all get eaten by Beasts.
We can send up a flare so the Mainland can see that we're all safe.
It's probably best that you stay here with me and Peeps.
Only if you'd like to, though. I am a witch after all.

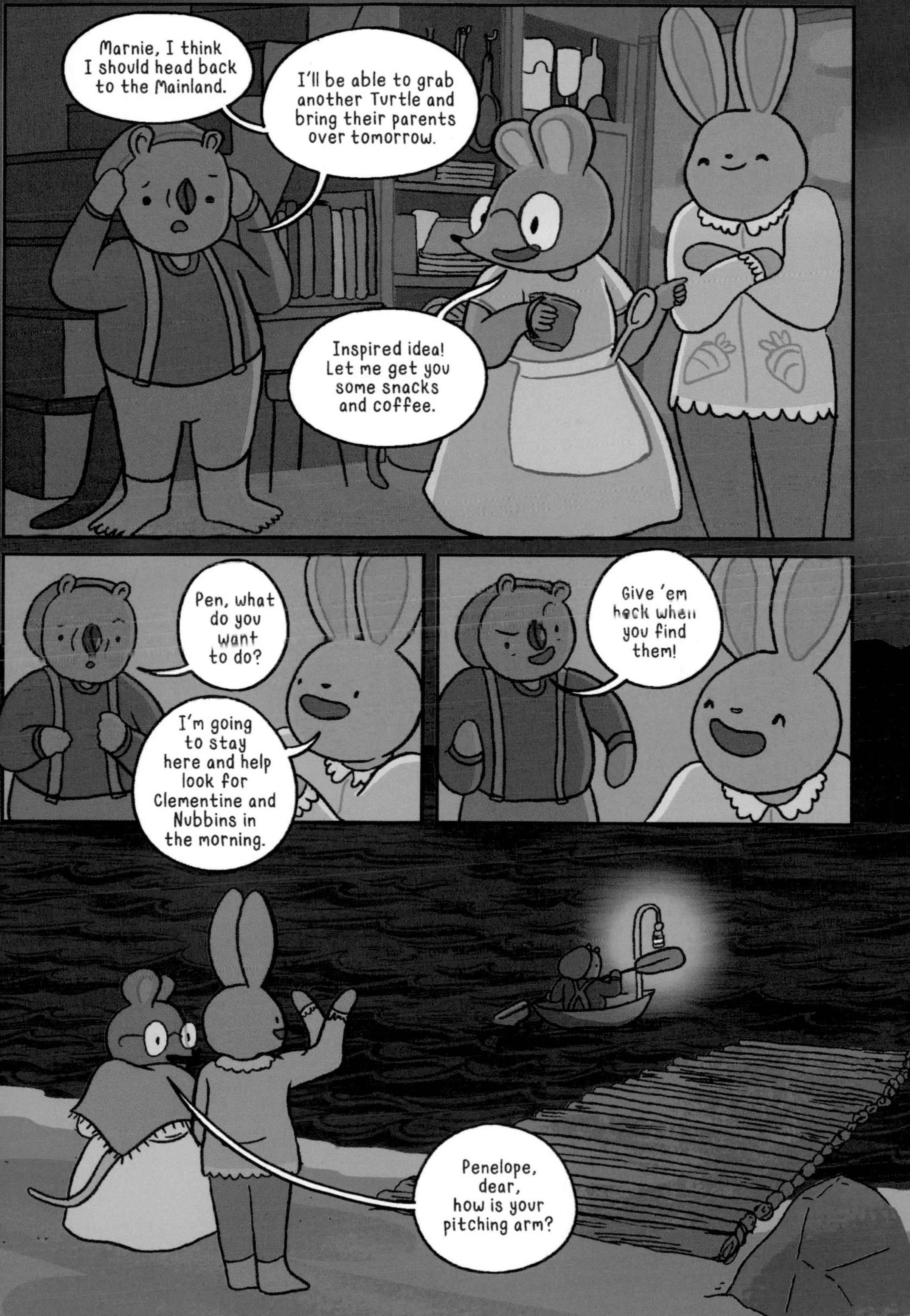
Marnie, I think I should head back to the Mainland.
I'll be able to grab another Turtle and bring their parents over tomorrow.
Inspired idea! Let me get you some snacks and coffee.
Pen, what do you want to do?
I'm going to stay here and help look for Clementine and Nubbins in the morning.
Give 'em heck when you find them!
Penelope, dear, how is your pitching arm?

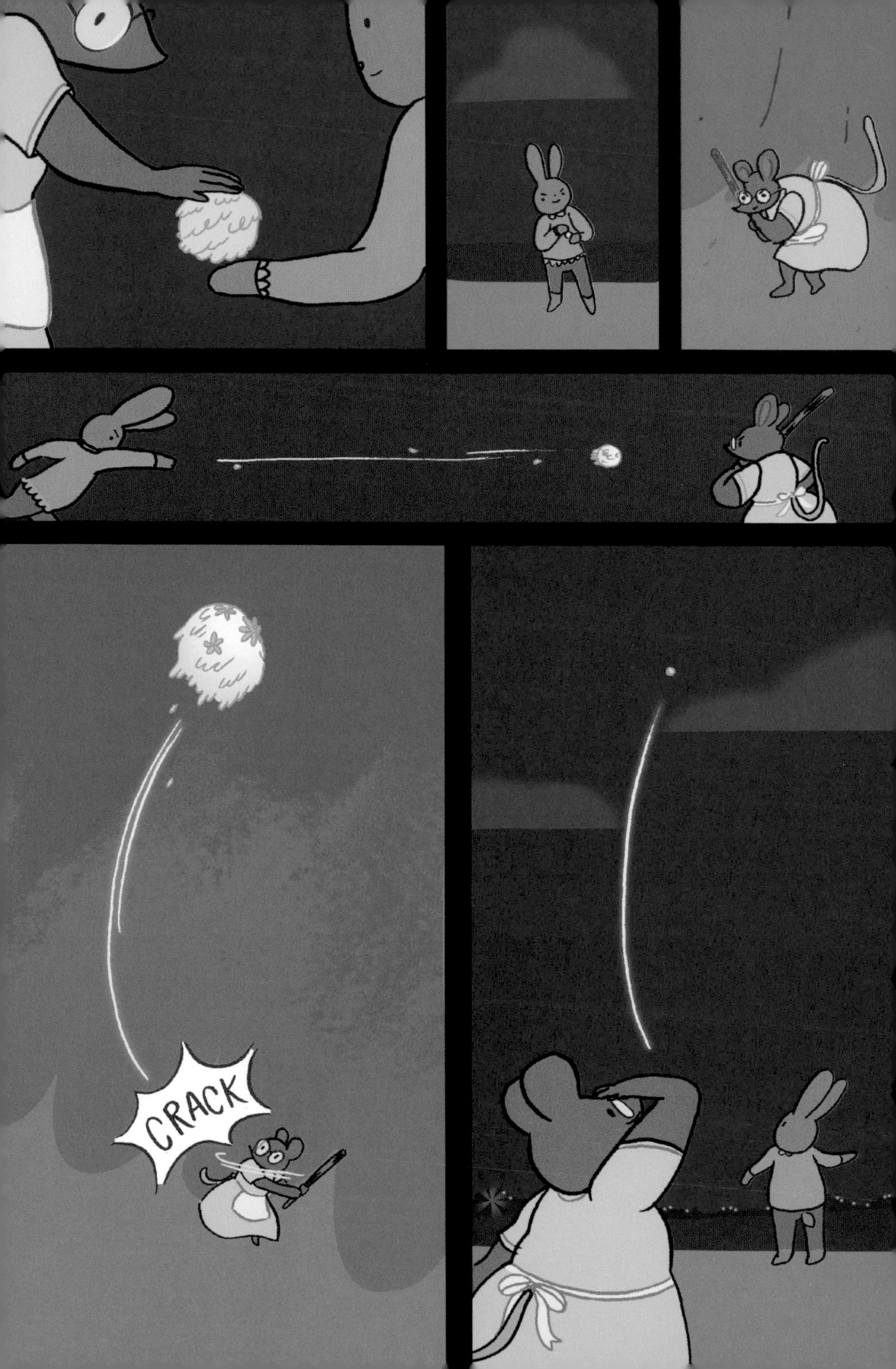
CRACK

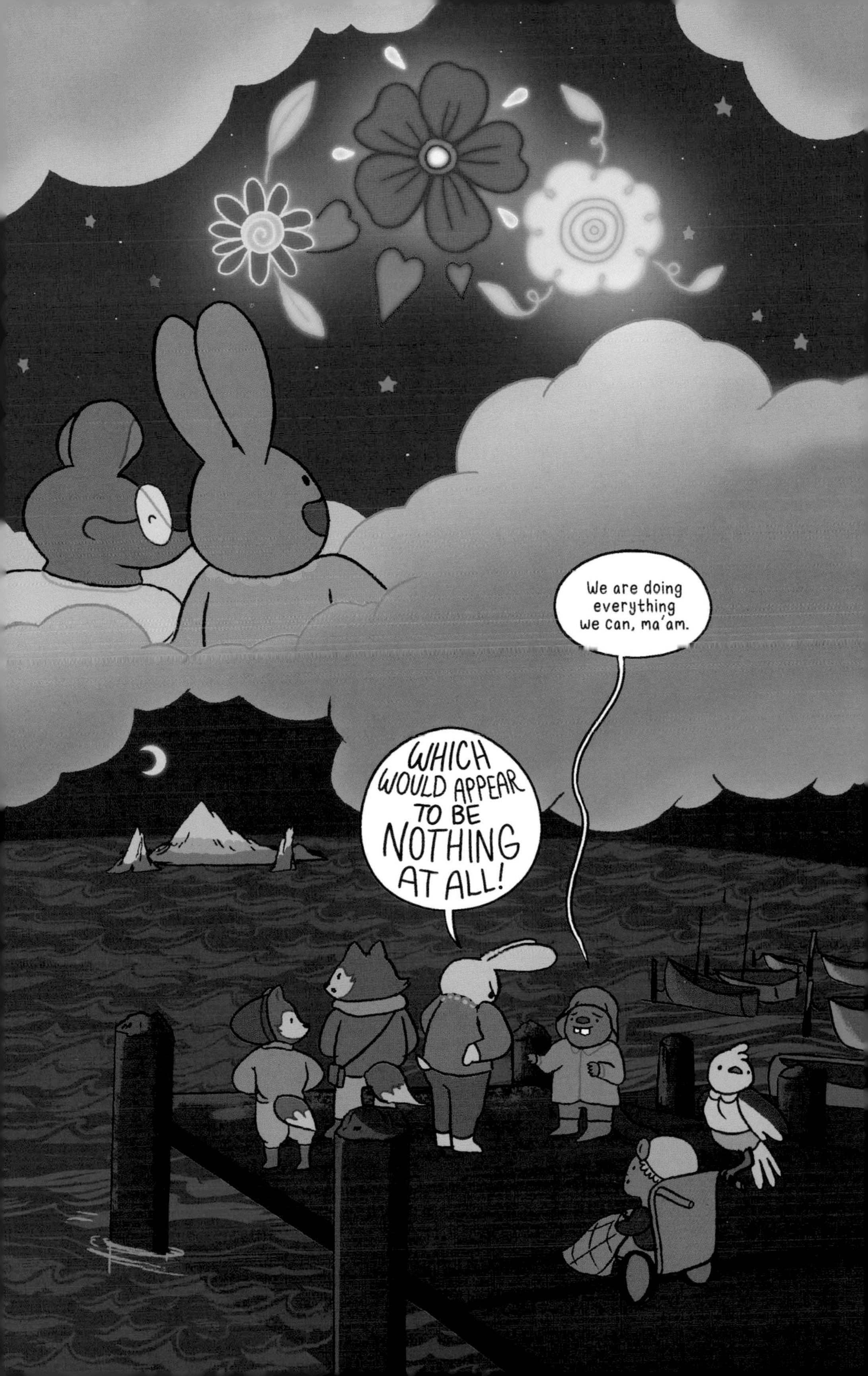
We are doing everything we can, ma'am.
WHICH WOULD APPEAR TO BE NOTHING AT ALL!

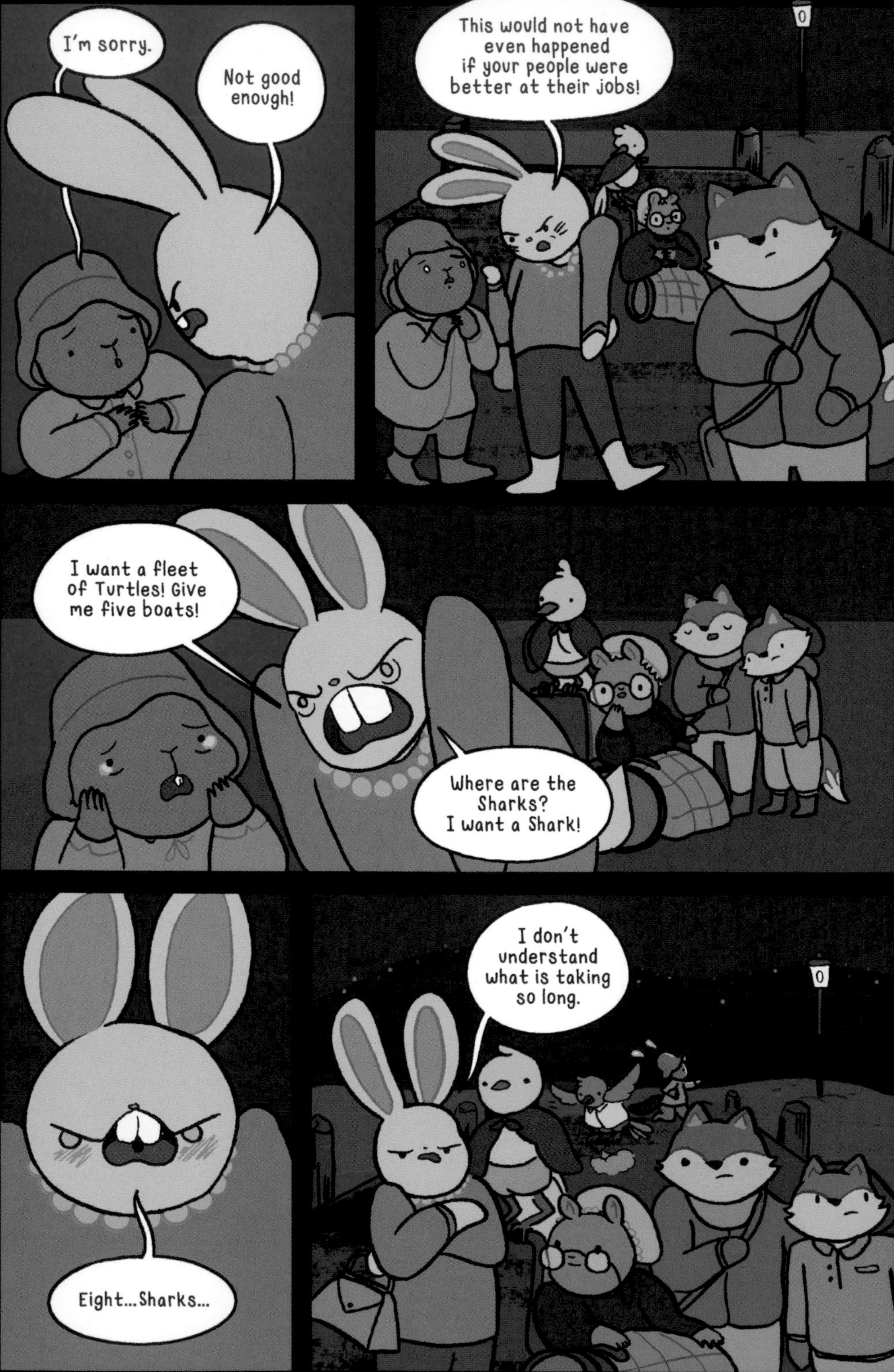
I'm sorry.
Not good enough!
This would not have even happened if your people were better at their jobs!
I want a fleet of Turtles! Give me five boats!
Where are the Sharks? I want a Shark!
Eight...Sharks...
I don't understand what is taking so long.

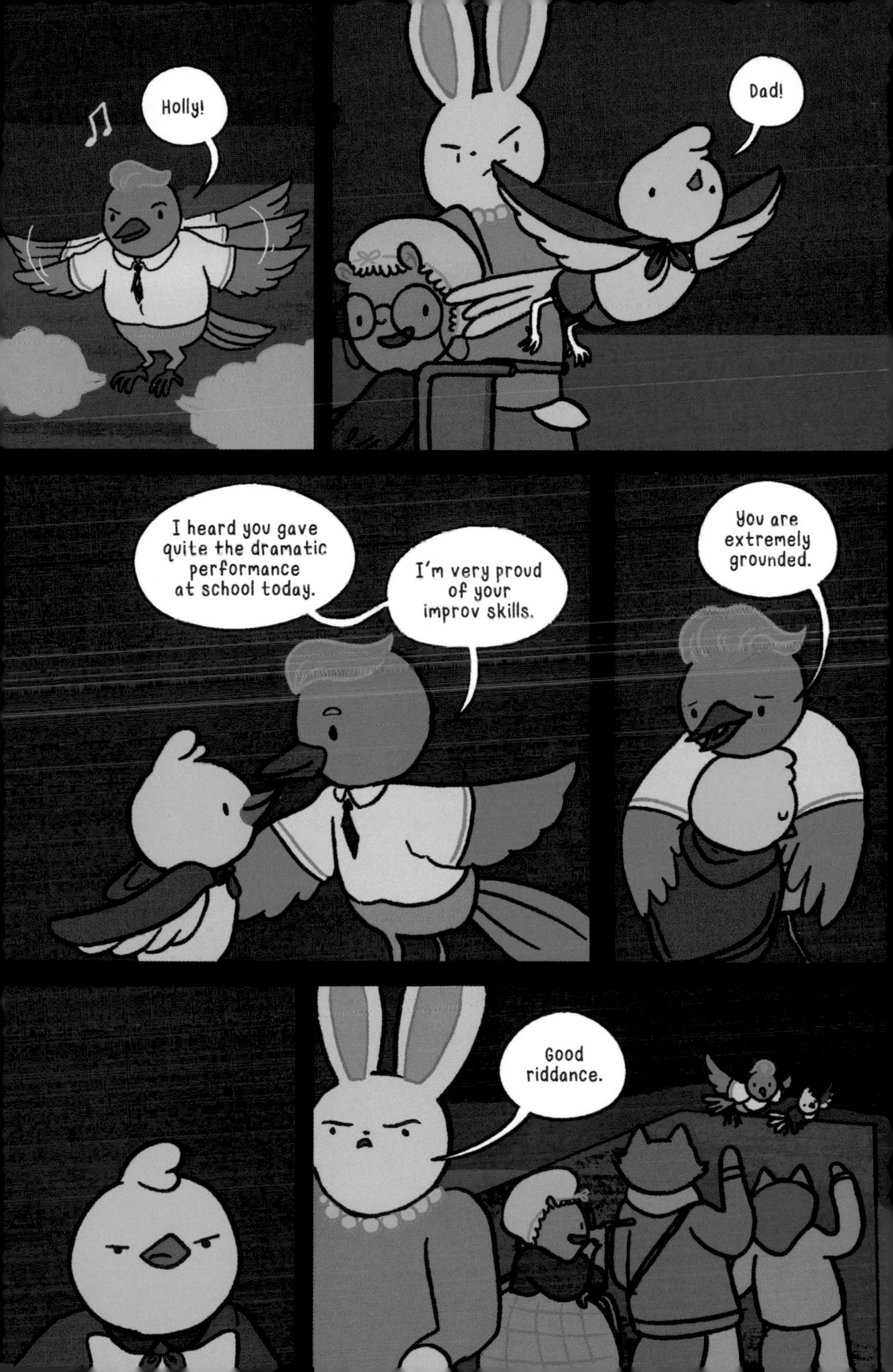
Holly!
Dad!
I heard you gave quite the dramatic performance at school today.
I'm very proud of your improv skills.
You are extremely grounded.
Good riddance.

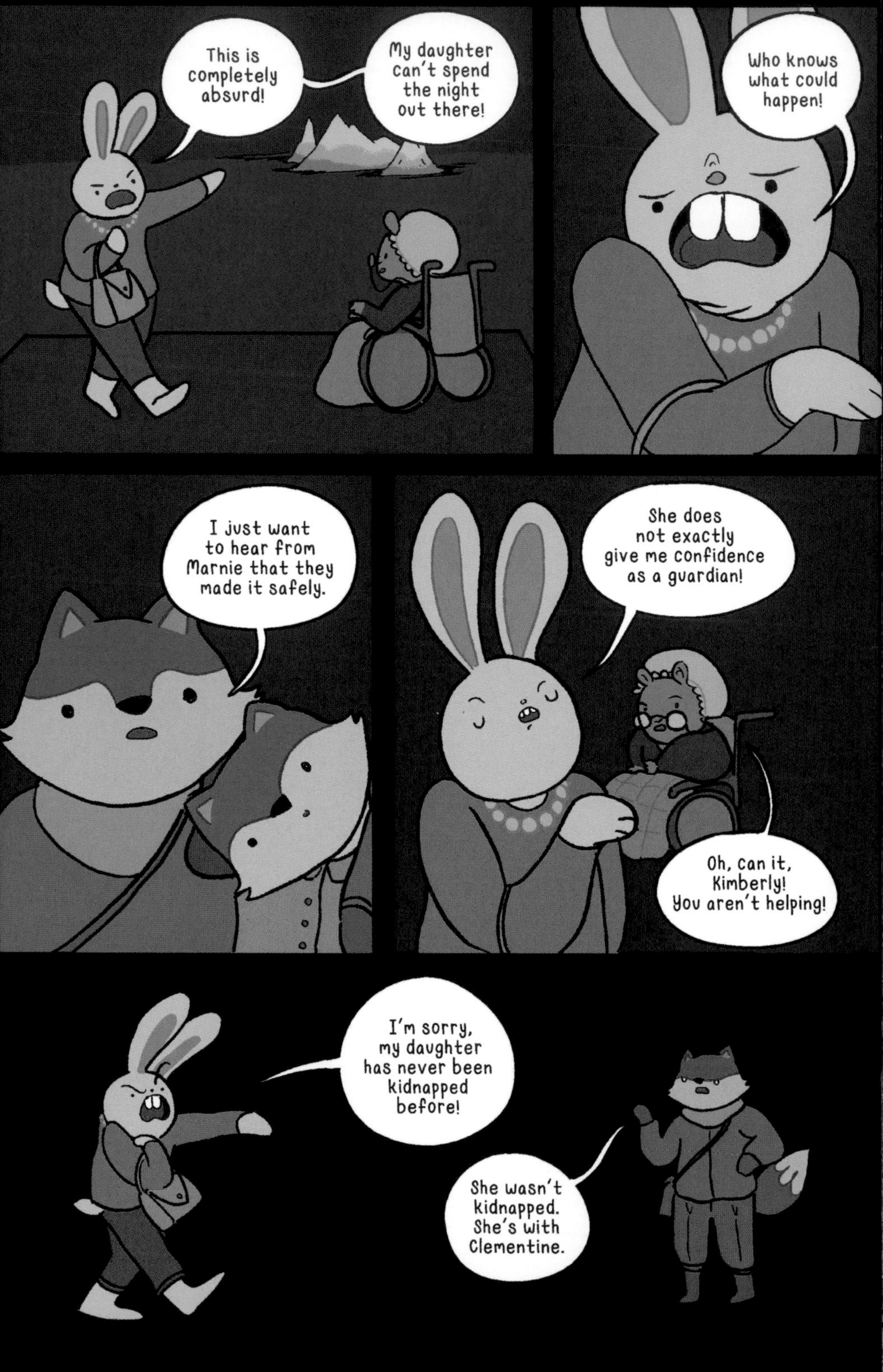

This is completely absurd!
My daughter can't spend the night out there!
Who knows what could happen!
I just want to hear from Marnie that they made it safely.
She does not exactly give me confidence as a guardian!
Oh, can it, Kimberly! You aren't helping!
I'm sorry, my daughter has never been kidnapped before!
She wasn't kidnapped. She's with Clementine.

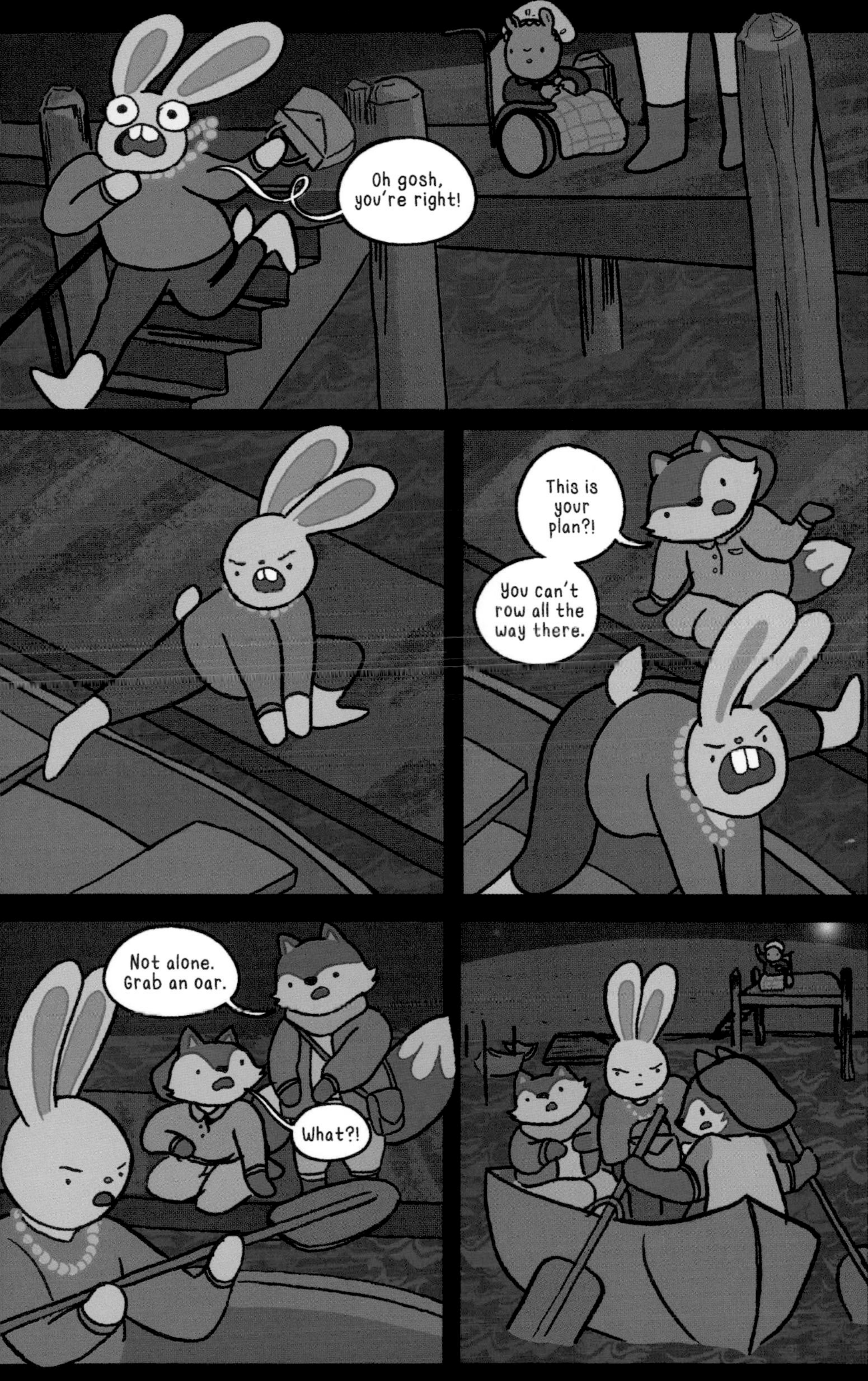
Oh gosh, you're right!
This is your plan?!
You can't row all the way there.
Not alone. Grab an oar.
What?!

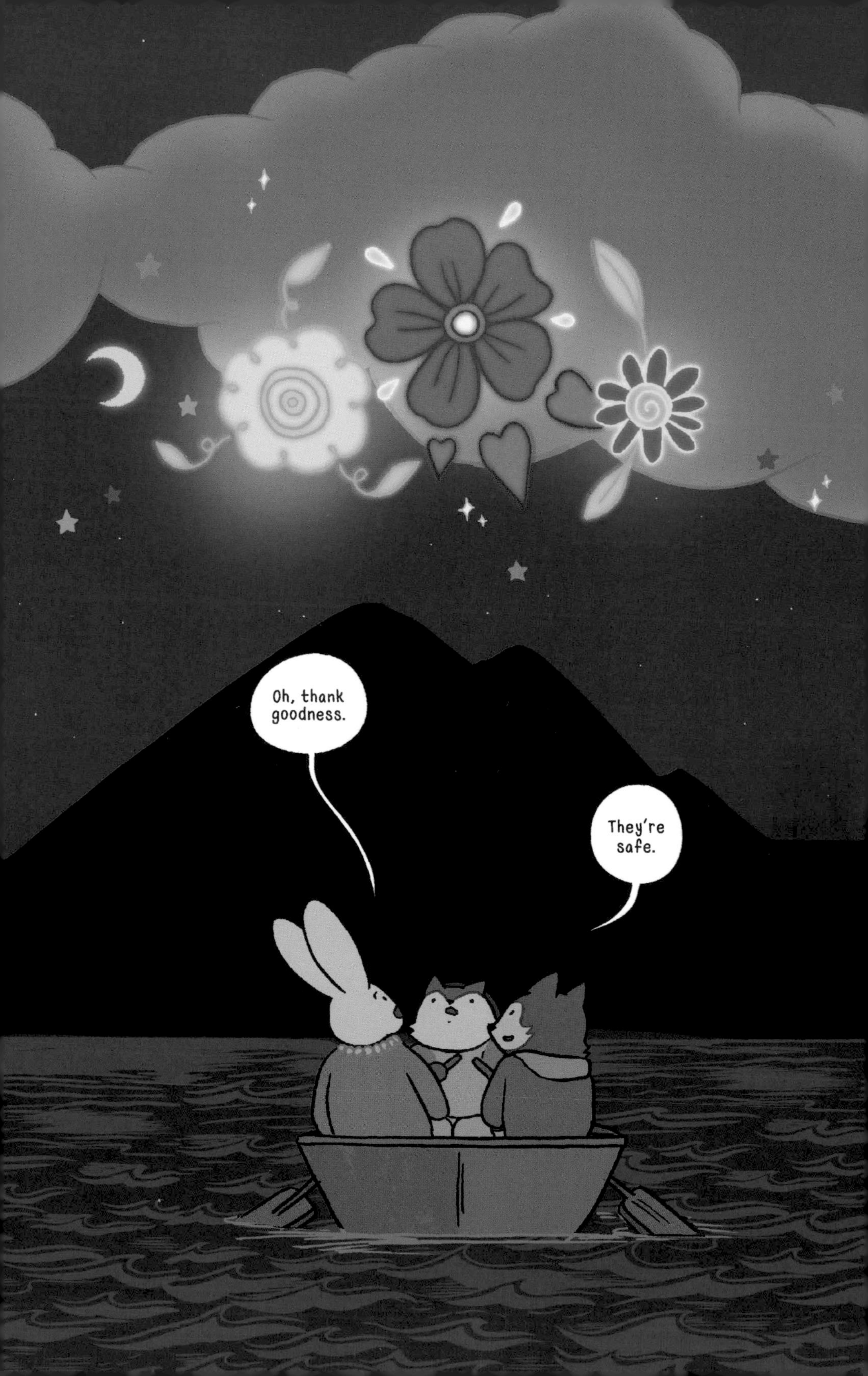
Oh, thank goodness.
They're safe.

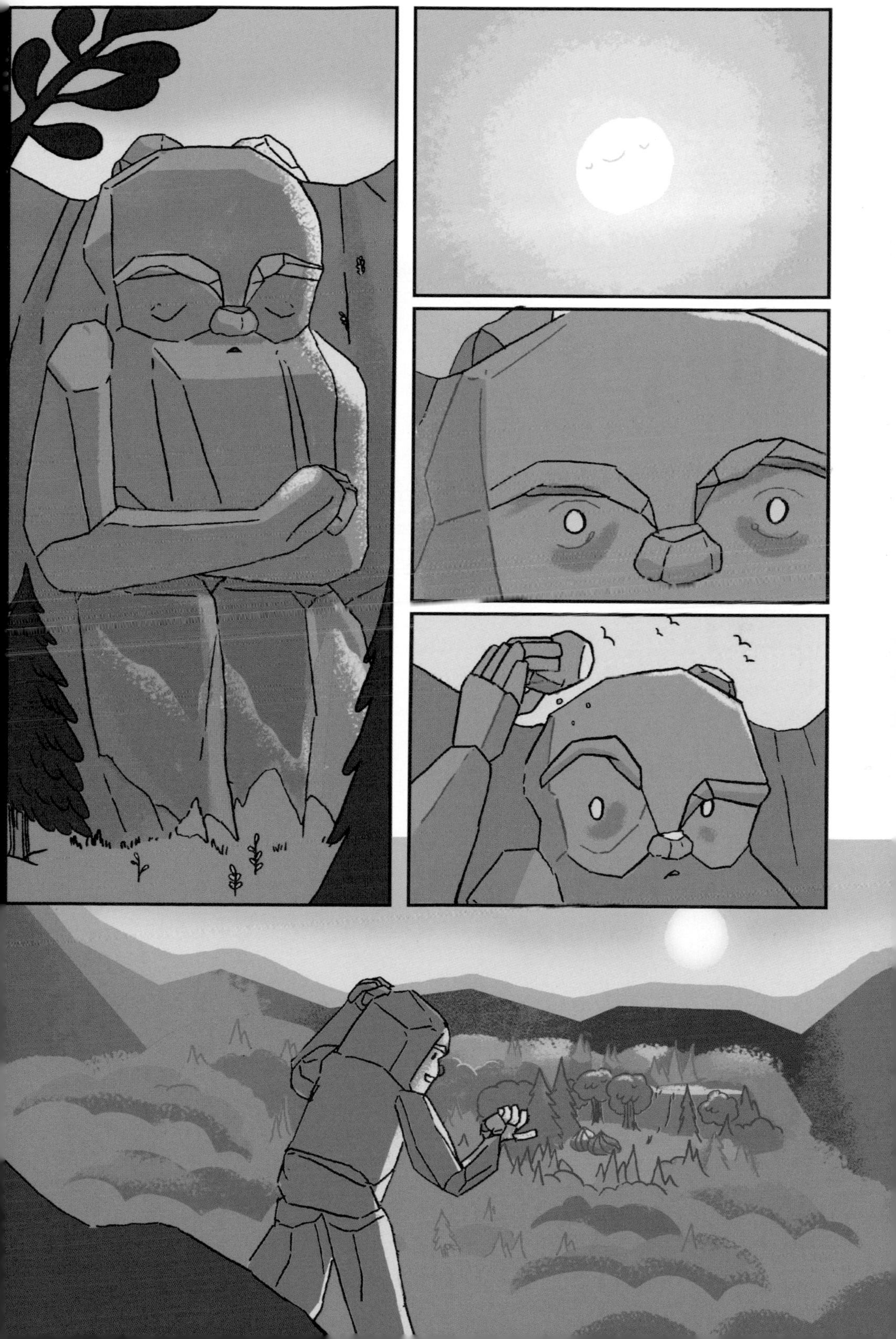

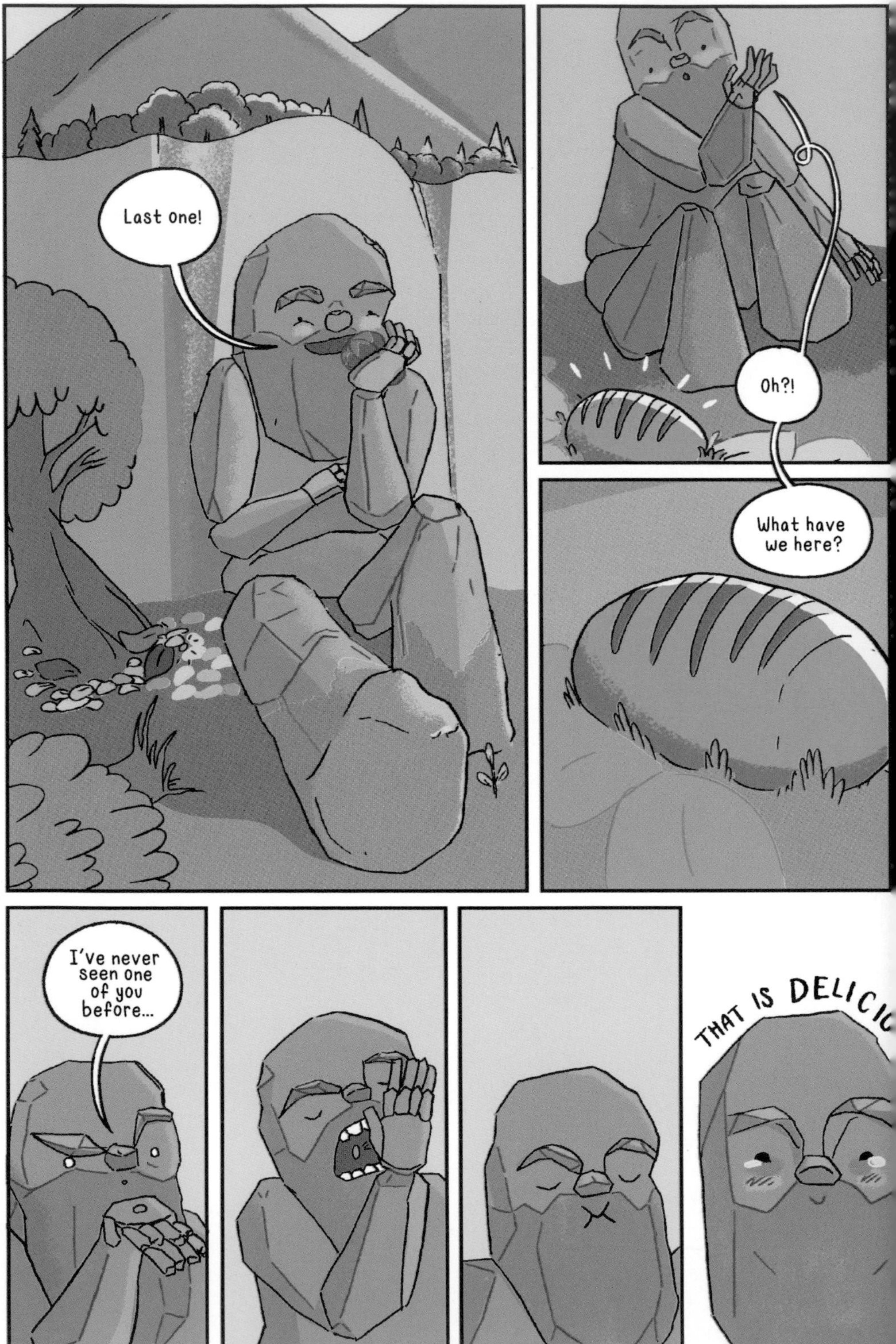
Last one!
Oh?!
What have we here?
I've never seen one of you before...
THAT IS DELICIO

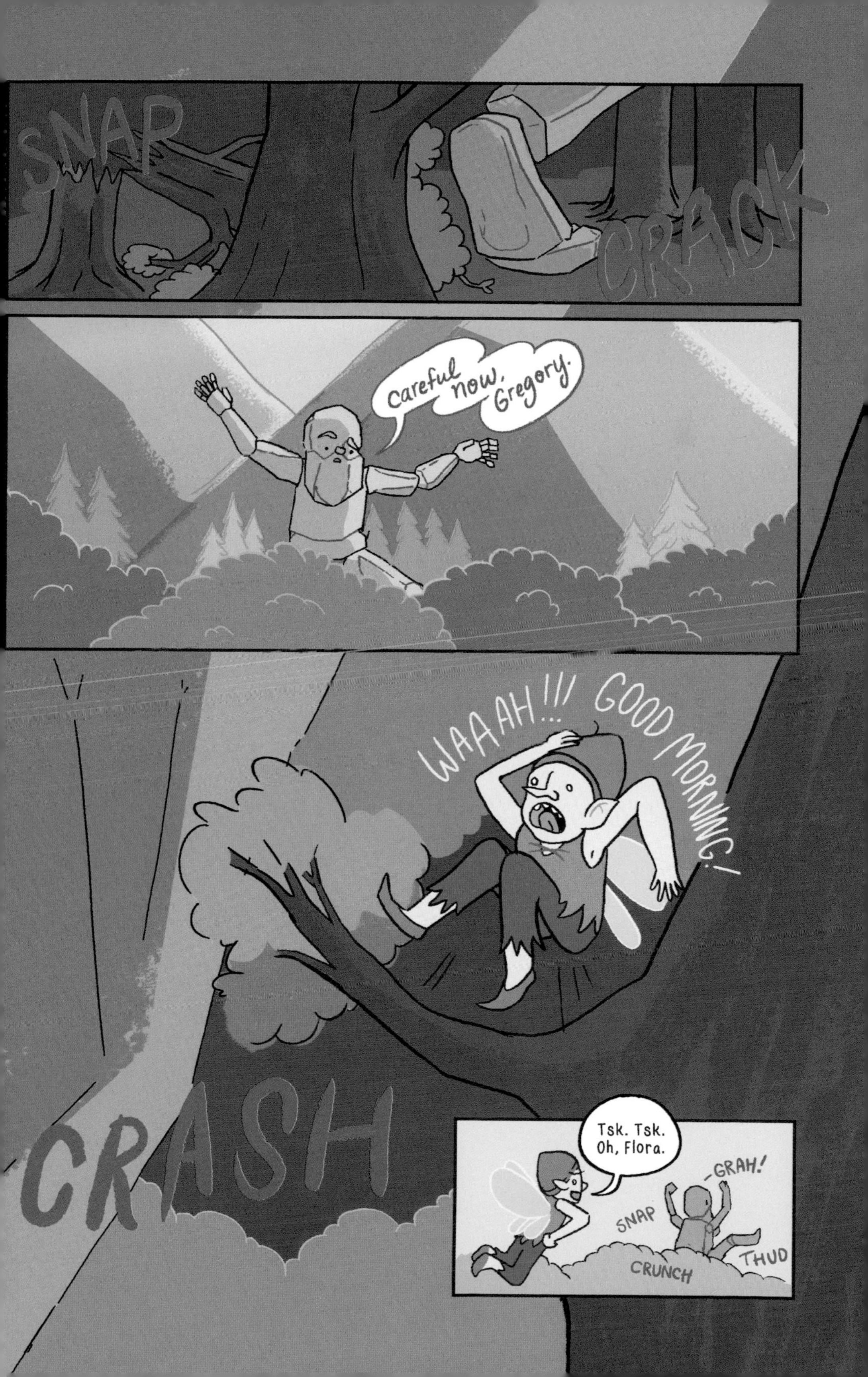
SNAP
CRACK
Careful now, Gregory.
WAAAH!!!... GOOD MORNING!
CRASH
Tsk. Tsk. Oh, Flora.
-GRAH!
SNAP
CRUNCH
THUD

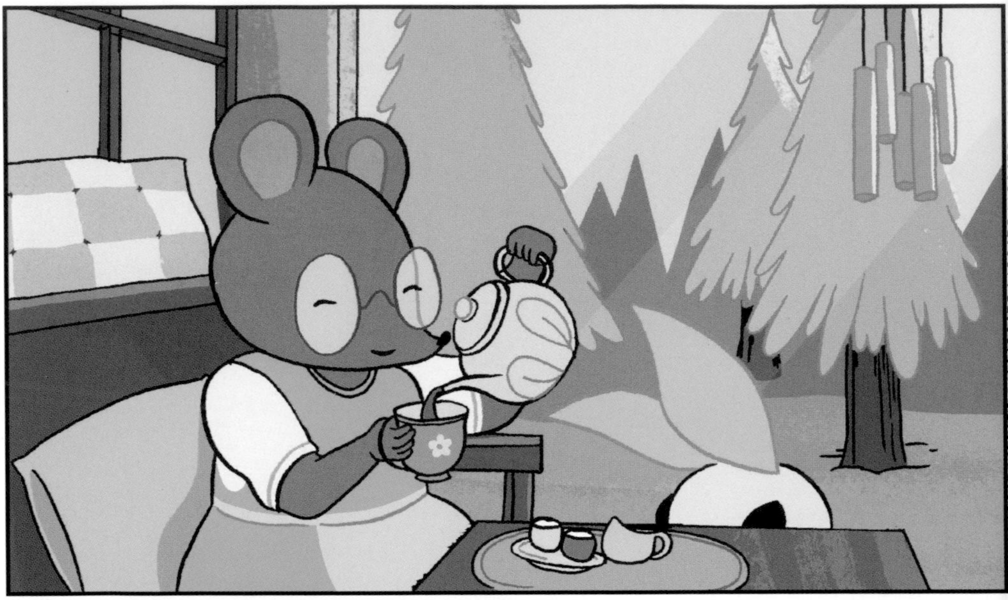

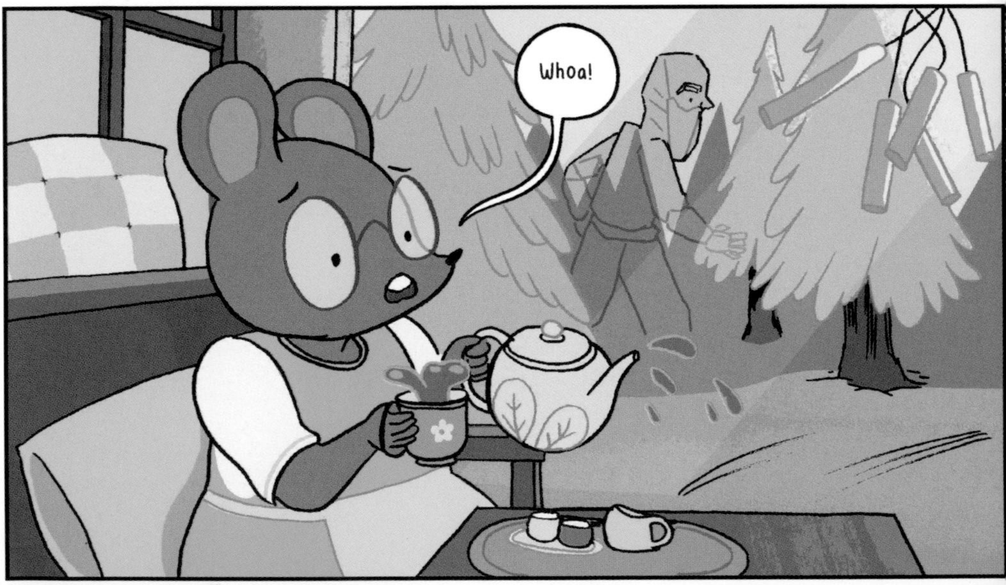
Whoa!

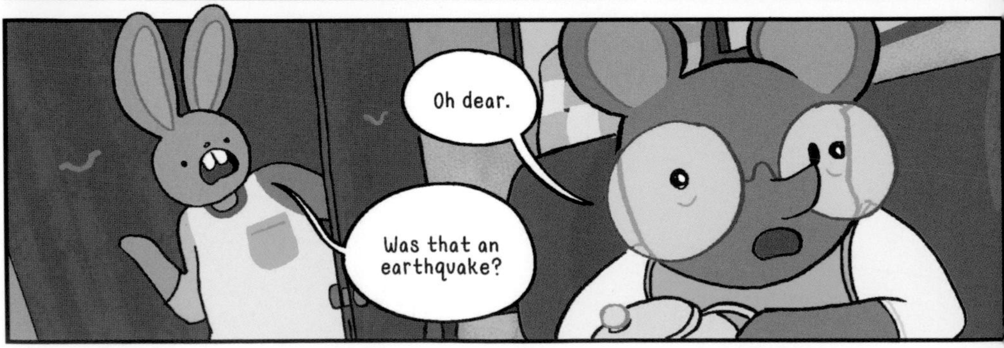
Oh dear.
Was that an earthquake?

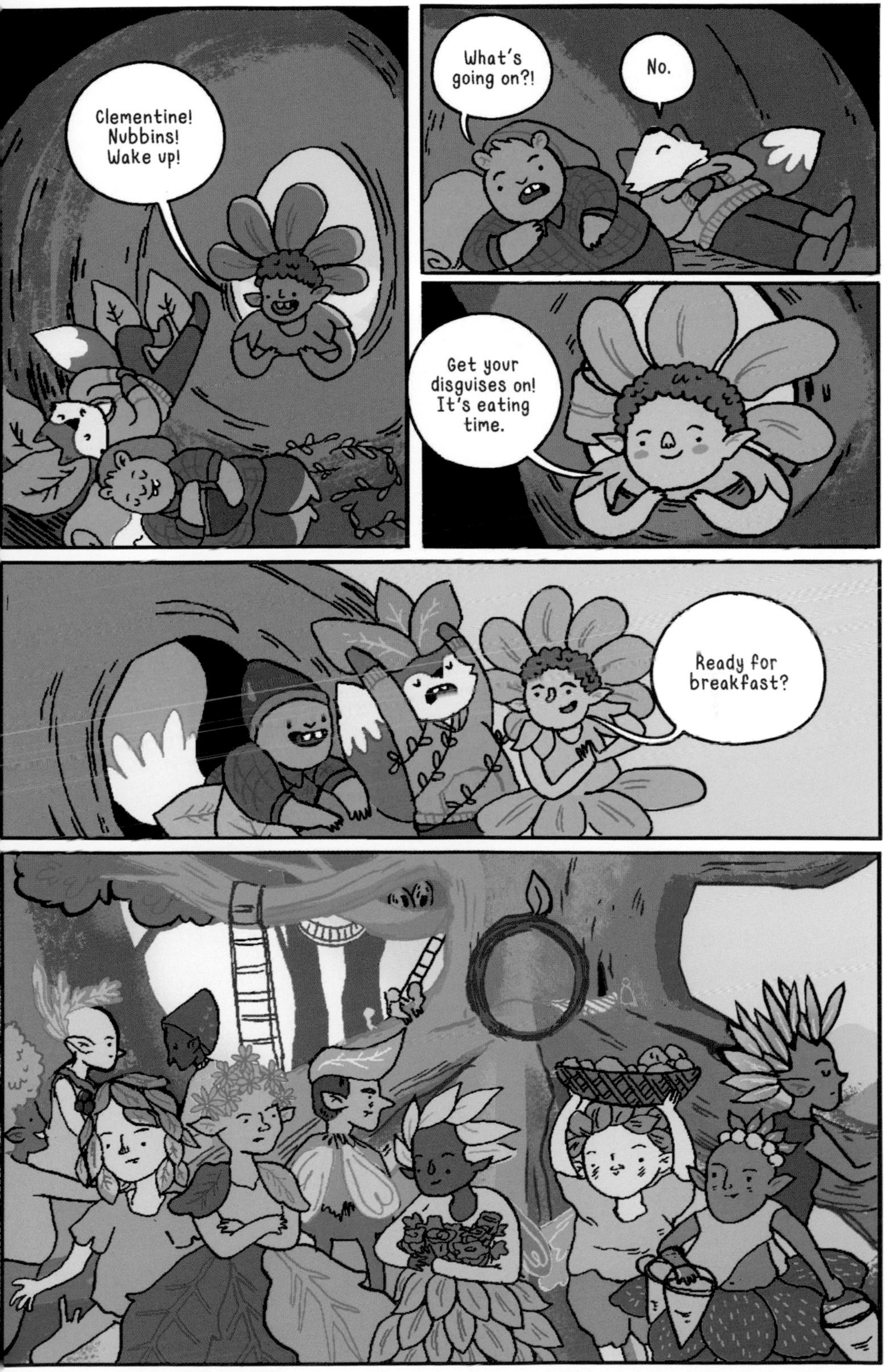
Clementine! Nubbins! Wake up!
What's going on?!
No.
Get your disguises on! It's eating time.
Ready for breakfast?

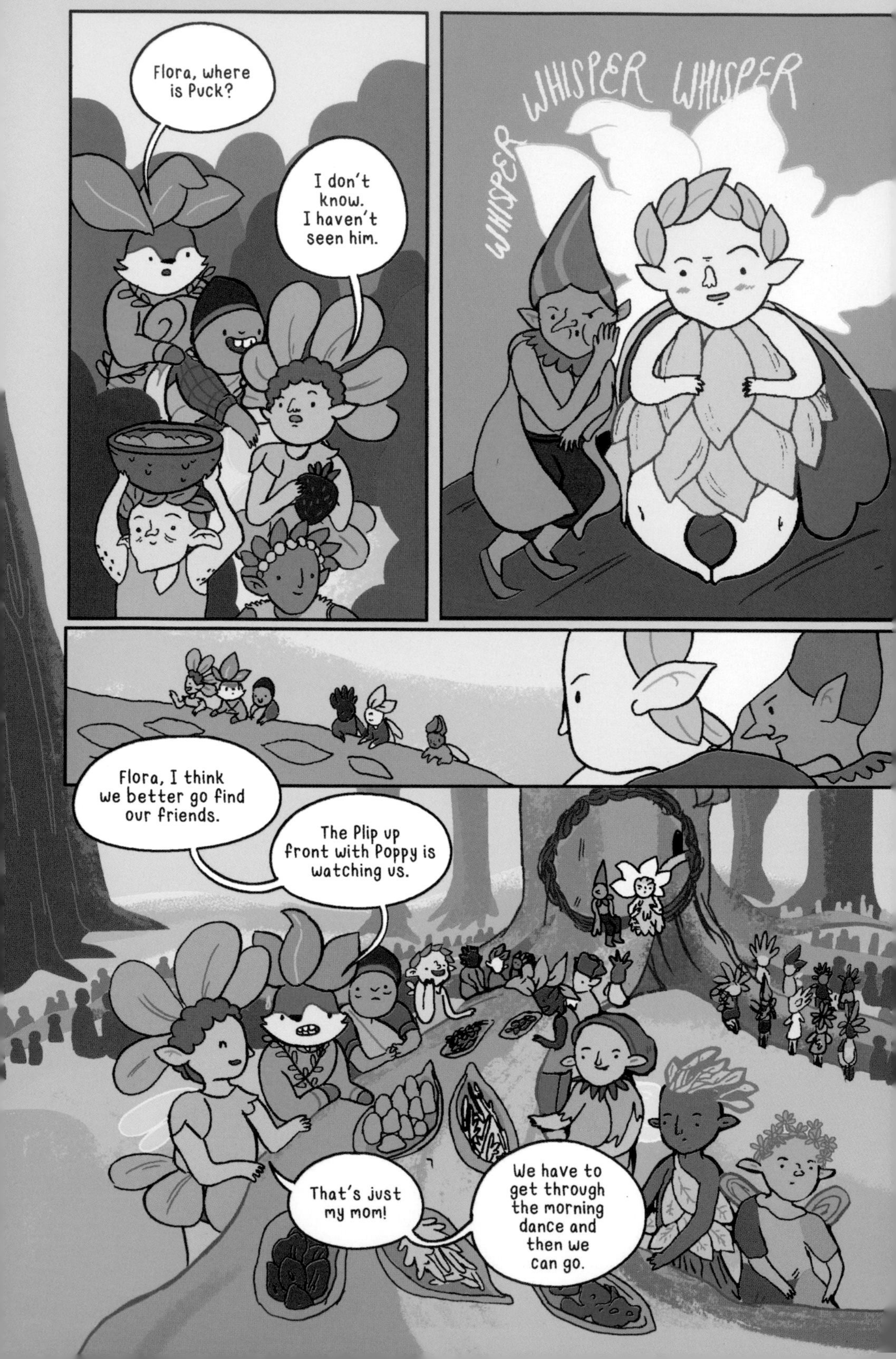
Flora, where is Puck?
I don't know. I haven't seen him.
WHISPER WHISPER WHISPER
Flora, I think we better go find our friends.
The Plip up front with Poppy is watching us.
That's just my mom!
We have to get through the morning dance and then we can go.

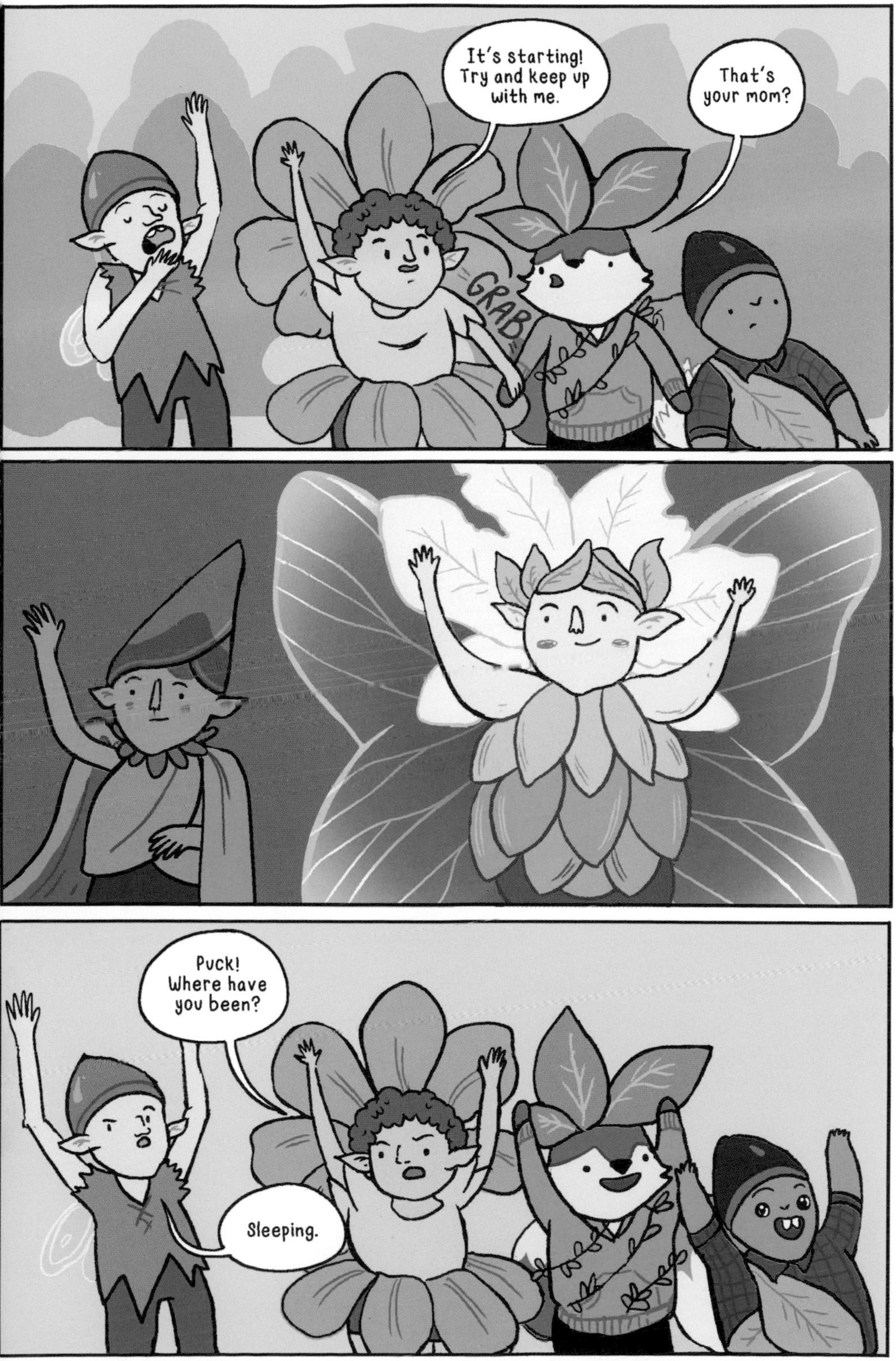
It's starting! Try and keep up with me.
That's your mom?
GRAB
Puck! Where have you been?
Sleeping.

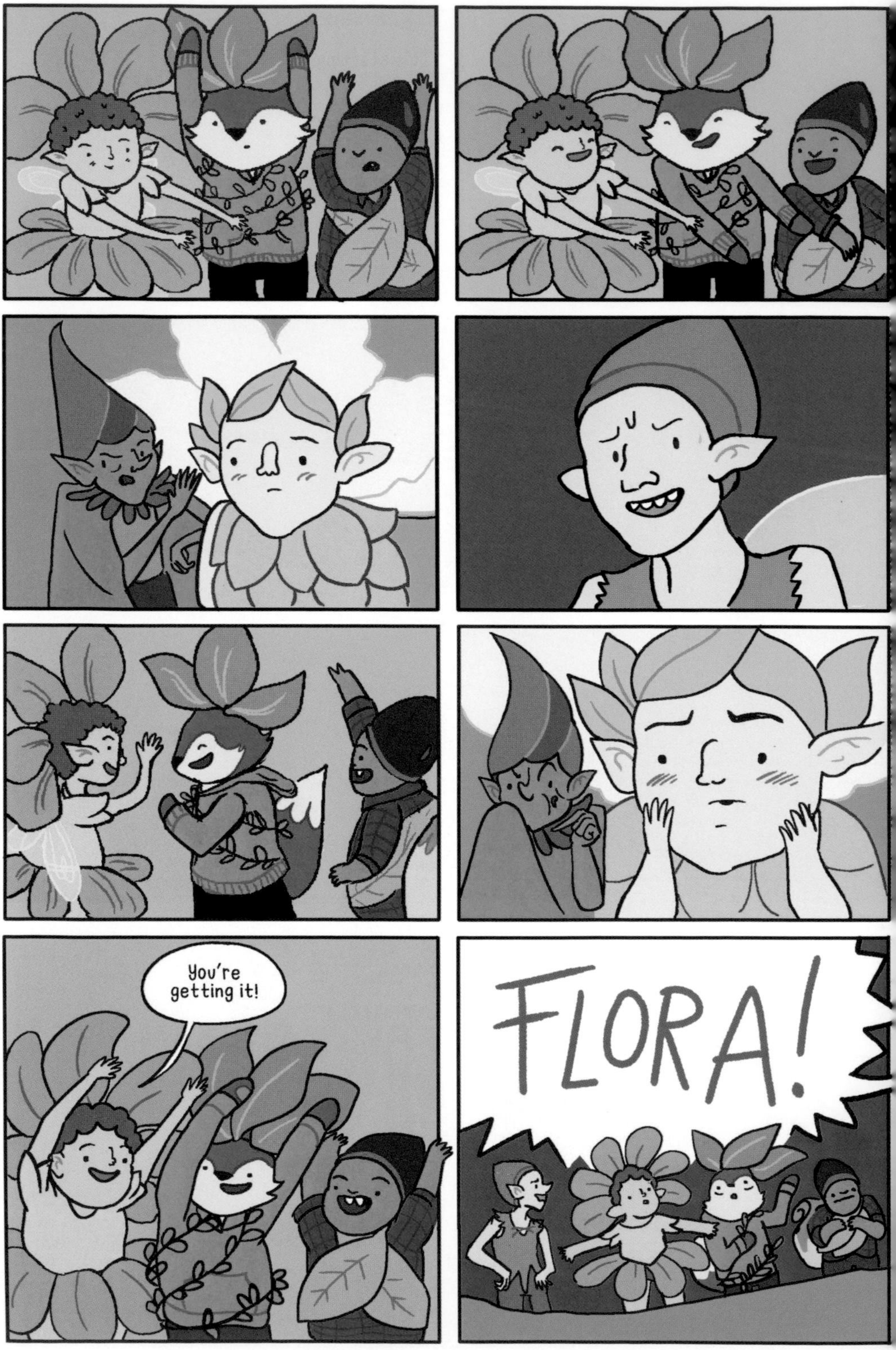
You're getting it!
FLORA!

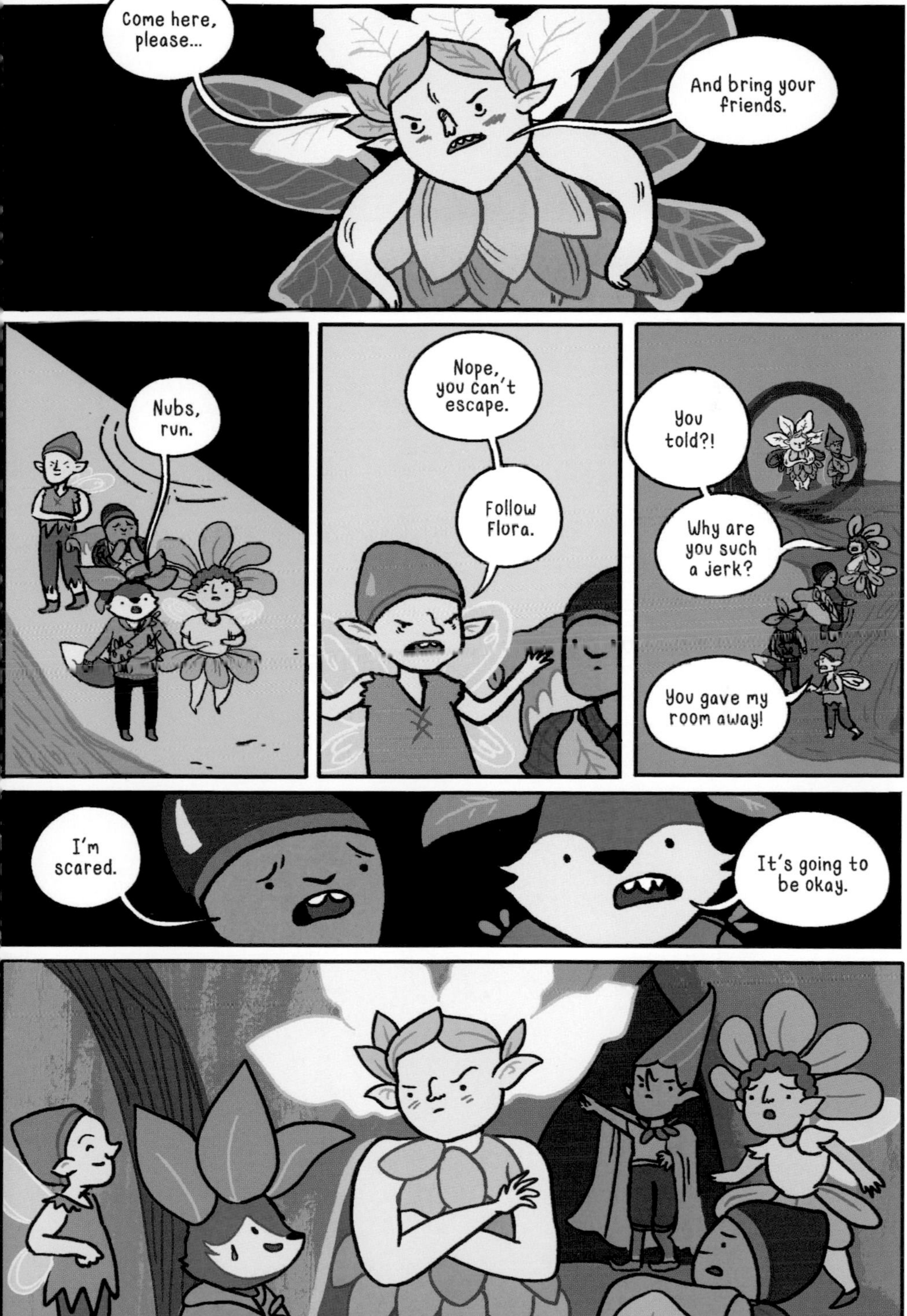
Come here, please...
And bring your friends.
Nubs, run.
Nope, you can't escape.
Follow Flora.
You told?!
Why are you such a jerk?
You gave my room away!
I'm scared.
It's going to be okay.

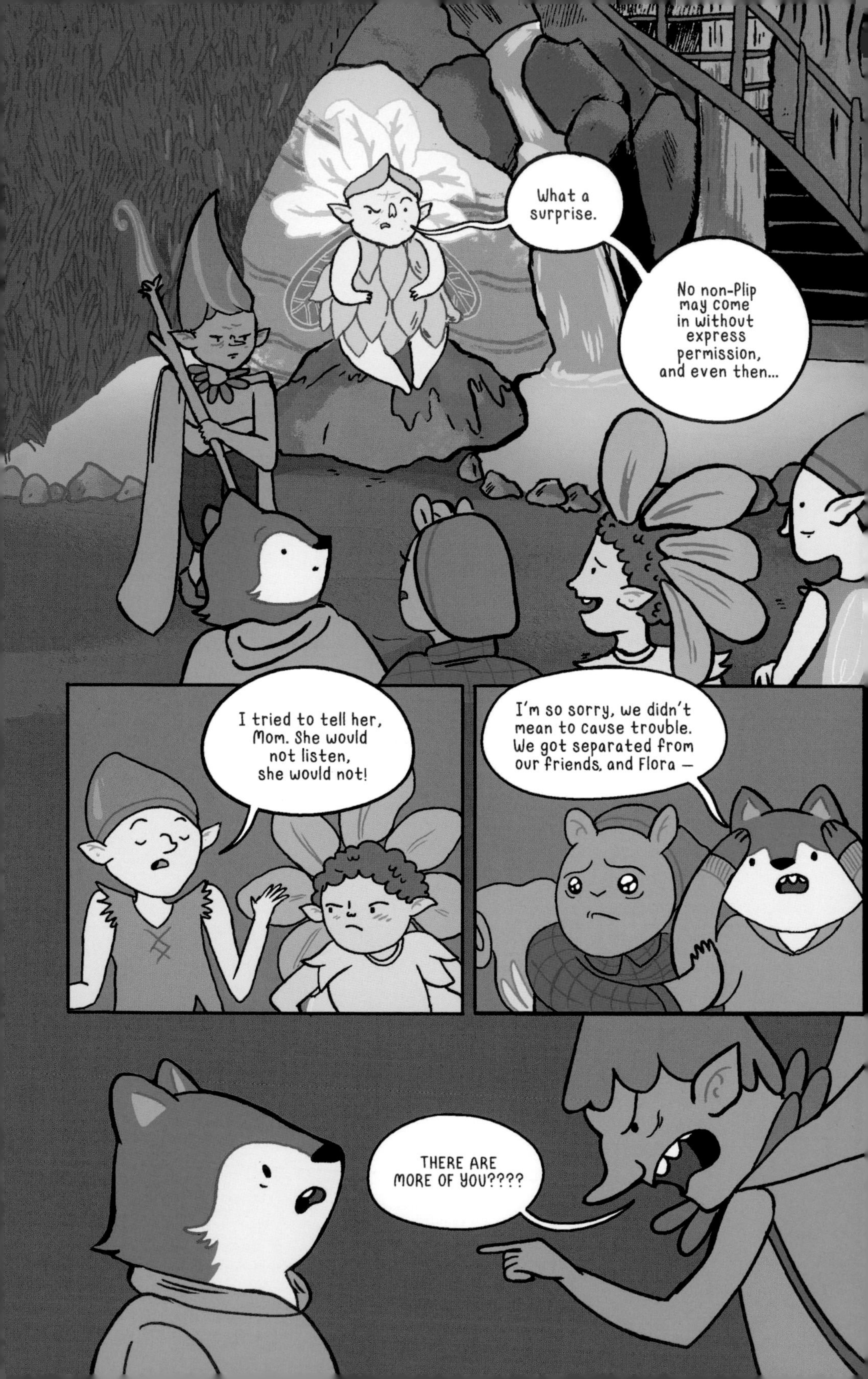
What a surprise.
No non-Plip may come in without express permission, and even then...
I tried to tell her, Mom. She would not listen, she would not!
I'm so sorry, we didn't mean to cause trouble. We got separated from our friends, and Flora —
THERE ARE MORE OF YOU????

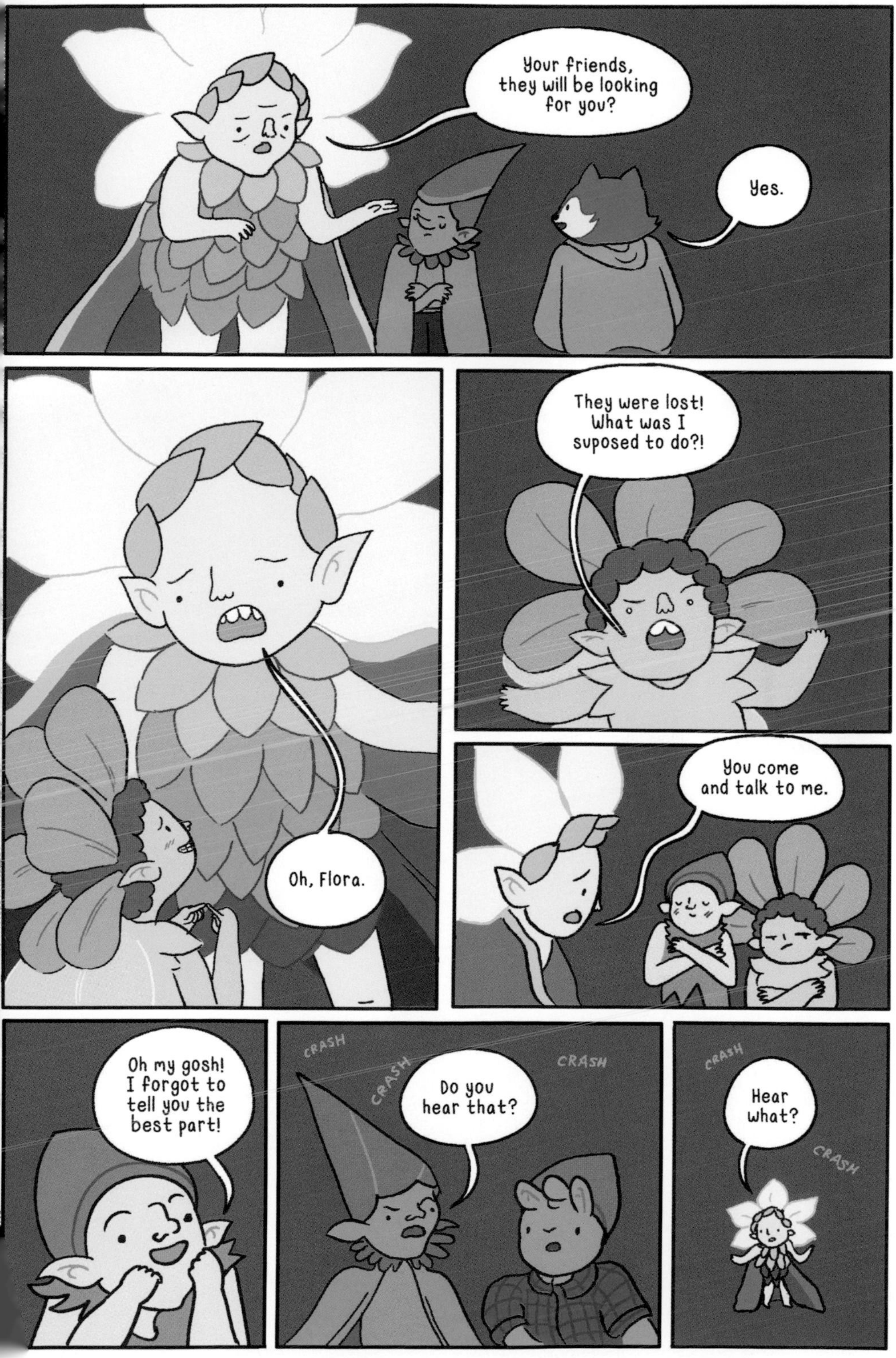
Your friends,
they will be looking
for you?
Yes.
Oh, Flora.
They were lost!
What was I
suposed to do?!
You come
and talk to me.
Oh my gosh!
I forgot to
tell you the
best part!
CRASH
CRASH
CRASH
Do you
hear that?
CRASH
Hear
what?
CRASH

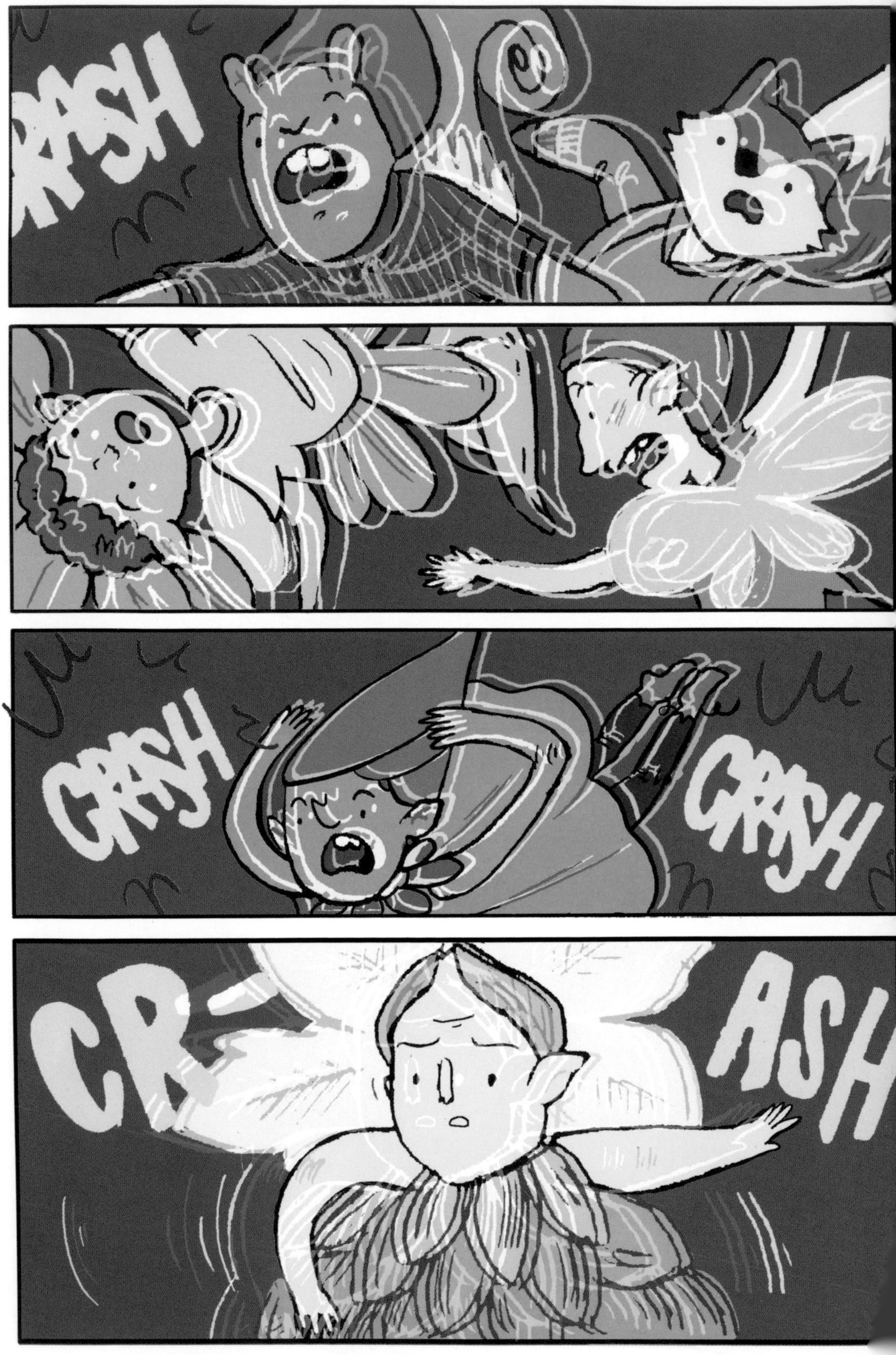
RASH
CRASH
CRASH
CR-
ASH

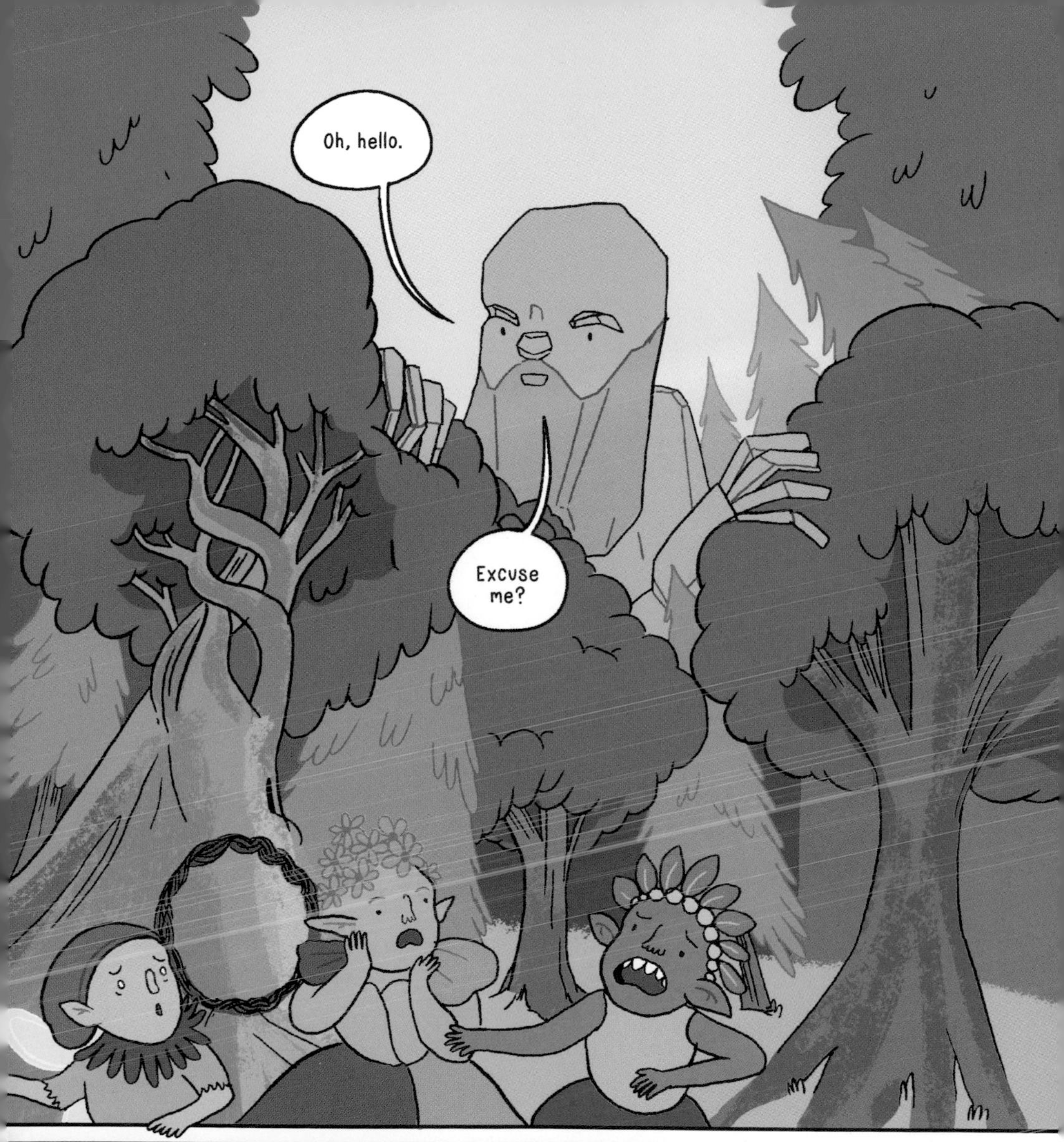
Oh, hello.
Excuse me?
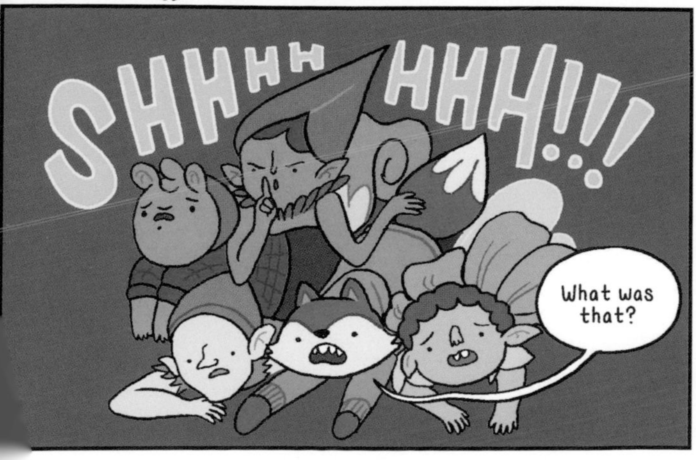
SHHHHHHHH!!!
What was that?
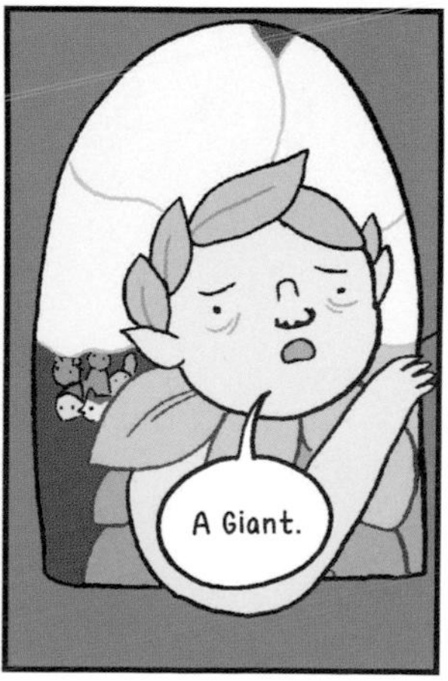
A Giant.

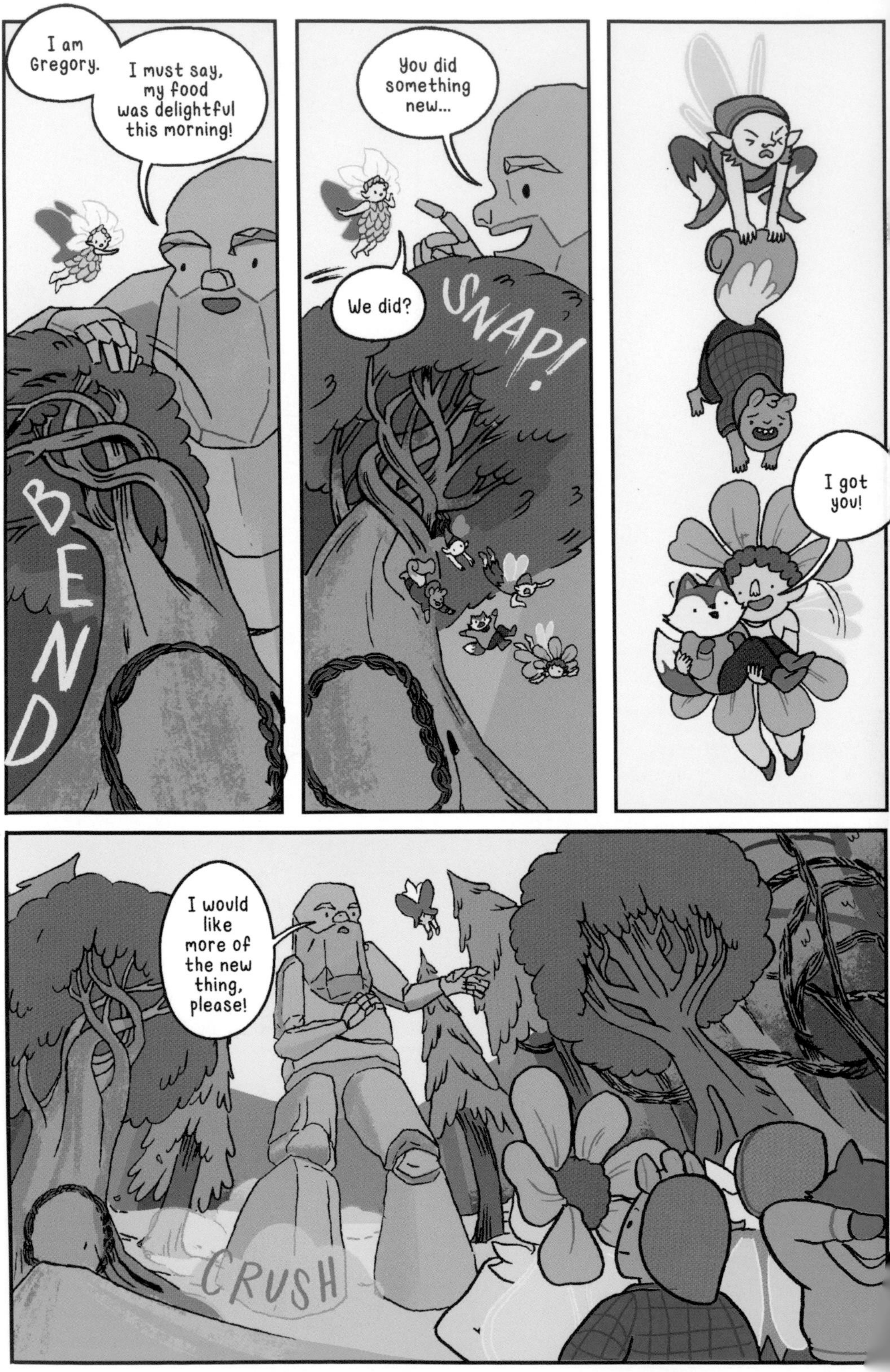

I am Gregory.
I must say, my food was delightful this morning!
BEND
You did something new...
We did?
SNAP!
I got you!
I would like more of the new thing, please!
CRUSH

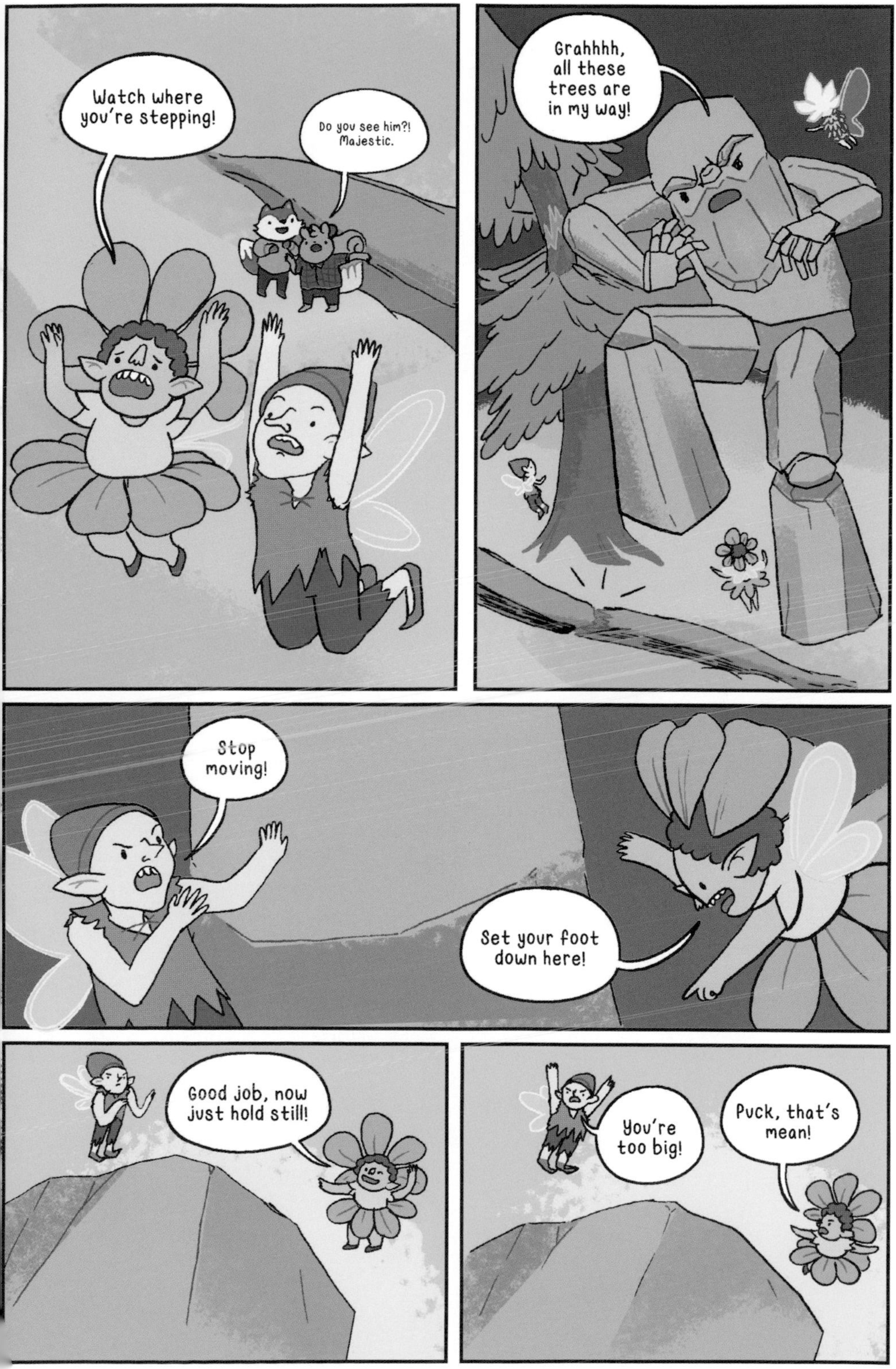
Watch where you're stepping!
Do you see him?! Majestic.
Grahhhh, all these trees are in my way!
Stop moving!
Set your foot down here!
Good job, now just hold still!
You're too big!
Puck, that's mean!

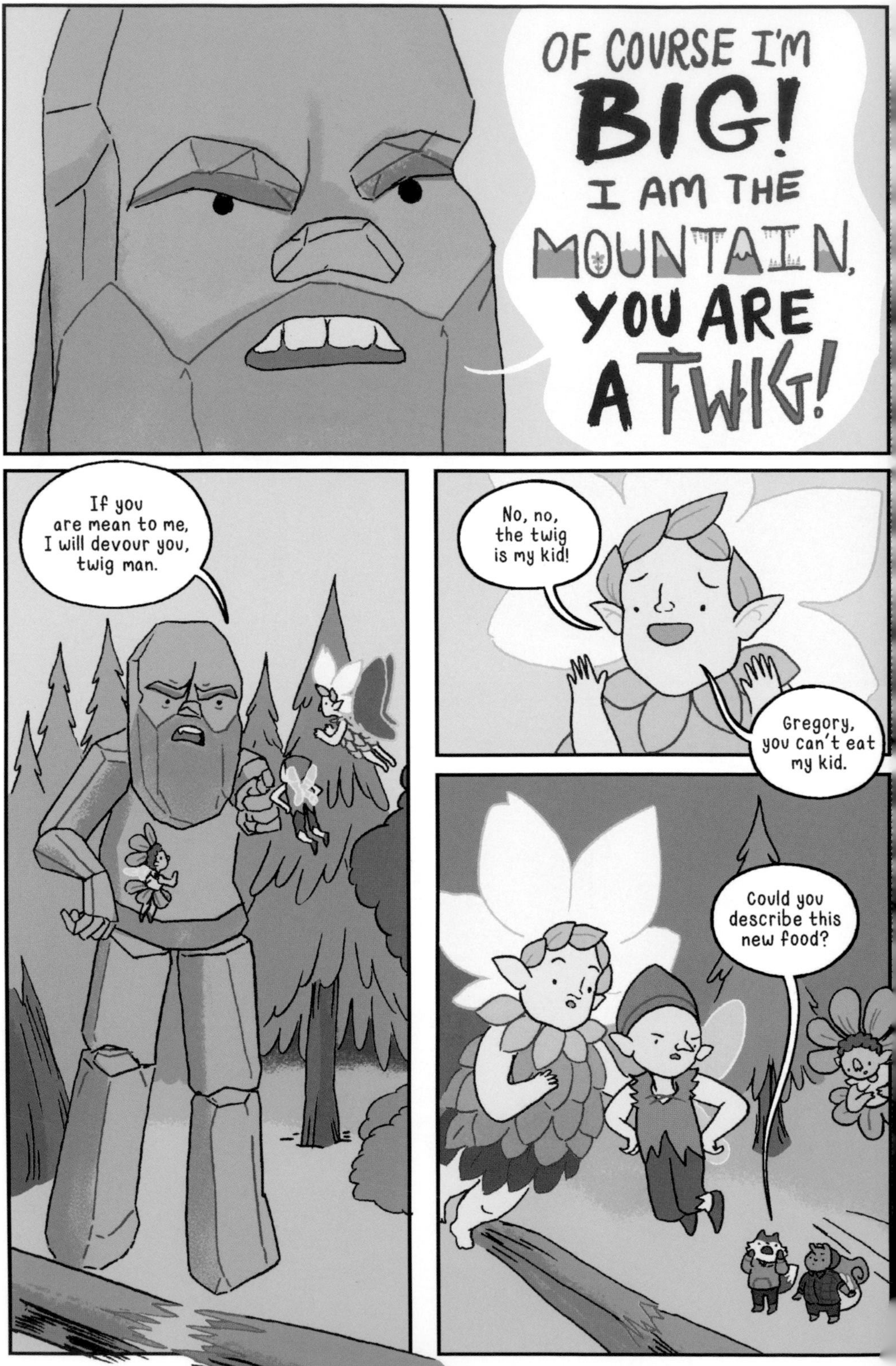
OF COURSE I'M BIG! I AM THE MOUNTAIN, YOU ARE A TWIG!
If you are mean to me, I will devour you, twig man.
No, no, the twig is my kid!
Gregory, you can't eat my kid.
Could you describe this new food?

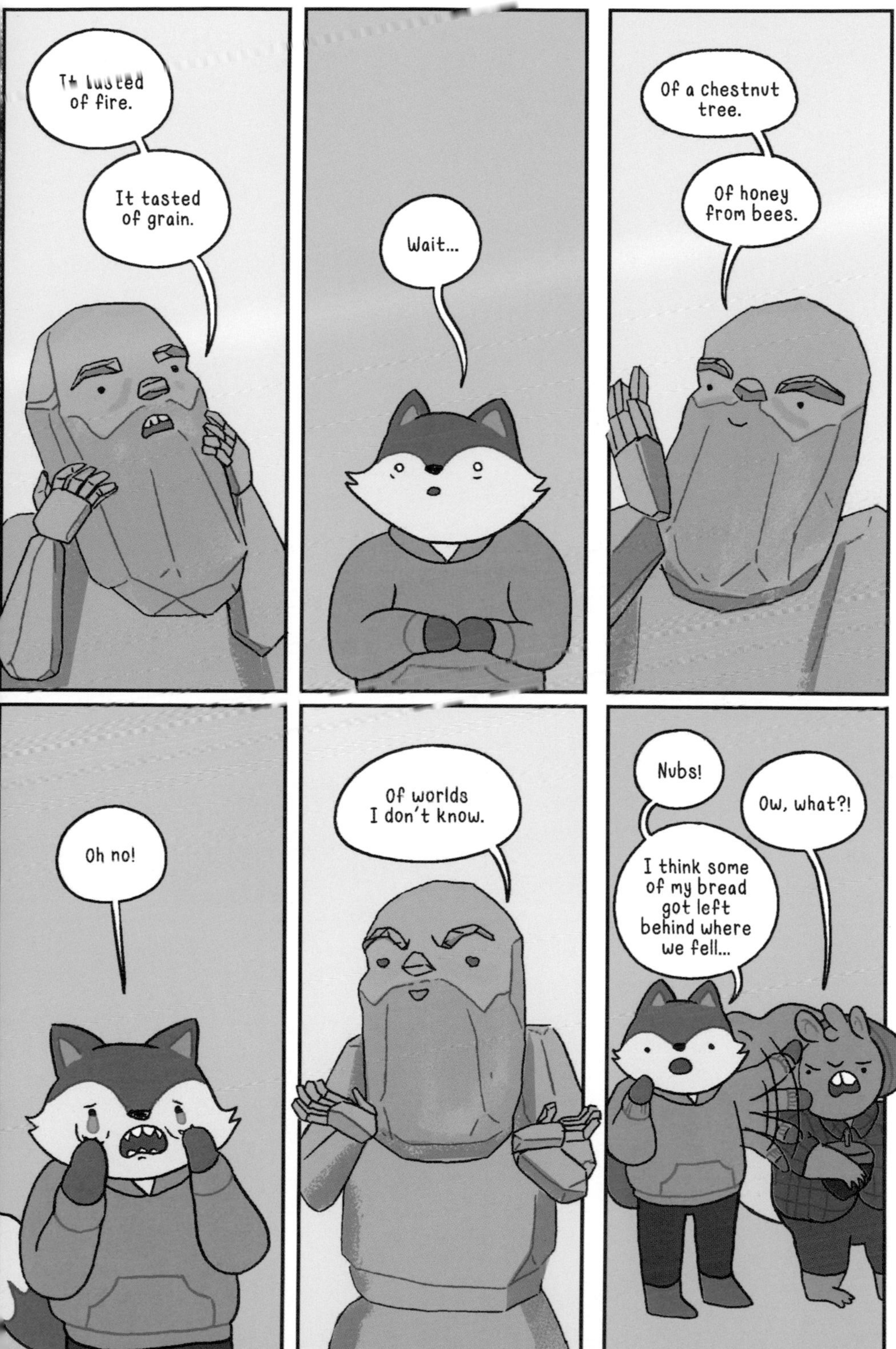
It tasted of fire.
It tasted of grain.
Wait...
Of a chestnut tree.
Of honey from bees.
Oh no!
Of worlds I don't know.
Nubs!
Ow, what?!
I think some of my bread got left behind where we fell...

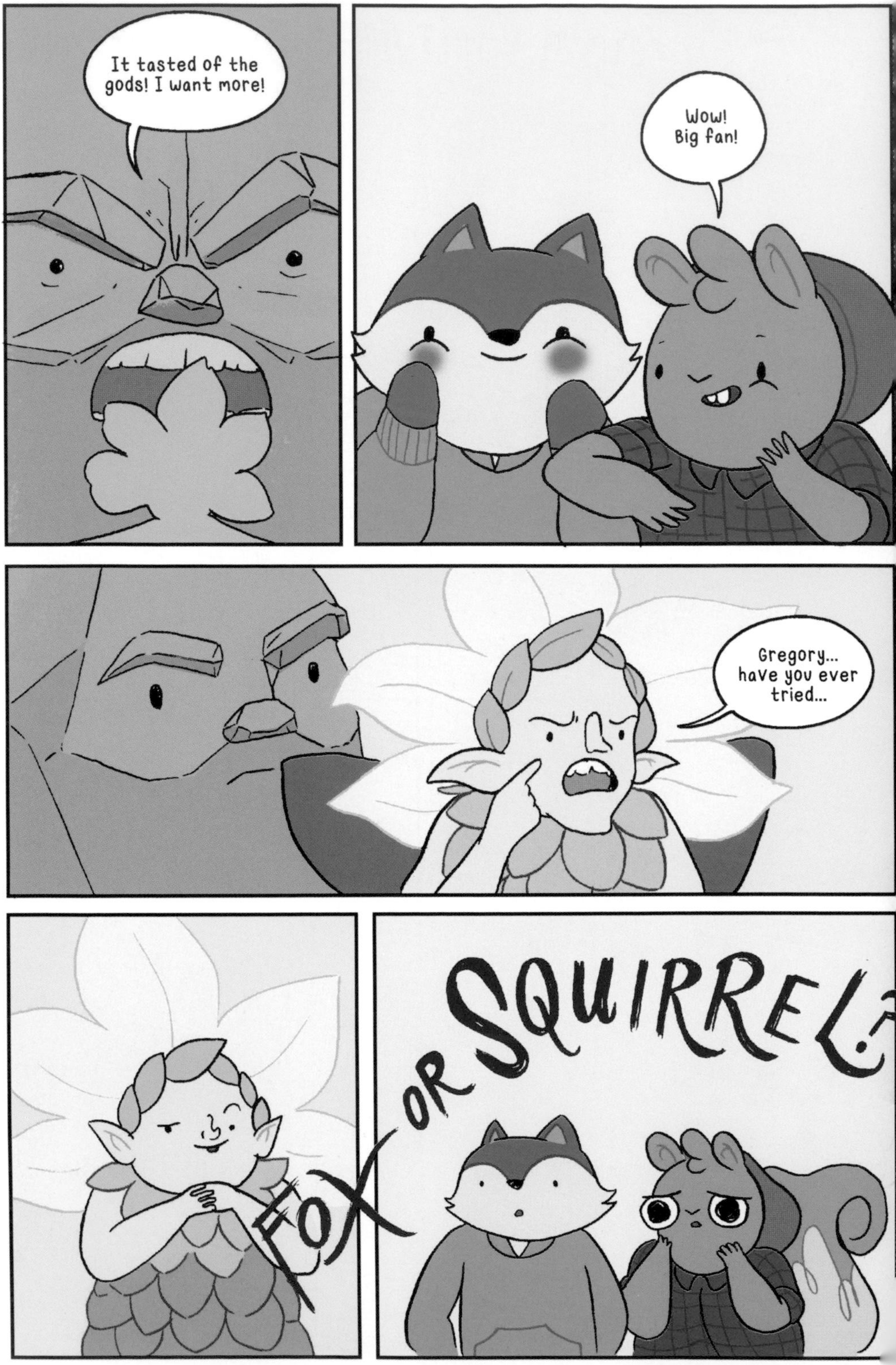
It tasted of the gods! I want more!
Wow! Big fan!
Gregory... have you ever tried...
FOX OR SQUIRREL?

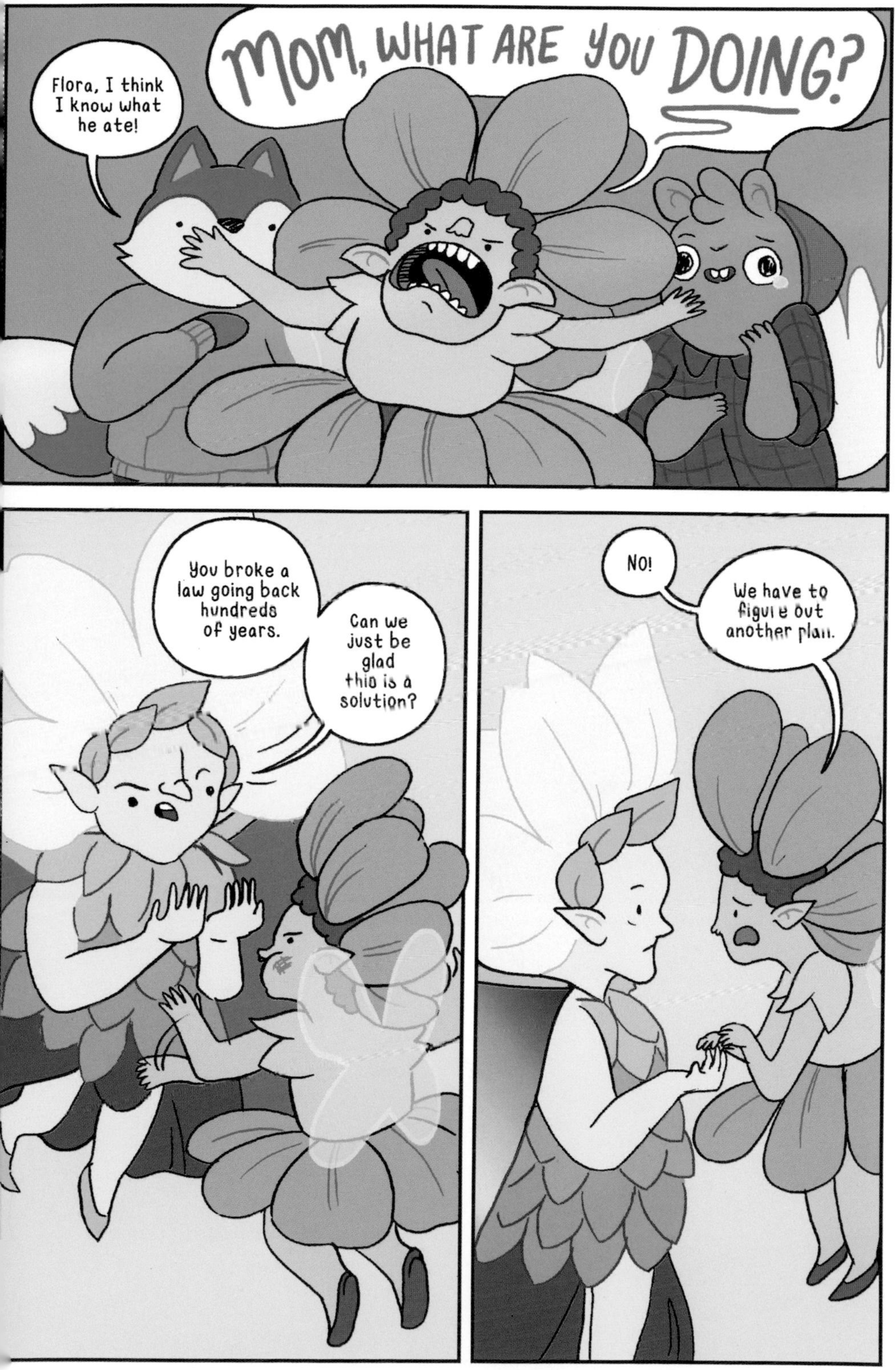
Flora, I think I know what he ate!
MOM, WHAT ARE YOU DOING?
You broke a law going back hundreds of years.
Can we just be glad this is a solution?
NO!
We have to figure out another plan.

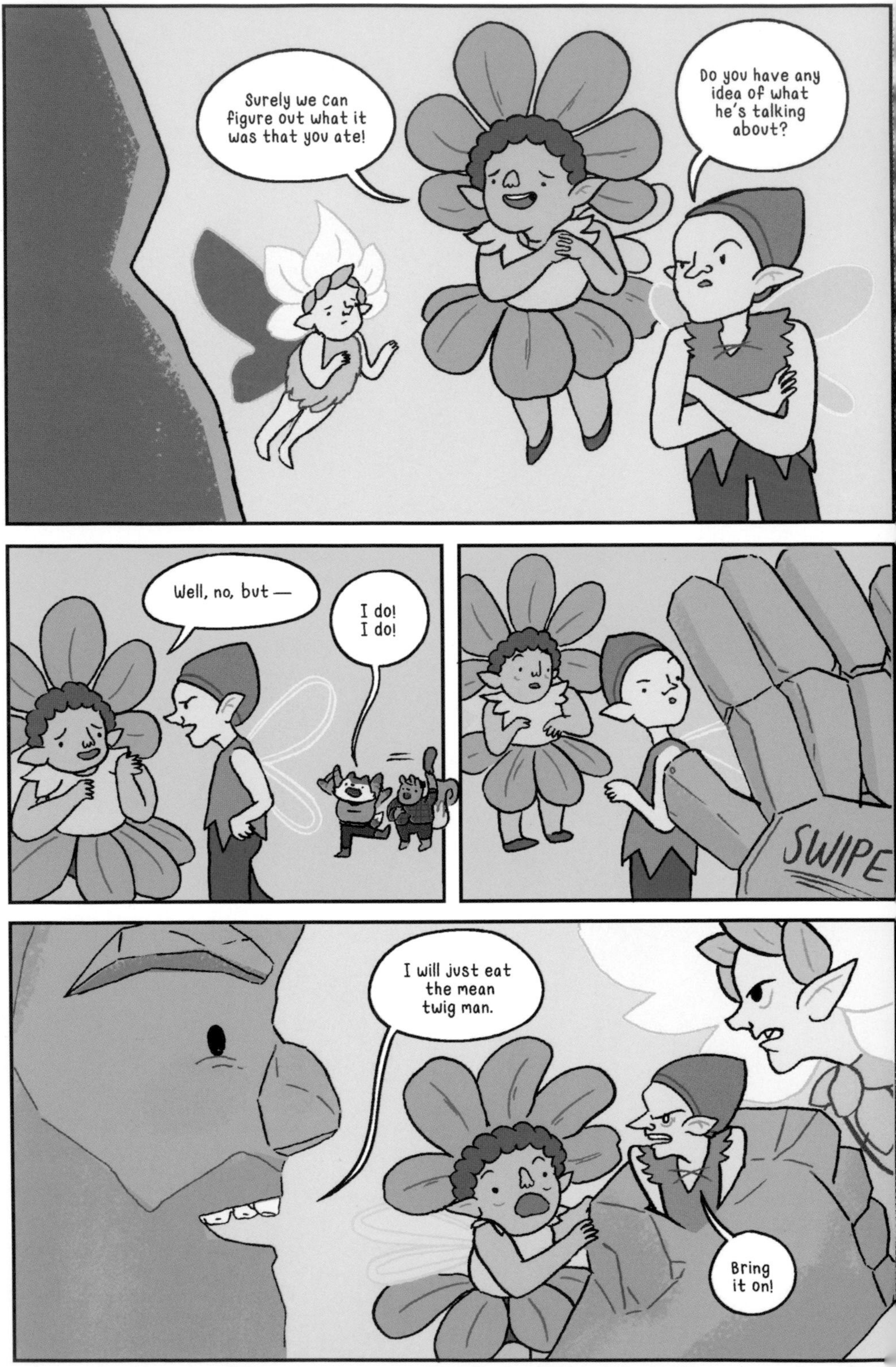
Surely we can figure out what it was that you ate!
Do you have any idea of what he's talking about?
Well, no, but —
I do! I do!
SWIPE
I will just eat the mean twig man.
Bring it on!

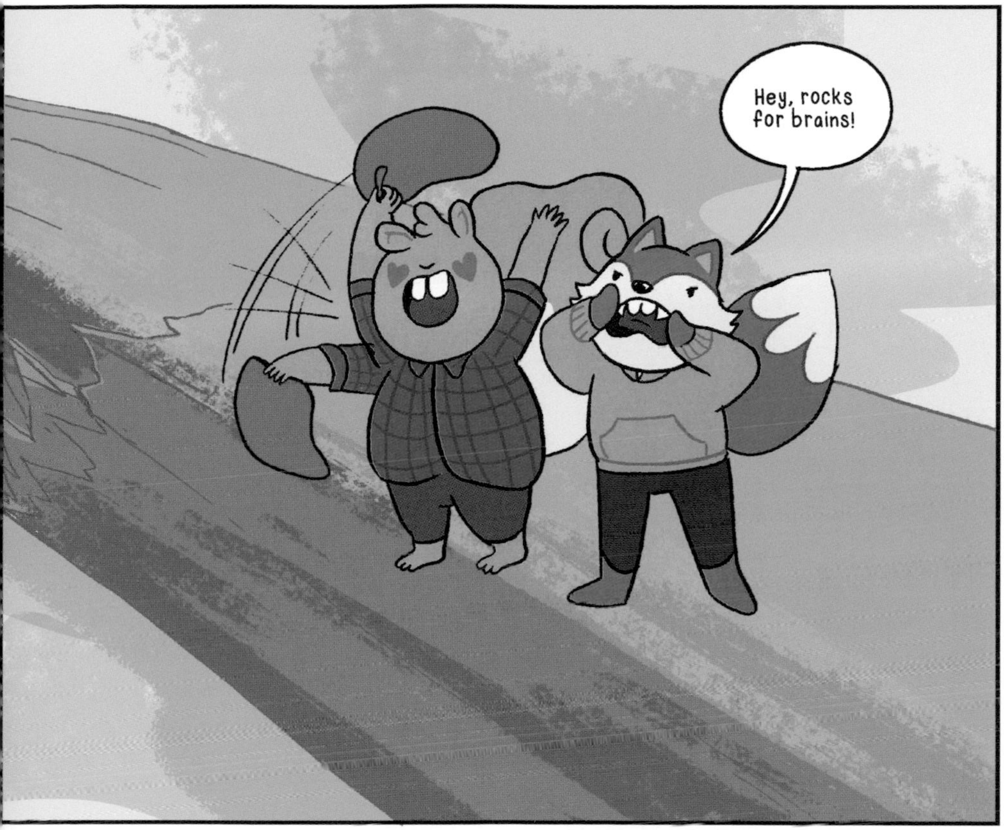

Hey, rocks for brains!

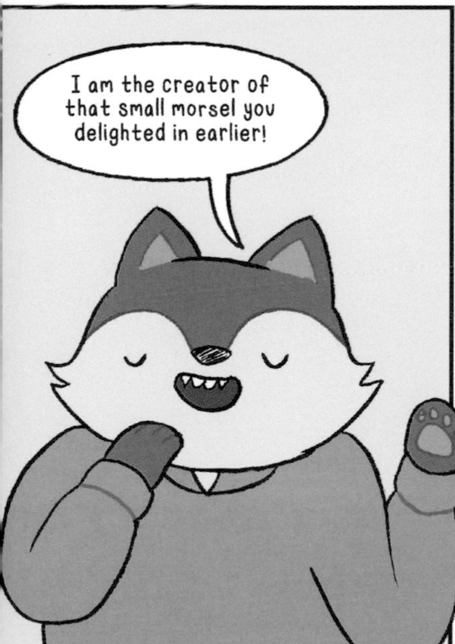

I am the creator of that small morsel you delighted in earlier!

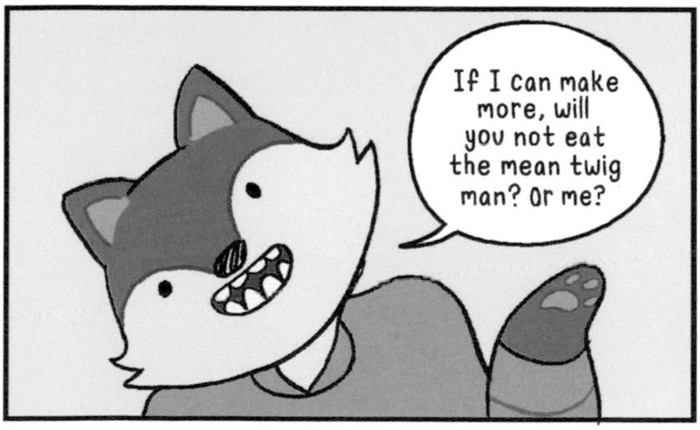

If I can make more, will you not eat the mean twig man? Or me?

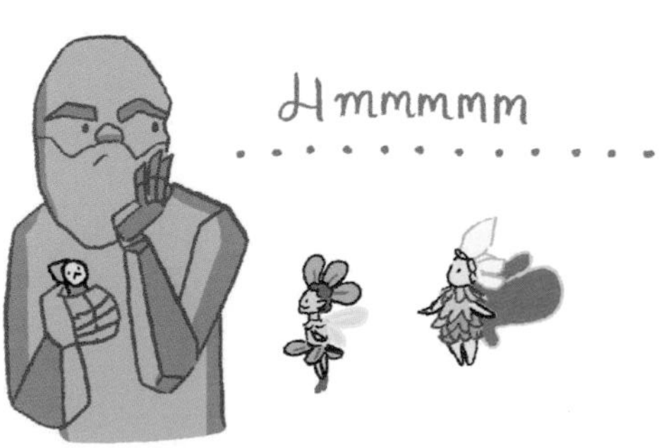

Hmmmmm

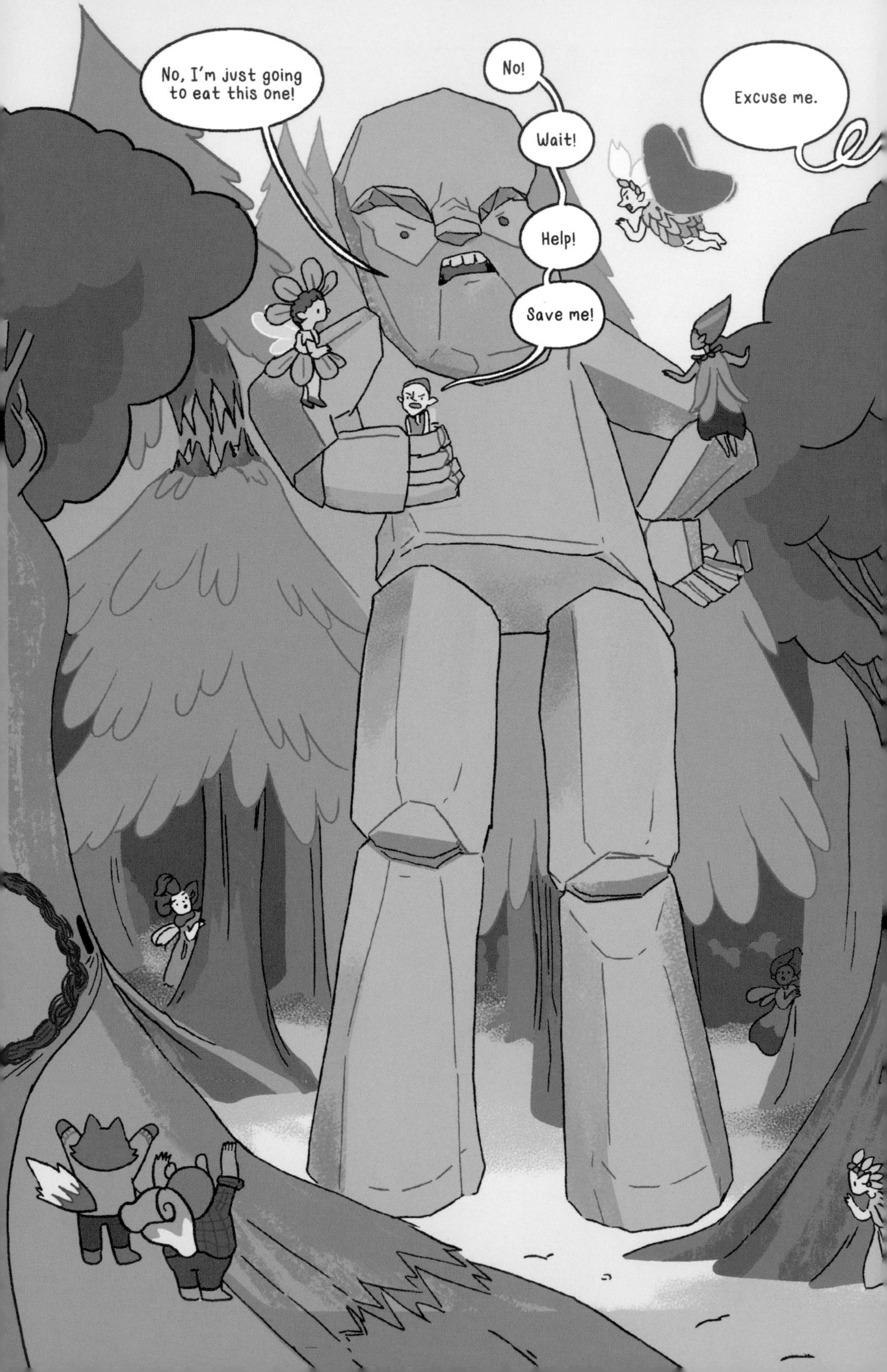
No, I'm just going to eat this one!
No!
Wait!
Help!
Save me!
Excuse me.

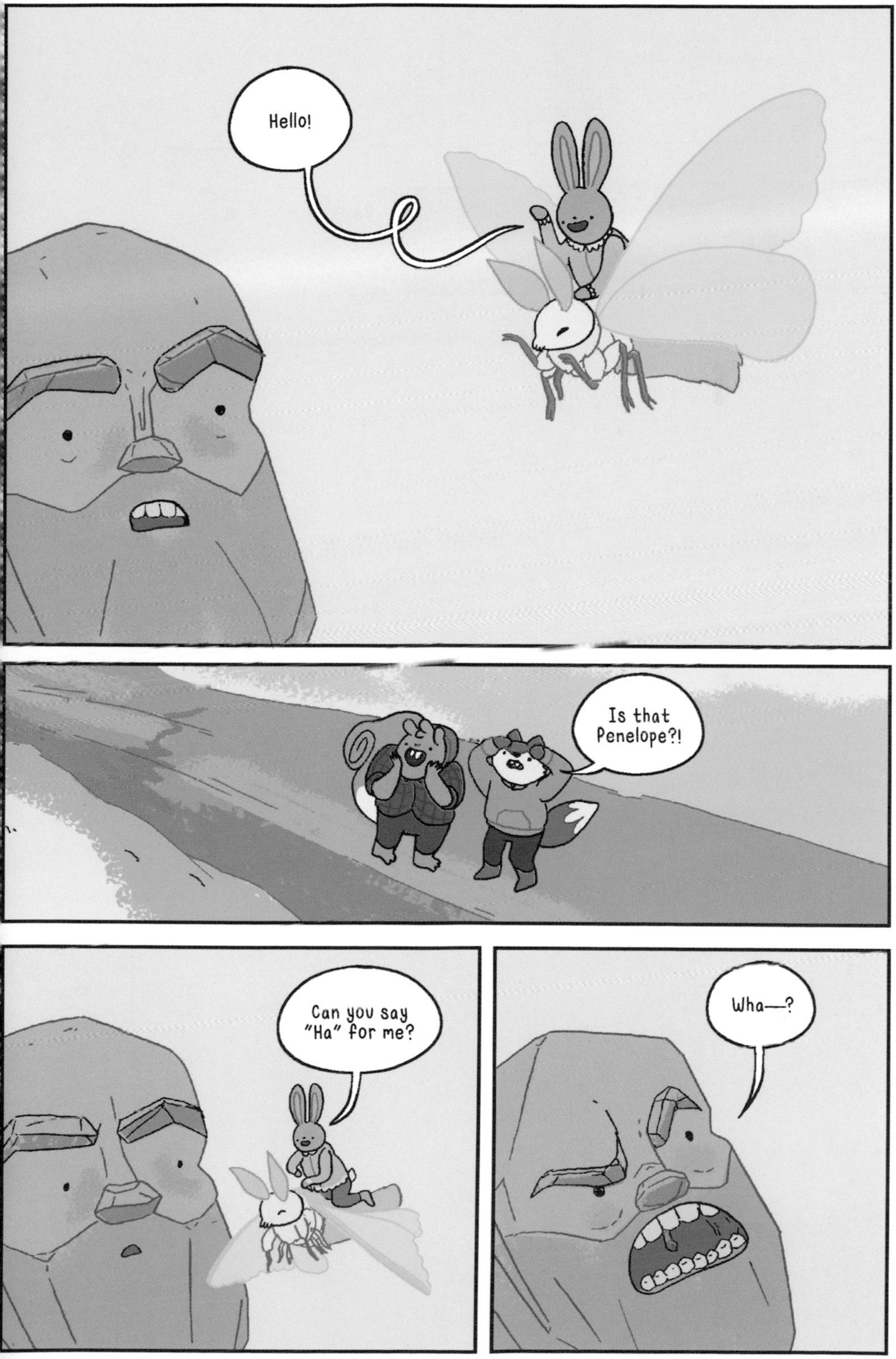
Hello!
Is that Penelope?!
Can you say "Ha" for me?
Wha—?

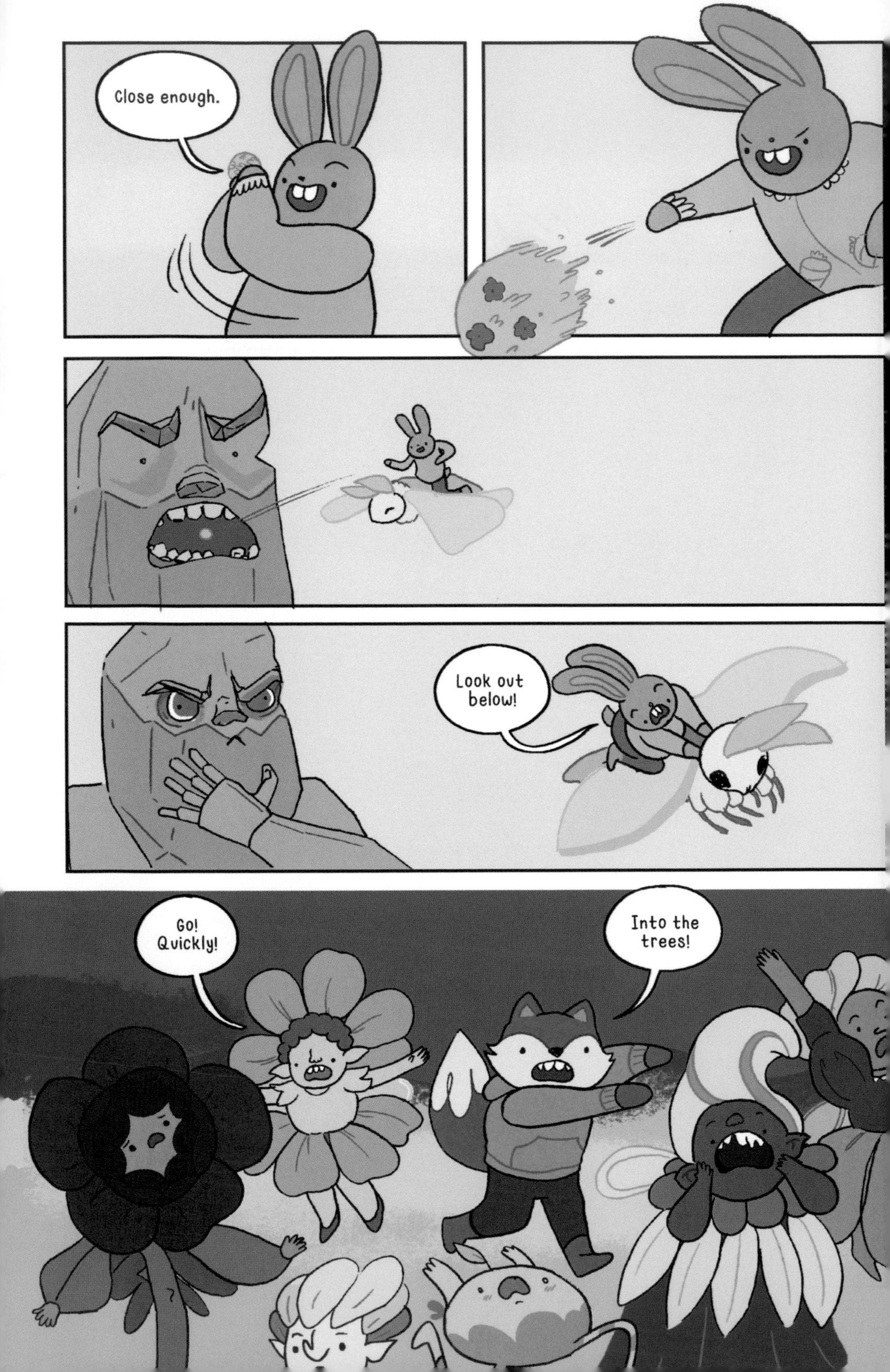
Close enough.
Look out below!
Go! Quickly!
Into the trees!

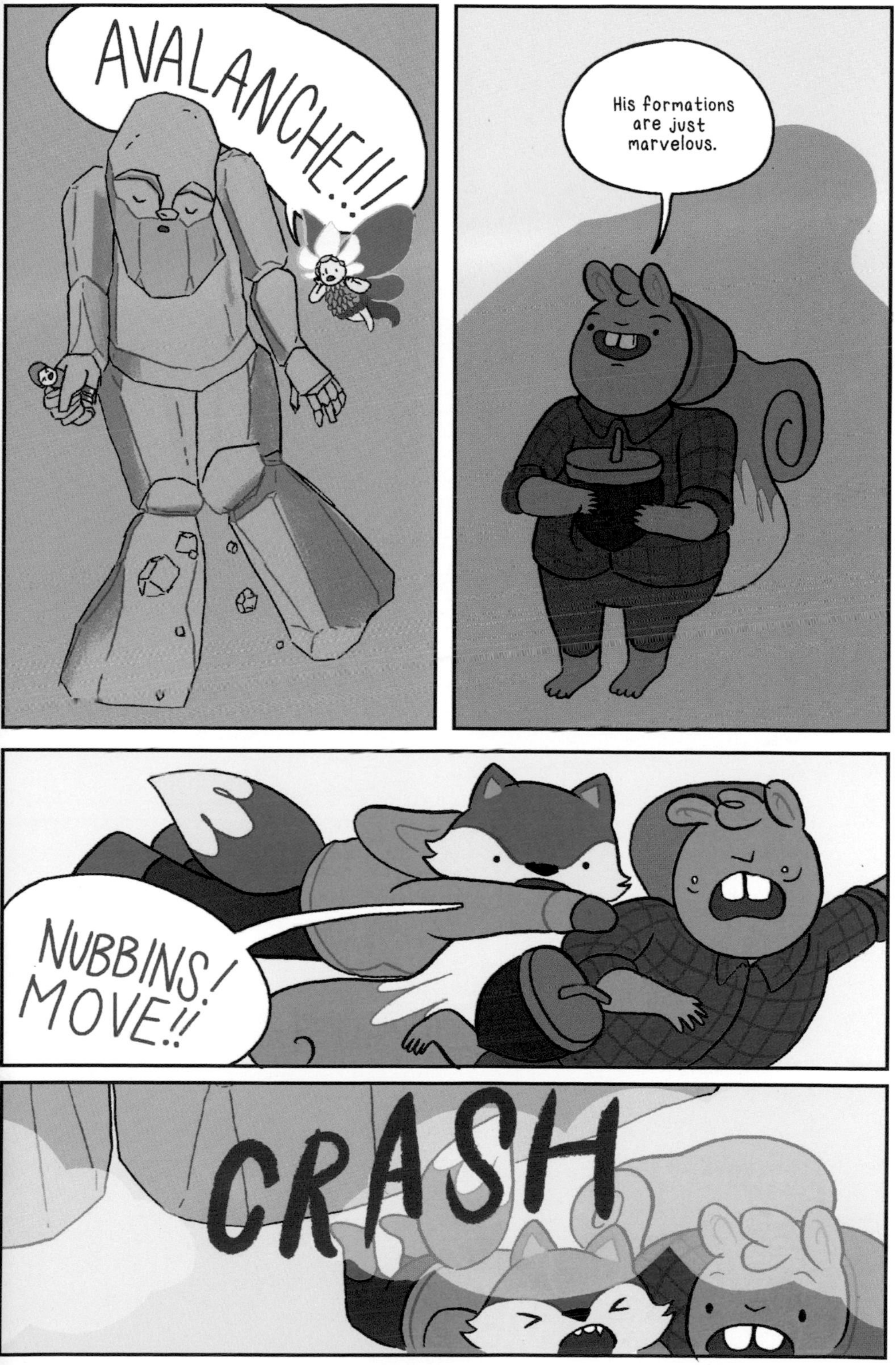
AVALANCHE!!!
His formations are just marvelous.
NUBBINS! MOVE!!
CRASH

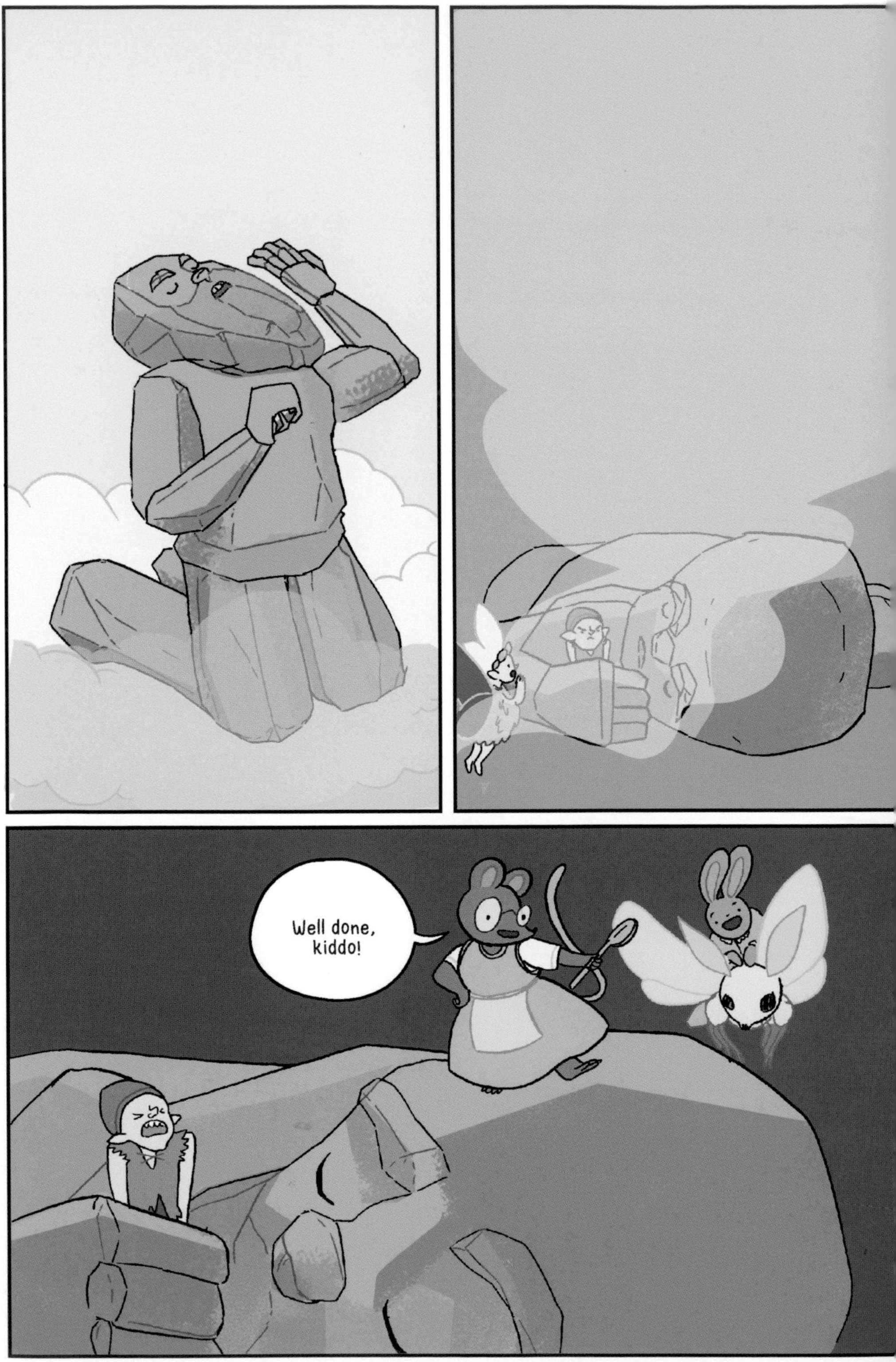
Well done, kiddo!

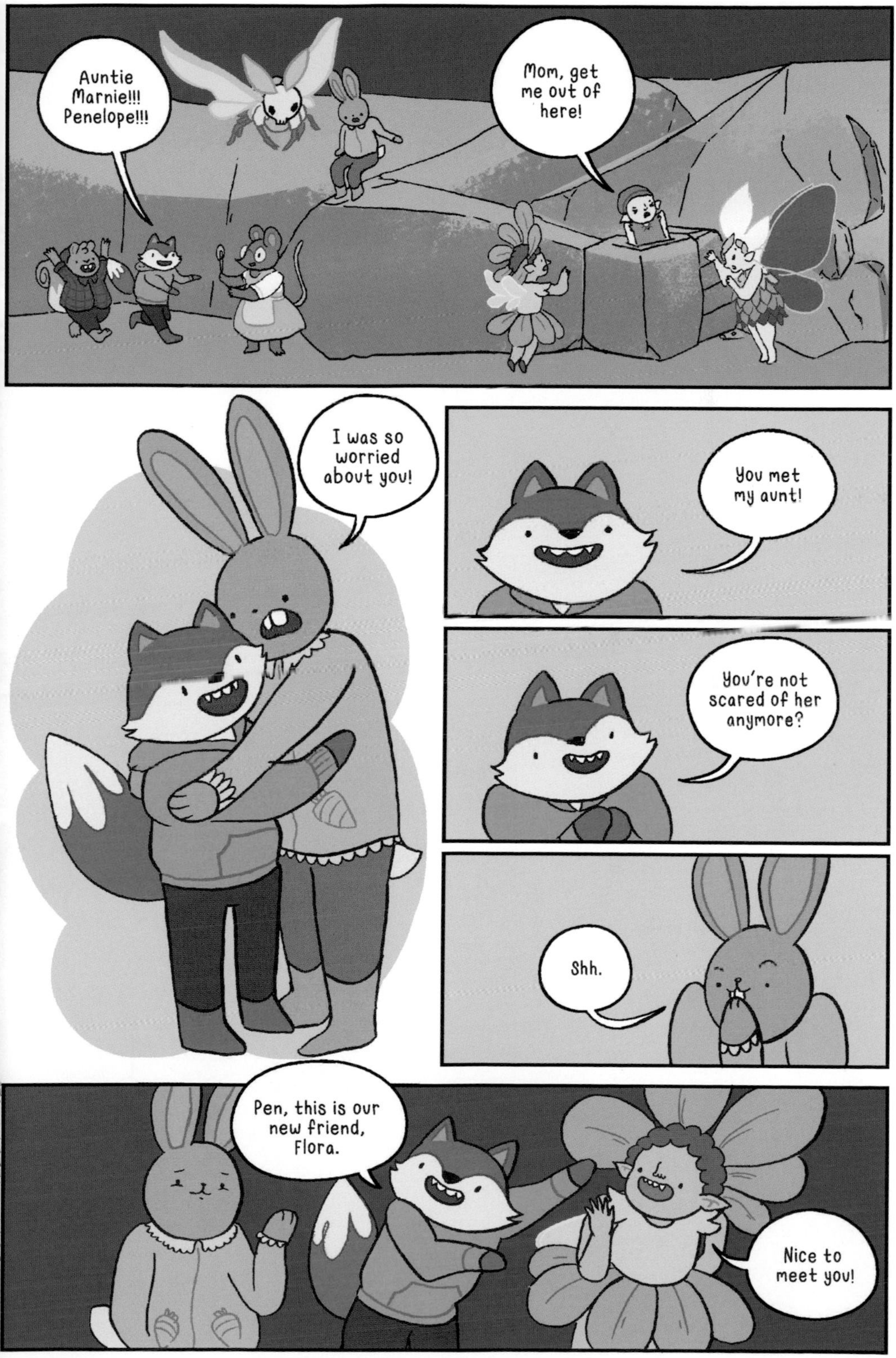

Auntie Marnie!!! Penelope!!!
Mom, get me out of here!
I was so worried about you!
You met my aunt!
You're not scared of her anymore?
Shh.
Pen, this is our new friend, Flora.
Nice to meet you!

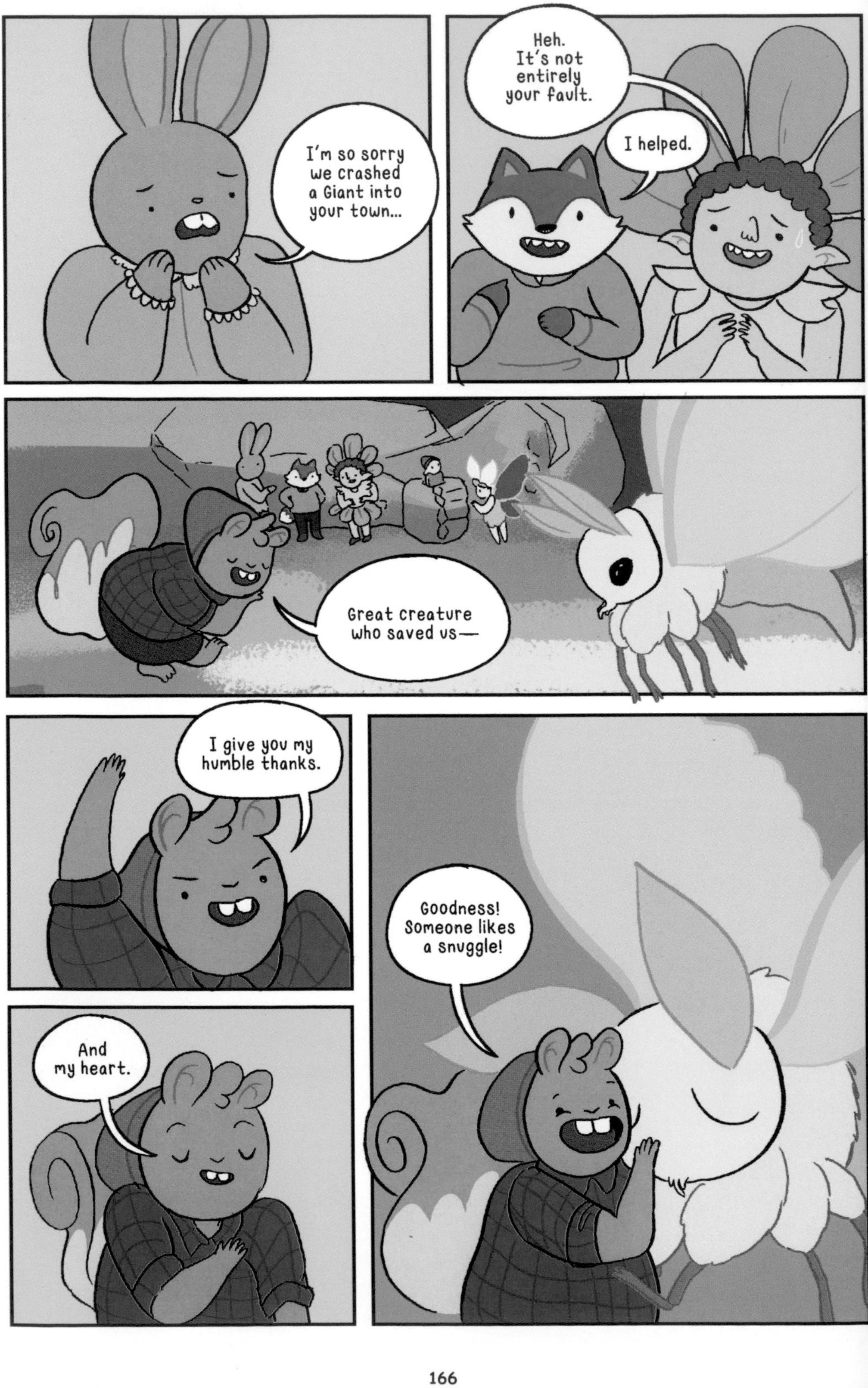
I'm so sorry we crashed a Giant into your town...
Heh. It's not entirely your fault.
I helped.
Great creature who saved us—
I give you my humble thanks.
And my heart.
Goodness! Someone likes a snuggle!

Aww. New friends!

We'll figure out how to get you out of there, Puck.

Would anyone like some tea?

Tea, Marnie? Now?!

It'll help settle everyone down.

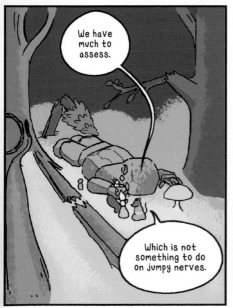

We have much to assess.

Which is not something to do on jumpy nerves.

For example, Lily, your attempt to sacrifice my niece.

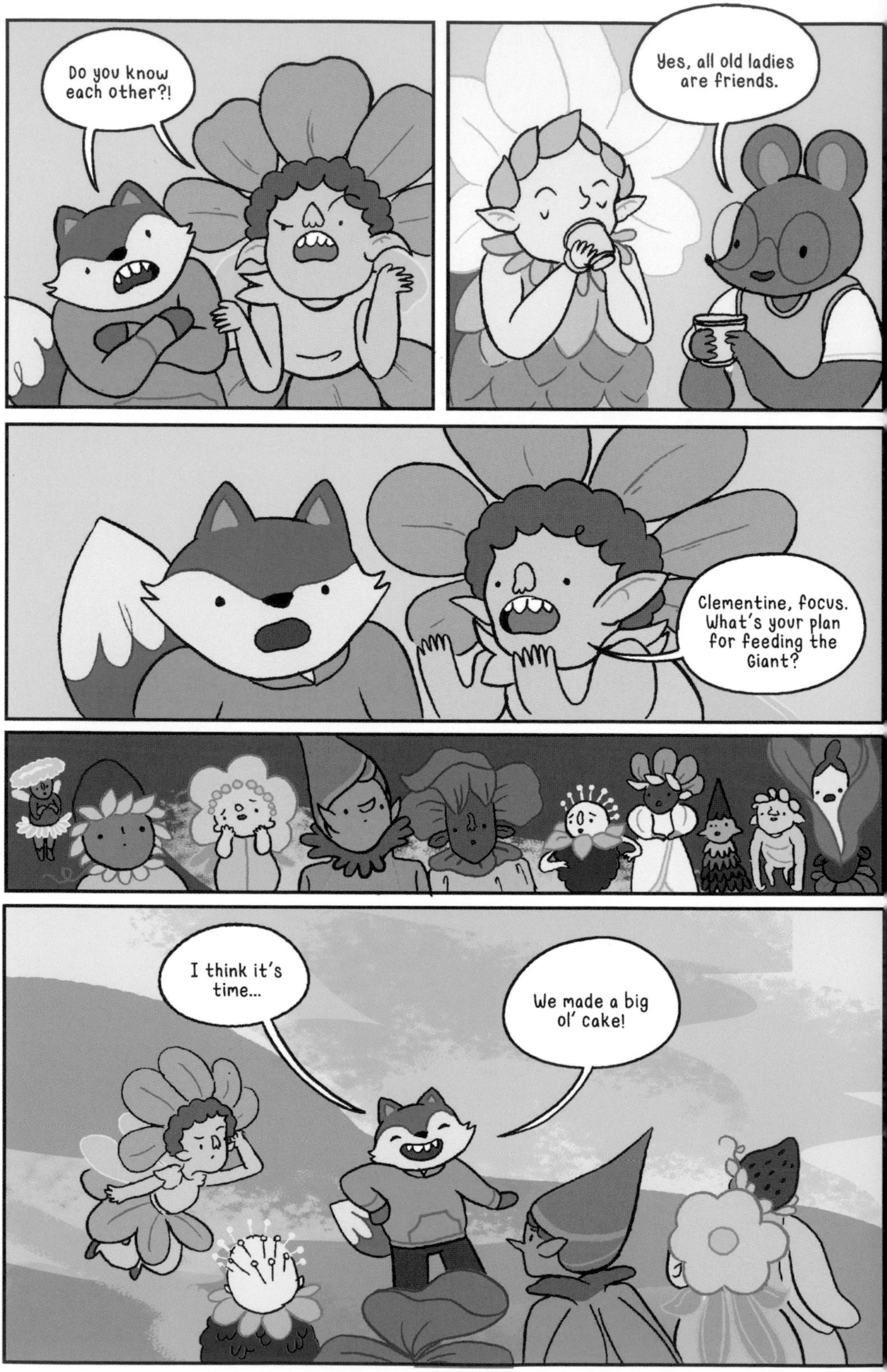
Do you know each other?!
Yes, all old ladies are friends.
Clementine, focus. What's your plan for feeding the Giant?
I think it's time...
We made a big ol' cake!

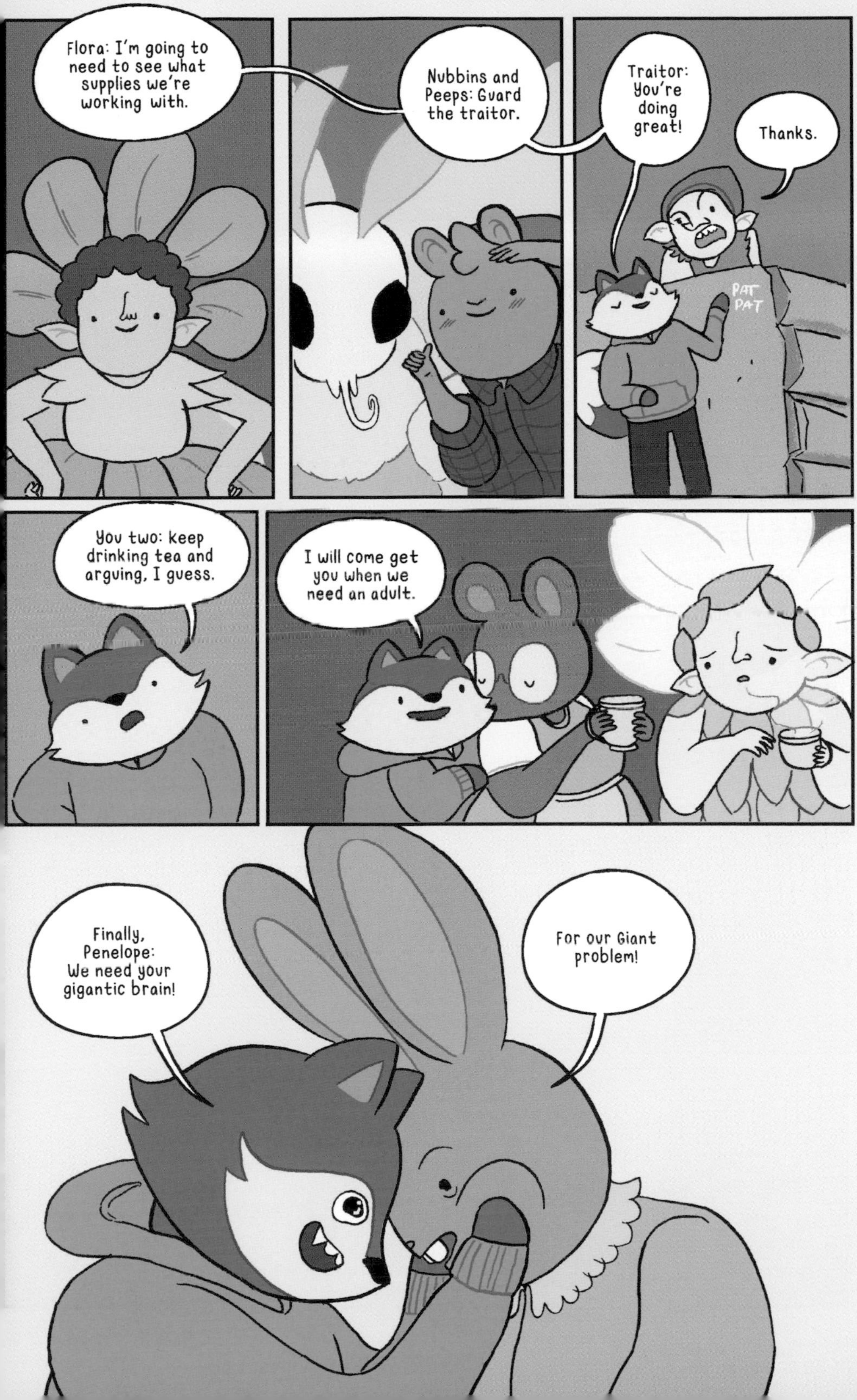
Flora: I'm going to need to see what supplies we're working with.
Nubbins and Peeps: Guard the traitor.
Traitor: You're doing great!
Thanks.
PAT PAT
You two: keep drinking tea and arguing, I guess.
I will come get you when we need an adult.
Finally, Penelope: We need your gigantic brain!
For our Giant problem!

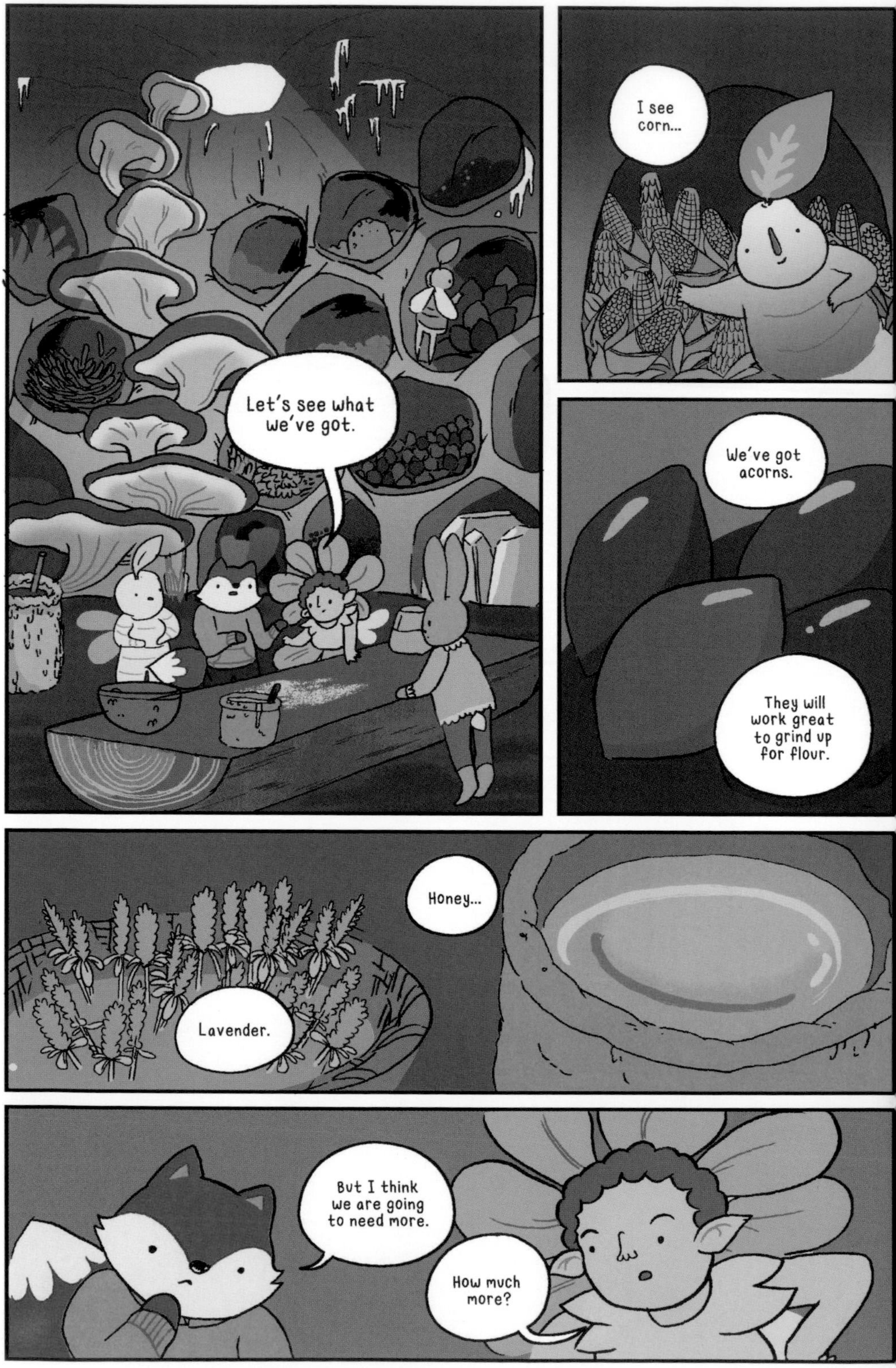
Let's see what we've got.
I see corn...
We've got acorns.
They will work great to grind up for flour.
Honey...
Lavender.
But I think we are going to need more.
How much more?

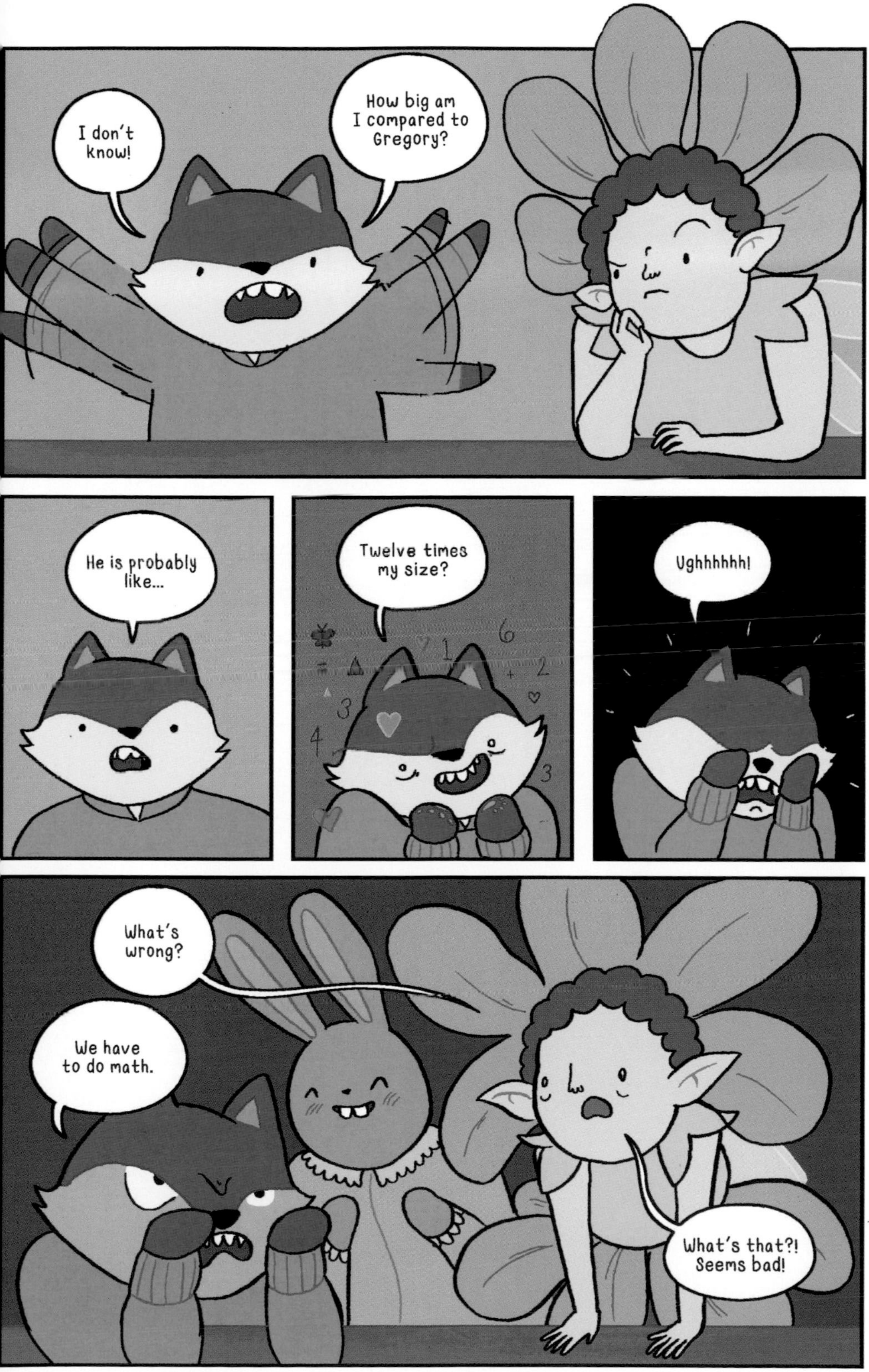
I don't know!
How big am I compared to Gregory?
He is probably like...
Twelve times my size?
Ughhhhhh!
What's wrong?
We have to do math.
What's that?! Seems bad!

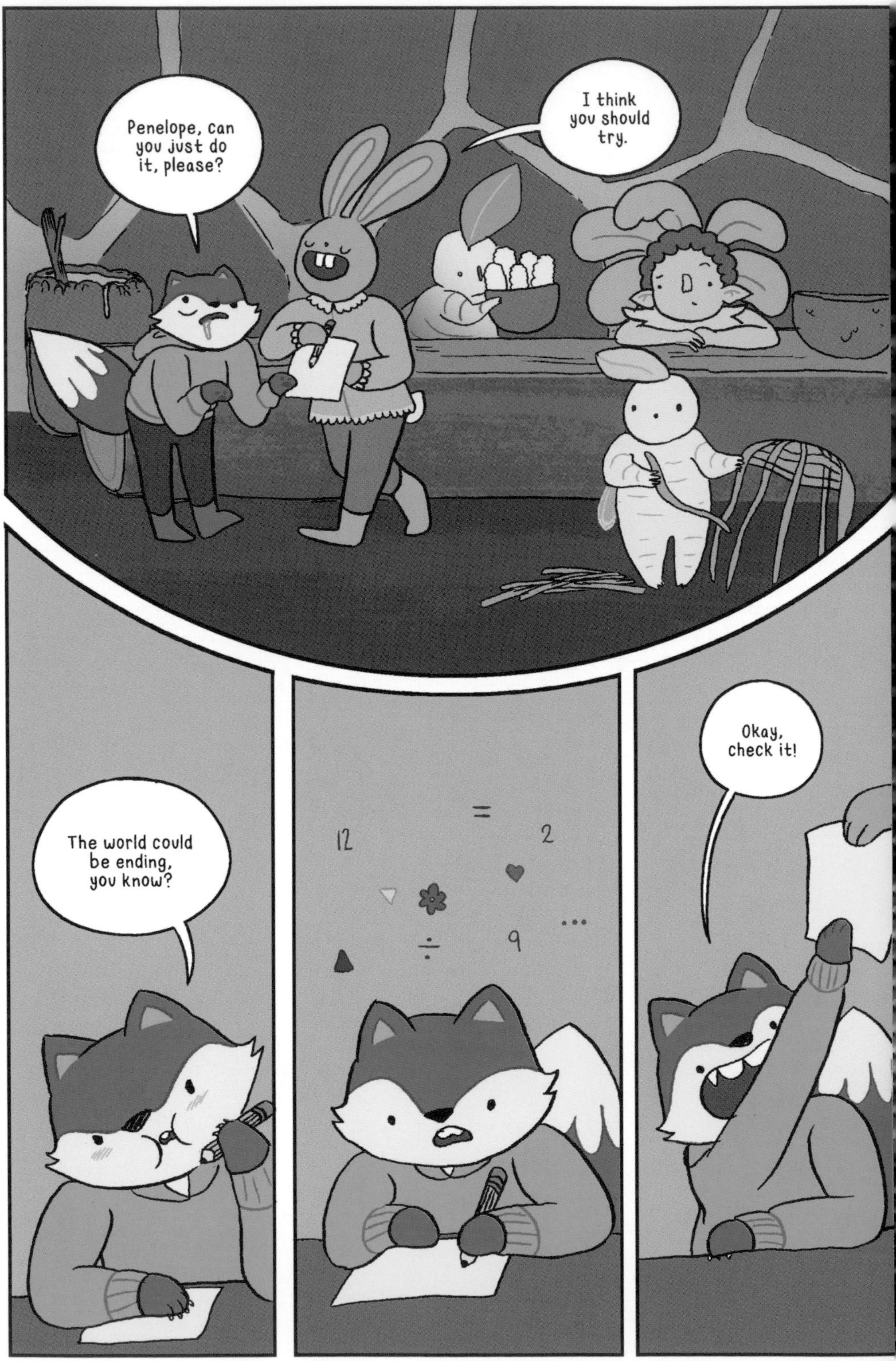
Penelope, can you just do it, please?
I think you should try.
The world could be ending, you know?
12 = 2
÷ 9
Okay, check it!

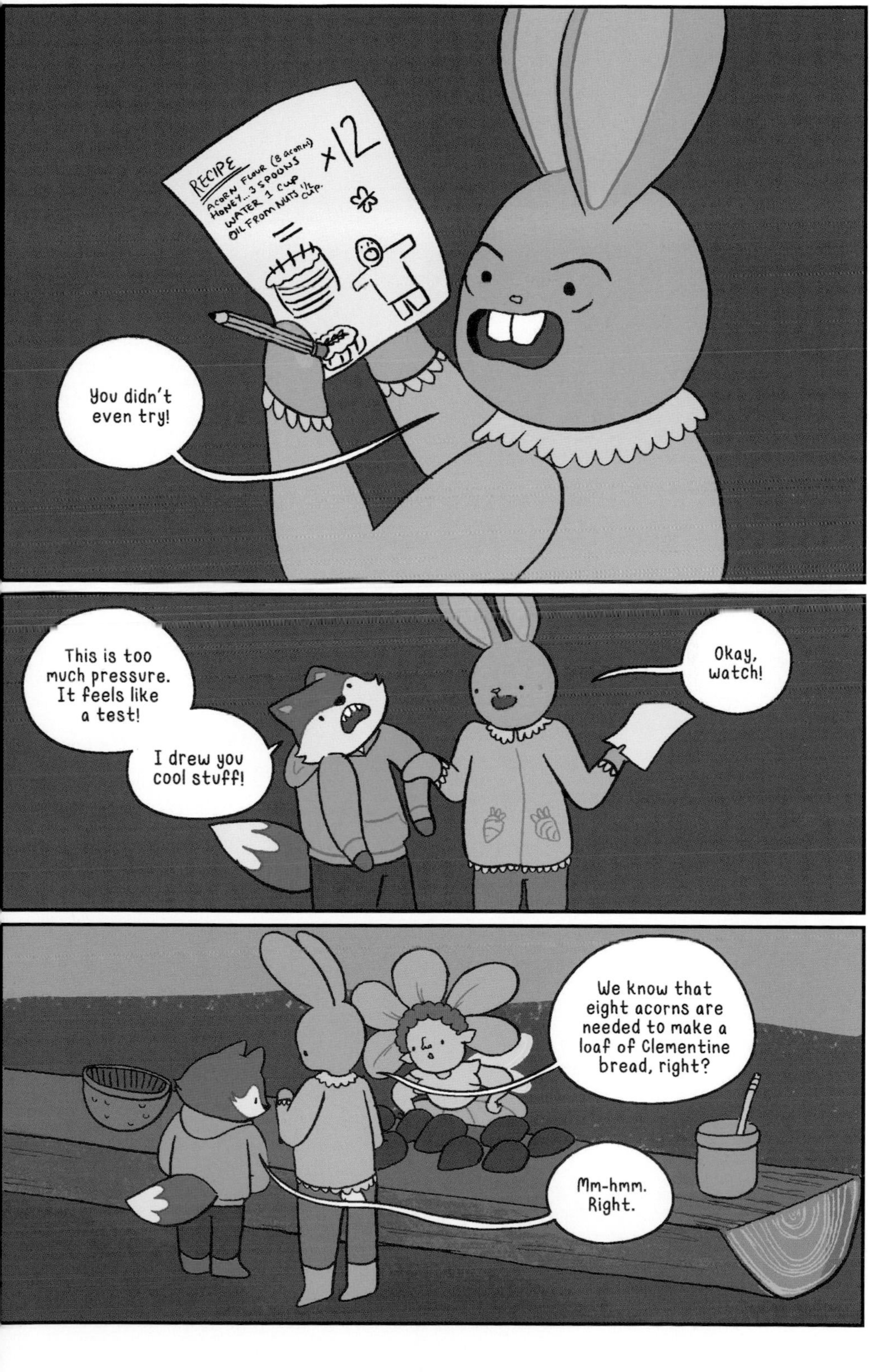
RECIPE
ACORN FLOUR (8 acorns)
HONEY...3 SPOONS
WATER 1 CUP
OIL FROM NUTS 1/2 CUP.
x12
You didn't even try!
This is too much pressure. It feels like a test!
I drew you cool stuff!
Okay, watch!
We know that eight acorns are needed to make a loaf of Clementine bread, right?
Mm-hmm. Right.

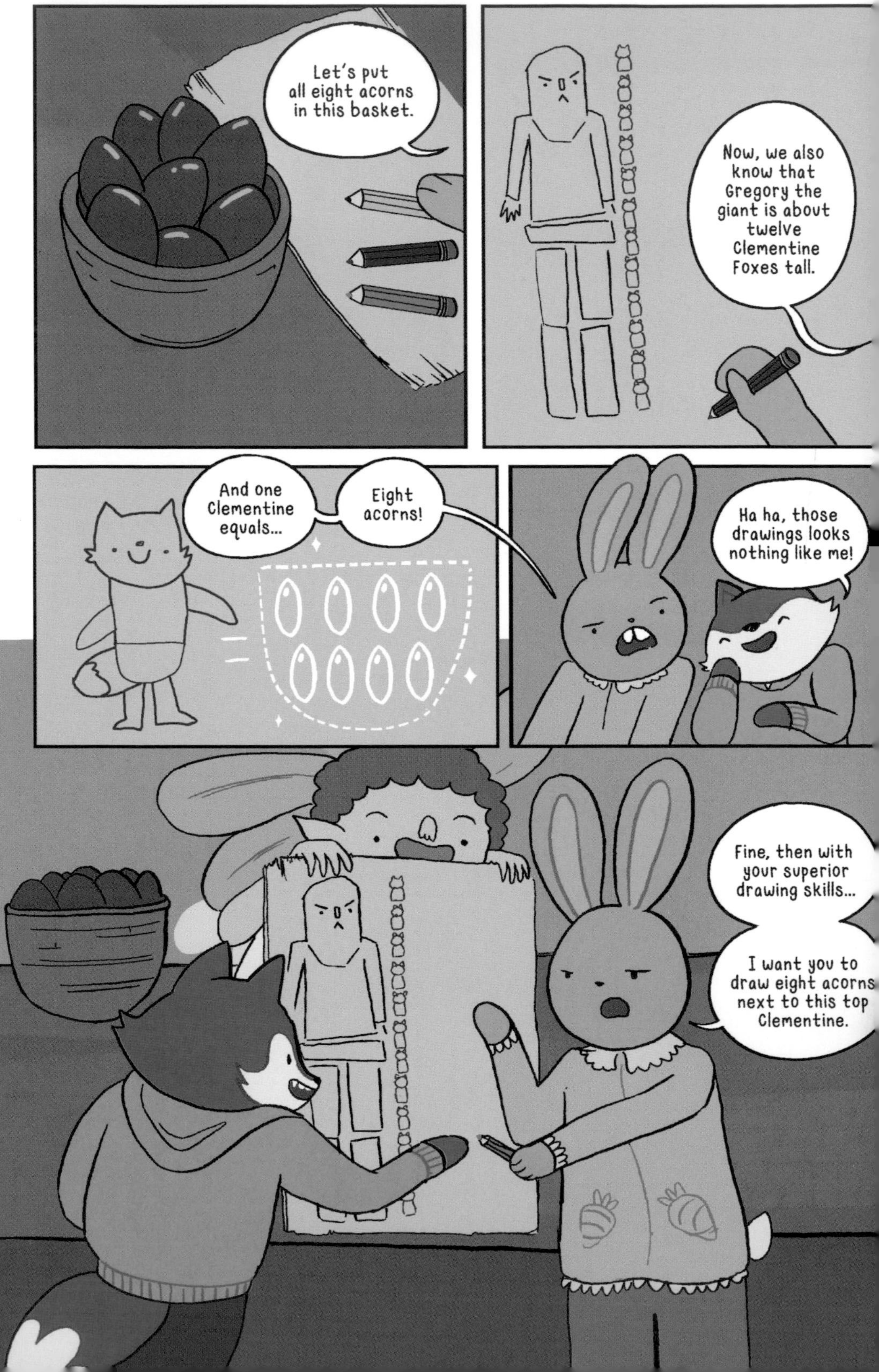
Let's put all eight acorns in this basket.
Now, we also know that Gregory the giant is about twelve Clementine Foxes tall.
And one Clementine equals...
Eight acorns!
Ha ha, those drawings looks nothing like me!
Fine, then with your superior drawing skills...
I want you to draw eight acorns next to this top Clementine.

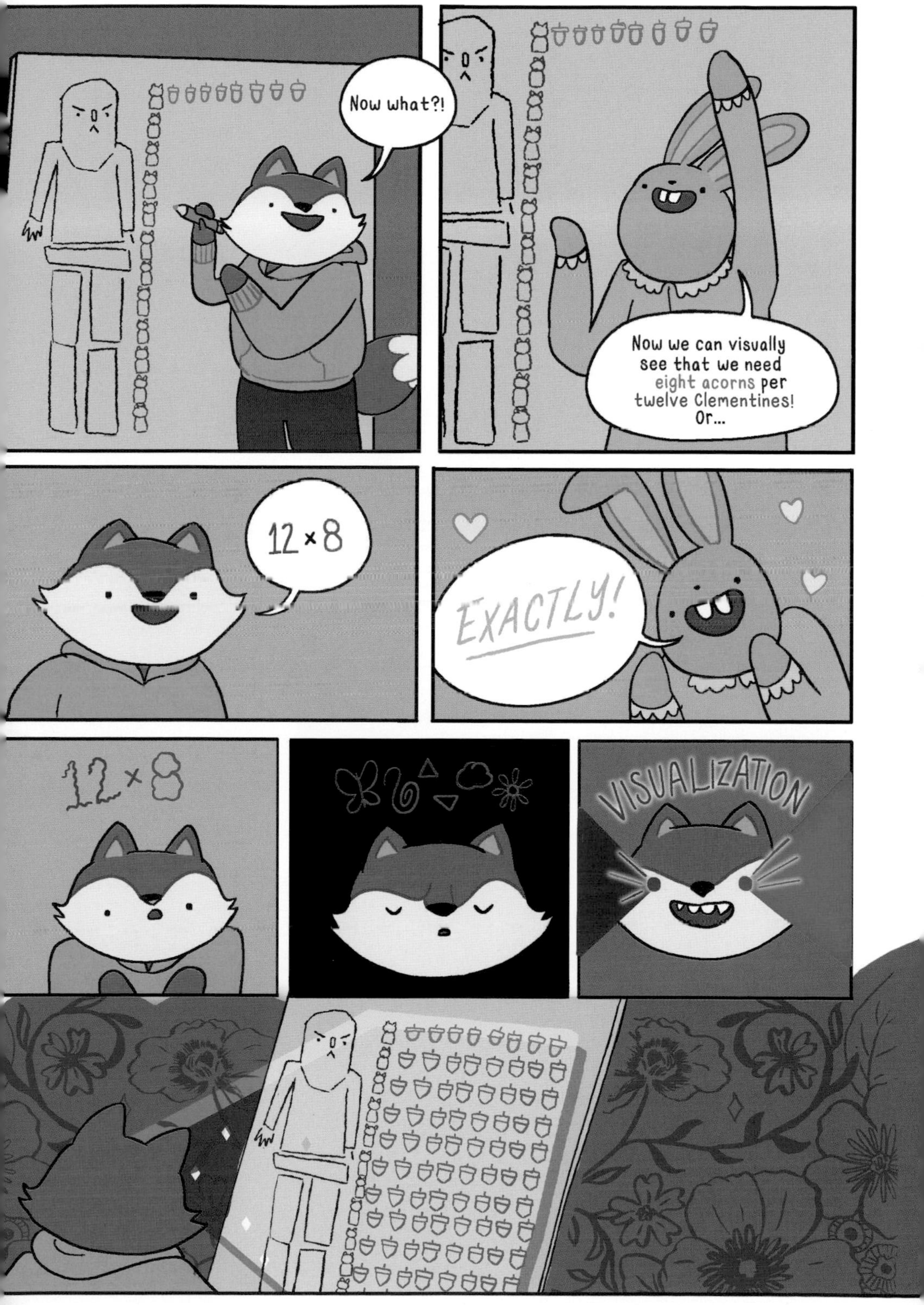
Now what?!
Now we can visually see that we need eight acorns per twelve Clementines! Or...
12 × 8
EXACTLY!
12 × 8
VISUALIZATION

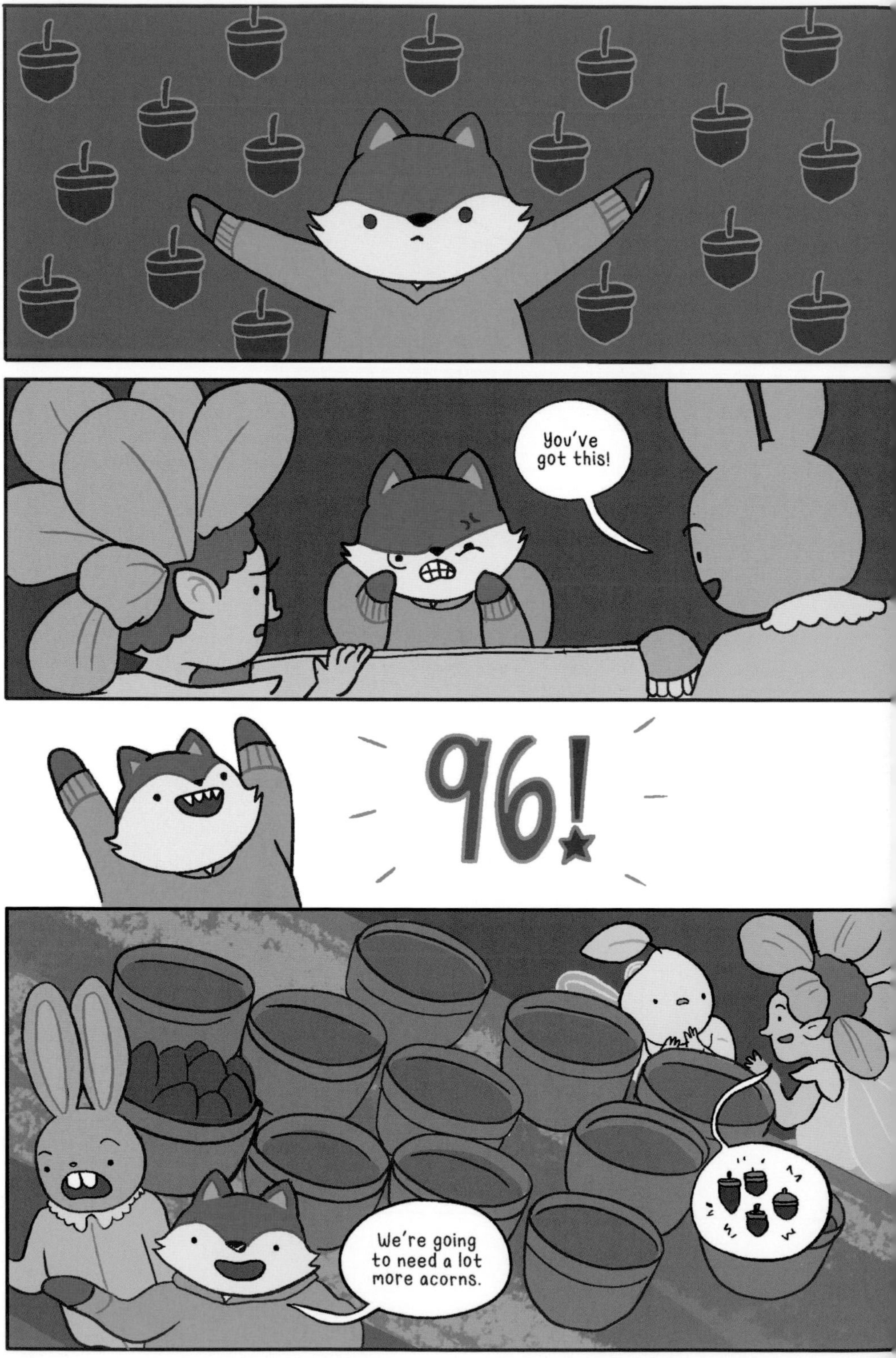
You've got this!
96!
We're going to need a lot more acorns.

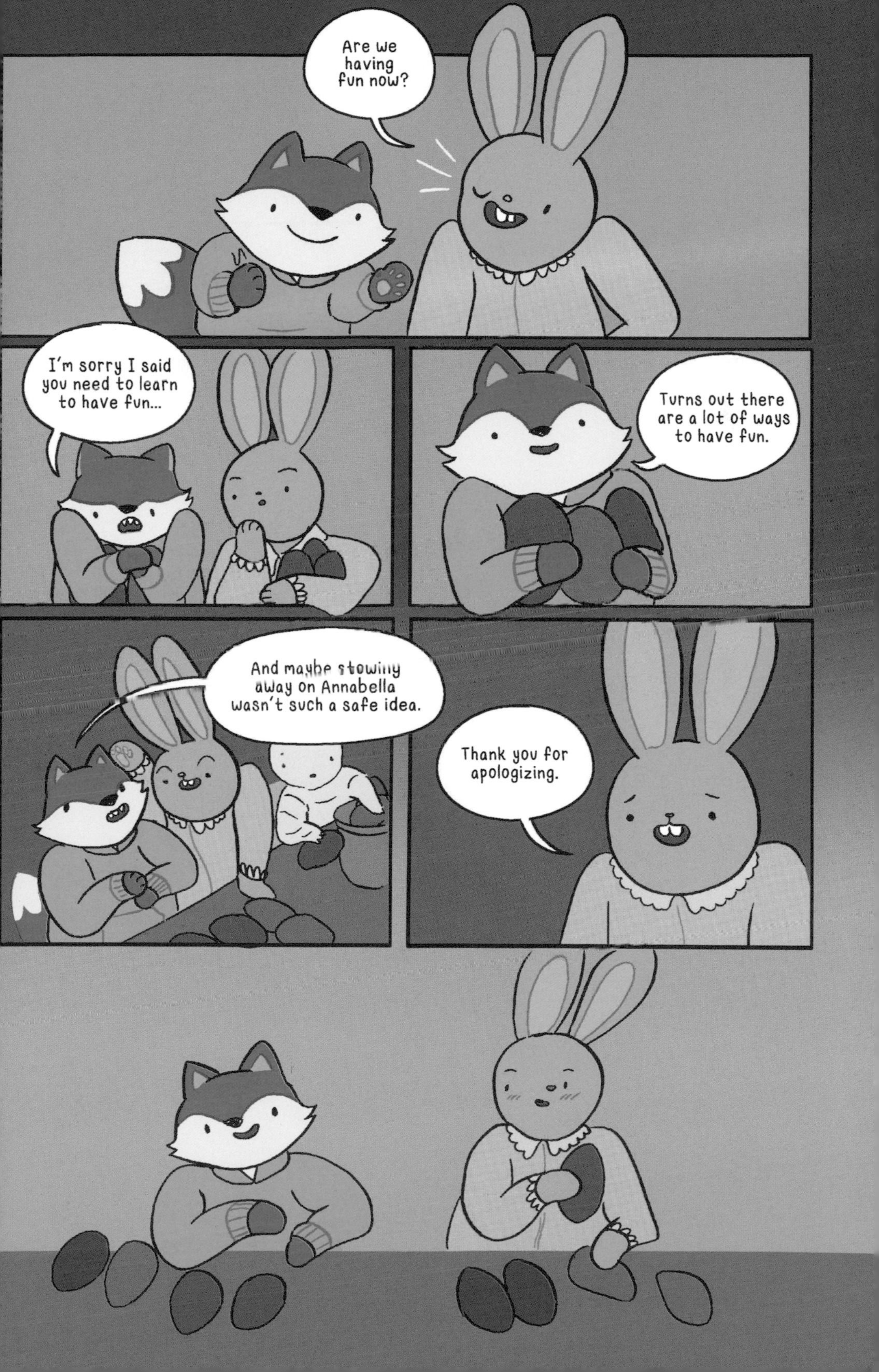

Are we having fun now?
I'm sorry I said you need to learn to have fun...
Turns out there are a lot of ways to have fun.
And maybe stowing away on Annabella wasn't such a safe idea.
Thank you for apologizing.

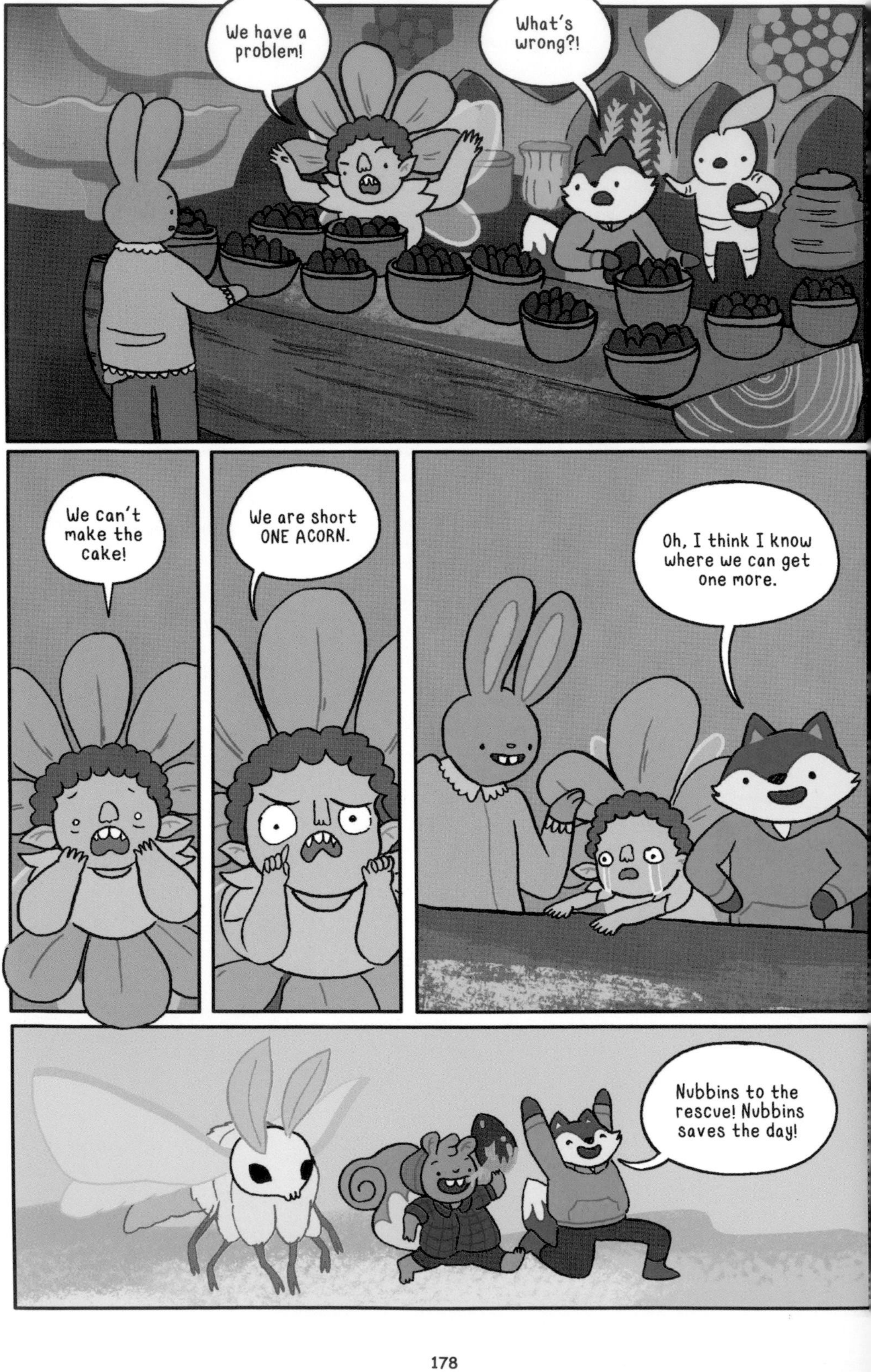
We have a problem!
What's wrong?!
We can't make the cake!
We are short ONE ACORN.
Oh, I think I know where we can get one more.
Nubbins to the rescue! Nubbins saves the day!

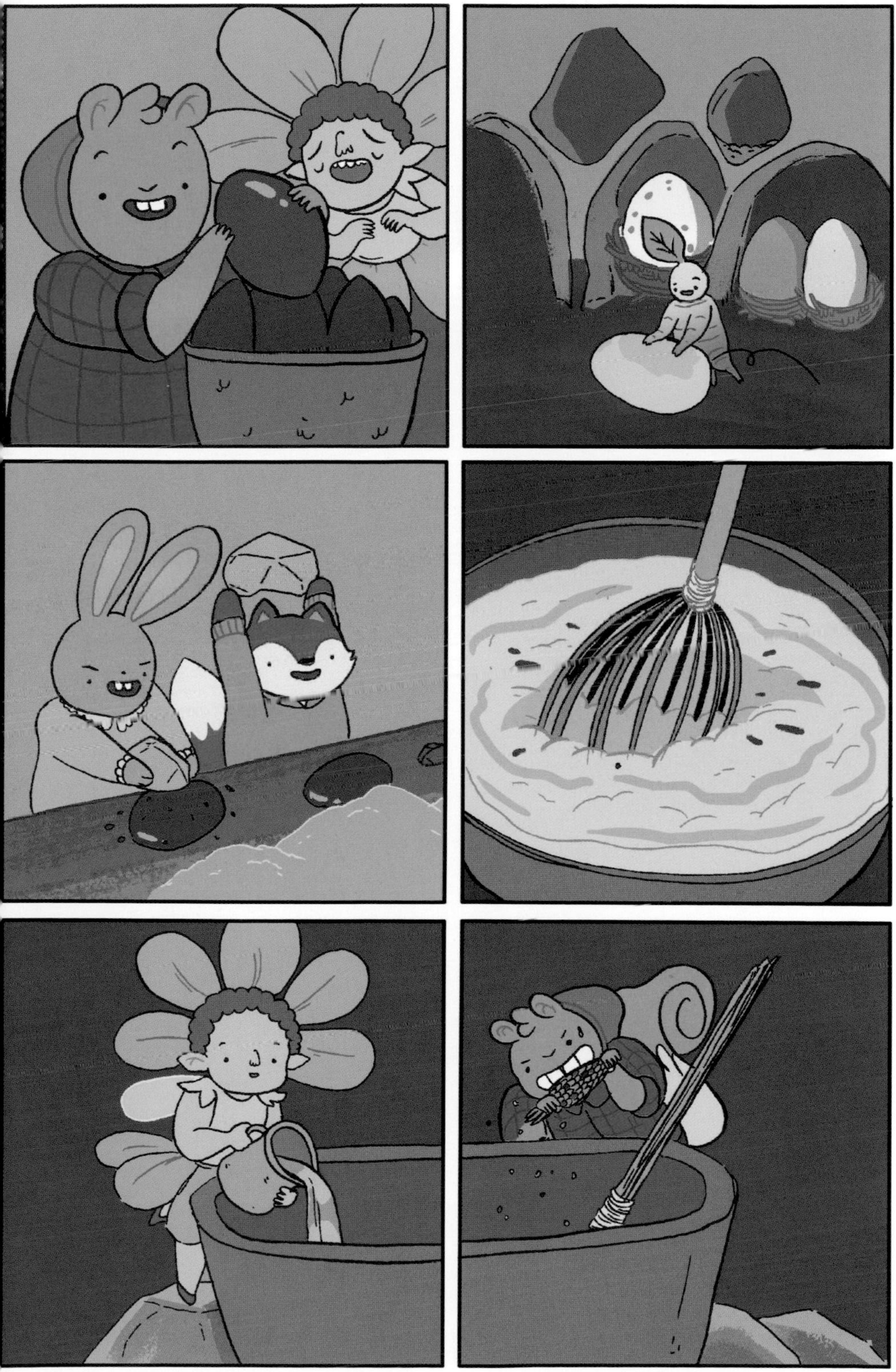

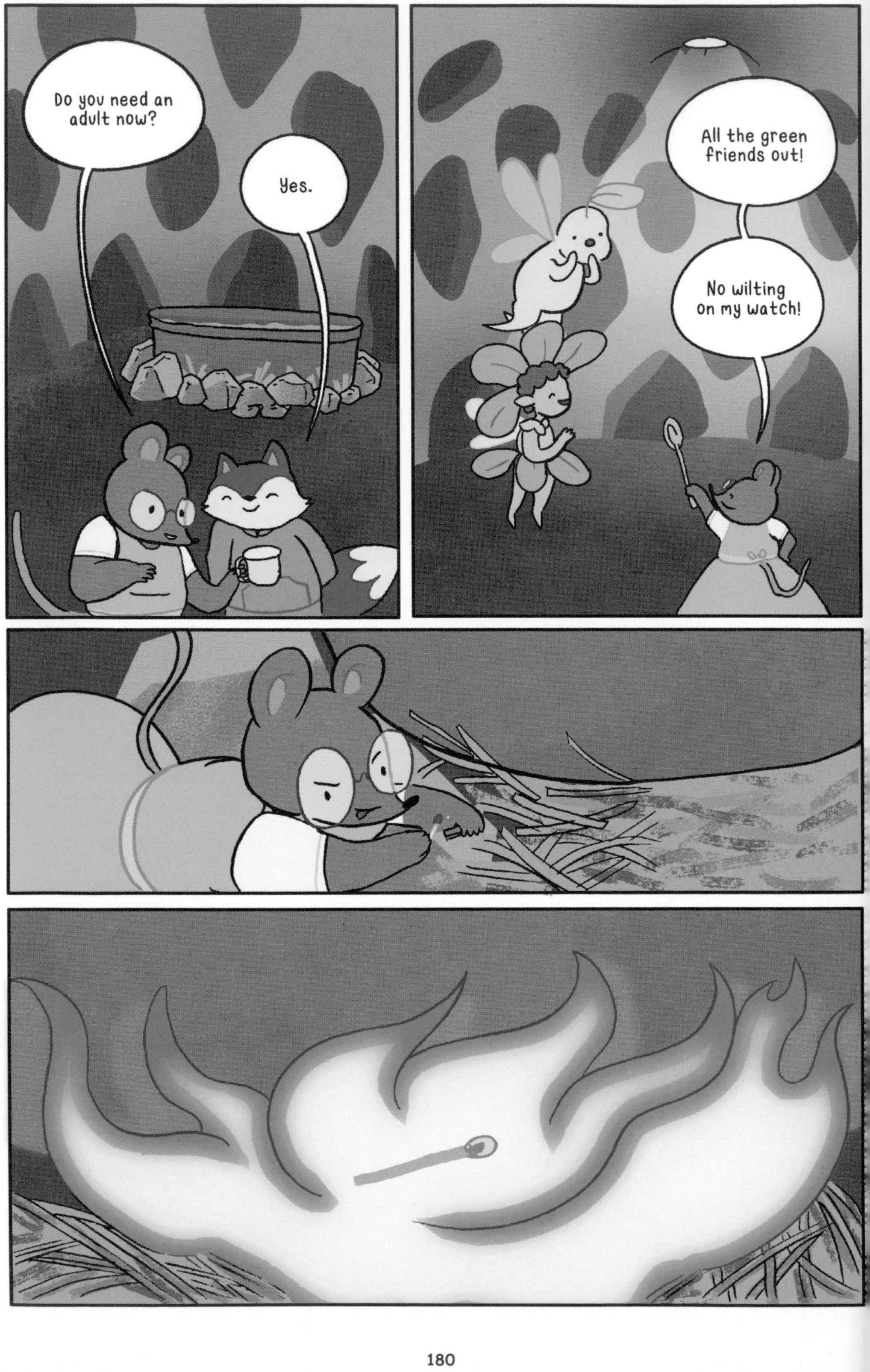
Do you need an adult now?
Yes.
All the green friends out!
No wilting on my watch!

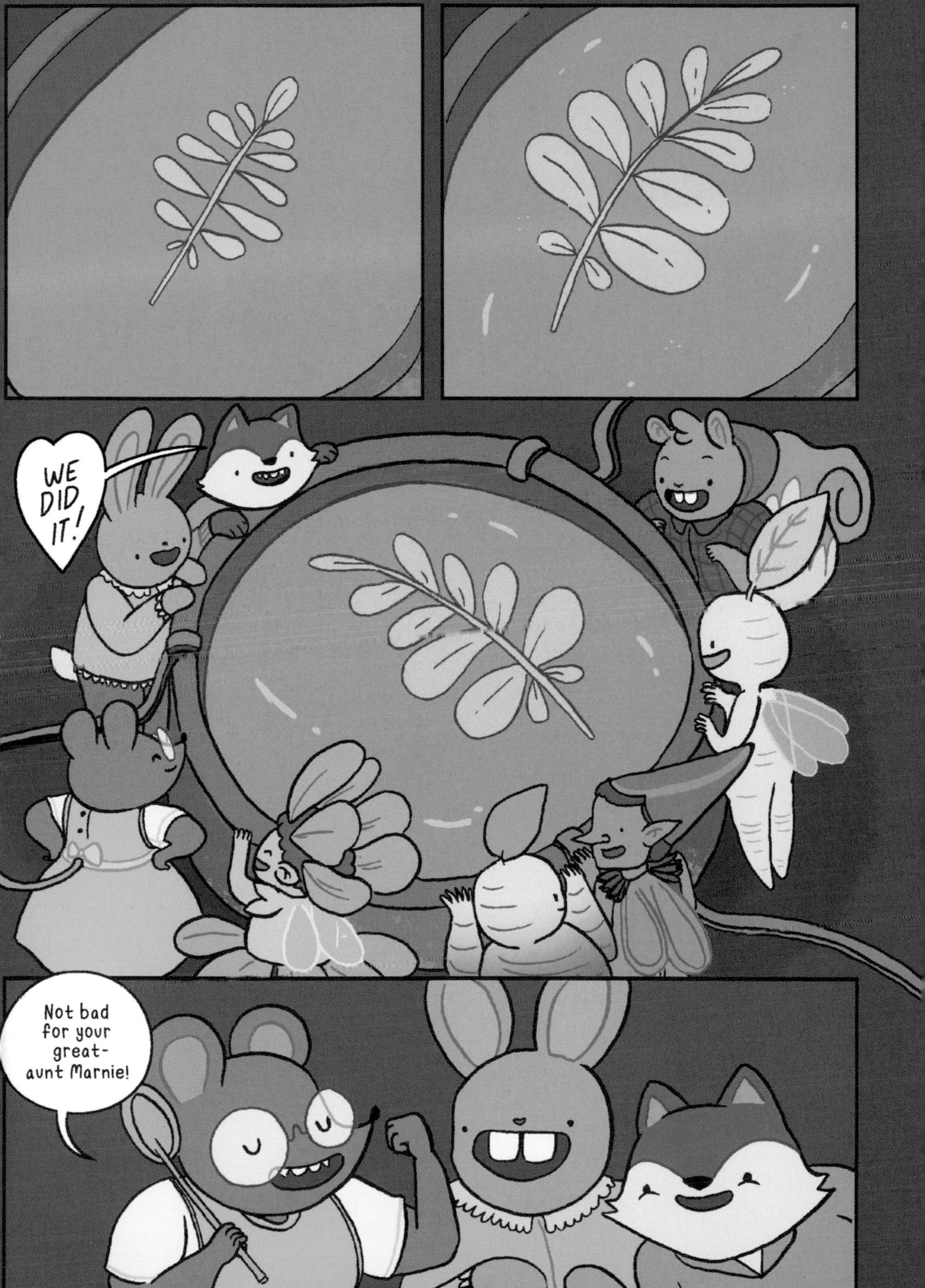
WE DID IT!
Not bad for your great-aunt Marnie!

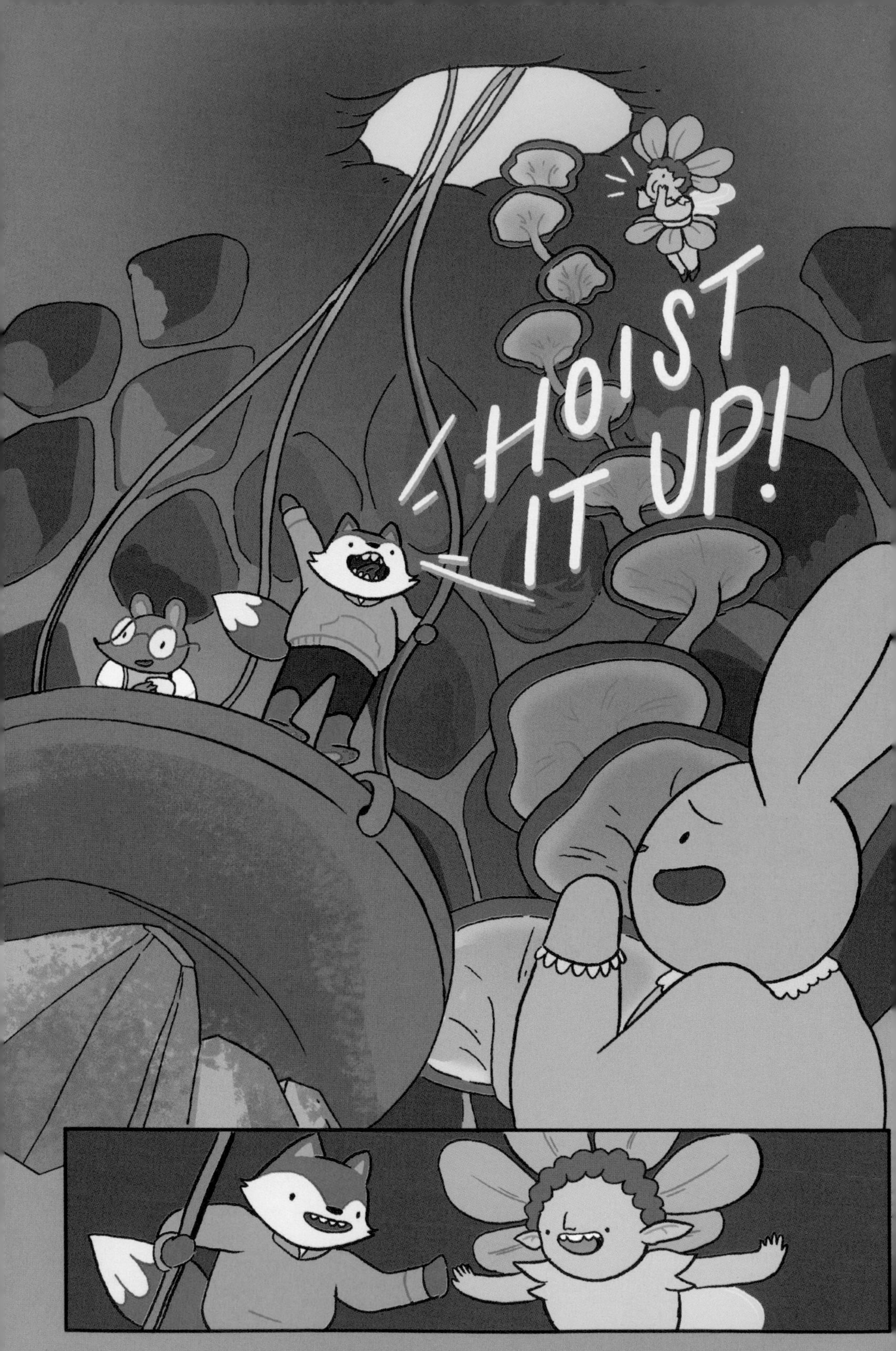
HOIST IT UP!

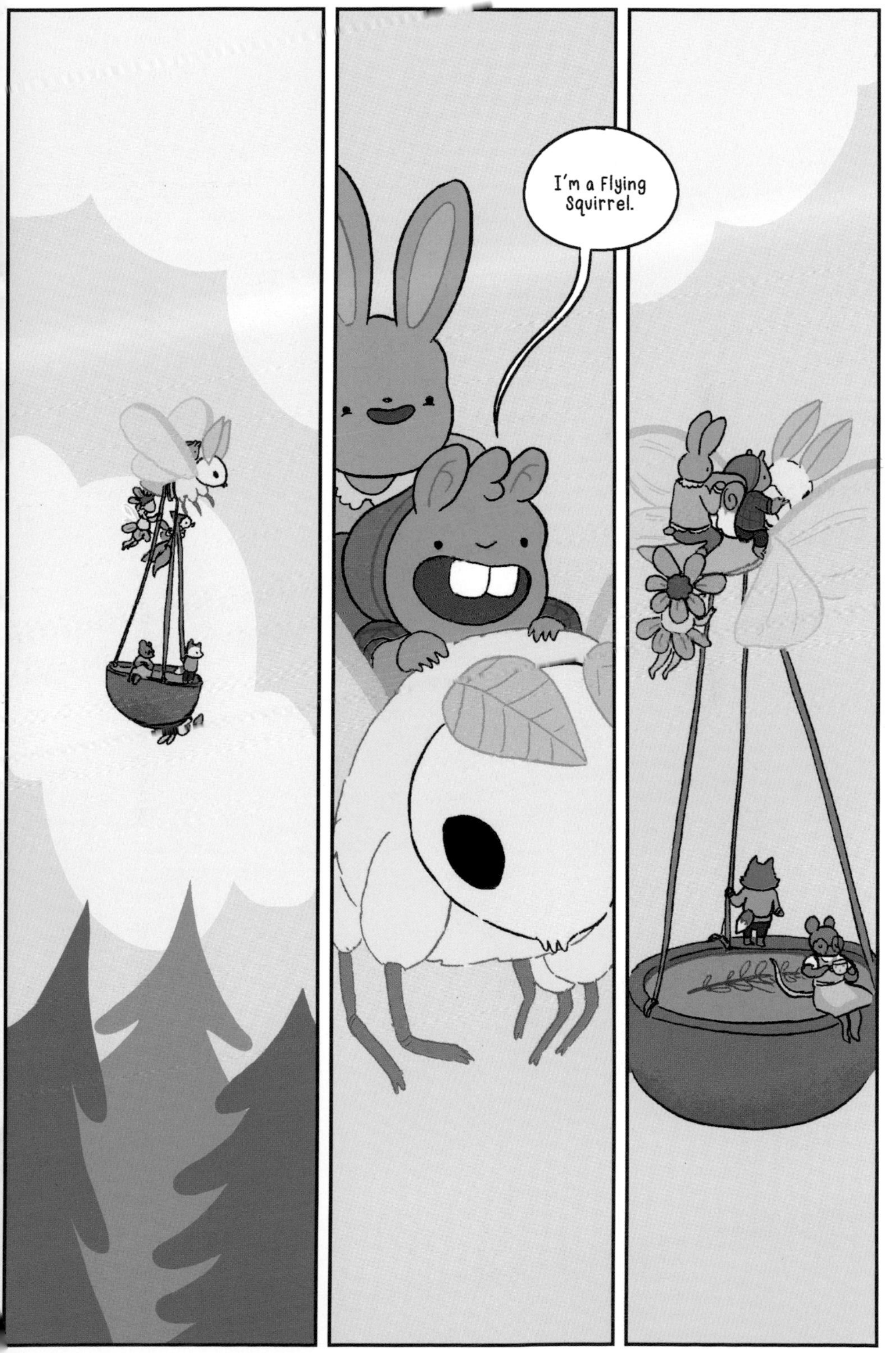
I'm a Flying Squirrel.

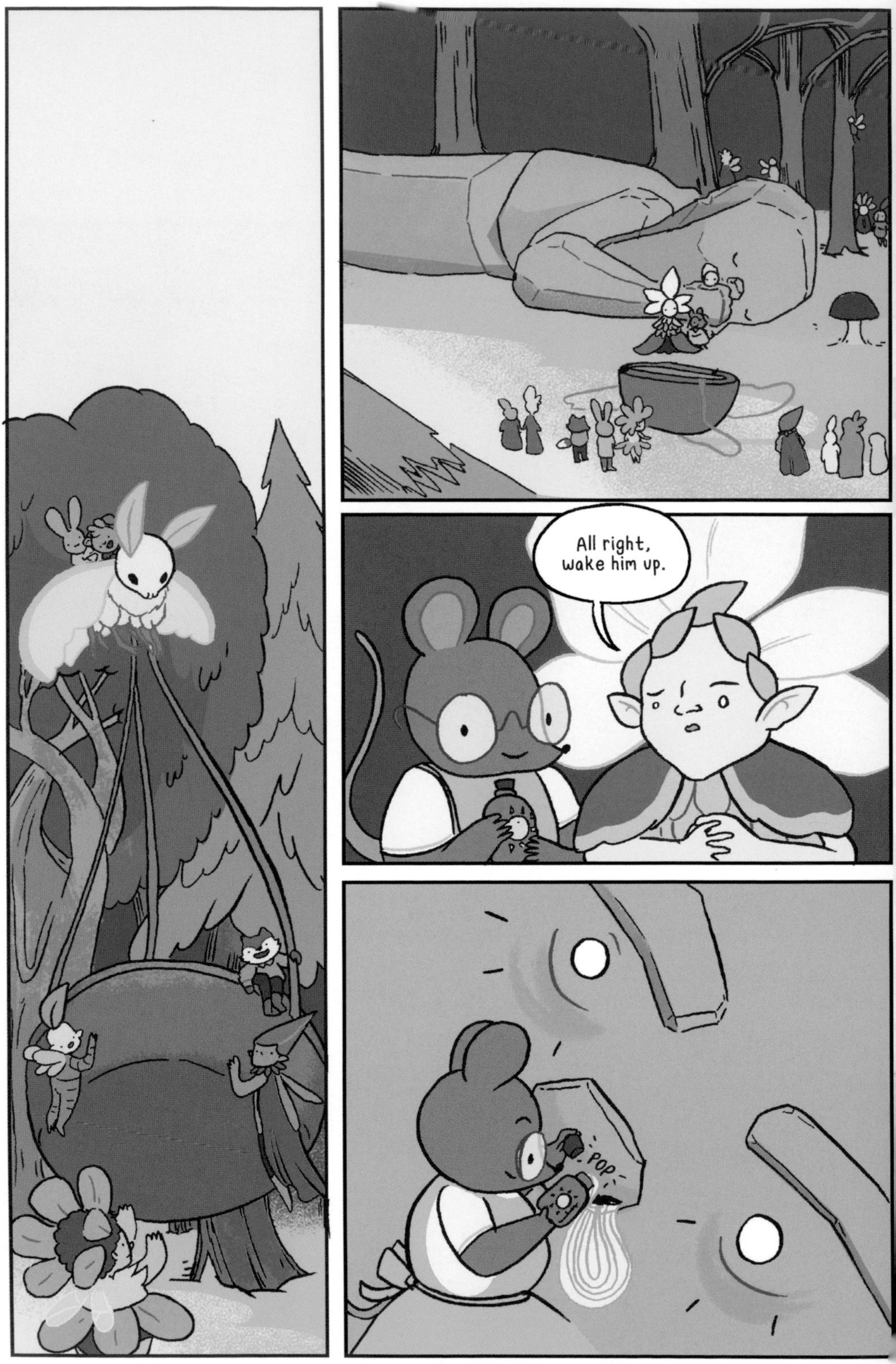
All right, wake him up.
POP

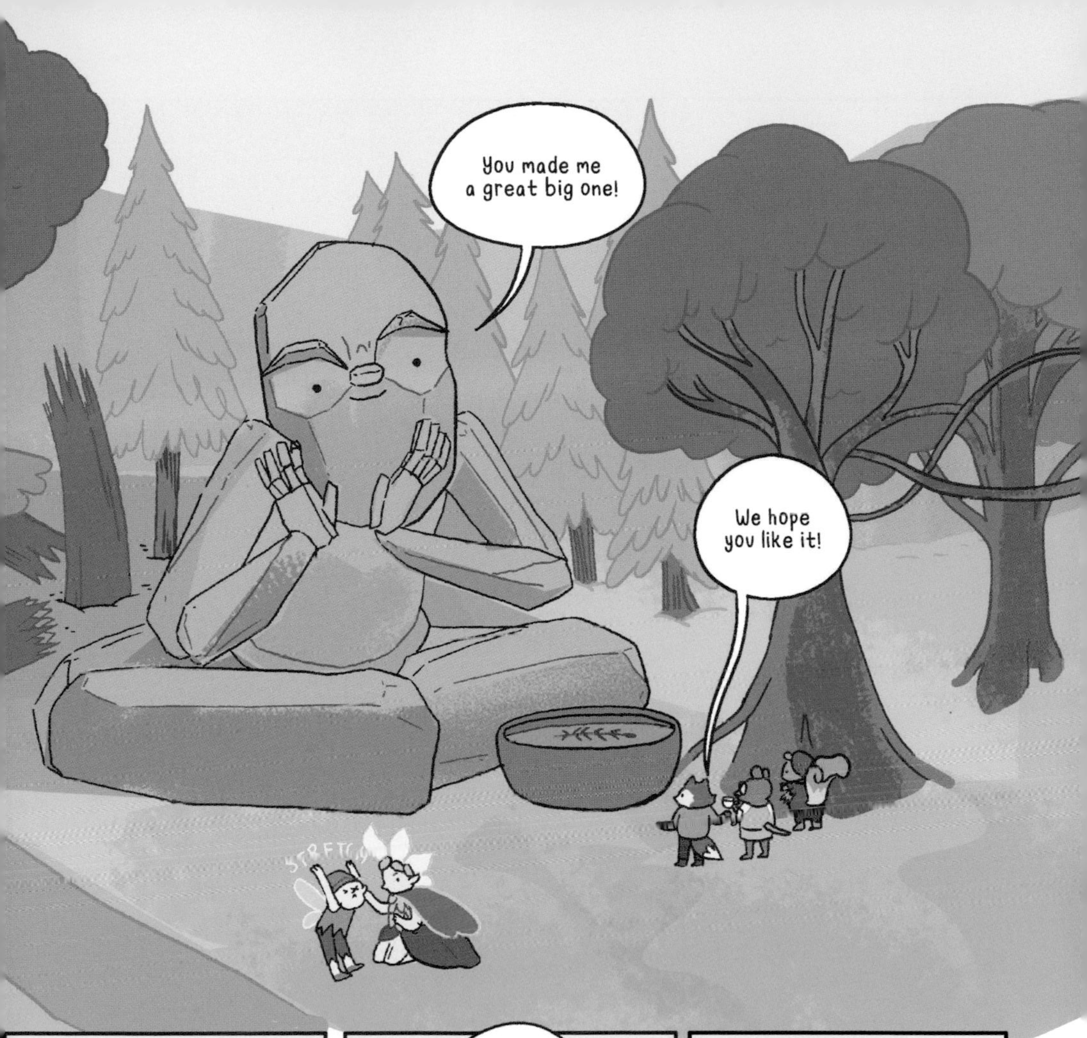
You made me a great big one!
We hope you like it!

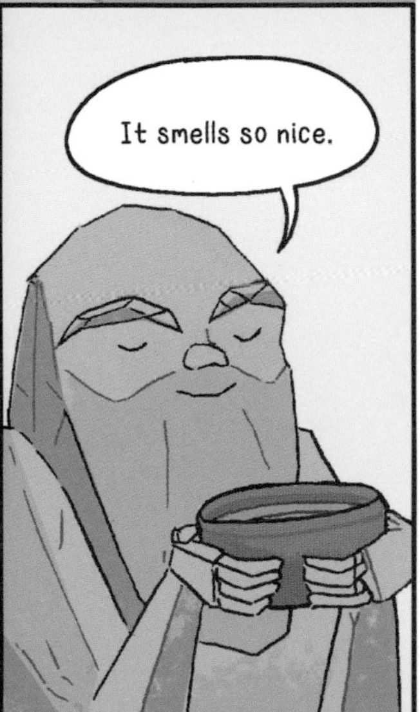
It smells so nice.

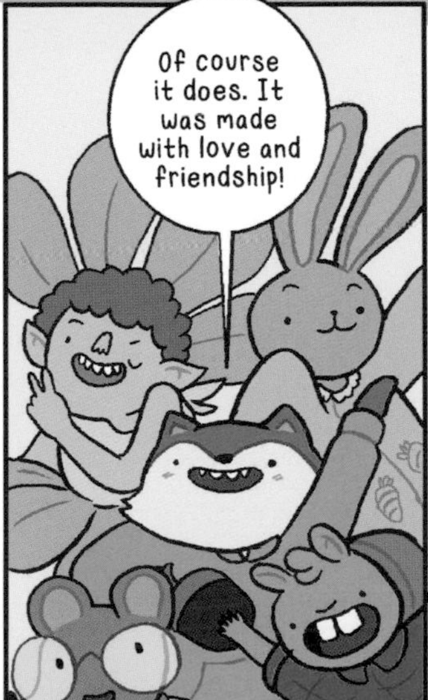
Of course it does. It was made with love and friendship!

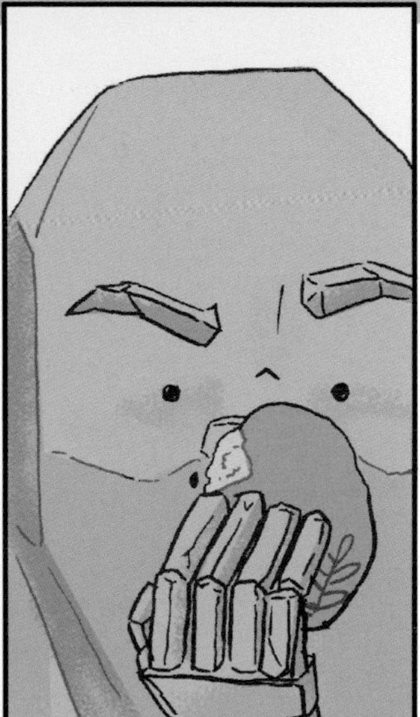

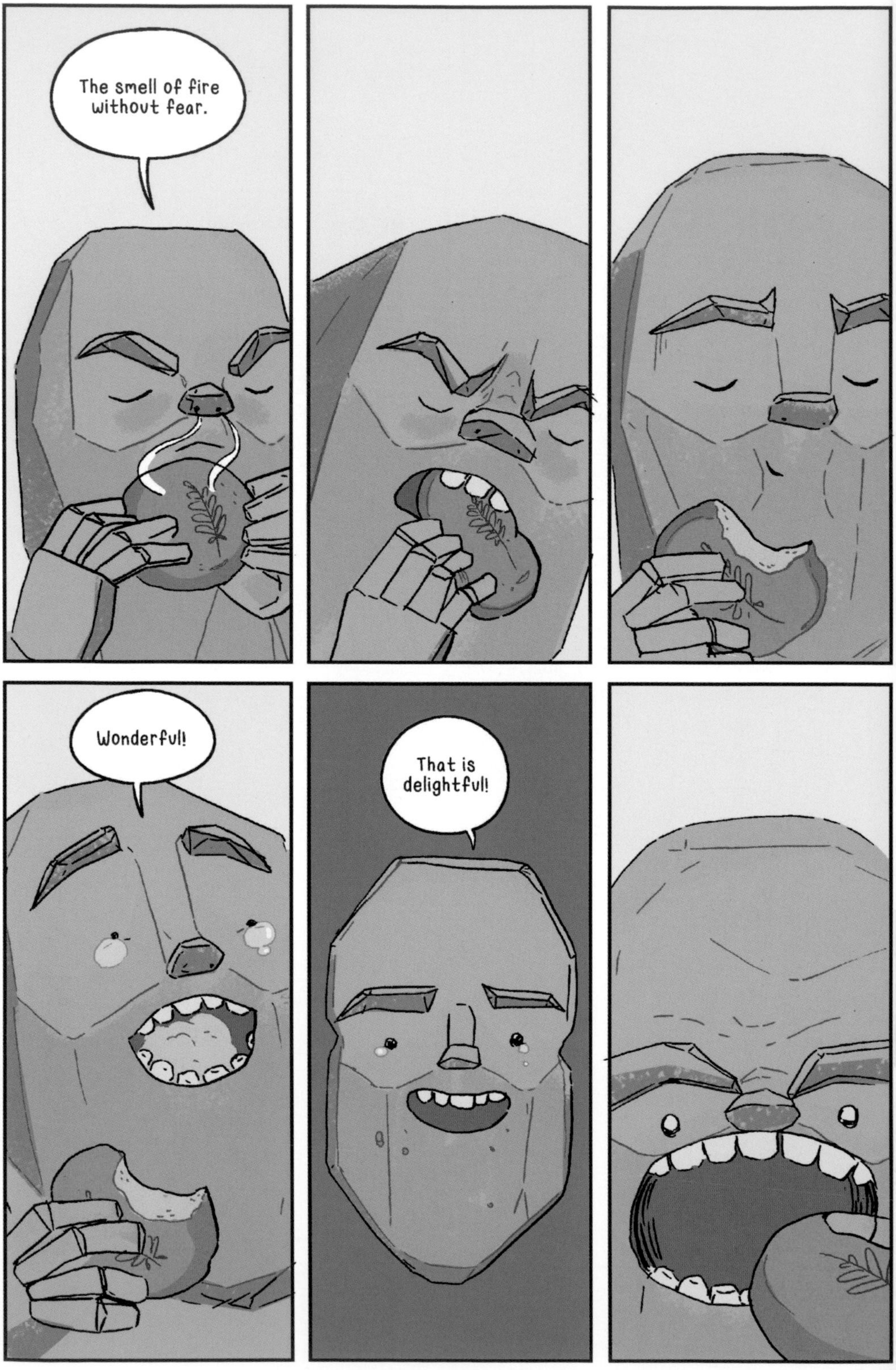
The smell of fire without fear.
Wonderful!
That is delightful!

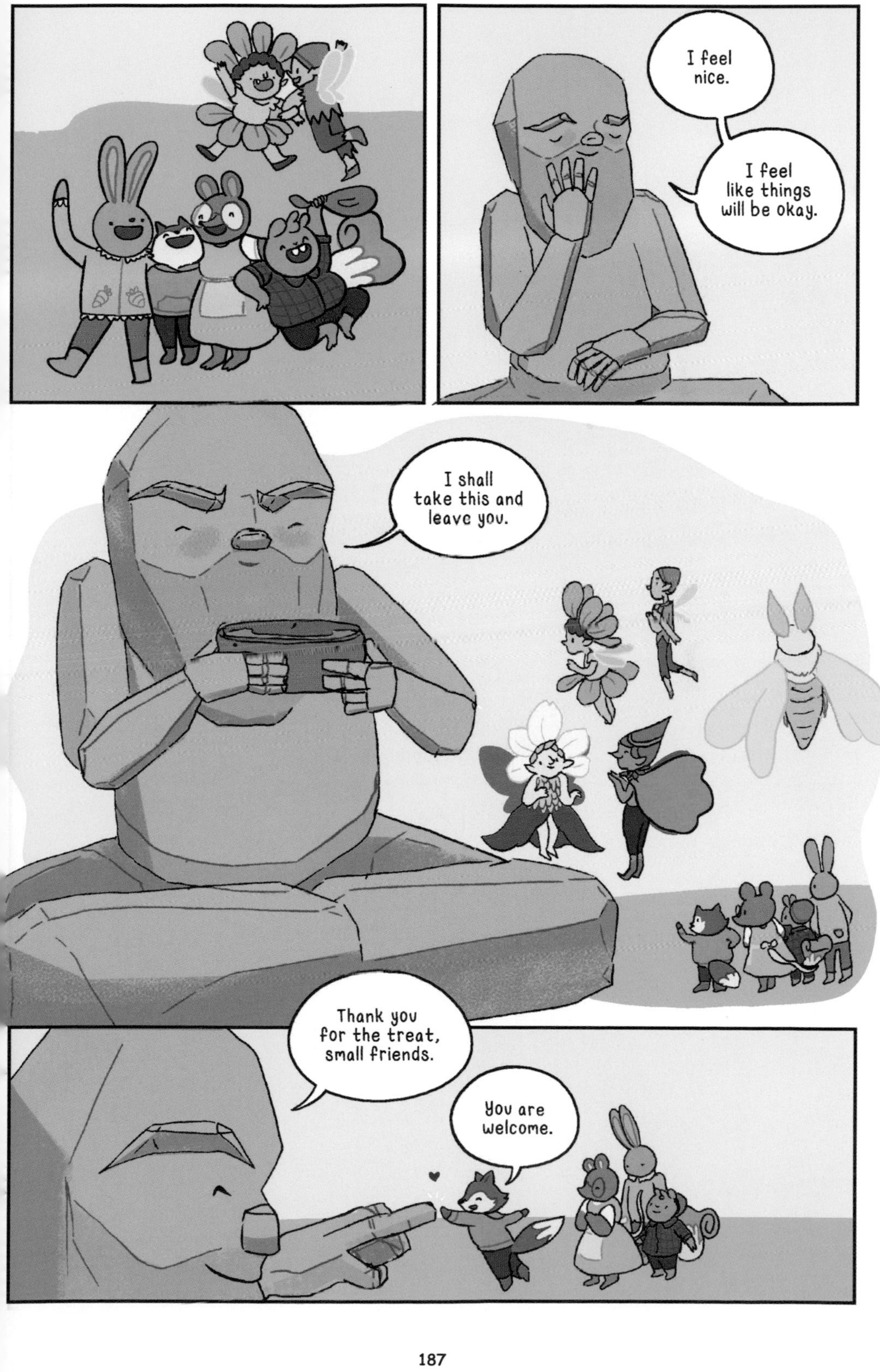
I feel nice.
I feel like things will be okay.
I shall take this and leave you.
Thank you for the treat, small friends.
You are welcome.

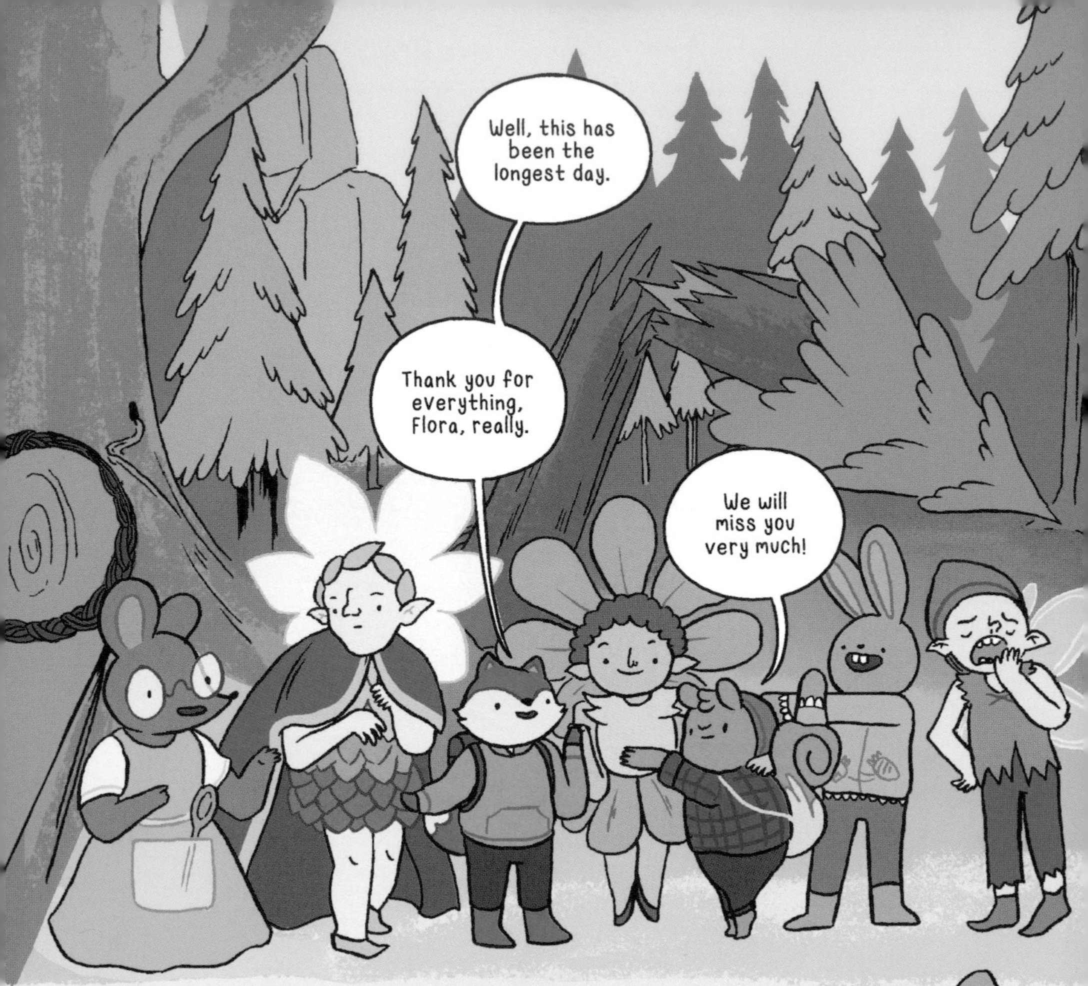
Well, this has been the longest day.
Thank you for everything, Flora, really.
We will miss you very much!

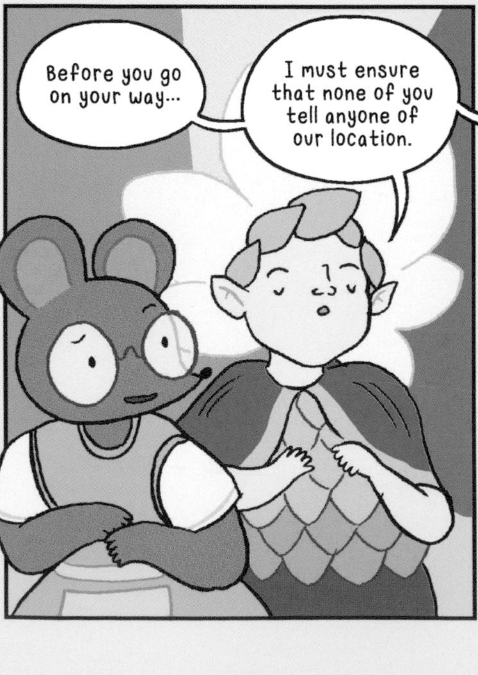
Before you go on your way...
I must ensure that none of you tell anyone of our location.

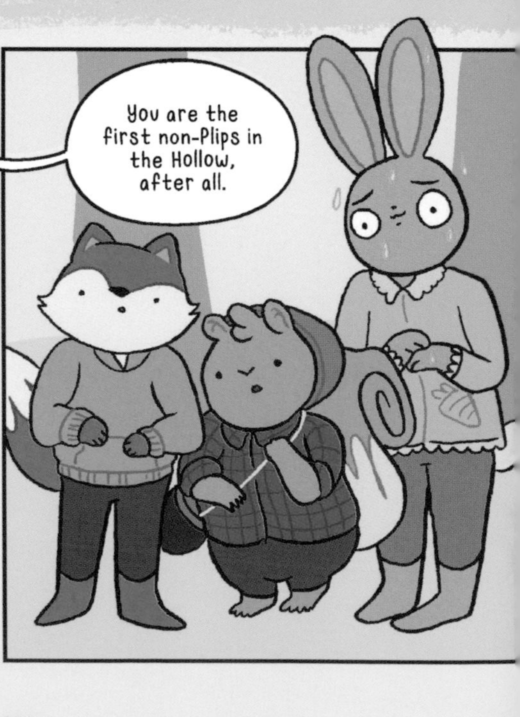
You are the first non-Plips in the Hollow, after all.

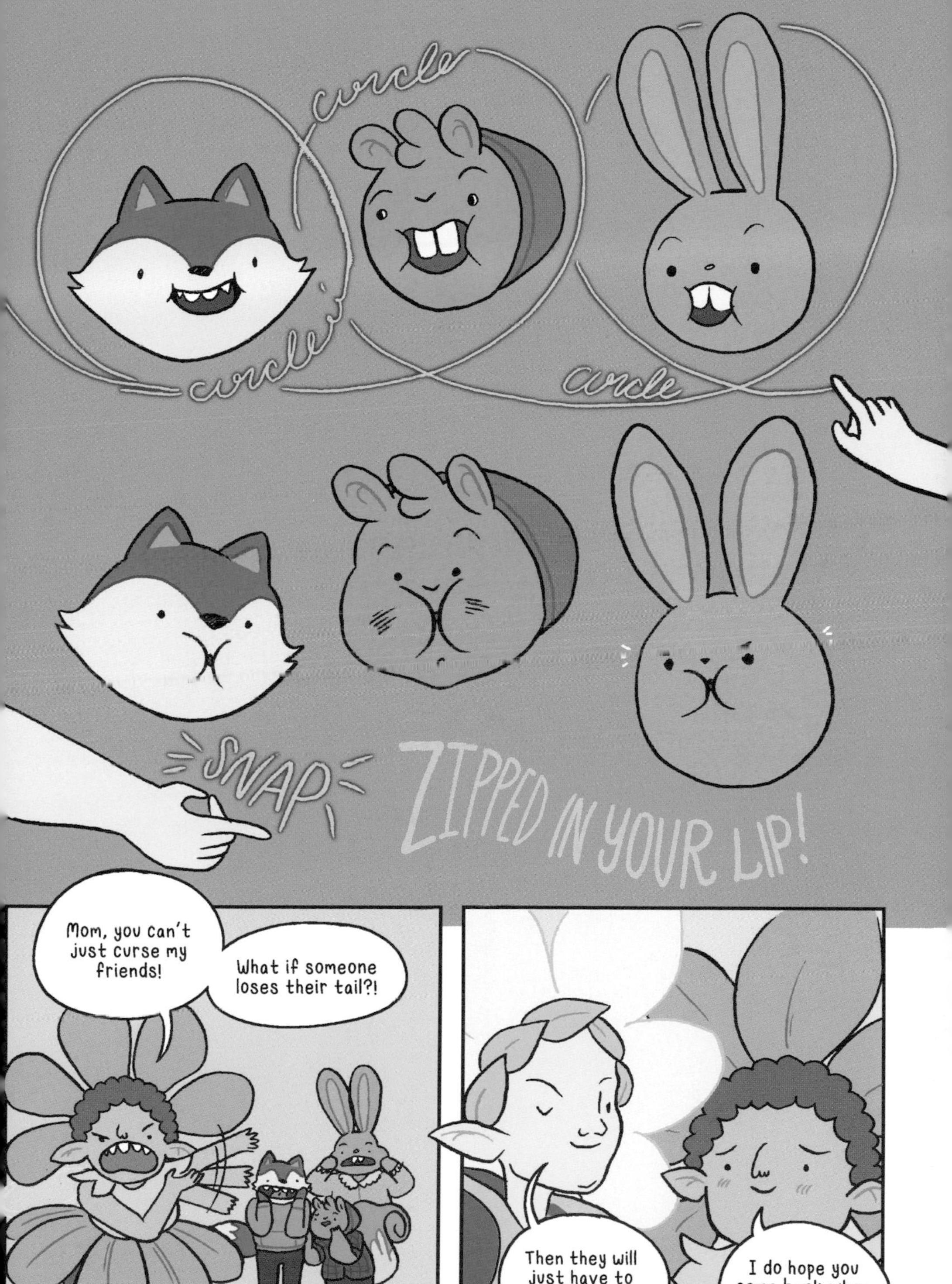
circle
circle
circle
circle
SNAP
ZIPPED IN YOUR LIP!
Mom, you can't just curse my friends!
What if someone loses their tail?!
Then they will just have to come back!
I do hope you come back when we're in bloom next year!

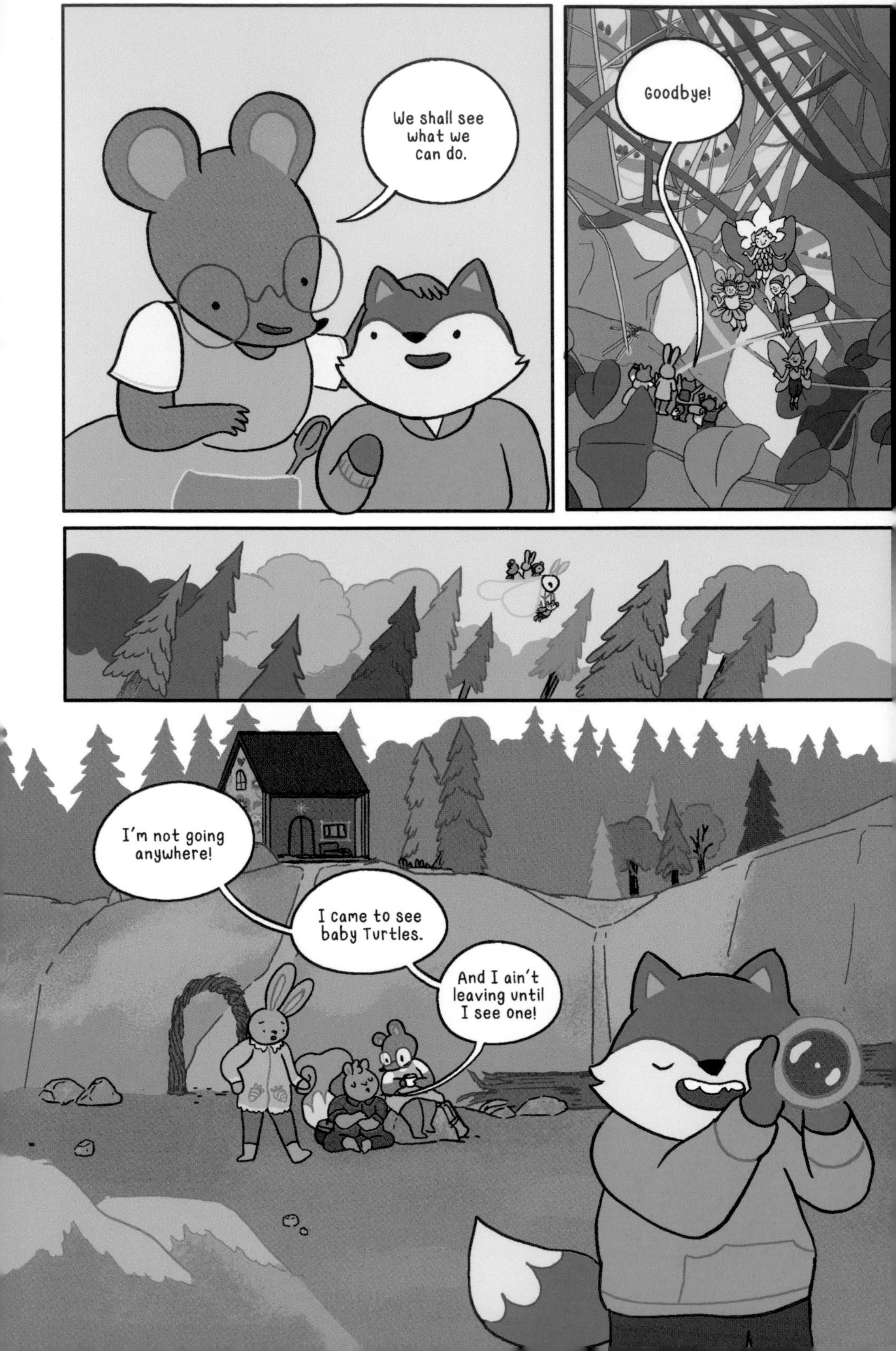
We shall see what we can do.
Goodbye!
I'm not going anywhere!
I came to see baby Turtles.
And I ain't leaving until I see one!

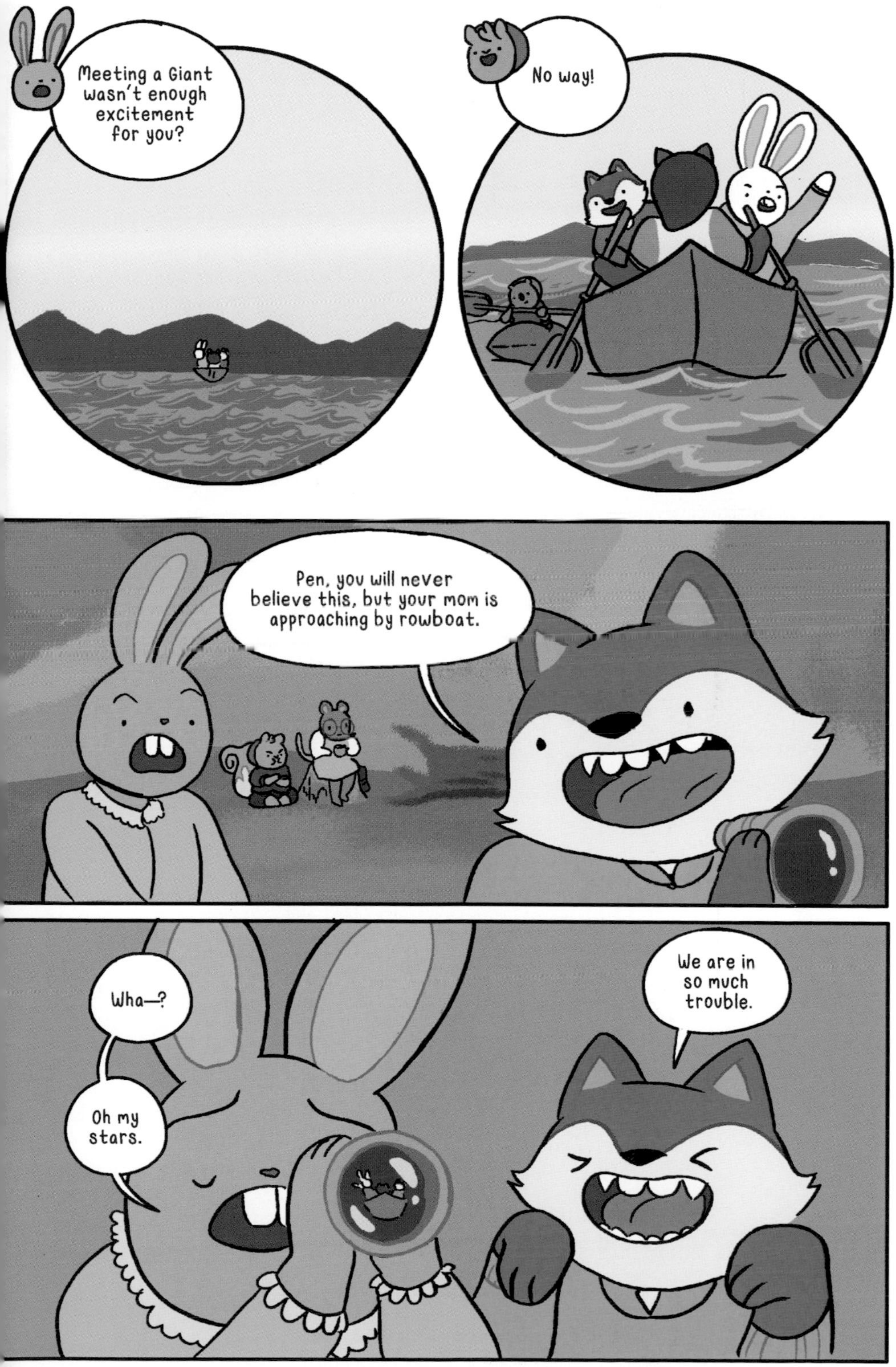
Meeting a Giant wasn't enough excitement for you?
No way!
Pen, you will never believe this, but your mom is approaching by rowboat.
Wha—?
Oh my stars.
We are in so much trouble.

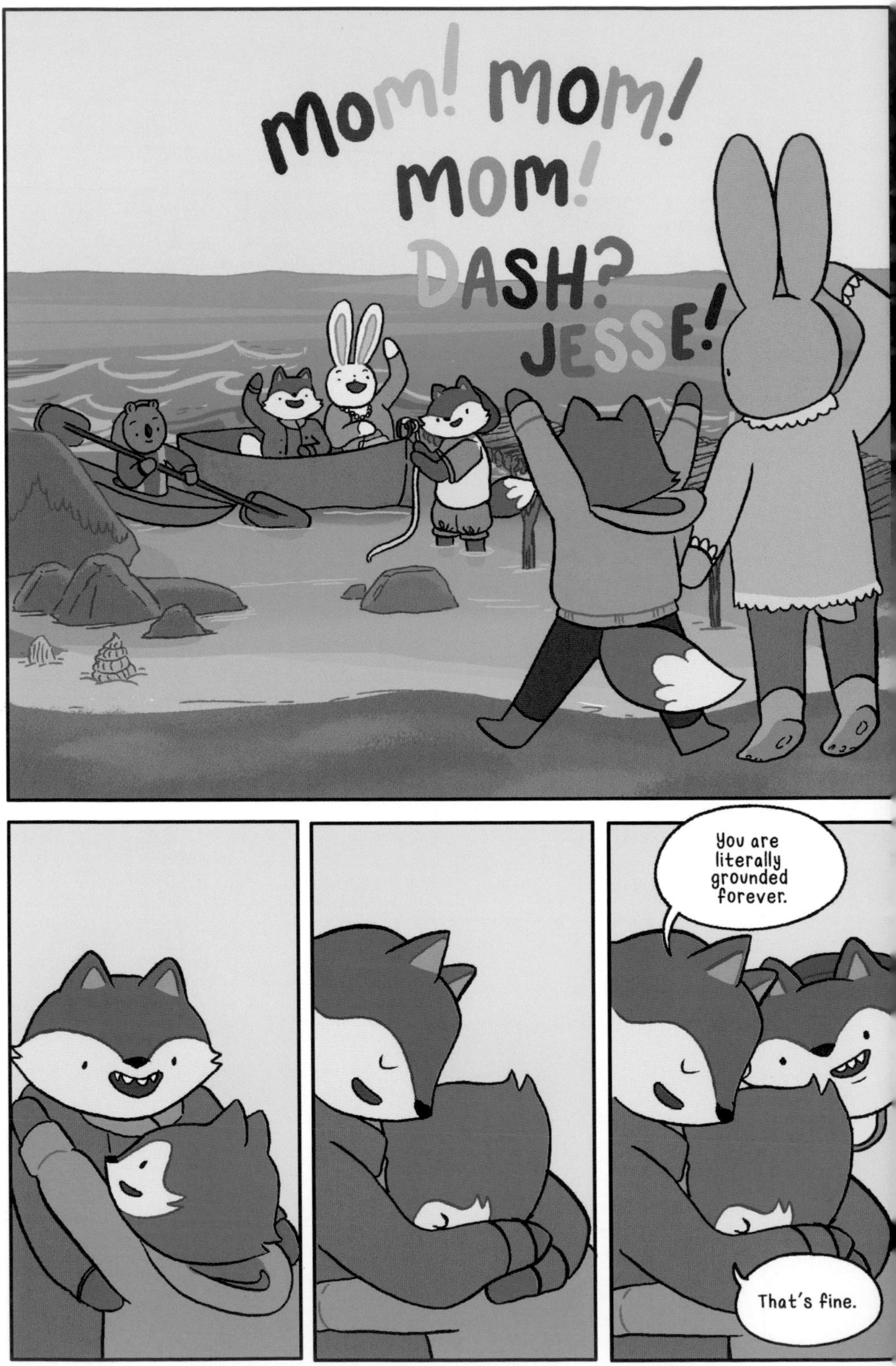
MOM! MOM!
MOM!
DASH?
JESSE!
You are literally grounded forever.
That's fine.

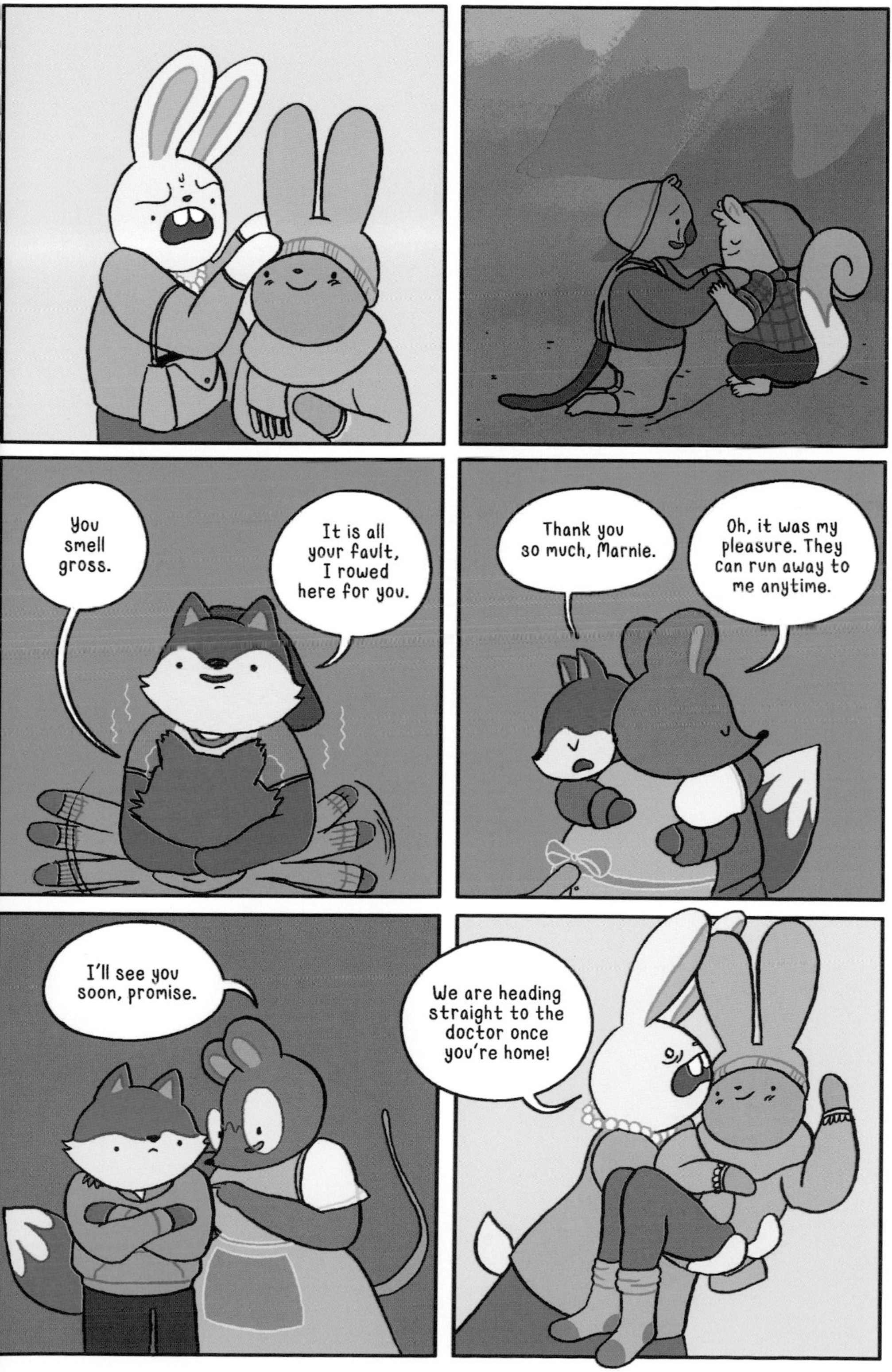
You smell gross.
It is all your fault, I rowed here for you.
Thank you so much, Marnie.
Oh, it was my pleasure. They can run away to me anytime.
I'll see you soon, promise.
We are heading straight to the doctor once you're home!

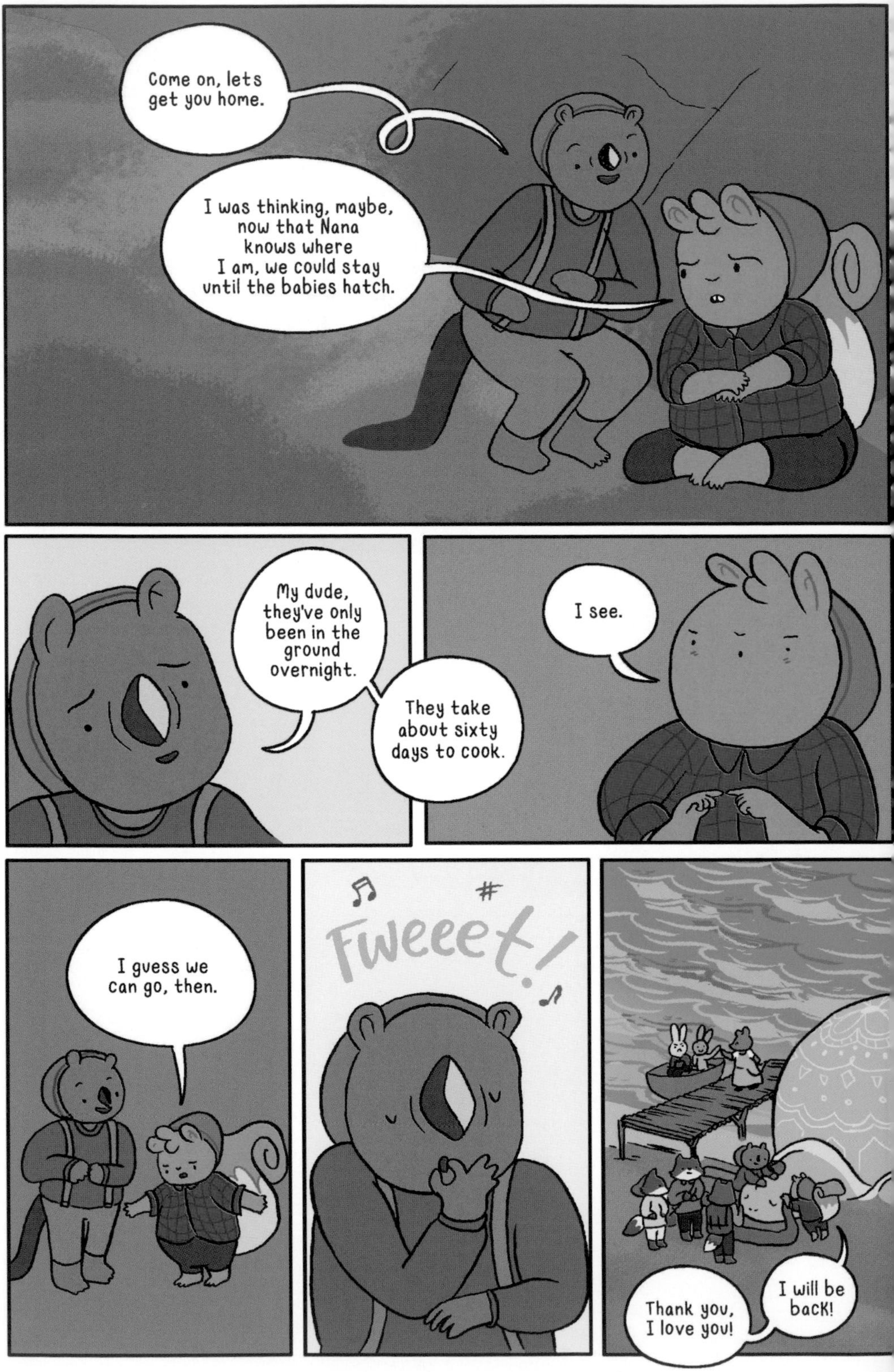

Come on, lets get you home.
I was thinking, maybe, now that Nana knows where I am, we could stay until the babies hatch.
My dude, they've only been in the ground overnight.
They take about sixty days to cook.
I see.
I guess we can go, then.
Fweeet!
Thank you, I love you!
I will be back!

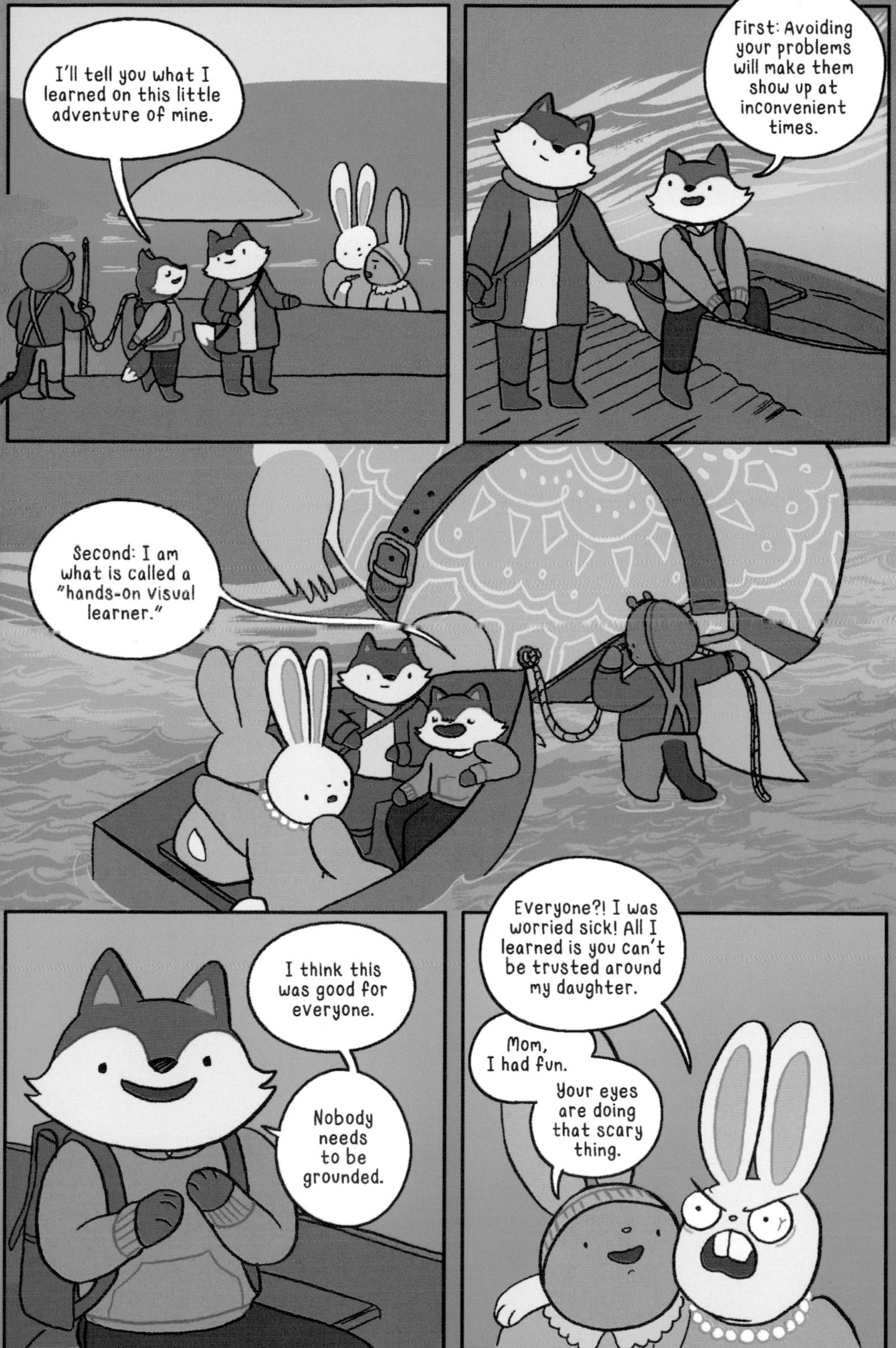
I'll tell you what I learned on this little adventure of mine.
First: Avoiding your problems will make them show up at inconvenient times.
Second: I am what is called a "hands-on visual learner."
I think this was good for everyone.
Nobody needs to be grounded.
Everyone?! I was worried sick! All I learned is you can't be trusted around my daughter.
Mom, I had fun.
Your eyes are doing that scary thing.

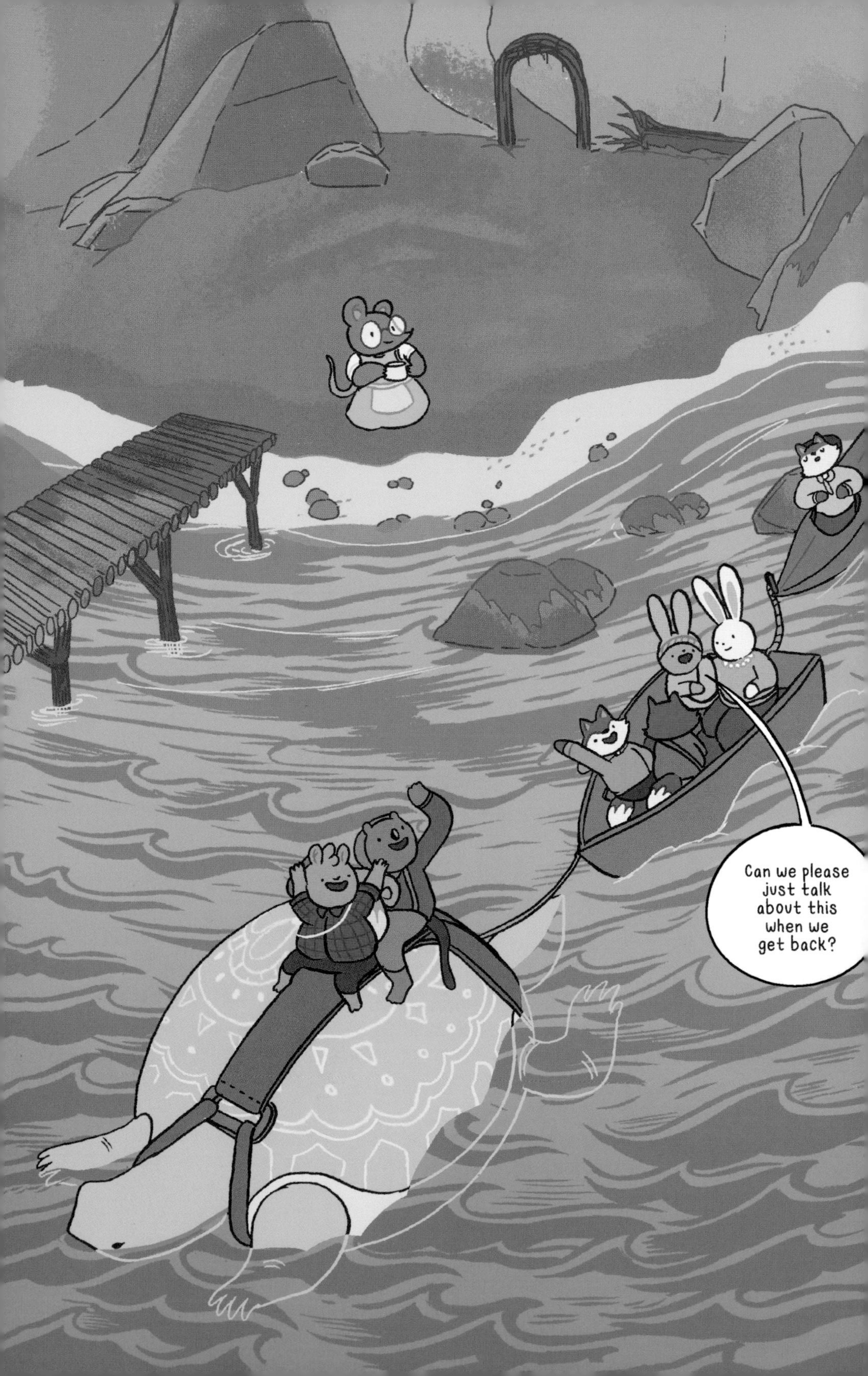
Can we please just talk about this when we get back?

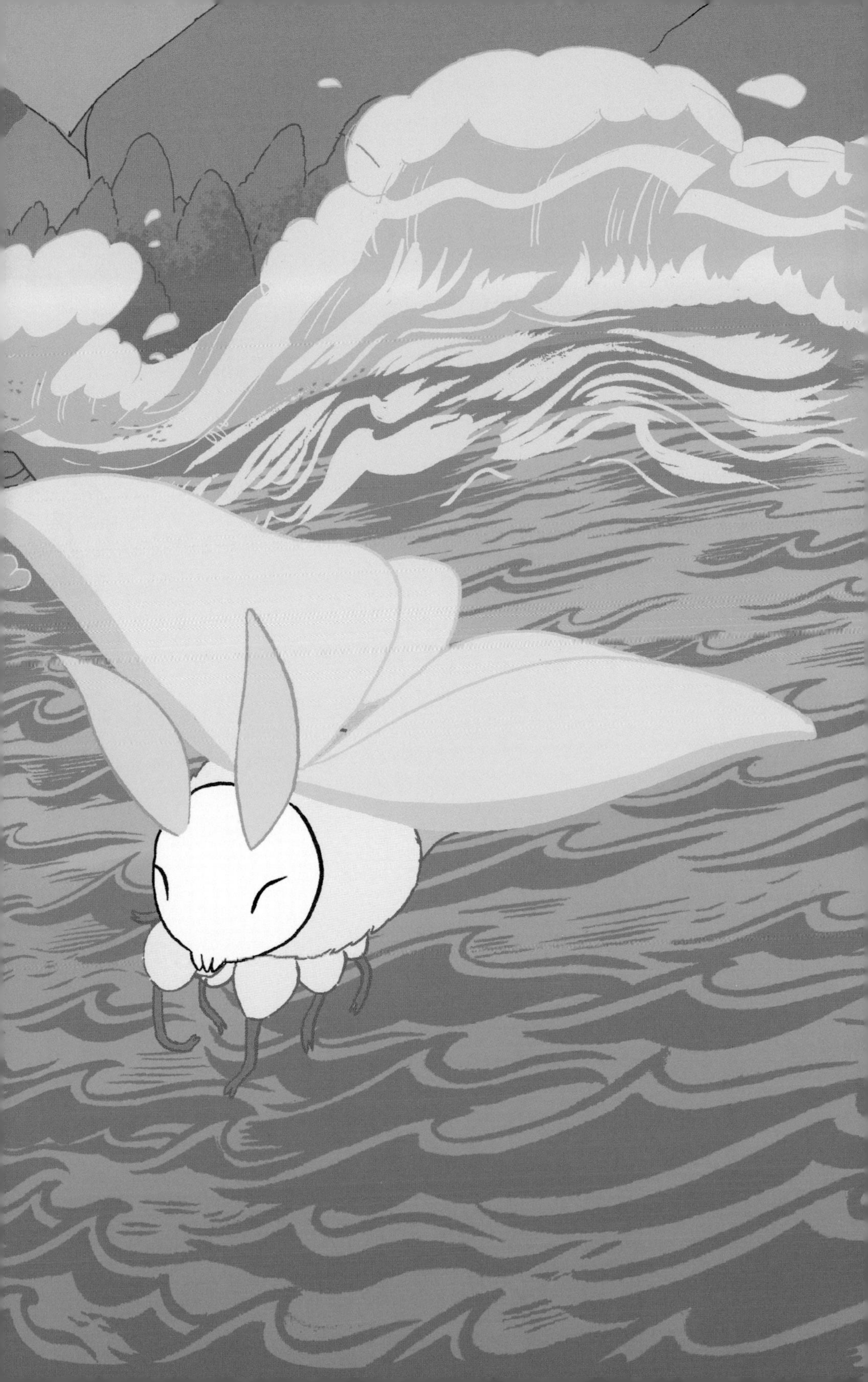

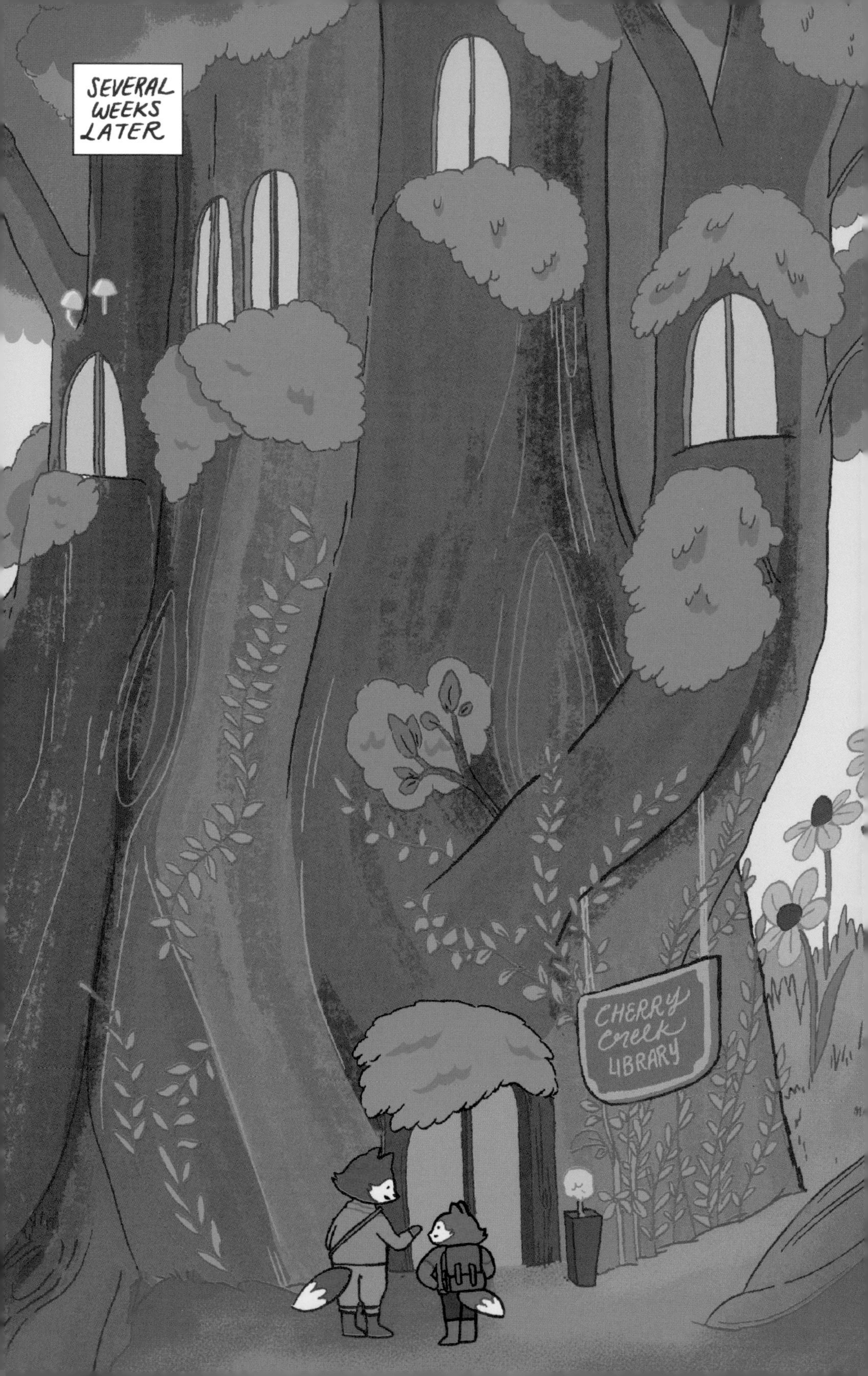
SEVERAL WEEKS LATER
CHERRY Creek LIBRARY

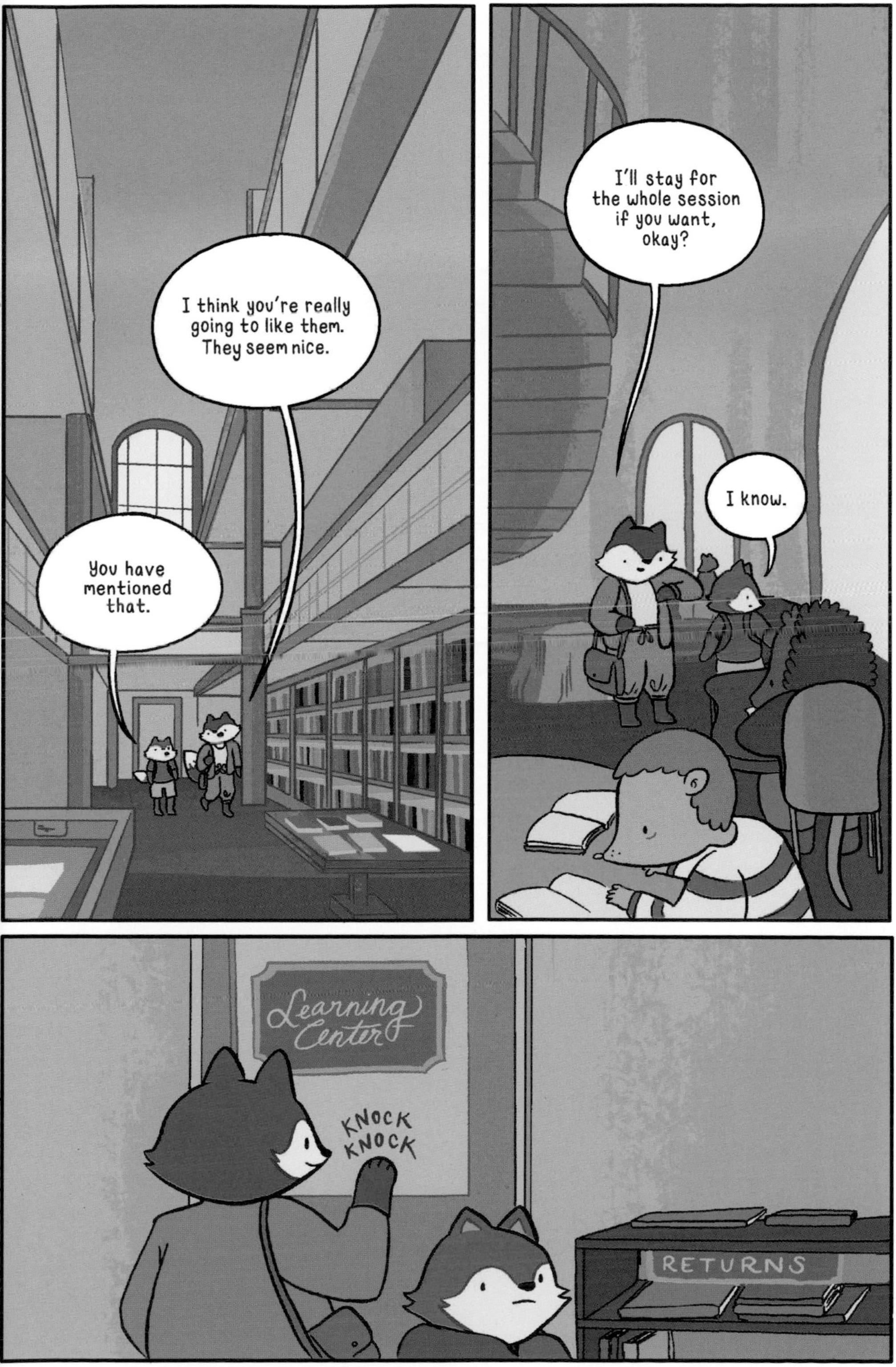
I think you're really going to like them. They seem nice.
You have mentioned that.
I'll stay for the whole session if you want, okay?
I know.
Learning Center
KNOCK KNOCK
RETURNS

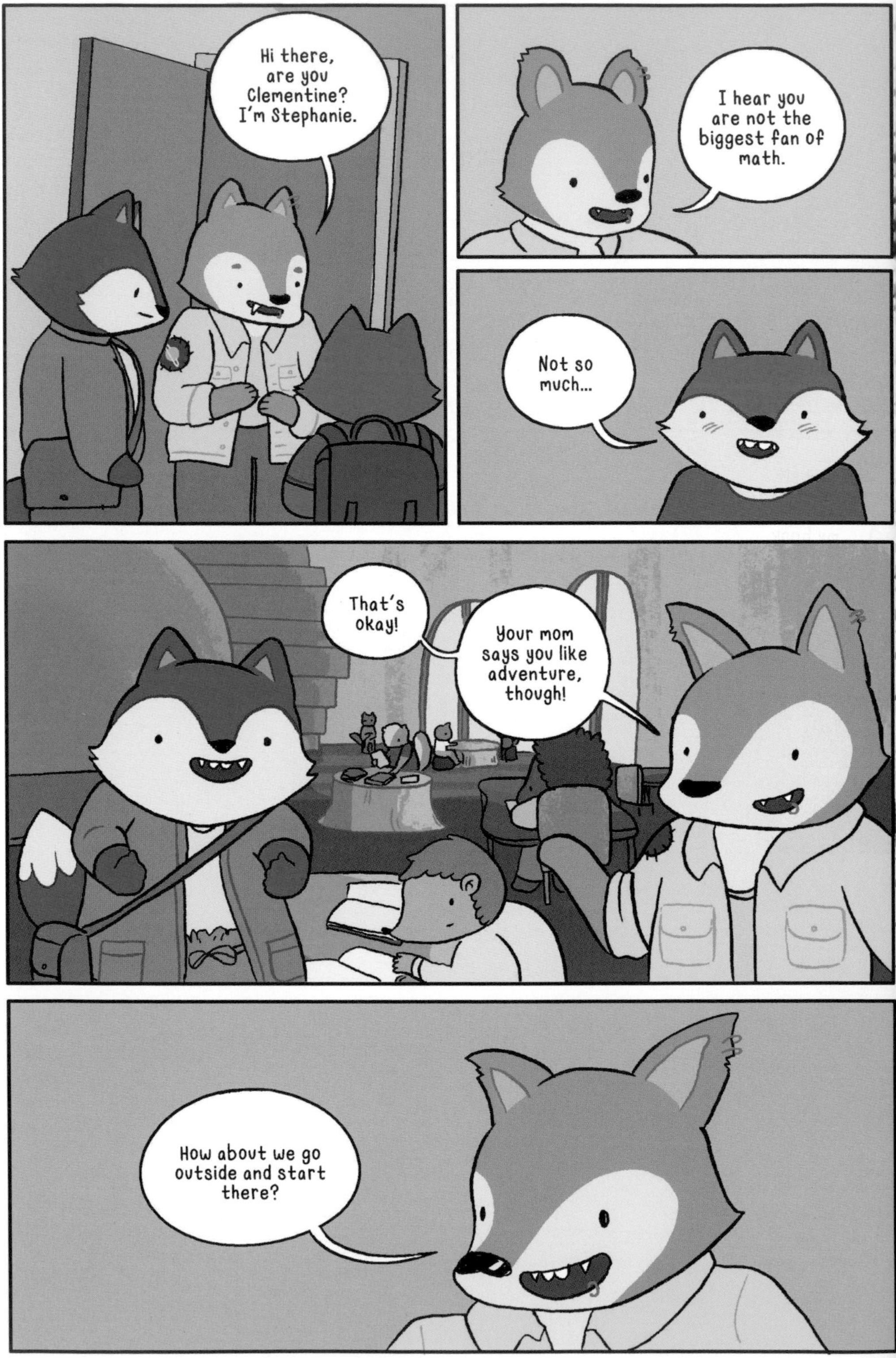
Hi there, are you Clementine? I'm Stephanie.
I hear you are not the biggest fan of math.
Not so much...
That's okay!
Your mom says you like adventure, though!
How about we go outside and start there?

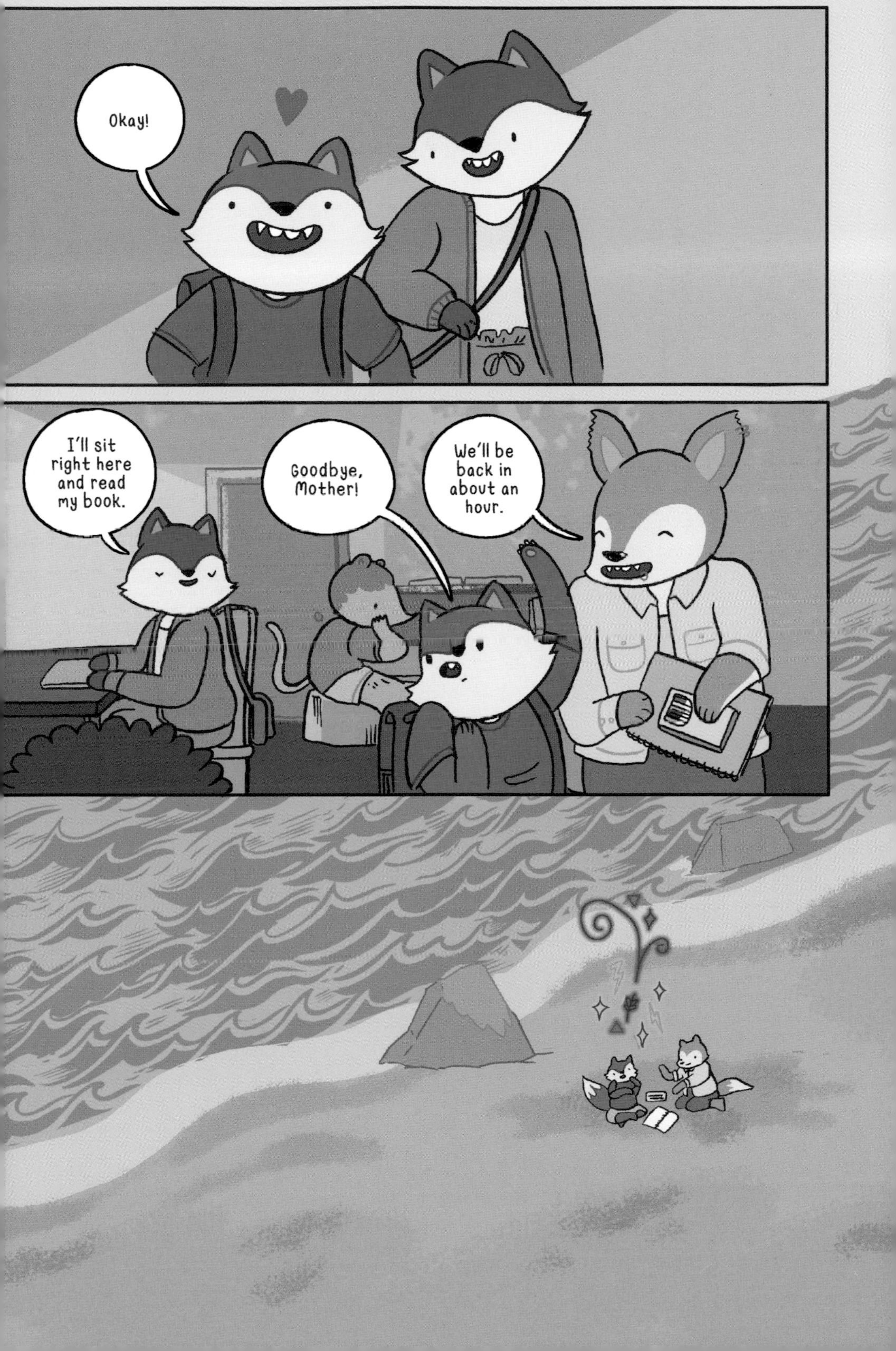
Okay!
I'll sit right here and read my book.
Goodbye, Mother!
We'll be back in about an hour.

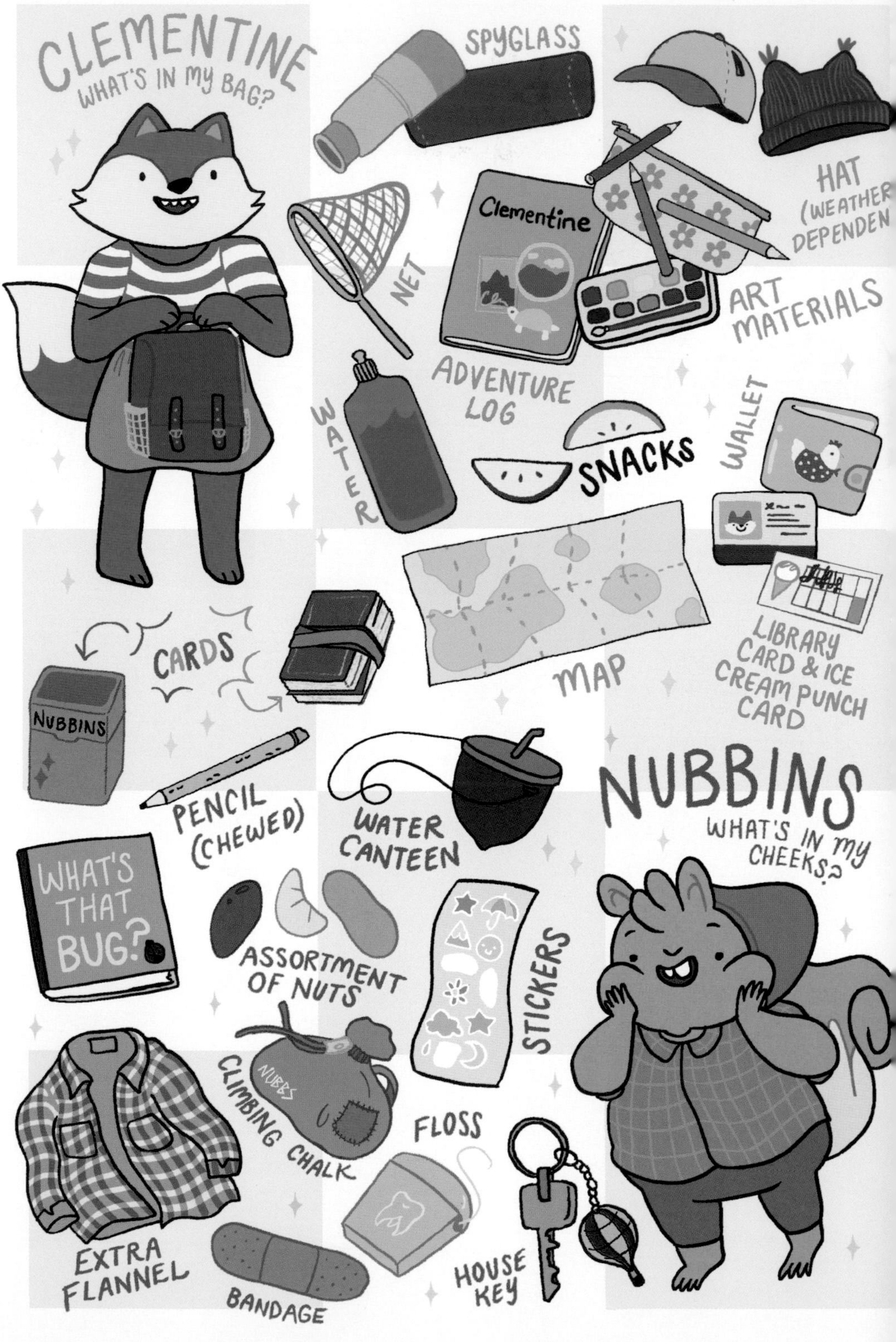
CLEMENTINE
WHAT'S IN MY BAG?
SPYGLASS
HAT (WEATHER DEPENDEN
Clementine
NET
ART MATERIALS
ADVENTURE LOG
WATER
WALLET
SNACKS
CARDS
NUBBINS
MAP
LIBRARY CARD & ICE CREAM PUNCH CARD
PENCIL (CHEWED)
WATER CANTEEN
NUBBINS
WHAT'S IN MY CHEEKS?
WHAT'S THAT BUG?
ASSORTMENT OF NUTS
STICKERS
NUBBS
CLIMBING CHALK
FLOSS
EXTRA FLANNEL
BANDAGE
HOUSE KEY

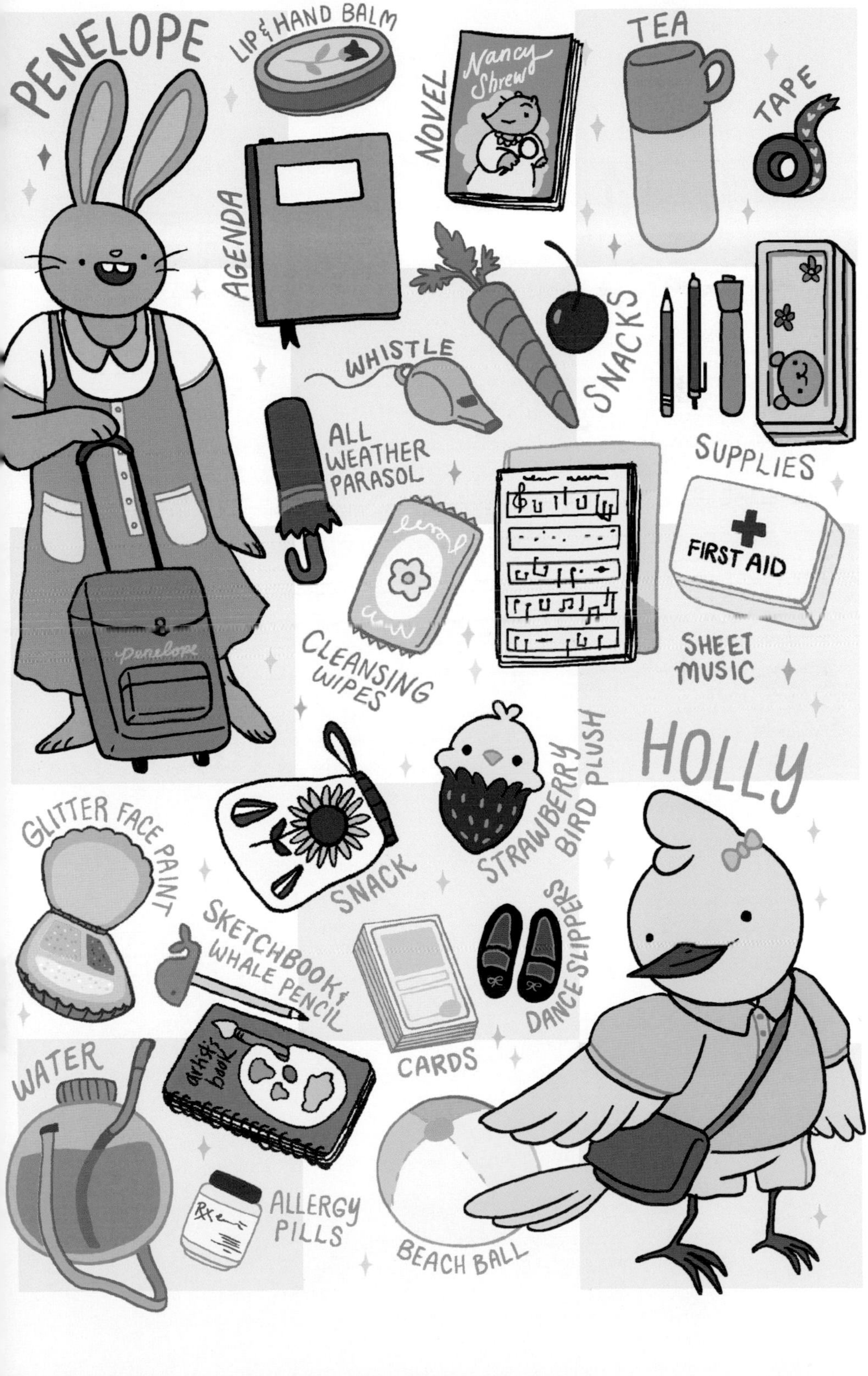
PENELOPE
LIP & HAND BALM
NOVEL
Nancy Shrew
TEA
TAPE
AGENDA
SNACKS
WHISTLE
ALL WEATHER PARASOL
SUPPLIES
FIRST AID
penelope
CLEANSING WIPES
SHEET MUSIC
HOLLY
STRAWBERRY BIRD PLUSH
GLITTER FACE PAINT
SNACK
SKETCHBOOK & WHALE PENCIL
DANCE SLIPPERS
CARDS
WATER
artist's book
ALLERGY PILLS
BEACH BALL

ACKNOWLEDGMENTS

A special thanks to Scholastic; my editor, Cassandra Pelham Fulton; and my agent, Jennifer Linnan, without whom Clementine would not be possible.

Additional gratitude to Shena Wolfe for originally believing in me and this project.

Thank you to Amish, Ashley, Ashlyn, Evan, Hilary, Kam, Paloma, Charles, and Rosemary, who heavily supported me while creating Clementine; my immediate family, Rachelle, Larry, and Lisa for their unwavering confidence; my loving grandparents; Paula and Phyllis for nurturing my artistic talents; and, finally, my incredibly caring friends.

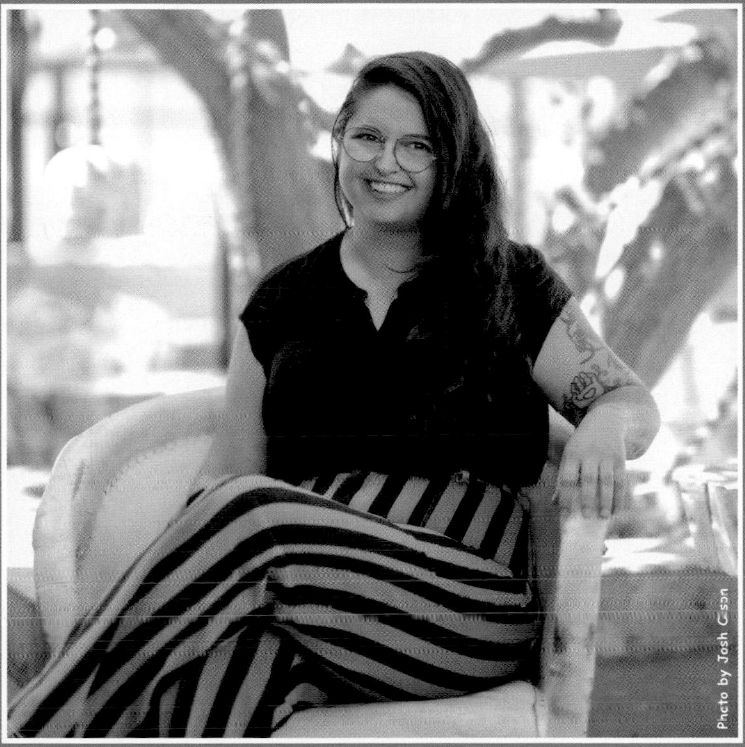

Photo by Josh C[illegible]son

LEIGH LUNA is a mixed Latina artist who was born in Albuquerque, New Mexico, and graduated from the Minneapolis College of Art and Design. In addition to making comics, she has worked in animation as a color designer on shows such as *Steven Universe* and *Centaurworld*. Her client list includes Cartoon Network, Nickelodeon, Disney/Hyperion, Target, AV Club, and BuzzFeed.

Leigh is passionate about color, comedy, and alternative learning. She lives in Los Angeles. Visit her online at leighlunacomics.com.

Clementine's Next Adventure is Coming Soon!

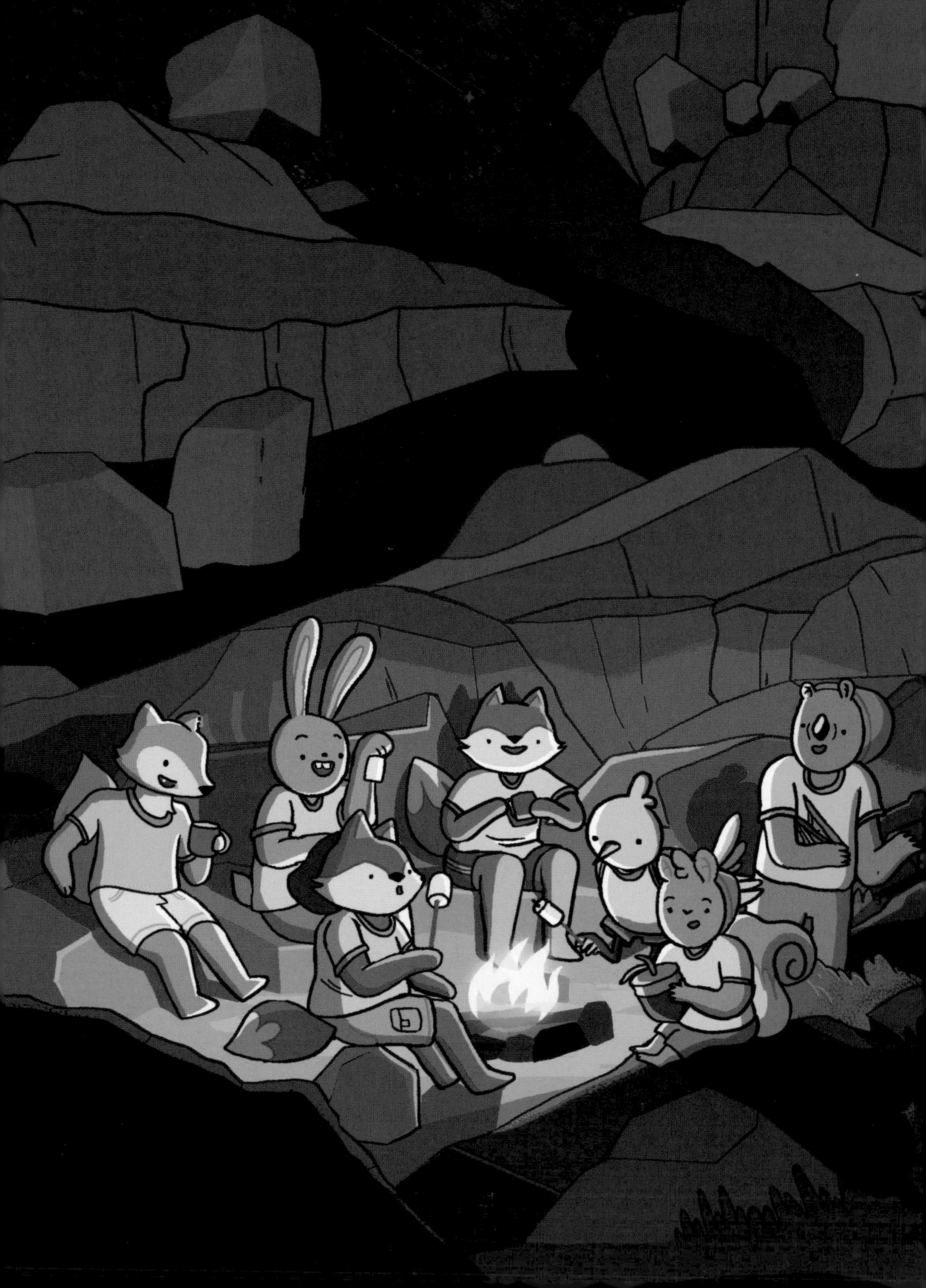

b